WITNESS
FOR THE
DEFENSE

Books by Jonnie Jacobs

The Kali O'Brien Novels of Legal Suspense

SHADOW OF DOUBT
EVIDENCE OF GUILT
MOTION TO DISMISS
WITNESS FOR THE DEFENSE

The Kate Austen Mysteries

MURDER AMONG NEIGHBORS
MURDER AMONG FRIENDS
MURDER AMONG US
MURDER AMONG STRANGERS

Published by Kensington Publishing Corporation

JONNIE JACOBS

WITNESS FOR THE DEFENSE

KENSINGTON BOOKS
http://www.kensingtonbooks.com

KENSINGTON BOOKS are published by

Kensington Publishing Corp.
850 Third Avenue
New York, NY 10022

All Kensington titles, imprints and distributed lines are available at special quantity discounts for bulk purchases for sales promotion, premiums, fund raising, educational or institutional use.

Special book excerpts or customized printings can also be created to fit specific needs. For details, write or phone the office of the Kensington Special Sales Manager: Kensington Publishing Corp., 850 Third Avenue, New York, NY 10022, Attn. Special Sales Department. Phone: 1-800-221-2647.

Kensington and the K logo Reg. U.S. Pat. & TM Off.

Library of Congress Card Catalogue Number: 00-107158
ISBN 1-57566-643-X

First Printing: April, 2001
10 9 8 7 6 5 4 3 2 1

Printed in the United States of America

To David and Matthew,
who have taught me so much and
enriched my life beyond measure

ACKNOWLEDGMENTS

My thanks once again to Margaret Lucke, Lynn MacDonald, and Camille Minichino for their insightful comments on the manuscript. Thanks goes also to Norman Ismari, who patiently answered even my silliest questions about firearms. He is a wealth of information. On occasion, I chose to ignore their suggestions, so the errors are all mine. And finally, I'd like to thank the many readers who've contacted me. Your letters, e-mails, and in-person comments are a powerful fuel for the fire.

PROLOGUE

The shot wasn't loud. Nothing more, really, than a sharp pop. Another pop followed maybe thirty seconds later. Barely discernible above the background din of a busy city.

Alexander Rudd wouldn't have thought twice about it if he'd been anywhere else. On any different errand.

He pulled the blue windbreaker across his chest in an effort to shield himself from the late-night fog—and the certainty that gunfire had erupted not more than fifty feet from where he stood.

Rudd cursed under his breath. He didn't need this. Not now. His legs moved of their own accord, away from the spot on the narrow street where the shots had been fired.

Getting involved was out of the question. It would mean explaining what he was doing out at midnight in a part of the city where he had no business being. The proverbial can of worms. Once the lid was opened, there'd be no putting it back.

He couldn't. Not now.

But how could he walk away?

Rudd pressed against the building, cloaking himself in shadow. He stood still, ears alert, eyes watchful.

The street was empty. Dimly and unevenly lit, although lights shown sporadically in the surrounding houses. And quiet. Even the wind seemed to have settled. In the distance, the roar of a motorcycle, the screech of sirens, the slamming of a car door. City sounds. Oddly comforting.

Funny, he felt no fear. Just the high-tension anxiety of moral dilemma. Clinging still to the thin edge of darkness, Rudd heard the soft tread of rubber-soled shoes, caught a glimpse of movement in the narrow sliver of public stairway on the other side of the road.

Street thugs, he told himself. A drug deal gone bad. Urban rats.

He tried to still the voice in his head, the voice that urged him to offer help. If there was a life in balance, he could tip the scales. Wasn't that what his own life had once been about?

Once.

A long time ago.

Out of the corner of his eye, Rudd caught the blur of movement heading his way. His heart quickened. He slipped into the tiny alcove of the building's entrance.

A darkened figure hurried past not ten feet from where he stood. Crossed briefly through the soft glow of a lone street light, and then once more into the cloak of night. But not before the picture had imprinted on Rudd's mind.

No city ruffians, after all.

Rudd wanted to slip away, forget he'd been here tonight. Forget the sound of gunfire. It wasn't anything that concerned him.

Except for that life that might be hanging by a thread.

Again, he cursed silently and crossed to the downhill side of the street. A stream of light angling from an opened doorway caught his eye. He hesitated, then started down the path that led to the entrance.

And then he saw it. Just inside the doorway, the crumpled form of a human body.

Rudd approached cautiously. A pool of blood had already begun forming on the tile floor below. He felt for a pulse, and found none. The flesh was still warm, but it wouldn't be for long.

The load of Rudd's moral dilemma lifted. There was nothing he could do.

CHAPTER 1

There are things you know before you know you know them. If I'd been listening to those cautionary whispers instead of silently debating my options for lunch, I might have turned Terri Harper away on the spot. Advised her to seek representation elsewhere.

As it was, she sat across from me, separated by the width of my faux-walnut desk, and regarded me earnestly with eyes the color of a summer sky.

"All we need," Terri said, "is someone to guide us through the legalities."

She tucked a strand of blond hair, highlighted by the hands of a professional, behind her ear. It was a gesture she'd made repeatedly since arriving at my office ten minutes earlier. Habit or nervousness? I couldn't decide.

"Mere paperwork and legal hoops," she added. "Nothing more."

I nodded, not convinced. Clients rarely understood that *mere paperwork* was an oxymoron. That every clause in a legal document, every word, in fact, was fraught with potential pitfalls.

Terri fingered the thin gold chain around her neck and smiled. She appeared to be in her early thirties, about my age or maybe a couple of years younger. A cotton sweater of warm taupe was draped casually around her shoulders, softening the formality of her linen slacks and white silk shirt. The diamond on her ring finger was the only thing about her that wasn't classically subdued.

"You come highly recommended, Ms. O'Brien. And I'd feel more comfortable working with a woman."

That was, as far as I could determine, my only real qualification for the job. "There are attorneys who specialize in adoption, who've got a network of contacts—"

"But I told you, we've already *found* a baby. That's the hard part. Believe me." Terri Harper's voice was girlish and dusted with the remnants of country twang, belying the model-like features and aura of sophistication that made such a striking first impression.

"It's an awful experience. An emotional roller coaster." The smile was gone. Her lovely features grew pinched at the memories. She looked down at her nails. "All those letters we sent out. Our life, our souls, reduced to a single sheet of advertising copy. And the waiting. The false hopes and leads that went nowhere . . ."

"That's why I was suggesting an attorney with experience in private adoptions."

Terri shook her head. "They don't understand either. For them, it's just a business transaction." She again tucked the errant honey-blond strand behind her ear. "Besides, that part is all behind us now. The mother, the birth mother that is, likes us. Really likes us. And she's committed to placing her baby for adoption. I'm sure she won't change her mind."

I looked out my office window to the blanket of gray that was just now beginning to break. Full sun was still an hour away. Summer in the city, Bay Area style. But at least here in Oakland we'd eventually see the sun. The same couldn't be said for the folks across the bay in San Francisco.

"How old is the baby?" I asked Terri.

"She isn't born yet. Melissa's due in a couple of weeks. Melissa Burke, she's the birth mother."

A couple of weeks. That was manageable. And maybe a couple of weeks on the other end. I'd just finished a big trial and there was nothing major looming on the horizon. Except bills. Straightforward and short-term were just what I was looking for. Breathing room. Money to tide me over until the rest of my life sorted itself out.

Terri leaned forward. "Steven had only nice things to say about you."

"Steven?"

"Cross."

My chest tightened. A name from the past. A name I'd had a hard time relegating to history.

Dr. Steven Cross had been an expert witness in a big case about seven years ago when I was still with Goldman and Latham. He'd advised us behind the scenes on another case a couple of years later, just before his wife and daughter were killed by a hit-and-run driver. I'd sent him a sympathy note and received in return a printed acknowledgment with a hand-scrawled *thanks for caring*. I still had the note, but we hadn't spoken in the five years since. I was sure it was for the best.

"He's the one who gave me your name," Terri said. "He knew I wasn't happy with the attorney we used before."

"Before?" I pushed the memory of Steven from my mind.

"A year and a half ago we were all set to adopt a little boy." Terri's voice broke and she paused, looking down at her hands until she'd regained her composure. "We'd brought him home, sent out announcements and everything, and then the birth mother changed her mind. Decided to marry the baby's father after all."

I'd read of such cases. Out of the thousands of adoptions that went smoothly, those that didn't were the ones that made headlines. California law streamlined the process in an attempt to avoid just that sort of heartbreak, but there were no guarantees.

"How terrible for you," I told Terri.

She nodded, took a gulp of air.

It was, I imagine, a wound that never healed. Which brought me back to her relationship with Steven Cross. Steven was a psychologist, formerly a consultant to the FBI, and now associated with UC Berkeley, but he probably saw private patients as well. I wondered in which role Terri Harper had made his acquaintance.

"What's your connection with Dr. Cross?" I asked.

With a quick brush of her hand, Terri again looped her hair behind her ear. "He's my brother," she said.

"Ah."

"Half-brother really. His father died when he was eight. Arlo married our mother a couple of years later and I came along ten months after the wedding." She capped the explanation with a smile, like she'd been down that road many times before.

"How's he doing?" I knew I would be better off not asking, but I couldn't help myself.

"He's doing okay," Terri said after a moment. "All things considered."

In general I shied away from clients with strings to friends or relatives, but Steven Cross wasn't really a friend. Certainly not anymore.

And I *could* use the income.

I uncapped my pen. "Let me get some information, and then we can map out what needs to be done. Does Melissa Burke live locally?"

Terri nodded. "In fact, she's living with us at the moment. It works out great because we know she's taking care of herself—not doing drugs or drinking or anything. You worry about stuff like that. I've been going to doctor appointments with her, too. And we're doing Lamaze training together."

"You and Melissa?"

"And my husband." Terri had the tact to laugh. "I know it sounds strange to people who haven't been there themselves. But open adoption involves rethinking lots of commonly accepted notions. It takes some getting used to, for everyone."

Frankly, I wasn't sure I'd have been up to it myself, either as prospective parent or birth mother. I was thankful I'd never been in a position to find out.

"How did you hook up with Melissa?"

"My guardian angel was working overtime. I swear, it would never have happened if somebody up there didn't care." Terri fingered the braided metal watchband at her wrist. "Losing Christopher was devastating for us. It put a lot of strain on our marriage." She paused and looked out the window. "There were some rocky times. But we finally pulled ourselves together and started in again with the newspaper ads, the letters to physicians, the ads on the Internet . . ."

"The Internet?"

"You want to cover all the bases. Anyway, we steeled ourselves for the inevitable crank calls and rejection. We'd barely gotten started when my husband broke a tooth. The dental receptionist remembered we'd been interested in adopting before. Her niece happened to know Melissa. The whole thing just fell into our laps."

"Amazing how that works."

"It is. Some things are just meant to be."

We covered the remaining points quickly. Terri's answers were concise and to the point, a far cry from what I get with some clients who ramble on, telling me everything but what I want to know.

Melissa Burke was nineteen. She'd come to California from a small town in Ohio last fall in order to establish residency for in-state tuition. She'd been sharing an apartment in Berkeley with three others until she'd joined the Harpers in their Pacific Heights home across the bay. At the time of the move, she'd quit her job making sandwiches at a local deli. The baby's father was a young man Melissa had known casually. There was no ongoing romance between them. Never had been. He had no interest in the child, and was relieved to be off the hook.

The Harpers and Melissa had already worked out the most troublesome aspect of an open adoption—the continuing role of the birth mother. Melissa wanted annual photos and updates, but no actual contact. The Harpers were more than happy to oblige.

"You must be thrilled to know you're going to have a baby soon," I said when we'd finished.

"Thrilled doesn't begin to describe it. Some days I have to pinch myself to make sure it's not all a dream." She practically glowed with pleasure. "I know you'll want a check, a retainer."

"If that won't be a problem."

"No, not at all." She reached for her purse. "Oh, I almost forgot. My husband's attorney suggested this affidavit. The man is obsessed with petty details."

Suddenly I was wary. "Your husband's attorney won't handle the adoption?"

"I wouldn't want him to. He's a grump who hasn't a drop of human blood in his veins." She pulled out a letter and handed it to me. "My husband couldn't come today but he signed this statement so you'll know we're together on this."

Buff-colored paper of the finest quality. Embossed letterhead. But what jumped out at me was the name at the bottom.

Terri Harper was the wife of Ted Harper, former star quarter-back for the 49ers and now the voice and face of TelAm Communications, hot new contender in the digital phone arena. His roguish smile graced billboards and print ads, but it was the sexy television commercials that swelled the ranks of his female fans.

Now that I knew who the players were, I remembered the earlier adoption fiasco well. The Harpers had fought to keep the child, but the law was squarely against them. That didn't stop the media, particularly the tabloids, from exploiting every possible twist and drawing the story out as long as possible.

"Will a thousand be okay?" Terri Harper asked. "I can make it for more, if you'd like."

"That will be fine."

She handed me the check. I hesitated a moment before I took it.

An adoption was an adoption, I reminded myself. But I had the feeling there'd be a lot of eyes watching this one.

CHAPTER 2

"Hey, boss." Jared stuck his head into my office. "Was that who I think it was?"

"Depends on who you thought it was."

"Ted Harper's wife?" It came out sounding more like a question than a statement.

"Right."

"Wow."

"And I don't like to be addressed as *boss*."

"So you've said."

I crossed my arms and looked at him. "Jared, listen to me. You may think that passing the bar exam is the only hurdle between you and success, but not pissing people off is equally important. Especially not your boss."

He grinned. "See, you said it yourself. You're the boss, so what's wrong with calling you that?"

"A few active brain cells will also stand you in good stead." I tried for a glower but found myself fighting the urge to smile.

Jared Takahashi-Jackson was working for me while awaiting bar exam results, the second time around. His failure to pass the first time was not actually his fault but the result of an overturned big rig that closed all but one lane of the Bay Bridge the second morning of the exam. And Jared, of course, hadn't timed his trip with any margin for surprises.

Jared was bright and hardworking, but not at all willing to temper his youthful brashness with anything akin to brown-nosing. He was, in many ways, a male version of the lawyer I wished I'd had the courage to be at his age.

"So," Jared said, leaning against the doorjamb, "are we handling a divorce here? Or maybe a postnup? Please don't tell me it's something dull like a testamentary trust."

"They're adopting a baby."

"The kid from before?"

I shook my head. "A newborn."

"Lucky kid." Jared looked almost wistful. His childhood had been anything but privileged.

"I think the Harpers consider themselves the lucky ones."

He rolled his eyes, like let's not get sappy about this, and started for the door. Then he turned back. "We don't have to do a lot of . . . of baby stuff with this, do we? I mean, we're not going to have an office full of pregnant girls crying their eyes out or anything?"

"We're just doing the paperwork."

Eat my own words.

I met with Melissa Burke the next day at The Barnacle, a restaurant along San Francisco's Embarcadero. As supportive as the Harpers might be, I didn't want them breathing down our necks while we talked. I had some rather pointed questions to ask Melissa, and anything less than absolute truthfulness would only sow the seeds for disaster down the road.

I picked Melissa out of the crowd immediately. A middle-America schoolgirl not long out of braces and gym shorts, with a bulging tummy and downcast eyes. Her hair was a muddy blond, shoulder length with feathered bangs. One hand was thrust into the pocket of a stylishly cut maternity dress, no doubt purchased by Terri. With the other, she clutched her pocketbook as though it tethered her in a roiling sea.

"Melissa?" She looked up. "I'm Kali O'Brien, the attorney hired by the Harpers to handle the adoption."

She extended a hand, her expression wary. "Pleased to meet you."

I'd reserved a table by the window, with a view of the water looking back toward Oakland and Berkeley. It also offered a bit more privacy. I'd worried initially that meeting in a public place might be awkward for her, but when I'd spoken with Melissa yesterday by phone, she'd leapt at the chance for lunch.

"This is really nice," she said now, primly unfolding her napkin onto her lap. "Very fancy."

"The food is good, as well. Or it used to be at any rate. I haven't been here in a couple of years, so we'll see."

"How come?"

A simple question to which I had at least ten variations of an answer. I opted for the short and sweet. "At one time I worked around here but I don't anymore."

That satisfied her.

We made small talk while we looked over the menu. Though there were only fifteen years between us in age, I found myself feeling unaccountably old. Like a maiden aunt entertaining a long-lost niece. It wasn't a role I relished, though some days it seemed one I was destined to fill. A woman always on the periphery.

I ordered a crab salad and Melissa had a club sandwich with fries. We both had the iced tea; I took mine with artificial sweetener while she loaded hers with two helpings of sugar.

"The first thing you need to understand, Melissa, is that you're entitled to your own lawyer. At the Harpers' expense."

"Why would I want that?"

"In theory, your interests and the Harpers' are not necessarily the same. The right to independent counsel is written into the law to ensure that you aren't being coerced into giving up your baby."

"I'm not being coerced."

"I believe that, but you might still want someone who is your advocate."

She shook her head. "The Harpers have been very nice to me. And I have no intention of keeping this baby. I want her to have a good home with parents who love her and all, but I don't want to be involved. Maybe it sounds selfish, but I want my own life. I want to go to college, have fun. I'm not ready to be tied down to a baby."

"That doesn't sound selfish, it sounds very mature."

She wrinkled her nose. "*Mature* would mean not being in this mess to begin with."

She had a lot more faith in maturity than I did. "If you're sure about not wanting your own lawyer, I'll need you to sign a waiver."

"A waiver?"

"Acknowledging that you've been advised of your right to counsel and declined."

She gave a nervous laugh. "Sounds like that Miranda warning people get when they're arrested."

"The theory is the same." The waiter brought our food and I waited until Melissa had taken a couple of bites before hitting her with my next question. "I need to ask about the baby's father," I said. "I'll need his name and a way to contact him."

She dunked a French fry in catsup and ate it without answering.

I waited. "Will there be a problem? Terri seemed to think he'd be happy to be freed of any obligations."

"Do we really have to involve him?"

"I'm afraid so. You don't have to talk to him if you'd rather not. I can handle it myself. But we do need to notify him of the adoption and hopefully get a signed consent."

She ate another French fry in silence.

"Even if he doesn't sign the consent," I explained, "we can go ahead. But he has to be notified."

She wiped her mouth with her napkin.

"Does he know about the baby, Melissa?"

"That's all he has to do, sign a paper that says it's okay to place the baby for adoption?"

"Right. And like I said before, even without his signature, it's okay as long as he's notified and doesn't protest." This was a legality that provided for fathers who were wary about acknowledging paternity on paper. A not uncommon phenomenon.

Melissa looked out the window. A pair of tug boats was herding a large cargo ship as it passed under the Bay Bridge. Finally she shook her head. "I don't think there will be a problem. Let me talk to him first, then you can do whatever is necessary."

I felt a weight I hadn't even been aware of lifted from my shoulders. I leaned back. "What was your relationship with him, if you don't mind my asking."

Melissa shrugged. "Wasn't much of a relationship. Just, you know, one of those things."

Unfortunately, I knew exactly. Only I'd been lucky enough, or smart enough, to avoid finding myself in her position.

"Someone your own age?"

She raised her eyes, gave me a funny look, then turned to again gaze out the window. "He's a couple of years older, I think." Her tone put an end to further inquiry.

We talked some about her home in Ohio (no, her parents didn't know about the baby and she wanted to make sure they never found out), about her plans for college (she wasn't sure what she'd major in yet, but not anything related to math or science), the decision to give birth (she was raised Catholic so abortion was never a consideration), and the Harpers. Melissa was clearly in awe of them, more, I feared, because of their wealth and reputation than because she thought they'd be good parents.

"You're entitled to counseling," I told her. "It's your right by law. And it might help you."

"I don't need counseling. I'm fine with what I'm doing." She sounded almost defiant.

"Okay. I'll draw up the consent forms. It's best to have a medical history, too. Then, after the baby is born, there'll be another couple of forms to sign. The rest of the procedure involves filing papers with the proper court. That's not anything you need to be involved with."

The waiter cleared our plates and handed us dessert menus. Melissa ordered a slice of chocolate mousse cake and milk. I had black coffee.

Over dessert, Melissa oscillated between talkative moods, mostly about Ted and Terri, and periods where she was so quiet I felt as though I were being forced to deliver a soliloquy.

"You want me to give you a ride somewhere?" I asked when I'd paid the check.

"No thanks. I've got the Explorer."

Confusion must have registered in my expression because Melissa patted her belly and explained. "It's Ted's, but he hardly drives it. They let me use it whenever I want. Safety for the baby and all. They've even talked about letting me keep it when I leave."

No longer for the baby's safety, I gathered. "That's very generous of them."

So generous, in fact, it made me uncomfortable. While it wasn't unusual for adoptive parents to provide some limited financial assistance to the birth mother during the pregnancy—usually in the form of medical bills and housing—anything that smacked of baby buying was a crime. On the other hand, she *was* living with them, and use of a family car could hardly be classed as criminal.

We parted at the restaurant entrance. "You won't forget to put me in touch with the baby's father, will you?"

Melissa took a breath and shook her head. "I'll talk to him right away. I don't expect there to be a problem."

CHAPTER 3

True to her word, Melissa called Thursday afternoon to say that she'd talked to the baby's father, Gary Ellis, and that he would come by my office the next morning to sign papers.

He showed up about ten, looking painfully, and understandably, uncomfortable. He shifted from one foot to another and jingled the change in his pocket.

"Thank you for coming by so quickly," I told him, trying my best to sound reassuring. "This won't take long, and then you can put the matter behind you for good."

"All's I'm doing is saying it's okay for the baby to be adopted, right?"

"Right. As a matter of fact, signing the consent relieves you of responsibility. After this, you're off the hook."

The news didn't appear to offer him much relief. He continued to avoid my gaze as he dropped into the chair I'd indicated.

I slid the document across the desk toward him, and while Gary studied it, I studied him. He looked to be a few years older than Melissa, maybe twenty-one or twenty-two, but he was still very young. About my height, with a beer gut and dark hair that needed both a barber's scissors and a vigorous shampooing. My first thought was that Melissa had to have been very lonely, or very horny, to end up in bed with Gary Ellis.

He scrawled his name quickly, shoved the paper back across my desk, and rose, again thrusting his hands into his pockets. "That's it then?"

"It would be helpful to have a health history."

He looked at me as though I'd suggested he strip for a complete physical on the spot.

"There's a standard form," I told him. "Family history of diseases, allergies, that sort of thing."

"Uh-uh. Melissa said all I had to do was sign."

"Why don't you take it with you. It doesn't have to be filled out today."

He snagged the form from my hand and was out the door so fast it took me a moment to realize he was gone.

I don't often slip into sentimentality, but I experienced a moment's sadness for the baby girl who would someday wonder about her birth father. I hoped she would never learn the truth.

I jotted down a brief summary of the conversation and filed the adoption folder in the outer office. I was making due at the moment without a secretary. Without a lot of things, in fact.

My tenure in the office was supposed to be temporary, an assignment to fill in for a friend from law school who had become ill. Our well-laid plans had begun to unravel almost at once, however, and temporary had stretched on for longer than either of us expected. I carried what was left of her case load, and had taken on a few clients of my own, but I felt as though I were treading water. Keeping myself afloat while I decided which shore to head toward.

I'd returned to the Bay Area from Silver Creek, where I'd moved several years earlier and made a new life for myself—but that life hadn't worked out so smoothly either. Still, there was a limit to how long a person could live in limbo.

I was getting ready to call Terri Harper to tell her that we had the father's release, when she called me.

"Ted and I are having a small get-together this Sunday at our place in Napa. Very informal, just a few friends and family. If you're not already busy, why don't you come by. You'll have a chance to meet Ted, and you can bring the papers for Melissa's signature."

The Napa Valley, renowned for its many vineyards and wineries, also lays claim to some of the state's most idyllic surroundings. It took me about two seconds to mentally rearrange my plans for the day. I could pull weeds anytime.

"I'd love to come," I told Terri.

"Great." She gave me directions. "See you about eleven."

Jared was close to collapsing under the weight of his envy. "A party at the Harpers'! Geez. Can't I go as your date or something?"

"Afraid not. But I'll give you a full report on Monday."

He looked glum. "No offense, boss, but it's not the same."

I handed him a file folder. "How about spending some time in the shadow of the limelight, then?"

"Huh?"

"I want you to do a bit of a background checking on Melissa Burke and Gary Ellis. Nothing exhaustive, but look into marriage records, general lifestyle, and so forth. I'd like to avoid any last-minute surprises."

He scratched his cheek. "Does that happen often?"

"Statistically it's a very small percent, but that's little consolation when your case is the one that blows up."

Sunday dawned bright and warm, a rare event during summer in the Bay Area, where coastal fog often lingers until past noon. It was going to be downright hot in the Napa Valley.

With the sky such a glorious blue, I passed on exercise class at the gym in favor of a brisk walk. I was counting on the fact that I'd burned off enough calories for at least two extra canapes.

Driving north, I turned on the radio looking for something lively and festive. Something with solid rhythm and a quick tempo. What I got was the strident voice of Bram Weaver, talk show host with a mission. In Weaver's never humble opinion, feminism and the so-called "liberation of women" were at the root of everything wrong with society today. And in case his listeners hadn't noticed, there was plenty wrong.

That morning, he was railing against women who refused to take their husband's name at marriage.

"The greatest gift a man can give," he bellowed, "is his name. I ask you, what kind of woman would refuse? Isn't marriage about two people becoming one? If she doesn't love you enough to take your name, fellows, think what trouble you're going to have down the road!"

When a caller, a woman, suggested that a man might take on the wife's surname, he grew belligerent and launched into another of his tirades. "You women are all alike. You want to have your cake and eat it too. Give me special treatment in the job market, give me family leave, gimme, gimme. You never think about giving back."

I sometimes listened to Weaver's program, largely because it was such fun to argue with him in my head. Even on those rare occasions when I agreed with him in principle, I took umbrage at his single-focused, and largely misguided, attacks on women. It would have been easy to laugh them aside if he didn't also have a book on the bestseller list and a growing audience.

I punched the buttons until I found a classic rock station, then sang along with the Beatles about yesterday as I headed up Highway 29.

Following Terri's directions, I wound past acres of vineyards and old stone wineries, then turned and climbed into the hills. The grapes were beginning to hang heavy on the vines and the grasses beyond had turned to summer gold.

The Harpers' house was set back from the road through a gated driveway, and overlooked the valley below. Actually, *house* was much too prosaic a word. Villa or estate would have been more apt. The main building was a sprawling structure that looked like something out of one of those glossy, twelve-dollar-an-issue magazines. The central portion of the house was constructed of heavy, natural stone reminiscent of the original wineries in the vicinity, though it had clearly been remodeled and updated. The remainder of the house was wood and glass—a more modern design that blended beautifully with the old stone.

The Harpers' *small, informal gathering* totaled probably forty people, many of whom were dressed far more elegantly than met my definition of casual. Thank goodness I'd decided to wear rayon slacks and shell with a linen overshirt rather than the khakis and T-shirt I'd pulled from my closet initially.

I stood in the stone-floored entryway and looked around for famous faces. Names I could drop to needle Jared. Didn't recognize a soul.

Terri waved to me from the main room—a room built for throwing parties from the looks of it—just as a waiter held out a silver tray of bubbling champagne glasses. I snagged one and moved toward Terri. She was wearing black slacks and a white silk shirt that combined the best of sophisticated and relaxed.

"Did you have any trouble finding us?" she asked.

"Your directions were perfect."

"Good. There really aren't many ways to go so it's hard to get too lost."

We were standing by French doors that opened onto a deck. I

turned an admiring eye to the view. "Your place is beautiful," I told her.

"It's a wonderful retreat. We bought it when Ted was still playing ball." She laughed. "And still making big money. It's actually nicer than our house in the city."

She turned away to say a few words to a couple who were passing by. "Yes, we are. So thrilled. Nice to see you, too."

"You're busy," I said. "I should let you get back to your hostess duties."

She gave me an impish grin. "I hate playing hostess. Most of these are Ted's friends, anyway."

"Where is he?"

"He and my father wanted to check on some grapes. They should be back soon."

"Your parents live nearby?" I tried to recall if Steven had mentioned them. I didn't think he had.

"In Carmel. We see them fairly often, and I'm sure we'll see even more of them after the baby is born." She made the comment with a straight face, but I could tell by the glint in her eye that it would be something of a mixed blessing. "My mother adored Rebecca," Terri added soberly.

Rebecca. Steven's seven-year-old daughter. Dead, along with her mother, because some idiot had driven through a red light at close to fifty miles an hour. And he'd kept right on going.

"I gather they're excited about the baby," I said, pushing the memory of the accident aside.

Terri nodded. "Excited is putting it mildly. Some people don't feel an adopted baby is a *real* grandchild, but thankfully my parents aren't like that. They've been waiting so long I don't think they'd care if the baby arrived via UPS." She looked at my empty glass. "Can I get you more?"

"I should probably take care of work first. Is Melissa around?"

"Upstairs. She said she was tired, but I imagine it's more that she doesn't like mixing with a bunch of people she doesn't know. I told her I'd send you up to see her when you arrived." She hesitated. "You said the paperwork from the baby's father is complete?"

"Except for medical information, which isn't required."

"What's he like?"

"You've never met him?"

She shook her head. "Melissa was so reluctant. We were afraid that if we insisted, we'd lose her. So all we know is what she's told us. To tell you the truth, I was kind of worried there might be a problem."

I described Gary Ellis in the most flattering light possible, but the fact that he'd finally given his consent was the attribute that outweighed all others in Terri's mind. Then I headed up a curving stairway to the second door on the left, as she had instructed.

I knocked. "It's Kali. Can I come in?"

"Sure. The door's not locked."

Melissa sprawled on the sofa in what appeared to be a library. The leather furniture and oriental carpets lent a heavy, masculine feel to the room. Richly stained wooden shelves lined one whole wall, though books were noticeably lacking. Two VCRs, a large-screen television, and a sound system filled the cabinetry instead. Melissa was watching a cartoon program I didn't recognize.

"Terri said you had some papers for me to sign." Melissa hit the remote and the wild screams from the screen went mute.

"Right." I sat in a chair kitty-corner from her. "Gary came to see me on Friday. I appreciate your getting in touch with him so promptly. I hope it wasn't too hard on you."

She kept her eyes on the television screen. "Not really."

I couldn't help myself. "Was he surprised to hear from you?"

"Probably, but it's not like we have deep feelings for each other."

I handed her the two documents—a health history and the Declaration of Mother, which is the official document relating to parentage. She signed the latter after a cursory glance, and filled out the former with almost equal haste.

"Terri requested medical records after we first met," Melissa said testily. "She probably knows more about my health history than I do."

"You sound weary," I told her. And a little angry, but I didn't say that.

"I guess I am. It's hard to sleep when there's a baby partying inside you."

"Rough night?"

She shrugged. "And now *they're* all partying down there, and I'm up here, big and fat and ugly." She blinked away tears.

"Maybe spending so much time with the Harpers isn't a good

idea. You have your own life, after all. Your own friends. Do you see them much?"

"A little. I haven't exactly been a zippy person to be around these last few months. Besides, I like Ted and Terri. I really do."

Except they were a dozen or so years older, a married couple with interests and preferences that had to be very different from Melissa's. "Another month, right? And then you can reclaim your life."

Melissa brushed her eyes with the back of her hand. "Yeah, my wonderful life." Her voice was heavy with sarcasm.

"I can imagine this hasn't been an easy experience. It will be good to have it behind you."

"Whatever," she said with a lack of interest, and turned her attention back to the soundless screen.

Downstairs, I was immediately summoned by Terri, who introduced me to her parents, Lenore and Arlo Cross. They were both tall, like Terri, and her mother had the same slender figure and honey blond hair. Her father, however, was a big man, broad through the shoulders and the middle, but solidly built. Even his nose and mouth were large, as was his voice.

"Pleased to meet you," he boomed, though I was standing not an arm's length away.

"So am I," Lenore added. "Glad to know that Ted and Terri have finally got an attorney lined up. I don't know why they were so slow about getting this process underway. I've been telling them they shouldn't leave these things to the last minute."

"Mother, I've explained this I don't know how many times. Throw too much legal stuff at people before they're ready, and they run." Terri's voice held an edge of irritation.

"Just because that first birth mother changed her—"

Terri interrupted. "We wanted Melissa to feel comfortable."

"Well, she certainly does feel that." Lenore Cross gave a little laugh.

"A solid personal relationship is more important than a bunch of meaningless forms anyway," Terri said.

"Yes, dear, but one can never be too careful."

Arlo Cross held out his empty champagne glass to be refilled by a passing waiter. "Well, they've got someone on top of things now. That's all that matters."

Out of the corner of my eye I saw Ted approach. Though I'd never seen him in person, I recognized him in a flash. Dark eyes, dark hair, and shoulders so broad he looked almost top-heavy. He was not quite as handsome in the flesh as on screen, but there was no getting around the fact that he was a man who stood out in a crowd. And he knew it. He eased into our cluster and slid a hand along Terri's shoulder. She turned and smiled at him.

"Ted, this is Kali O'Brien. The adoption attorney. The one who's a friend of Steven's."

Ted extended a hand. "Pleased to meet you."

Jared would no doubt have appreciated the moment more than I, but I was not entirely immune to the aura of stardom. I felt my skin tingle at the warmth of his handshake.

"Do what needs to be done to make it airtight," Ted said. "Money's not the object here."

"The fees are fairly straightforward," I told him, "as is the law. Melissa is the only unknown in the equation, and you both seem comfortable with her."

"She's a sweetheart," Ted said.

A man of similar age and build buddy-punched Ted in the shoulder. "Hey, looking good, Harper."

"Charlie. Great to see you." The two moved off toward the deck.

Lenore, who'd been quietly studying her champagne glass, looked at me. "I didn't know you were a friend of Steven's."

"Friend is probably not the right word. We worked together on a couple of cases."

A truth of sorts. This was the lawyer's art, recasting facts without actually lying.

Lenore's face grew pinched. Despite similarities in appearance between herself and Terri, the age difference was clear if you looked closely. "Did you know his wife, Caroline, too?"

Even the name, so casually dropped, sent my stomach into spasms. "I'd met her."

"And Rebecca?"

I shook my head. "I certainly heard about her, though." Another careful adaptation of reality. Steven had been careful to keep his home life private.

"Such a tragedy. Rebecca would have been twelve next month.

Almost a teenager." Lenore Cross was silent a moment. "It changed Steven."

I didn't trust myself to say anything. Wasn't sure that if I opened my mouth, I might not blurt out the truth.

"He's coming today, isn't he?" Lenore asked, addressing Terri. "I expected him before now."

"He said he'd try to make it, but he'd be late. You know how hard it is to pin Steven down to anything."

I felt panic building in my veins. I didn't want to see Steven Cross again. Couldn't imagine what I'd say.

"I hope he's not bringing Myra," Arlo said. "That woman brings out the worst in me."

"Who's Myra?" I asked before I remembered I didn't want to know.

"Someone he's been dating for the last, what"—Terri turned to her mother—"six months?"

Lenore nodded. "Off and on."

Dating. A tiny bubble caught in my throat. Of course he'd be dating. Did I think he'd put his life on hold?

I reminded myself that my mission at this gathering was purely business. Get it done, get out.

Ted rejoined the group. "Sorry to run off like that. But it wouldn't do to snub Charlie."

"Ted," I said, turning toward him, "if you've got a few minutes, I'd like to run through the adoption procedures with you. I explained them to Terri last week, and I'm sure she's filled you in, but just to make sure there aren't any loose ends . . ."

"Sure, no problem. Just let me get a fresh glass of champagne. Would you like one?"

"I'll pass for now."

"Meet you in my office at the end of the hallway then. I won't be but a minute."

When he joined me there maybe five minutes later, I'd already made my way down the wall of photographs—mostly publicity pictures of Ted and society shots of Ted and Terri, but there were a few of family as well. I lingered over one with Steven, Caroline, and Rebecca at the beach.

"Terri calls that my ego wall," Ted said, setting his glass on the polished wood credenza next to a bronzed trophy cup.

"There are some striking photos of Terri, too."

Ted laughed. "I think she'd say that was part of the ego trip." He sat at the desk and propped his feet on an open file drawer. "So, what did you need to tell me?"

There was a smooth assurance about his manner. Not arrogance exactly, but close to it. Impatience maybe. It didn't surprise me, in any event.

"I want to make sure that you and Terri are in agreement—"

"Absolutely." He gestured with his hand, a knifelike movement that underscored the point.

"And you have no concerns about Melissa's role down the road? About sending her pictures and so forth."

He shook his head. "She's a sweet girl. It's like she's become a friend of the family."

I went over the steps we'd be taking. "The baby will come home from the hospital with you and Terri," I concluded. "As soon as she's released, Melissa can waive her right to revoke consent, and that's it. The adoption won't be final legally until there's been a court decree, but that part is pretty much a formality."

Ted crossed his arms behind his head and grinned. "We're ready." He laughed. "Even if it does mean more visits from the in-laws."

Just then Melissa appeared at the doorway looking as white as a sheet.

"Hey, Mel, what's up?" Ted straightened, put his feet on the floor.

Melissa clutched her belly. "I feel kinda funny."

"Funny?" Ted asked.

"I think it's . . ." She grimaced and bent forward at the waist. "I think I'm in labor."

CHAPTER 4

I was home watching *The X-Files* when the phone rang later that evening. I sprinted to answer it, sure it would be one of the Harpers calling to announce the birth of the baby. Instead, it was Jared.

I was both annoyed and amused. "Couldn't you wait until to-morrow morning to hear about the party?"

"I've got a dentist appointment."

"You aren't going to spend all day at the dentist, are you?"

"Maybe half the day. It's a double crown and—"

I sighed heavily into the phone. "Please don't tell me you are one of these people who goes ga-ga over famous names."

He laughed. "Not the male ones, for damned sure. I'm not call-ing to hear about the party anyway."

"That's a relief." Jared had been working for me only a couple of months. So far it was an easy relationship, but I often found myself braced for surprises. "There isn't much to report, in any event," I told him. "No starlets or Hall-of-Famers."

"Not that you'd have recognized them."

My turn to laugh. "So true." I told him about Melissa's labor and could practically feel him recoiling over the phone line. Jared hadn't sweated through three years of law school to talk about babies. "So why'd you call?"

He hesitated. "Since I won't be in tomorrow morning, I thought I'd better let you know now about the Coles."

I punched the remote to lower the volume. I had the feeling this was not good news. "Who are the Coles?"

Another pause. "The couple who think they're adopting Me-lissa's baby."

"What?" I switched the phone to my other ear, in case I'd simply misunderstood. "How can they think that?"

"Well, they shouldn't be thinking it anymore since they haven't seen her for two months. But you know how it goes, desire springs eternal."

"Hope. Hope springs eternal."

"Same idea. They want the baby and they refuse to believe she's changed her mind about them."

"Whoa. Back up. How do they know Melissa?"

"She answered their ad. One of those *Loving couple want to adopt* things. They talked on the telephone, met face to face, and hit it off right away. Or so Mrs. Cole says. Melissa apparently told them she wanted them to have her baby. Then out of the blue, she sent them a note saying she'd changed her mind and chosen another couple."

"She's within her rights to do that." Though I wished she'd told me about it herself.

"I know," Jared said. "And so should the Coles, but they found some hotheaded lawyer and they're threatening to sue."

"On what grounds?"

"I'm not sure. Probably fraud or emotional distress or something."

"That's crazy. It will be tossed out of court." Or it would be if the system worked as it was supposed to. "Who's the lawyer, do you know?"

"Thatcher. She sounds like one tough cookie."

"You talked to her?"

"I was in the office this afternoon, working on the pleading for the Nelson case, when she called. Didn't seem at all surprised to find someone there on Sunday."

"Maybe she's one of those lawyers who doesn't know what the word *weekend* means. Do you know anything about this couple?"

"Only that they live in San Jose and they're bent out of shape about losing the baby. I suspect they're hoping Melissa will decide to give them the baby after all just to avoid the legal hassles. Even if there's no chance in hell they'll win, it kinda puts a kink in things."

"It's Melissa's choice who she wants for parents. The Coles can sue her all they want but it won't affect the Harpers' adoption." Nonetheless, it was a discomfiting twist.

"Thought you'd want to know," Jared said.

"Thanks."

He paused, then asked sheepishly, "Seeing as how you're on the line anyway . . . uh, how was the party?"

The phone was silent for the remainder of the evening. I paced around the apartment like an expectant aunt, too nervous to settle into anything for long.

The house felt empty without the company of my housemates Bea and Dotty, two retired sisters to whom I'd rented the house during my sojourn in Silver Creek. Since my return to the Bay Area, they'd graciously sublet the downstairs in-law unit back to me with shared kitchen privileges. I'd been unsure about the arrangement at first, but with housing prices being what they were, I'd given it a try—and grown to appreciate their companionship, not to mention their cooking.

They'd taken the Gambler's Special to Reno for the weekend, as excited as school kids before summer break. I couldn't imagine the trip would live up to their expectations, but then I couldn't imagine anything pleasurable about forty-eight hours of stale, smoky air and raucous noise either. A casino is not my idea of a good time.

I tried calling the Harpers about ten that night and got the answering machine. I called again the next morning from work and this time reached Ted, who sounded exhausted but happy.

"Six pounds, two ounces," he said. "The cutest little thing you ever saw." I could practically hear him grinning over the telephone wire.

"So everything's okay?"

"Melissa had to have a C-section and they wouldn't let us be present for that, even though they routinely let *biological* fathers attend." There was just the briefest trace of bitterness in his voice. "The baby is doing fine and so is Melissa, but she's still pretty doped up."

"I guess congratulations are in order."

"The doctor says the baby should be able to come home in a couple of days. Her lungs are real well developed and everything. God, she's beautiful, and so tiny. Terri and I each got to hold her. It was an incredible high."

"Does she have a name?"

"Hannah Elizabeth Lenore Harper. A big name for such a little thing, but she'll grow into it."

"I'll see if we can expedite the signing of the waiver." Generally it couldn't be signed until the mother had left the hospital, but there was an exception for cases where she remained after the baby had been released.

"That would be great," Ted said. "We don't want this to drag on any longer than it has to."

I decided the best way of dealing with the Coles was to ignore them. Now that the baby had been born, Melissa had only to sign the waiver of consent, and the matter would be settled for good. To that end, I stopped by the hospital that afternoon. Melissa was still pretty groggy and was clearly in no state to sign anything.

Hannah went home with the Harpers the following day, and on Thursday Terri called.

"Have you seen Melissa yet?" she inquired.

I'd seen her three times in as many days, but what Terri was asking, I knew, was whether Melissa had signed the final adoption papers.

"She's not a happy camper at the moment," I explained. "It's not only the Cesarean, but she's developed an infection as well."

"Does that mean she hasn't signed them?"

"Not yet."

"How much concentration does it take to sign your name, for God's sake." There was a harshness to Terri's tone I'd not heard before.

"It doesn't mean she's changed her mind, Terri, just that her mind is on other things."

"Can't you nudge her a little?"

"She could always claim duress. The law is pretty clear about the mother's state of mind. Besides, pressuring her might backfire."

There was a moment's silence from the other end of the phone. "Until she does sign," Terri said, "Hannah isn't really ours."

I was as eager as Terri to see things handled expeditiously, but it was also important they be done correctly. "Don't start imagining trouble where there isn't any. This is a process that has to move at its own pace."

"I just want everything to be settled."

"I can understand that."

"Come see Hannah, why don't you. She's amazing."

We set a time for later that afternoon.

I skipped lunch and went shopping for a baby gift instead. The move struck me as totally illogical on a number of fronts. I was a lawyer not a godmother, for one. And babies had never held much fascination for me. But I did it anyway, and didn't even try to figure out why.

Afterward, I stopped by the hospital again to see Melissa, who was looking better than she had the previous day. She was propped up in bed, leafing through *People* magazine. A large and colorful bouquet of flowers rested on the small dresser across the room.

"They're from Terri and Ted," Melissa said when she saw me looking.

"They're lovely." There were no other flowers or cards in the room.

She nodded, and made an effort to sound sprightly. "The doctor says he'll probably release me on Monday."

"That's good."

"Except it's going to be lonely living by myself."

"You've got friends. And you'll meet new people once school starts."

She looked skeptical. Her eyes began to tear up.

"You're doing the right thing, Melissa. Giving the baby a happy home with two parents who love her and can care for her."

"I know that. It's not that I have doubts about what I'm doing."

"Do you think you're ready to sign the final papers?"

Given her mood, I expected her to hesitate. But she didn't. "Then it will be official, right?"

"For all intents and purposes. There are a few legal hoops we have to toss papers through, but as far as you're concerned, it's a done deal."

"Do you have them with you?"

I pulled the folder out of my briefcase, relieved that I would bring Terri the best baby present of all. Melissa took the pen I offered, scanned the page, and signed her name. Then wiped away a tear.

"There," she said, handing the packet back to me. "My baby has a good home."

Hannah was in good hands, but it was clear Melissa wasn't. Whoever her friends were, they had not rallied to offer support.

"You need any help getting settled, give me a call, okay? I'm great at lining shelves and toting boxes."

She smiled, and I realized it was the first time I'd seen her do so. "Thanks. I appreciate it."

From the hospital, I went to see Hannah.

The Harpers' San Francisco house wasn't as plush as their "weekend" place in the Napa Valley, but it was still large and imposing, situated near the crest of Pacific Heights. Another vignette of *life among the rich and famous* to share with Jared.

I'd arrived about ten minutes early, but I doubted Terri was punching a time clock. I rang the bell. The door opened immediately.

I blinked and stepped back. "Steven!" It was more an utterance of surprise than greeting.

"Hello, Kali." He looked as startled as I felt, but he recovered much more quickly. He actually managed a smile. "Good to see you again."

At first impression, Steven looked just as I'd remembered. The unruly buckskin brown hair that hung over one eye, the slightly asymmetrical features, the five o'clock shadow at midday. But he'd changed too. A little older, a little heavier. His face had more tension to it, his eyes weren't as lively. He had a worn look, I thought. Like faded denim.

"I was just leaving," Steven said.

Probably because he knew I was scheduled to arrive soon. He couldn't have been any more anxious to run into me than I was him. Yet he'd referred Terri and Ted to me.

I stepped back to allow him room to pass. "Thank you for giving Terri my name."

He nodded. "I heard you were back in town. And Terri needed a lawyer who was user-friendly, so to speak. I thought of you immediately."

User-friendly. Not the highest compliment among lawyers, who prefer to be known for their sharp minds and tongues, but among psychologists it probably amounted to praise.

We stood awkwardly for a moment, then Steven nodded again, for no reason. "Well, I'd best get going."

Suddenly, I felt I had to say something. "Steven, I wish I—"

He held up a hand. "I know, Kali. Believe me, I know. But beating yourself up over something that's done serves no purpose." He paused, started to say something, then changed his mind and started down the stairs. "Go take a look at Hannah. She's a beauty."

I watched Steven's retreating form for a moment longer, then turned and let myself in, surprised to find that my legs were wobbly.

In the marble-tiled entry, I paused to breathe deeply and steady myself. Then I called out to announce my arrival.

Terri appeared at the top of the stairs. "Hi, Kali. Come on up. Did you see Steven? He was just here."

"He let me in."

The entry was large, with an antique chest and a Miro-like painting on the wall above it. My eyes made a quick sweep of the artist's signature at the bottom. The genuine article.

Terri led me to the nursery. A sunny room done in shades of yellow and adorned with enough stuffed animals to fill an ark.

"Here she is," Terri said proudly.

Hannah was indeed a beautiful baby. Bright blue eyes that shone with curiosity, clear skin, and a downy, golden blond fuzz that would grow into real hair with time. She was tucked into an infant seat, swaddled in a creamy white hand-crocheted blanket.

I felt unexpected maternal stirrings somewhere behind my ribs and made a concerted effort to ignore them.

My biological clock, ticking away right when I'd finally come to accept the fact that I was alone. Whether by fate or choice, I hadn't yet decided.

I touched the top of Hannah's head with my fingers. Soft and warm. I could feel her tiny pulse beating just under the skin. "She's lovely," I said.

"She is," Terri agreed. "In every way."

For years I'd attended friends' baby showers and christenings. I'd oohed and aahed like a pro, but it never seemed any different to me than looking at vacation slides of a trip to the Grand Canyon. Lately, though, I'd noticed a tug somewhere deeper. Hannah's newborn helplessness practically knocked me over.

Terri adjusted the blanket even though it was fine as it was. "Can I get you some coffee or something?"

"No thanks. I can't stay long." I handed her the brightly wrapped gift. "For Hannah."

"You didn't need to do that." But Terri had begun tearing into the paper before she finished speaking. "Look, Hannah, a doggie. And a book. *The Runaway Bunny.* This is one of Mommy's favorite stories, Hannah." She turned to me, hugging the stuffed terrier to her chest. "This was so sweet of you. Thank you."

"It will be a while before Hannah is old enough to enjoy them, I guess."

"Not that long really. And we'll be sure to tell her how grateful we are for your help."

"Speaking of which, I have an even better present. Melissa signed the consent papers. The adoption is about as final as it can get without being totally official."

Terri threw her arms around me. "That's wonderful news. We should break out the champagne this minute."

"Better to save it for when Ted is home."

"Melissa called here last night," Terri said. "She didn't mention anything about the consent, but she did ask to stay with us awhile."

"What? Absolutely not."

"That's what I say, but Ted thinks maybe we should let her. Just until she gets her strength back. The C-section and infection were more than she bargained for."

"It's not a good idea, Terri. In fact, it's a bad idea. No matter how open the adoption, Hannah is your daughter now. Having Melissa move in will only complicate things. For her as well as you all."

Terri nodded silently.

"She has a place in Berkeley, doesn't she? Ted said you'd found it together."

"Right. We even paid the first couple of months' rent."

"You've done more than can be expected."

"I know, it's just so. . ." Hannah started to whimper and Terri picked her up to comfort her. "It's just that Melissa is, well, so needy."

"You're adopting Hannah, remember, not Melissa." I'd been wondering how and when to bring up the Coles. This seemed as good a time as any. Now that Melissa had signed the final papers, they weren't a threat to the Harpers. But I thought Terri should know nonetheless.

I started to explain but Terri interrupted. "Melissa was up front with us about that from the start," Terri said. "The Coles were, are, nice people, I'm sure. But they can't offer Hannah what we can. Melissa liked them because they are Catholic like she is, but she never felt comfortable with them."

Nor had they been able to offer her use of a car, rent, or temporary room and board in Pacific Heights. But it also helped explain why Ted and Terri were so solicitous of Melissa. She'd changed her mind once and they didn't want her to do so again.

Fortunately, that was all behind them now.

"Concentrate on being Hannah's mother," I told Terri. "Melissa will figure out how to take care of herself."

I was in court all day Friday on a slip-and-fall case. From there, I went straight to the gym. I knew if I went home first, I'd find some excuse to keep me there. Or I'd putter around the house until it was too late, then curl up with a glass of wine and a book, and promise myself that tomorrow, for sure, I'd do a healthy workout.

I started in the weight room, surrounded by grunting testosterones and biceps as big as my waist—and I'm no Scarlett O'Hara. Finally, I moved on to the treadmill. Here at least, the women held their own, in numbers if not in intensity. And many of both sexes were in worse shape than me, which I found heartening.

On the way home, I picked up a veggie burrito and held off eating it until I'd poured myself a glass of wine. Bea and Dotty were out for the evening—I couldn't remember whether Fridays were ballroom dancing or Italian cooking—so I sorted through the mail and listened to my messages while I munched. I tried not to dwell on the fact that I was once again home alone on a Friday night.

Jared had called asking me to phone him when I got in.

I half suspected he wanted a rundown on the Harpers' Pacific Heights house and thought about putting off the return call. Prudence won out, however, and I picked up the phone.

"Hey, boss," Jared said. "We got a problem."

"It can't wait?"

"I don't think so."

"Can you handle it yourself?" For a guy who saw himself as the Perry Mason of the new millennium, Jared was sometimes maddeningly unwilling to step up to the plate.

"Bram Weaver was here, boss."

"Weaver? The talk show host?"

"Yep. The man women love to hate."

Not all women. There were a surprising number who ate up his sermonizing about *a woman's role.* "What did he want?"

Jared paused. "His daughter."

"His—"

"He claims he's the father of Melissa Burke's baby."

CHAPTER 5

"What do you mean she's not here?" I stared in disbelief at the exhausted-looking woman seated behind the hospital reception desk. "She's been here all week."

"She checked out about four hours ago."

"Monday," I protested. "Melissa was supposed to be discharged on Monday. Not today."

After the call from Jared, I'd headed straight for the hospital to talk to Melissa. No telephone calls, no passing Go, no collecting anything, even my wits. And I was still too late.

The woman sighed, clearly exasperated by a long day of dealing with people like me. "You might try one of the nurses. Third floor. Take the elevator to your right."

The third-floor nurse, crisp and efficient, could tell me nothing beyond fact that Melissa Burke had left that afternoon, without waiting for the doctor's release. "It's against policy," she said, "but we aren't a jail. We can't force people to stay if they don't want to."

"What made her decide to leave?"

The nurse shrugged and went back to the sorting of files I'd interrupted. A moon-faced black woman, a patient rather than nurse, addressed me. "You asking about Melissa, that young girl had a C-section?"

"Right."

"Was her father. He come here today ready to whup her ass."

"Her father?"

"What she says. Acted like a father, too. All mean and nasty."

"Her father?" I asked again, puzzled. She'd said her parents didn't even know she was pregnant.

"Didn't hardly seem old enough to be her daddy," the woman added. "Must'a knocked up her mama when he was still a kid his-self."

Her father or birth father? "What did he look like?" I asked.

"Pointy nose, thin lips. Light complexion. Wasn't no toad, but not a prince neither."

"Did she leave with him?"

"Nah. She didn't want nothing to do with him. But once he was gone, so was she. Outta here fast as a rabbit on speed."

I'd seen Bram Weaver's picture only once, when one of the national magazines did a feature on him, but the description fit. And his visit lent credence to his paternity claim.

"Any idea where Melissa went?" I asked the black woman. She shook her head.

"Thanks for your help." I addressed the comment to both women, but the nurse didn't even raise her eyes.

Ten o'clock on a Friday night and I was wound up tighter than a coiled spring. I thought about hitting the gym for a second time that day, then decided I preferred wine. My unfinished glass of Merlot was still sitting on the counter where I'd left it before head-ing off in search of Melissa. I picked it up and took a swallow on my way to the phone.

There weren't many people I felt comfortable phoning at that hour, but my sister Sabrina and I had a long history of ignoring the trappings of comfort.

"Hey, Kali." Sabrina sounded understandably wary. "Why are you calling?"

"I want to scream, is why." After a childhood spent at odds, Sabrina and I had worked out the parameters of a more or less peaceful coexistence. That I would turn to her in my frustration said a lot about how far we'd come.

She laughed. "Well, I'm the right person for that. Only you'll have to get in line. I seem to be a magnet for anger these days."

I reached for the wine bottle and refilled my glass. "How are you doing?"

"Cut the Hallmark stuff and tell me what's got you pissed."

I told her about Terri and Ted, and Hannah and Melissa, with-out using last names. But since Bram Weaver wasn't a client, I didn't feel the same constraint.

"The guru of public morality?" Sabrina asked, incredulous.

"Wannabe guru is more like it. Have you ever listened to him?"

"All the time." She paused and I heard the clink of ice cubes. Sabrina prefers the hard stuff to wine. "I know he's controversial," she continued, "but if you put aside his arrogance, some of what he says is pretty sound."

"Women barefoot and pregnant. No such thing as date rape."

"So he's a little extreme. But you have to agree that the radical feminists are too. They've given women a bad name."

That Sabrina sometimes lumped me with the *radical feminists* seemed to have slipped her mind, but I wasn't in the mood to argue. "Anyway," I continued, "if he's really the baby's father, the whole adoption will be thrown out. My clients will be heartbroken."

"Can you imagine being Bram Weaver's daughter?" She giggled, a sure sign that the ice cubes weren't cooling a glass of ginger ale.

"Her name is Hannah. Although I guess it might not be for long. Weaver's bound to choose something different."

"You think a judge would choose Weaver over your clients?" Her tone suggested the idea was inane, despite her professed admiration for Weaver.

"It's not a matter of choosing."

"But your clients are a married couple. Stable, probably well off, right?"

"Doesn't matter. You can't terminate parental rights simply because there are better options." In fact, fathers' rights was one of Weaver's rallying cries.

Another clink of ice against glass. "You sure pick 'em, Kali."

"Don't I." The vision of Hannah and her bright blue eyes haunted me.

"How'd you end up with this one, anyway?"

"Terri is Steven Cross's sister. Half-sister, actually. He gave her my name."

"Steven?" There was a moment of silence. "God, Kali, what were you thinking?"

"It didn't seem like any big deal at the time." Liar, I told myself.

"Liar," she said.

In a moment of wine-induced honesty not long after the accident, I'd confided in my sister. She was the only one who knew the whole story, and as much as I later regretted having told her, I found it also something of a relief. Secrets are a terrible burden to bear alone.

"It was supposed to be a simple adoption," I said. "Besides, what's wrong with taking his half-sister on as a client?"

"Weren't you the one who insisted it would be best if you and Steven never crossed paths again?"

I could think of a dozen snappy retorts, but the bottom line was, she was right. Six degrees of separation between you and the rest of the world. If you wanted to keep your distance from someone, you didn't cultivate ties that might bring you closer.

"Right now," I said, "my bigger concern is Bram Weaver."

"If anyone can find a way to make it right, Kali, you can."

I appreciated her confidence, though I couldn't help but think it was misplaced.

My doorbell rang the next morning a little after nine. I was up, but barely. My head hurt from too much wine and my muscles were tired from a restless night's tossing and turning. I waited for Bea or Dotty to get the door, but when the buzzer sounded again, I realized they must have gone out.

I trudged upstairs myself and opened the door. Then blinked in surprise.

"I need to talk to you," Melissa said, shoving her hands into her jacket pockets.

"Damn right you do."

She looked up. A host of emotions played across her face. "You've talked to him then," she said warily.

"Not directly, no." I stood back, inviting her in.

She stayed put. "Are you mad?"

"Of course I'm mad. I'm furious. But not half as mad, or hurt, as Ted and Terri will be."

"Do they know?"

"Not from me. Yet." I waved her in. "Come inside, I promise not to bite. You want some coffee?"

"Tea?" She followed me into the kitchen, moving gingerly, like an old woman.

"How are you feeling?"

She groaned. "If I'm ever again tempted to sleep with some guy, I'm going to remember what it's like to have your belly cut open and stapled shut."

At least her sense of humor was intact.

Melissa eased herself into one of the kitchen chairs, wincing as she bent forward. "If I hadn't had to stay in the hospital so long, he'd never have found me."

"Maybe, maybe not." I put the kettle on to boil and took a bag of Constant Comment from the cupboard. "What's your relationship with Bram Weaver? Besides the obvious."

Her eyes welled with tears. She shook her head, waved her arm through the air in a gesture of helplessness.

"If you have any doubts about paternity, a blood test can settle the question once and for all." I was ready to grasp at whatever hope there was.

Melissa took a breath. "There's no need."

I was sure the Harpers would insist on one anyway.

"He's the baby's father," Melissa said, looking past me.

"What a mess!"

She nodded mutely.

"Why didn't you tell me the truth up front?" It was all I could do to keep from screaming.

"Because I knew he'd cause trouble. Because I hate him and couldn't face even thinking about him." The tears spilled over and she began to cry in earnest.

"Who is Gary Ellis then?"

"A guy I used to work with at the deli. I paid him to say he was the father."

"Paid him?"

"With money I got from the Harpers."

Money again. I groaned inwardly at the thought. But I had bigger troubles to worry about. "Do they know Gary Ellis lied?"

"No. They have no idea about any of it." Her voice was small.

"You swore under penalty of perjury that you were telling the truth, Melissa. Didn't you read the documents I had you sign?" No, of course she hadn't. She was nineteen and looking for an easy fix to troubles of her own making.

"It would have been okay," she said. "He'd never have known

I was pregnant except for Hank, this guy who lived downstairs from me in Berkeley. He's a friend of Bram's. He saw me that day we had lunch in the City. Saw that I was pregnant."

I handed her a tissue and she blew her nose.

"If he hadn't seen me, everything would have worked out just fine."

"Maybe." I pulled out a chair and sat at the table next to her. "I want to know about you and Bram. The truth this time."

"There's not much to tell."

"Try it anyway. I don't need the sordid details, just the bigger picture."

"It's all sordid."

She'd met Bram through Hank, a dimwit who was getting divorced from his wife and spent most of his time bad-mouthing her. He used to invite Melissa and her roommates downstairs for beer and pizza, and since none of the girls was over twenty-one, they weren't about to pass up the opportunity for free beer. Hank usually had a few guys over too, and that was how Melissa met Bram.

"At first I thought it was cool, him being older and everything," Melissa said. "And he was so different from anyone I knew back home. Bram acted like he really liked me. He talked about how alive I made him feel. How different I was from other women, who never appreciated him." She hesitated, then finished the thought in a rush. "We drank a lot and somehow ended up in Hank's bed."

"It was just that one time?"

"There were a couple of other times too." She had her arms crossed over her chest, hugging herself. "He had a key to Hank's apartment. We used to meet there."

"How long were the two of you dating?"

"We weren't. Dating, that is."

There was something about her tone that made the picture instantly clear. "You never went on a real date with him?"

"He kept talking about it." She looked embarrassed.

"What happened then?"

"After a couple of weeks, he told me . . ." Her voice wavered. "He told me that he wasn't desperate enough to keep doing it with someone as fat and stupid as me."

"What a piece of shit!" No wonder she didn't want to tell him about the pregnancy.

She nodded. "I guess by then I was already pregnant."

"You guess?"

"I mean I was. Though I didn't realize it at the time."

"How terrible for you. Weaver is scum." He was also a hypocrite with his sermonizing about the role of women as caretakers. Although Melissa had certainly taken care of *his* needs.

"I didn't know who he was," she said plaintively. "Just that he had some talk show on the radio. I listened once. It was so boring I turned it off."

"Oh, Melissa." I leaned over to pat her knee but ended up hugging her instead. That started her crying again.

"I hate him," she said between sobs. "I hate him so bad it hurts. But I hate myself more."

"Hating yourself won't change anything."

"I was so lonely. Being on my own in a strange city. I hardly knew anyone except for my roommates, and they weren't interested in being friends."

"We all make mistakes, Melissa. The trick is to learn from them."

She nodded, wiped at the tears. "What's going to happen now?"

"Well, first off, we're going to have to tell the Harpers. It's going to break their hearts to lose another baby."

Melissa's face registered alarm. "What do you mean? Bram can't take the baby away from them, can he?"

"He's the father."

"But he's a horrible person. You said so yourself."

"He's not who I'd choose—"

"I don't want him raising my baby," Melissa insisted.

"She's his baby too."

"I carried her, I gave birth to her. He didn't do anything but use me for sex."

"Under the law, that's enough."

Melissa shook her head violently. "There must be some way to stop him."

"There will be a hearing. He'll have to prove paternity. He'll also have to show that he didn't know of the pregnancy in time to exercise his parental rights earlier."

She looked like she might be sick to her stomach.

"If the Harpers want, I'll fight it every way I can, including in the press, which just may be Weaver's most vulnerable spot. But bottom line is, a birth parent has rights."

"Birth parent." She spat out the word. "The guy's an asshole. I won't let him near the baby."

"It's not your decision, Melissa."

"There's got to be *something* I can do."

I hesitated. "You could raise her yourself."

"You mean quit school, give up my life, and become a single mother?"

"Yeah."

Melissa pressed her palms to her forehead. "My parents would find out. I'd be stuck in some stupid, low-paying job trying to make ends meet. My life would be ruined."

"It would certainly take a turn in a different direction."

"This sucks."

"Right," I agreed. "It does."

"I could have had an abortion and Bram wouldn't even have known."

And if he'd known, he couldn't have stopped her. That was one of the ironies.

"Let's take it one step at a time. Nothing can happen without a hearing. And I'll break the news to the Harpers unless you want to do it yourself."

She looked agitated and scared. "No, they'd kill me."

CHAPTER 6

In general, I don't subscribe to the theory that unpleasant tasks are best confronted at once, but in this case I thought it necessary. I called Terri and asked if I could come by later that day.

"Is it important? We're kind of busy today."

"It's important. I won't stay long."

"More papers, I bet. Can you make it this morning? We're expecting friends in the afternoon." She laughed. "We can't help showing off Hannah."

My throat constricted. I swallowed hard. "I can be there in an hour. Is that too early?"

"It's fine."

Ted answered the door. He was dressed casually in a T-shirt and shorts. His shoulders were so broad, his arms so thick, I wondered if he had to have his shirts custom made.

"I'll let Terri know you're here," he said, ushering me past the large, formal living room into a smaller, more comfortable sitting area off the kitchen. He disappeared and I heard him calling Terri's name.

The mantel above the fireplace was lined with cards welcoming the new baby. A pile of baby gifts, largely unopened, was spread on the credenza. I sat on the beige chenille sofa, wishing I were somewhere else. Anywhere else. I hoped Ted and Terri didn't confuse the messenger with the message.

Terri came through the doorway followed by Ted.

"Sorry to keep you waiting," she said. "I was putting Hannah down for a nap. Can I get you some coffee?"

"No thanks."

Ted sat down, leaning forward with his arms on his knees. He tapped his foot impatiently. "Terri said you had some more papers for us to sign?"

"No, that's not why I'm here." My mouth was so dry I was having trouble talking. "There's been a complication."

Terri had been standing. Now she, too, sat. "What do you mean? What kind of complication? Melissa signed the waiver of consent."

"Gary Ellis may not be . . . isn't Hannah's father. He's just someone Melissa worked with. The true birth father is a man named Bram Weaver. You may have—"

Terri let out a gasp and turned white.

"The guy with the radio show?" Ted stopped his foot-tapping.

I nodded. "And he says he's not going to agree to an adoption."

There was a moment of absolute silence, and then Ted exploded.

"What? Can he do that?" The vein in Ted's temple pulsed. With his bulky shoulders and powerful neck, he looked something like a bull staring at a red cape.

"He came to my office yesterday afternoon. I was in court so I haven't talked to him, but my associate did. And I talked to Melissa this morning. She confirmed that he is Hannah's father."

Ted slid an arm protectively around Terri's shoulder. "It's a little late for him to be getting involved, isn't it?"

"He claims not to have known about the pregnancy before now."

"What does this mean, exactly?" Terri's voice was so soft it was a struggle to hear her. "Can he really stop the adoption?"

"I'm afraid so. We'll demand a paternity test. And maybe we can show that he did know Melissa was pregnant. If that's the case, and he made no effort to assert his paternal rights before now, then we may have a leg to stand on."

"And if not?" Ted asked.

"Then I'm afraid the adoption is in jeopardy. The law is clear."

"She's ours." Terri choked. Her eyes welled with tears. "We can't lose her. We can't lose another baby."

Ted squeezed her shoulder. "We won't, honey. We'll fight him on this."

"I have to warn you, your chances aren't good." It wasn't a

pleasant role, being the bad guy. But I thought they needed to know what they were up against. "It might be easiest to bow out now rather than prolonging the ordeal."

"Roll over and give up? Not on your life." Ted was at the helm, ready to do battle.

"You may have to eventually," I cautioned. "And by then you'll be even more attached to Hannah, and she to you." I was sure I didn't need to remind them about Baby Jessica, whose adoptive parents fought to keep her for three years, only to eventually lose her.

Terri wiped her eyes, but the tears continued to come. "She isn't a piece of property, Kali. She's our daughter."

"Hit him with the heavy artillery," Ted bellowed. "Hell, nuke him if you have to. I don't care how much it costs or who gets hurt. We're not giving up our daughter."

Neither, apparently, was Weaver. Tuesday we received official documents from his attorney demanding that the Harpers withdraw from the adoption and turn Hannah over to him.

I called to deliver the news.

"I've been checking into this guy," Ted said. "He's an ass."

"If you're looking for an argument, you're not going to get one from me."

Ted was breathing heavily into the phone. "Have you ever listened to his show?"

"The white male reigns supreme."

"Heck, I'm a guy, about as white as they come, and he makes *me* uncomfortable."

"If he's Hannah's father, though, all of that other stuff is irrelevant."

"How can the court choose a man like that over us?" Ted's voice sparked with indignation.

"It isn't the court's role to *choose*."

"Someone's got to."

"This is different than contested custody in a divorce," I explained. "There the judge looks at what's in the best interests of the child. That's not a consideration here."

"Maybe it should be."

"I know how painful—"

"With all respect, Kali, you don't know. You can't know until you've been there yourself." His venom was directed at me this time.

"You're right. Whatever I imagine, the reality is probably a hundred times worse. But that doesn't change the fact that the rights of the biological father take precedence."

"Not this time," Ted said. "We're going to do whatever it takes to keep her."

I set Jared to work trying to dig up dirt on Weaver. I peppered Melissa with questions about what he might have known when. I called Weaver's attorney, who told me there was nothing to discuss unless the Harpers were willing to relinquish Hannah.

I held out hope that Weaver's interest in Hannah was a superficial one, like a boy with a new toy at Christmas, and that he'd lose interest when faced with the rigors of litigation—and the time to reflect on the challenges of child rearing.

Or that in the alternative, he might care deeply about his daughter, and be swayed by the Harpers' sincerity. To that end, I'd tried to speak with him directly. But he never returned my phone calls.

Two weeks later we assembled in Judge Nye's courtroom for a preliminary hearing concerning the Adoption of Hannah B. Ted and Terri sat rigidly and silently, eyes straight ahead. Seated behind them, Melissa slumped, curling in on herself as though she were being pulled into the fetal position.

Bram Weaver's attorney caught my eye and started to approach. He looked to be in his mid-forties, ruddy-faced and fashionably dressed in a European-cut suit of dark gray. I moved to meet him midground, beyond earshot of the Harpers.

"Bill Trimble." He winked at me as we shook hands. "Pleasure to finally meet you, Ms. O'Brien."

It was all I could do to keep from wiping my palm on my skirt.

He nodded in the direction of Ted and Terri. "That the couple who were hoping to adopt the child?"

I was sure his use of the past tense was intentional. *"Are* hoping," I said.

He gave me a supercilious smile and said nothing.

"Your client will be here today, won't he?"

"Any minute."

"I'd like to talk to him. We might be able to work this out our-selves, without involving the court. My clients are a warm and caring couple. They would provide a—"

"Save your breath, my dear. Bram wants his daughter."

Before I had a chance to argue further, the courtroom door flew open and a whippish, narrow-faced man with a cleft chin burst into the room. I instantly recognized Bram Weaver from the magazine photograph I'd seen, but he wasn't nearly as tall, or devilish, as I'd envisioned. His dark hair, trimmed close at the sides, was beginning to gray near the temples, and he wore silver-rimmed glasses, which had been absent in the picture.

Weaver strode to the front of the courtroom, took his attor-ney's arm, and whispered something in his ear. Then he turned, casting a quick glance around the room.

As his eyes met Melissa's, she flinched and turned away. Terri, by contrast, stared at him with a hateful glower. If her eyes had been lasers, Weaver would have been toast.

"All rise."

Judge Robert Nye entered the courtroom and took a seat at the bench. His face was pinched, whether from displeasure or habit it was hard to tell. He motioned for us to be seated.

"Bill, you're representing Mr. Weaver, correct?"

"Yes, Your Honor."

Not a good sign. The judge and Weaver's attorney were on a first-name basis.

Judge Nye looked toward the table where I sat with the Har-pers. I rose. "Kali O'Brien representing Edward and Theresa Har-per."

"Is the natural mother here as well?" Nye asked.

Melissa stood, awkwardly, and then quickly returned to her seat.

"Is the child in court today?"

I took the question. "No, Your Honor. She's at home with her grandmother, Mrs. Cross."

Weaver tossed his head back. "She's not the baby's grand-mother any more than those people"—he pointed to the Harpers—"are her parents."

Nye rapped his gavel. Trimble leaned over and said something to his client.

"I'll have no more outbursts in my courtroom, is that under-stood?"

Trimble nodded. "We understand, Your Honor."

Judge Nye folded his hands in front of him. "I've read the pleadings. Let me make sure I have the facts straight. The baby in question was born to Melissa Burke. She and the Harpers have initiated proceedings for an independent adoption, correct?"

"Yes, Your Honor," I said.

"And Mr. Weaver has just recently learned of the pregnancy?"

"Correct." This time it was Trimble who answered.

Nye stroked the corners of his mouth. "Go ahead, Bill, you may proceed."

Trimble rose and stepped out from behind the counsel table. "Bram Weaver is the father of the baby herein known as Hannah B. He was not aware that the baby's mother, Melissa Burke, was pregnant until several weeks ago when a mutual acquaintance caught sight of her on the streets of the city. When the acquaintance told my client about seeing Melissa, who was noticeably pregnant at the time, my client took immediate action to establish his parental rights. He tried to contact Melissa where she'd lived and worked at the time he knew her. When he determined that she'd gone into hiding—"

"Objection. She wasn't hiding."

Nye waved a dismissal my way. "This isn't a trial, Ms. O'Brien. It's an informal hearing."

Be that as it may, the casting of facts was often as important as the facts themselves.

Trimble continued as though he'd merely paused for a breath. "My client tried contacting her roommates, who claimed to know nothing about Melissa's departure. He tried by several other means to locate her. All to no avail. He checked birth records and contacted local hospitals several times a week. His efforts finally paid off when he found that Melissa Burke had given birth at California Pacific. He went to see her the very afternoon he located her. He wanted to assume his parental duties, to offer financial and emotional support. He wanted to meet his baby daughter."

Trimble paused, ostensibly for a drink of water, but more likely for effect. "You can imagine," Trimble continued, "how devastated my client was to learn that Melissa Burke had given the child away."

There we were with the casting of facts again. Trimble made it sound like Melissa was tossing the baby out with the recycles. I bit my tongue.

"Mr. Weaver immediately voiced his displeasure. He agreed to take on full financial and custodial responsibility, and to raise the child himself. But Melissa Burke has refused to cooperate. He now seeks to establish his parental rights through the court of law."

Nye's features squeezed more tightly. "Ms. O'Brien, did you make any effort to notify Mr. Weaver of the impending birth and to obtain his consent to the adoption?"

I'd known this moment was coming, but that didn't make it any easier. I hated pointing a finger at Melissa, especially because it ended up making me look foolish. But there weren't a lot of options.

"I was operating under the belief that a different young man was the baby's father," I said, choosing my words carefully. "And that may yet prove to be the case. Mr. Weaver hasn't established paternity."

Trimble was on his feet immediately. "He's more than happy to undergo a paternity test. The sooner, the better."

Nye pressed his knuckles into the furrows of his forehead. "Ms. Burke, perhaps you could help us out here."

All eyes turned in her direction. "I . . . I . . ." She swallowed. Her eyes held a look of panic. I'd warned her not to give away the store. If Bram wanted to establish paternity, let him take the lead and prove it. Melissa lifted her chin. "I'm sorry, sir, I can't."

"Are you saying you don't know who is the father of your baby?" Nye came across like a stern and reproachful parent. I suspected it was a role that came naturally to him.

Melissa didn't look at him. "Right."

"Liar." Weaver's face turned red. "You know that baby is mine. I was your first, remember?" His tone was nasty, like a slap in the face.

But Melissa didn't falter. While she'd avoided looking directly at the judge, she faced Weaver squarely. She stood straighter and managed a haughty shrug. "You might have been first, but it's rather presumptuous to assume you were the *only* one."

Weaver's fist clenched into a ball. His eyes darkened and he muttered under his breath.

Judge Nye banged his gavel. "Enough. Both of you." He paused to let his words sink in. "Ms. Burke, why didn't you tell Mr. Weaver about your pregnancy?"

"I didn't want him involved." Melissa's composure surprised me.

"Is there something that makes you think he might be a danger to the baby?" Judge Nye asked.

"No, not exactly."

Nye leaned back and crossed his arms. "You don't want this child of yours, but you don't want Mr. Weaver to have her either?"

"I don't want him near her at all." Melissa's voice was filled with loathing.

"Yet you can give me no reason."

Melissa said nothing.

"You're coming from a position of revenge maybe?"

I'd had enough. "Your Honor. Ms. Burke is perfectly within her rights to place the child for adoption in a loving, two-parent home."

"Unless the natural father objects," Trimble added.

Nye sighed. "What's clear," he said, "is that we can't proceed in any direction until paternity is established. Let's get the testing done and then we'll reconvene. Until then, the baby will remain with Mr. and Mrs. Harper." He reached for the gavel.

Trimble was on his feet again. "If I may, Your Honor."

Nye raised an eyebrow.

"Mr. Weaver would like to visit his daughter. He hasn't even seen her except briefly through the glass at the hospital nursery."

Terri whimpered.

"Your Honor," I said, rising also. "We have nothing but Mr. Weaver's unsubstantiated contention that he is the baby's father. There may well be no blood relationship at all, in which case Mr. Weaver has no rights with respect to the child. We can't allow wide-open visiting privileges to every person who wants them."

Judge Nye made an elaborate show of looking around the room. "I don't see anyone else waiting in line to visit the baby, Ms. O'Brien. We're talking about one man, a man who willingly stepped forward to take on the lifelong and serious responsibility of parenthood."

Ted and Terri had clasped hands, holding on tightly to each other for support.

"She's only three weeks old," I said.

"If Weaver is the baby's father," Nye said, "he will be the one raising her. I think it would be beneficial for both of them, father and daughter, to spend time together early on."

"And if he's *not* the father," I pointed out, "visitation will have been granted to a complete stranger."

Trimble cleared his throat. "We're only asking for a short visit. Say, an hour or so."

"In the unfortunate event that this matter should become a legal battle . . ." Nye looked toward the Harpers, making it clear the ball would be in their court. "If it comes to that, you, Ms. O'Brien, will be the first to argue that the child has bonded with her adoptive parents and that it will be detrimental to remove her from their home. I am only trying to anticipate your concerns."

Bullshit. But I kept the thought to myself. Instead, I said, "The welfare of a young baby is at stake, Your Honor."

"Precisely." Nye cleared his throat. "The court sanctions a supervised visit of one hour, to be arranged within the next week. This hearing is continued until such time as the paternity testing has been completed."

The whole thing took less than thirty minutes. Terri was shaking by the time the judge's gavel sounded. I could practically hear the outrage boiling inside her.

"Can he do that?" she sputtered. "Can he make us let that man take Hannah, even for an hour?"

"Yes," I said, "he can. But Weaver won't be alone with her. A third person will be present as well."

Terri was hyperventilating. "She's *our* baby. I'm her *mother*. I can't just leave her with strangers."

When we reached the hallway, I cupped Terri's elbow, pulling her and Ted off to the side. "This probably isn't the time for a discussion, but I'd like the two of you to think again about the wisdom of fighting Weaver."

Terri leaned back against the wall, moaning. Ted shoved his hands into his pockets. "I understand what you're saying, but we just can't do—"

Terri let out a sharp wail. Suddenly she flew across the floor in a rage and began clawing at Bram Weaver, who'd stopped to get a drink of water from the fountain.

"No way in hell you'll get your hands on my daughter," she shrieked.

Weaver held up an arm to defend himself and Terri kicked him in the shins. "You're nobody in that child's life."

Ted pulled at Terri's arm. She fought him as well, broke free and pummeled Weaver with her fists.

"Fucking doesn't make you a parent," she screamed.

Trimble joined Ted in restraining Terri. Weaver stepped back and brushed himself off.

"In this case," he said with a smirk, "it did. You'd better get used to the idea."

"And you'd better watch your back." She spit at him. "I'd kill you before I let you have Hannah."

Weaver offered a resigned smile to the sea of faces watching the spectacle. "And to think some people say women are the weaker sex."

"You okay?" Trimble asked his client.

"I'm fine. And I've got great material for my show tonight." He started for the elevator.

Ted turned to Terri. "Jesus, what were you doing?"

"He can't have Hannah," she wailed. "I won't let him."

"Honey, I don't like the idea any better than you do. But beating up on the guy isn't going to accomplish anything."

"What are we going to do?" Terri was sobbing now, her anger overshadowed by grief.

"We'll figure out something. Come on, let's go home." Ted turned to me. "But keep on this, Kali. We're not giving up."

I watched them depart, leaning on one another for support, then looked around for Melissa. She appeared to have slipped quietly away when I wasn't looking.

I was headed for my car when I saw Weaver approaching. Instinctively, I braced myself for an attack. I wasn't sure if it would be verbal or physical.

Weaver surprised me with his even tone and cordial manner. "Your clients don't have a leg to stand on, you know."

"At the moment, they're Hannah's parents."

"They have temporary custody. That doesn't make them parents." Again the soft drawl, the nonthreatening stance.

"Why are you doing this?" I asked.

Weaver looked at me, eyes a cool gray like the ocean on an overcast day. "She's my daughter."

"Even if she is, the Harpers are a couple who desperately want a child. You're single."

"Single women raise children all the time. The number of fatherless households is astounding."

One of his pet harps. I wasn't about to get into a philosophical argument.

"You think a single man can't be a decent father?" he asked.

"I didn't say that. But I'm a little perplexed that you're so eager to take on the responsibility."

"Feminists have been trying for years to emasculate men. To do away with fathers." The words had a preachy, almost belligerent tone. Like on his radio shows. Then he smiled again. "Sorry, I sound like I'm on the air, don't I? But the truth is, that's the way I feel. My child belongs with me. Your clients can find another baby. I have only one daughter."

There were days I thought brain surgery might be a simpler profession than law.

CHAPTER 7

The media had a field day with the story. A contested adoption involving two public figures—it was the stuff headlines were made of. Reluctantly, Ted and Terri agreed to a few brief interviews. Weaver, on the other hand, sought them out. He also used his radio program to expound on the plight of fathers, who were, he said, too often ignored, overlooked, and relegated to second-class status.

Weaver was on a roll. The Harpers were terrified.

Ted called me at work first thing Tuesday morning. "I found out he's already got a kid," Ted announced. "A son who's fifteen."

"Are you talking about Weaver?" I slipped my left foot out of my shoe and scratched the sole with my other foot.

"Weaver completely ignored the boy until recently. If he's so interested in family, why didn't he take on some parental responsibility the first time?"

Interesting question, though I doubted it made a difference in terms of the law. "Where's the boy live?" I asked.

"With his mother. Bram's ex-wife. They were divorced when the kid was a baby. She remarried and Bram apparently washed his hands of them."

"No involvement at all?"

"Not from what I found. There were some articles on him. I can bring them by. Maybe if the judge sees what kind of guy Weaver really is—"

"I wouldn't count on that making any difference."

Ted was quiet a moment. "We're not going to give up."

"I'll fight for you, if that's what you want. But I don't think you should have any false hopes."

"Sounds like that's the only kind there are." Ted's laugh was bitter. "There's no way around Friday's visitation, is there?"

"I'm afraid not."

"You'll stay there to keep an eye on things?"

"Right." Since there were independent agencies that routinely supervised such visits, I'd been surprised the Harpers had requested, and Judge Nye had agreed to, a visit in my office.

"Unfortunately, I have to be out of town then," Ted said. "TelAm's had this commercial shoot scheduled for weeks. I wish I could cancel, but there's no way. Lenore will stay with Terri so she won't be alone."

"I can't imagine there will be problems with the visit. It's what comes after that we have to worry about."

Friday afternoon, twenty minutes before Weaver's scheduled visit with Hannah, the door to my outer office flew open and a jowly man scurried inside. His arms were laden with a stuffed bear, a bottle warmer, an infant seat, and a large camera bag.

"What's this?" I asked as he stormed past me to the loveseat in the reception area.

"Stuff Bram Weaver wanted." The man's protruding belly, showcased in a too-tight turtleneck jersey, jiggled as he moved.

"Weaver wanted it here?"

"This is where the meeting is, isn't it?" The man set his load on the seat cushions.

"What meeting?"

"The visit with his kid."

Bram had been cooperative about the logistics—he didn't much care whether the person supervising the visit was me or someone from an independent agency, but he hadn't mentioned that he'd be bringing reinforcements. Or paraphernalia.

"Who are you?" I asked the man. "Weaver's assistant or something?"

"The photographer." He patted his bag.

"Photographer?"

"Bram wanted some photos. You know, of him and the baby."

Photos that would no doubt find the shortest path to the press. Bram seemed determined not to pass up any opportunity for publicity.

"No way," I said. "The court order is for a visit. Period."

"You going to deny a father pictures with his kid?" Spittle sprayed when the man talked.

I crossed my arms and stepped back, distancing myself from the spray. "Yes, that's exactly what I'm going to do."

"Bram's gonna be pissed."

"Let him be."

The man shrugged and plopped heavily onto the seat cushion next to his stash. "All the same, I'll wait."

Terri arrived on the hour exactly, accompanied by her mother. Hannah was asleep in a plastic infant seat nestled under a yellow baby blanket. Both women appeared wan and edgy.

"An hour max," Terri said. "That's all the judge ordered."

I nodded.

"He shouldn't feed her anything," Lenore added. "Or change her. He shouldn't even wake her up, but he probably will. The poor child won't know who he is."

It seemed to me that Lenore was only adding to Terri's anxiety, but I realized this couldn't be easy for her, either.

Terri's eyes darted around the room, lighting briefly on the photographer. She tensed. Before she could say anything, I led her and Lenore into my inner office.

"Who's he?" Terri asked, clutching Hannah's infant seat to her chest.

"A friend of Weaver's. Don't worry, I already told him it was just Bram and Hannah. That's it."

"And you."

"And me." I'd moved the furniture in the conference room to accommodate the visit. When Weaver arrived, I'd put him there and then bring in Hannah myself. "There's a coffee house down the street," I told them. "You might find it easier to pass the time there than here in my office."

Terri shook her head. "I don't think so."

"This way," Lenore said, "we'll be nearby in case there's a problem."

Like a hostess awaiting the guest of honor, I flitted from room to room, all the while keeping my eye on the door and my ear tuned for the telephone. The photographer stepped outside once to smoke, then returned to the couch. Terri and her mother sat in silence while Hannah slept.

At quarter past the hour I called the number on Weaver's card and got an answering machine. I tried his attorney next.

"What do you mean he's not there?" Trimble barked.

"He hasn't shown up."

"Must be a major traffic jam. I can assure you he hasn't changed his mind."

It would have been nice if we could use the incident to argue that Weaver was unreliable and shouldn't be trusted with a child. Unfortunately, the issue before the court wasn't one of parental fitness but of biology. And on that point, there was little we could do.

At two twenty-five Bram strutted into the office without an apology or explanation for the lateness of his arrival. "Are we ready?" he asked.

"Hannah is here with her mother, but—"

"Melissa's here?"

"I was referring to Terri Harper." Something I imagined he already knew. "I've arranged the conference room for your visit. I'll bring Hannah in just as soon as you're settled. You've only got about half an hour of the scheduled visit left."

I expected an argument about the timing, but Weaver merely nodded.

"And no photographer."

"What?"

"You heard me, no photographer. That wasn't part of the agreement."

"What's the matter with taking a few pictures? Everybody takes baby pictures."

"Not you. Not today. We can argue about it but you'll be wasting your breath—as well as your visiting time with Hannah."

Begrudgingly, Weaver waved his photographer friend away.

I showed him to the conference room and closed the blinds on the interior window. Then I went to my office to retrieve Hannah. Terri had tears in her eyes as she kissed the baby's head and handed her to me.

"Watch him closely," she said. "Make sure he treats her right."

Hannah was still asleep when I set her infant seat on the conference table in front of Bram. I hoped she stayed that way. I had the feeling neither of us would know what to do with a crying baby.

Bram peeled the blanket back from around her face. "So tiny," he said. It sounded more like a clinical observation than an expression of sentiment.

I sat in a chair in the corner and tried to make myself invisible. Bram continued to gaze at Hannah, murmuring to her now and then as he touched a foot or hand, but mostly regarding her in silence. When she woke and started fussing, he tried rocking the seat, then finally, when the whimpers grew louder, he took her out and cradled her awkwardly in his arm.

It was clear from watching him that he hadn't had a lot of experience dealing with infants.

When holding failed to quiet her, Weaver bounced her on his knees, which only made her cry harder. He looked at me, and I shrugged. I wasn't about to coach him in parenting, even if I'd known how. Finally, ten minutes before the end of his already truncated hour, he handed her back to me.

"Your allotted time isn't up," I told him.

He checked his watch. "Close enough. I've got a busy afternoon."

I left to take the howling baby to Terri. She and Lenore were waiting by the door when I emerged.

"I thought you were going to stay in my office," I said.

"I heard her crying."

I handed Hannah to Terri. She held the child against her chest and gently patted her back. Hannah quieted.

Weaver was in the doorway. "Has she had a sample taken for the paternity test?"

"Yesterday." Terri had been relieved to learn that it required only a saliva swab and not the drawing of blood.

"Good," Weaver said, heading for the door. "I went in earlier this week. The baby ought to be able to come home with me by the end of the month."

"I hope that man rots in hell," Terri said.

Despite the fact that nothing much had happened for the entire hour, the air had been thick with tension. I was glad to have the office to myself again.

Without waiting for Jared's help, I began rearranging the furniture in the conference room, putting it back the way it was. When I heard a tentative knock on the outer door, I poked my head into the reception area thinking maybe Weaver had returned to sling some final barb my way.

A blast of canine energy greeted me instead.

"Loretta!"

The dog made a beeline for me, her stubby tail wagging so furiously I couldn't understand how she managed to stay upright. She pushed against my legs with the full force of spaniel energy. It had been a long time since I'd experienced such enthusiasm at my mere presence.

While I was scratching her ears, I looked up at Tom standing in the doorway. I knew he had to be somewhere close by since he'd been keeping Loretta for me.

"What are you doing here?" I was hoping he'd attribute the waver in my voice to surprise and nothing more. The truth was, seeing him called forth a jumble of feelings that left me a little breathless and short of rational thought.

Tom was part of my life in Silver Creek. We'd been seeing each other. Seriously, I'd thought. But when Tom's estranged wife decided that being divorced wasn't such a hot idea after all, he'd taken her back. For the children's sake, he told me. My head understood, but not my heart.

This wasn't the first time we'd been together since I'd returned to the Bay Area last winter, but the other times had been back in Silver Creek. And always with advance planning.

"No one was at the house," Tom explained, "so we came by here." His voice was warm but I could see the uncertainty in his eyes. "You alone or have you got clients?"

"Alone. The clients have gone and Jared left early for a weekend at Tahoe. Why, you in need of a good attorney?"

He hesitated and then laughed. It was the same wonderful laugh I'd grown to love. "All my quick comebacks are double entendres, probably best left unsaid. But no, that's not why I'm here. Lynn and I had a fight."

"You're looking for a place to stay?" *And maybe an old girlfriend to pick up with again?*

Tom looked embarrassed. "No, sorry. Not that kind of fight." He paused. "We had a fight about Loretta. Lynn doesn't want the dog around anymore."

I felt a stab of anguish. It hurts enough to get dumped, but when a guy dumps your dog as well, you know it's over.

"It's not Loretta's fault," Tom added. "She's been great."

"But?"

"Well, there's the connection with you." He paused for a sardonic smile. "It's hard to work on a marriage when your husband has his ex-lover's dog underfoot."

"Really?" I loaded the word with disbelief.

"No need to lay on the sarcasm."

I went to the coffee room and filled a bowl with water for Loretta. Tom followed, leaning against the doorjamb to watch me.

"You could have called," I said. "I'd have come and gotten her."

"I guess I was looking for an excuse to get away." He paused, rubbing his palms against his jeans.

"That bad, huh?"

"This isn't easy, you know."

I crossed my arms. "Don't expect me to feel sorry for you."

"I'm not asking for your sympathy, Kali. Just your understanding. As a friend." When I didn't say anything, he stuck his hands in his pockets. "So how are things going here? You think you'll stay?"

"I haven't decided yet." I wondered if Tom knew he was a big part of the equation.

"You'll be able to keep Loretta, won't you? I mean, it won't be a problem?"

I thought of the yard, which wasn't fenced; the traffic, which she wasn't used to; the narrow and steep streets near my house that made walking difficult. But truth was, I'd missed her. After years of staunch independence, of never taking on so much as the responsibility of an African violet, I'd inherited Loretta when my father passed away two years ago, and discovered the comfort of unconditional love. It was probably the only place I'd ever find it.

"I'm glad to have her back," I said. "It was lonely without her."

"That Barrett trial made headlines, even in Silver Creek." He cocked his head. "You're a star."

"Hardly that."

"Still, you did a good job, Kali." Tom's voice held genuine admiration.

"Thanks."

We stood in silence for a moment. Then Tom ran a hand along Loretta's neck and patted her sides. "I'm going to miss you, girl."

I wondered briefly if he was talking to me as well as the dog.

"Well," he said, straightening. "Guess I should be going."

"You headed back tonight?"

"I think that's best." He hesitated, then crossed the room and pulled me close in a quick, amiable hug. "We were friends once, Kali. We ought to be able to do it again."

I wasn't so sure. I returned the hug, then pulled away quickly. "Drive carefully."

Standing at the window, I watched his truck pull away from the curb and found myself filled with immeasurable sorrow.

The conference room furniture could wait. Loretta and I headed home.

Bea and Dotty were out for the evening, which was probably a good thing given my mood. While Loretta explored her new home, I watched *Seinfeld* reruns on TV, drank more wine than I should have, and cried. I couldn't decide how much of it was Tom, and how much simple loneliness.

I woke in the morning to the sound of voices. My head throbbed. I turned gingerly and looked at the clock. Ten o'clock.

I never sleep that late.

But I wasn't ready to get up either. I knew Loretta would have been let out and fed by now. The sisters had been ecstatic when they'd come home last night and learned that she was joining our household.

The voices grew stronger. Bea's and Dotty's I recognized, but there was a male voice as well. Low and resonant, like a rumbling of stones. Slowly, I pulled myself out of bed, and padded to the window. A police car was parked on the street in front. Had Loretta managed to get into trouble already? Then I saw the SFPD logo on the car. San Francisco, not Berkeley. I slipped into jeans, rinsed my mouth, and stumbled upstairs.

"Kali, we were just coming to get you," Dotty said. "There's a policeman here to see you."

A black officer. Male and young. Despite the dog prancing at his feet, he was all business. "Are you Kali O'Brien?" he asked, chewing on a wad of gum.

I nodded.

"Can you tell me how you're acquainted with Bram Weaver?"

"Is he in trouble?"

The dark eyes didn't blink. "I believe I asked a question, ma'am."

Ma'am. Like I was his mother's age or something. "I'm an attorney," I explained. "I represent a couple who are trying to adopt a baby Weaver claims is his."

"Ted Harper and his wife, right? I heard something about it on the news."

I nodded.

"When did you last see Weaver?"

I thought a moment, still befuddled by the shadow of a hangover. "Yesterday, in my office."

"About what?"

"It was a court-ordered visitation with the baby."

"Did you have any contact with him after that?"

"In what, all of the eighteen hours since the visit? Hardly. Now will you please tell me what this is about."

The officer tapped his pen against his notebook. "Weaver is dead, ma'am."

CHAPTER 8

I blinked. "You mean he was murdered?"

The young officer gave a look that was immediately suspicious. "What makes you say that?"

"Why else would you be here?" My brain was finally beginning to function. "How did Weaver die?"

The man ignored both questions and asked one of his own instead. "Who was present at the visit in your office?"

"Terri Harper and her mother, Lenore Cross. Weaver, of course. And a photographer friend of his. But for the actual visit, it was just the baby, Weaver, and myself."

He scribbled briefly in his notebook. "Your card was on the counter by Weaver's phone. Any idea why?"

"He must have picked it up yesterday in my office."

"And you're sure you haven't talked with him since?"

"I'm sure. When was he killed?"

The officer made another notation in his book. "Sometime last night."

"Where? How?"

He packed away his notebook and started for the door. "Thanks for your help, ma'am."

I'd gotten all the information I was going to get.

By the time I returned from ushering him to the front door, Bea had the morning newspaper open and was running her finger down the pages, column by column.

"I don't see a word about it anywhere," she said, clearly disappointed.

"Here, give it to me." Dotty elbowed her sister aside and reached for the magnifying glass she kept close at hand.

"I'd guess Weaver's body wasn't discovered in time to make the paper," I said. "Let's see if the radio has anything."

Seven minutes to the top of the hour. I turned the radio to KCBS. We sat through four long commercials, financial news, traffic and weather, and then a five-minute wrap-up of national news. But Weaver's death led the hour as the top local story. Unfortunately, the report was short on detail.

The body of Bram Weaver, talk radio host and author of the controversial book, *On Being Male*, had been found that morning in the entryway of his Twin Peaks condo. He'd been shot in the stomach and head. Police were asking anyone with information about the crime to contact them. The announcer read off the police hotline number, then shifted to a reporter in the field who fed us taped reaction from people on the street.

"Shocking."

"No one is safe anymore."

"I'm not surprised. He made plenty of people mad."

And the official reaction from the San Francisco Women's Alliance, *"While we disagreed with much of what Mr. Weaver stood for, we are steadfastly against the use of violence to solve problems. Our sympathy goes out to his family and friends."*

I'd barely known the man, and like some of those interviewed, I hadn't liked much of what I did know. Nonetheless, he'd sat in my office not twelve hours before his death. That gave the news a personal dimension that left me shaken.

But my mind had already jumped a step ahead. The Harpers could now adopt Hannah without a fight.

The newscast switched to coverage of a warehouse fire, and Dotty turned off the radio. She was a large-boned woman, tall and angular in contrast to her sister's softer, plumper figure.

"What was Weaver like in person?" she asked me.

"More mild-mannered than I expected."

She dusted the radio with her sleeve. "Did you ever listen to his show?"

I nodded.

"Nothing mild-mannered about him there," she said.

"He was so rude to callers," Bea muttered, "I wondered why they bothered calling."

"Nonetheless, he had plenty of listeners."

"I know his show was popular," Dotty said. "But I think a lot of people just tuned in to hear how outrageous he could be."

"Lots of his callers were outrageous too," Bea pointed out. "That's what made it interesting. Who wants to listen to bland, polite conversation?"

"Whatever the reason," I told them, "his audience was growing. There was even some talk of his running for office."

Bea put her hand to her forehead. "Heaven help us."

Dotty shot her sister a reproachful look. "You shouldn't speak ill of the dead, Bea."

"Why not?"

"It's disrespectful."

"Phooey." Bea turned back to the crossword puzzle she'd apparently been working on before the morning's excitement. "Truth is never disrespectful," she grumbled.

"Guess I'd better make some calls," I said, heading downstairs.

I phoned the Harpers, and when no one answered, I hung up without leaving a message. I tried Melissa next. She'd heard the news from a friend who'd caught the story on television that morning at the gym.

"I know I should feel sad or something," Melissa said, "but I'm actually kind of glad he's dead."

"Because of the adoption?"

"And because he was a creep."

I hesitated. "The police may want to talk to you."

"Me? Why would they talk to me?"

"I'm only guessing. They came to see me this morning."

"What did they want?"

"To know my connection with Weaver. Unless they have evidence that points to a specific suspect, they usually start by questioning people who knew the victim."

Melissa laughed nervously. "Guess I'd better not tell them what I just told you then. About not being sad he's dead, I mean."

"Probably a good idea. But don't wrap yourself in lies, either. The police are sure to figure out that you weren't happy about Weaver's interference in the adoption."

Melissa sighed. "Seems like all he's done since the moment I met him is cause trouble."

"How are you doing otherwise?" I asked, shifting focus. "You settling in to your new apartment?"

"Sort of. It's kind of lonely without Ted and Terri around." She was quiet a moment. "It's so weird him being dead and all. I guess maybe it *is* a little sad after all."

Sad, and in this case, unsettling. For the remainder of the afternoon, the pall of Weaver's murder clouded my mind like smoke from a grass fire. I switched on the radio every half hour, listening for updates. When it became clear there weren't going to be any, I took Loretta for a hike in the hills, off Grizzly Peak Boulevard. It was new territory for her and she clearly loved every minute of the three hours we were gone.

I was on the front porch trying to brush some of the dirt from Loretta's fur and checking her for foxtails, when Bea poked her head out the front door.

"You had a call from the police," she said. "About an hour ago. Same fellow who was here earlier. Said his name was Holbrook."

"Did he say what he wanted?"

"Couldn't weasel a thing out of him. And believe me, I tried."

I laughed. "I'm sure you did."

I took another few minutes to finish with Loretta, then went inside. Bea dallied about the kitchen, ostensibly wiping counters, while I returned the call.

"We haven't been able to reach the Harpers," Holbrook said, still popping a wad of gum.

"Ted is out of town on business. Terri probably went out for the afternoon with the baby."

"Her mother was there at the house. Says she doesn't know where Mrs. Harper is either."

"And you think *I* do?"

"Maybe," Holbrook replied. Smack, pop. "Seems logical that someone in her position might call her attorney first thing."

"Her *position?* What are you talking about?" But I thought I knew.

"Someone we might regard as a possible suspect."

At least he'd said *might.*

"You guys don't waste any time, do you?"

"No, ma'am. We don't."

"There must be no shortage of people with motives." I thought instantly of Melissa and bit my tongue. "I'm not talking about the adoption, but the rest of his life. He wasn't known as a controversial figure without reason."

A couple of quick pops. "You're sounding defensive, Ms. O'Brien. My question was simply if you knew where your clients were."

"Sorry, but I don't." Question answered, I hung up.

Bea looked up from the spot she'd been scrubbing for the last five minutes. "Trouble?"

"I hope not."

I tried the Harpers' number again, and again reached the machine. This time I left a message. "Mrs. Cross, if you're there, pick up. It's Kali O'Brien, Terri and Ted's attorney."

I'd just about decided she'd gone when the phone finally clicked in.

"Kali, this is Lenore Cross." I could hear the hysteria in her voice. "The police were here. They were looking for Terri. Why would they want to talk with her?"

"They're talking to a lot of people, Mrs. Cross."

"They think she might have something to do with that awful man's death, don't they?"

I banished Holbrook's words from my mind. "I don't think you should jump to conclusions. Do you know where Terri is?"

"No. I was heading home to Carmel earlier when I heard the news on the radio. I turned around immediately to come back. The police were here and Terri was gone."

"She's probably at the park," I said. "Or out shopping."

"That's what I thought at first. But a neighbor saw her with a suitcase. And Hannah's porta-crib is gone."

I sucked in a breath. "Have you tried to reach Ted?"

"I don't know where he's staying. Somewhere in San Diego is all I know."

"Maybe Terri decided to join him."

"Yes, that's probably it." She didn't sound as though she bought into the idea. "I called Steven, thinking she might have gone there. And the house in Napa. She wasn't at either place. I don't know why I didn't think of San Diego."

My guess was she hadn't thought of it because it didn't make much sense. Why would a woman with a newborn baby hop a plane on the spur of the moment to join her husband on a business trip?

"What did the police say?" I asked her. "Do you remember?"

"They asked about both Ted and Terri, but they seemed most interested in Terri."

"What did you tell them?"

"That I didn't know where Terri was." Lenore sounded nervous. More than nervous. Her voice was tight and thin. "I hadn't talked to the neighbor yet so I didn't say anything about the suitcase. When the police learned I'd spent the night, they wanted to know if Terri was home last night."

"Was she?"

"Of course."

There was something about her answer, the tone maybe or the quickness of the words, that gave me pause. "Just the two of you?"

"And Hannah, of course."

"What time did you leave this morning? I thought you were staying until Ted got back."

"That was the plan." She hesitated. "Terri said she wanted time alone. I left here about nine-thirty."

Wanting time alone didn't strike me as odd. But a sudden change of plans did. "Let me know if you hear from her," I said. "And in the meantime, don't worry. The police talked to me, too. They're just gathering information at this point."

"I'm going to head back home to Carmel in a bit. Let me give you my number there in case . . . in case anything comes up."

I jotted down the number she dictated, then hung up.

I tried to reassure myself. Once the police had finished their initial inquiries, Ted and Terri would be in the clear. The police would uncover some listener Weaver had angered or some colleague raging with jealousy. They'd get a match on the gun, maybe even a witness who could give them a description of the shooter. The set of possible suspects would gel to one or two, and the Harpers could go about their lives.

That was my hope anyway. But in the meantime, it was going to be a bumpy ride.

"It needs more garlic," Dotty said, swallowing a bite of cacciatore. She glared at her sister across the table. "I knew we should have used more."

Bea lifted her chin. "We used what the recipe called for."

"But you've got to cook by feel and taste. Isn't that what Fabiana keeps telling us? Recipes are guidelines, not formulas."

"Tastes wonderful to me," I chimed in truthfully. Bea and Dotty were taking an Italian cooking class and I was often their lucky guinea pig. I'd never had a meal they prepared that wasn't four-star.

Bea nodded. "Tastes fine to me too."

"I don't imagine Mr. Parsons likes a lot of garlic in his food anyway," Dotty said snidely.

"What does Mr. Parsons have to do with it?" Bea snapped.

"Don't tell me you aren't thinking about inviting him for dinner because I know you are."

"I am *not*."

"Oh yes you are."

"If I was, so what?"

Murray Parsons had called twice since the sisters' return from Reno, and although he'd invited both ladies to tea last Wednesday, it was Bea who'd charmed him. Dotty was obviously miffed.

"I bet Mr. Parsons would love a home-cooked meal," I said. "Maybe he has a friend who'd enjoy one too."

The sisters were busy giving each other annoyed looks and didn't respond.

Ted called just as we'd finished clearing the table. "Leave the dishes for me," I told Bea, and headed downstairs to talk to him in quiet.

"Have you heard about Weaver?" Ted asked. "Terri just told me."

"Terri's there with you?"

"No. I'm still in San Diego."

"Where's Terri?"

"Home, I guess." He sounded perplexed. "Why?"

I explained that a neighbor had seen her leaving. "The police want to talk to both of you."

"Us?"

"I think they're just covering all the bases. I wouldn't worry about it."

"Maybe that's why Terri left," Ted said. "She didn't want to deal with all that until I got back."

"Without telling you or Lenore?"

"It must have slipped her mind." He paused. "Terri didn't say where she was calling from and I never thought to ask."

"How did she sound?"

"Fine." His tone was tentative. It was clear I'd opened the door to worry.

"What did she say exactly? Do you remember?"

"Just that Weaver was dead. That Hannah was now ours." Ted was silent a moment. "I just assumed . . . I mean, that she was home. Why . . . why wouldn't she be?" His words, following his own internal thought process, were punctuated with pauses.

"Maybe the neighbor was mistaken," I told him. But when I called the Harpers after hanging up from my conversation with Ted, no one answered.

I tried again an hour later and got the same response. Ditto the next morning.

If Terri was home, she wasn't answering the phone. If she wasn't home, where had she gone?

CHAPTER 9

Terri finally called me late Sunday afternoon. I was sitting on the deck thumbing through the backlog of catalogs that had been littering the coffee table for months.

"Where have you been?" I sounded like a parent several hours past curfew.

"Visiting a friend."

"But you're home now?"

"Actually, I'm at the police station."

I dumped *Crate and Barrel* onto the pile at my feet. "San Francisco?"

"Yeah. They're asking me questions about Bram Weaver's death." She took a breath. "They said I had a right to have an attorney present. Can you come?"

"I'll be there as soon as I can. Don't say anything until I arrive."

A niggle of worry lodged in my chest. Terri's presence at the police station was not an encouraging sign.

During rush hour, the drive from Berkeley to San Francisco can take an hour, and Sunday afternoons are sometimes just as bad. But I was in luck. Traffic was light and moving faster than the speed limit. I parked across from the Hall of Justice on Bryant, where I had a choice of spots. During the week there wouldn't have been an inch of spare curb space for blocks around.

The building was largely deserted. Quiet in a hollow, ghostlike sort of way. I passed through the metal detector, then took the elevator to the fourth floor and pushed open the door marked HOMICIDE. The desk in the small anteroom was empty.

"Anyone here?" I called out.

A middle-aged man in a rumpled white shirt emerged from the doorway to my right. His hair was heavily grayed and his face lined in a fatherly way. "What can I do for you?"

"I'm an attorney here to speak with Terri Harper."

"You must be Ms. O'Brien. I'm Inspector Dennison."

"Where's Holbrook?"

"He'll be back in a minute." Dennison raked his chin, gave a sardonic laugh. "No need for your being here really. She doesn't need a lawyer at this point."

"What point is that?"

"We're trying to get the lay of the land, is all."

"But you told her she had the right to an attorney."

Dennison grinned sheepishly. "Just to cover the bases. You know how it works. Don't want to shoot ourselves in the foot from the get-go."

By briefing Terri of her rights, the cops ensured that anything she said could be used in court. Prudent, but not a common practice with nonsuspect witnesses. "I'd like to see her alone."

"Hey, have a heart. My partner and I are functioning on three hours' sleep. We're anxious to call it a day."

"Five minutes?"

"Better we just ask our questions and get it over with." Dennison's tone was cordial, but unyielding.

I didn't push it. "Where'd you find her?" I asked instead.

"We didn't. She found us. Said she heard we were looking to talk with her."

"She came here of her own free will?"

He nodded.

I felt the tension in my shoulders lessen. Terri wasn't being detained. Not that I saw any reason she should have been, but I'd worried the whole way over. Once the cops latch on to a suspect, it takes a lot of convincing to change their minds.

"Come on." Inspector Dennison nodded his head toward the doorway through which he'd emerged. "Your client's waiting in the interview room."

Seated at a pitted, gray laminated table with sleeping Hannah cradled in her arms, Terri looked tired and tense. But more angry than afraid. She glanced up as we entered.

"Thank goodness you're finally here."

Dennison pulled a chair to the table for me.

"I want to get it over with," Terri said to neither of us in particular. There was an undercurrent of irritability in her voice.

"So do we," Dennison said.

Terri adjusted the blanket around Hannah's face and turned to me. "I was trying to be a good citizen, to help the police. Instead of gratitude I get a Miranda warning."

"That's the way it works, Mrs. Harper." Dennison sat down opposite us. "I tried to tell you that."

She glared at him. "You did."

Dennison ran a hand across the back of his neck. "Sure you don't want anything to drink?" This was no doubt for my benefit. Reassure the lawyer that her client was being well treated.

Terri nodded and shifted Hannah slightly in her arms. She handled the baby with an ease I envied.

"I'm sure," she said. "Thank you."

Dennison didn't bother to extend the invitation to me.

Holbrook returned and nodded a greeting in my direction. "I see your attorney made it," he said to Terri.

"Can we please do whatever it is we have to do so I can get my daughter home?"

Dennison clicked on the tape recorder resting on the table, then in a monotone that bespoke countless similar interviews, logged in the date, time, and names of those present.

"You've come to talk about the death of Bram Weaver, correct?"

"Because *you* wanted to talk to *me*."

Dennison ignored the pique in her voice. "How did you know that?"

"My neighbor told me. And I had a message from my mother to the same effect." Terri looked at me. "Also from my attorney."

"Where were you yesterday afternoon?" This was Holbrook. His gaze had drifted to Hannah and he pulled it away.

"I drove up the coast. To Mendocino."

"Why?" His question echoed my own, silent one.

She shrugged. "I needed some time alone."

Mendocino, four hours to the north, seemed like a long way to go to get time alone.

"Was this a trip you'd been planning?"

"Not exactly. But I often go to Mendocino when I need to get away. A friend of mine runs an inn there."

"You went to see your friend?"

"Among other things. Mostly I went because I wanted to." Hannah whimpered and Terri patted her back softly.

"Without telling anyone you were going," Dennison added. His tone was neutral, but it was clear that his meaning was not.

Terri gave him a contemptuous look. "I'm an adult. I wasn't aware I had to ask permission."

"I wasn't implying that you did." Dennison smiled ever so slightly. Fatherly again, humoring a recalcitrant teen. "But it might have been prudent to tell someone."

"My mother had gone home," Terri explained. "My husband was out of town."

She appeared relaxed. Her answers were short and to the point, her manner believable. Still, Terri's explanation fell somewhat short of convincing. I knew the police would see the trip north as *flight* and therefore evidence of her guilt.

Dennison seemed to concede the point, however, and moved on. "When did you learn of Weaver's death?"

"I heard about it on the radio yesterday afternoon."

"When you were already on your way to Mendocino?"

"Right."

Holbrook twisted sideways in his chair. "What's your connection with Weaver?"

"You know that already," I said.

Terri acted as though she hadn't heard. She looked Holbrook straight in the eye. "He wanted my baby."

"The baby you're adopting? The one in your arms?"

Terri bristled. She pulled Hannah closer. "We've adopted her. She's ours."

"But Weaver claimed to be the father, right? Claimed the adoption wasn't legal because he hadn't given consent." Holbrook paused. When Terri didn't reply, he continued. "Now that Weaver's dead, he's no longer a threat to the adoption. That must make you mighty happy."

I interrupted, hoping to stave off any response on Terri's part that could go to motive. "If you've got questions, Inspector, ask them. But Terri doesn't have to sit here and listen to speculation and innuendo."

"Just showing you the way things look from our perspective," Holbrook said.

Dennison crossed his arms, appearing to gather his thoughts before speaking. "Where were you Friday night?"

"At home," Terri said.

"Alone?"

"With my mother and Hannah."

"All night?"

"Yes."

"Your mother can vouch for that?"

"Of course."

"What time did she go to bed?"

"I don't know exactly. I went to bed before she did."

"What time was that?"

"Early. About nine-thirty, I think. I had a headache."

"Did you take anything for it?"

"I may have taken some Tylenol, I can't remember."

"It was only two nights ago, Mrs. Harper."

I folded my arms on the table. "She said she can't remember."

Dennison exchanged glances with Holbrook. "Did you talk to anyone besides your mother that evening?" he asked.

"No." For the first time Terri looked nervous.

"Then there's no one besides your mother who can attest to your being home?"

Terri squinted. "No, I guess not."

"Let me make sure I've got this straight," Dennison said. "You went to bed with a headache, for which you may or may not have taken medication. Then you got up the next morning . . . By the way, was your headache better?"

Terri nodded.

"Your mother left for home and you took off for Mendocino?"

"Right."

I was hoping he wouldn't know to raise the issue that I found troublesome. Why did Terri send Lenore, who was planning to stay until Ted's return, home several days early?

"When was the last time you saw Weaver?" Holbrook asked.

"On Friday afternoon."

"His visit with the baby?"

Terri's expression was pained. "The judge said we had to let him."

"Did you talk to him after that?"

"I didn't talk to him that afternoon even, except in passing."

"Do you own a gun, Mrs. Harper?"

The question came out of the blue, no doubt intentionally. I glanced at Terri, who seemed unperturbed.

"No," she replied. "Guns make me nervous."

"Does your husband own a gun?"

"Not that I'm aware of."

"Have you ever owned a gun?"

Terri glanced my direction.

"If a gun was registered in your name," I told her, "the police will have access to the records."

An unregistered gun, of course, would present a different picture. But in general, the worst thing your client can do is trip herself up in lies and half-truths.

"My father gave me one when I moved to the city," Terri explained. "He believes women need to be able to protect themselves."

"What kind of gun was it?"

"I don't know exactly. Not big. It fit my hand."

"Did you ever fire it?"

"My father insisted I learn to shoot, but it didn't change how I felt about guns."

"What happened to it?"

I saw a shadow of alarm in Terri's expression. She licked her lips. "I don't know."

"What does that mean?"

"It means that I don't know what happened to it. I think it was probably stolen. We were missing a number of things after we had work crews in the house during the remodel."

"Did you file a report?"

She shook her head. "We didn't tie the missing things together until a year or so later."

Holbrook sucked on his cheek. "So maybe you do own a gun after all."

"I . . ."

"Why don't we come out and take a look for it?"

"I haven't seen—"

I cut her short. "If you want to look for it," I told Holbrook, "get a warrant."

"You don't really want us to do that now, do you?"

"I think this *friendly conversation* has gone far enough."

Dennison smiled at Terri. "See what happens when you call an attorney? They start making you sound guilty."

CHAPTER 10

"Thank God *that's* over," Terri said as we walked out into the hazy afternoon sunshine. She'd secured Hannah in a cloth sling across her chest and was now using her hand to shield the baby's eyes from the light.

The sidewalk was deserted except for the requisite smattering of homeless folk. A leather-skinned man with matted gray hair was propped against the rise of the stairs, sleeping. Halfway to the corner, a younger, wiry man was engaged in a frenetic shouting match with an invisible adversary.

"Where are you parked?" I asked her. "I'll walk you to your car."

"It's that blue Explorer." She pointed in the direction my own car was parked. "I appreciate your coming over here on such short notice. I hope I didn't interrupt anything important."

"Just cleaning out old magazines."

"I guess I shouldn't have been so eager to try to help them. Seems pretty stupid in retrospect, but I never thought they'd be suspicious of *me.*"

"Hard to tell how much of it is suspicion and how much is basic investigative procedure."

"It's unnerving, whatever it is."

We'd reached Terri's car, new and shiny with soft lambswool covers on the seats. She unlocked the car with the remote gadget on her key chain and gently pried the sleeping Hannah from her baby sling. Placing the baby into a rear-facing safety restraint, she adjusted the straps and secured a safety bar. I marveled silently, as I had on previous occasions, at the effort involved in simply transporting a child from one place to another.

"You've been a super traveler," Terri said, stroking the top of Hannah's head. "A perfect ten."

"It's a long trip to Mendocino," I said when she'd extracted herself from the car's interior.

Terri shrugged. "I don't mind the drive."

"I thought your mom was going to stay with you until Ted came home."

"That was the initial plan."

"So what changed?"

"I told you, I wanted some time to myself." Terri's tone was not snappish exactly, but close. She must have heard it herself because she backpedaled, softening her response. "Besides, Mom wasn't feeling well. I thought she'd do better at home."

Lenore hadn't seemed under the weather when I'd talked with her. "Nothing serious, I hope."

"No, just a touch of nerves, I think. I'd given her a couple of sleeping pills the previous night because she was feeling out of sorts. But I don't think she slept well." Terri started for the driver's door.

"Another thing—"

"Can we talk later? It's been a long day and I'd like to get home before Hannah wakes up hungry."

I stepped away from the car. "Sure." I had a couple more questions, but at this moment, they weren't at issue. With luck, they never would be.

Jared stumbled into work Monday morning looking like something the cat dragged in.

"You feeling okay?"

"Just tired is all. I didn't get much sleep this weekend."

"What were you doing?"

A smile tweaked the corners of his mouth. "Uh, boss, that's not a question you ask a red-blooded young man."

"Ah, that kind of tired. I hope you were careful."

He shot me a look between scorn and embarrassment. "Enough about my weekend, okay? Looks like I missed all the excitement, though. I saw the piece about Weaver's death in the paper this morning. Weird that the guy pops into our lives right before someone pops him."

Weird yes. I fervently hoped that it was no more than that.

"Guess Ted Harper and his wife will get to keep that baby after all."

"It looks that way." In fact, I'd already put in a call about the court date.

The phone rang and Jared reached for it. "Just a moment and I'll check." He put the caller on hold and looked at me. "For you, someone by the name of Steven. You want to take it?"

I nodded, then made a shooing gesture with my hands. Jared slid out the door and closed it behind him.

I took a deep breath to calm my stomach and picked up the phone. "Hi, Steven."

"Kali? Hi." A long pause. He cleared his throat. "How have you been?" Then he laughed. "Guess we did that already, didn't we? As I was leaving Terri's the other day."

I could hear the nervousness in his voice and that somehow made it easier. Put us on even footing in a way. "We did. And you were right about Hannah. She's wonderful."

Another pause. "Listen, I know this is awkward for both of us. But I think we're better off acknowledging that than pretending it isn't so."

The elephant in the middle of the living room. A favorite analogy among psychologists. Something so obvious everyone knows it's there despite an unstated conspiracy of silence.

"You're right," I conceded. "It is awkward. More than that even. I feel so—"

"Don't go there, Kali. That's not what I meant."

There was a moment's silence.

"I was surprised you gave Terri my name," I said at last.

"Why wouldn't I? You're just the sort of lawyer she needed. *Needs,* present tense. That's why I'm calling."

I slipped into my lawyer hat. "What's happened?"

"Nothing you don't already know. But I'm worried."

"In a case like this, the cops cast their net fairly wide."

"I understand that. But all this interest in her gun . . ." He paused. "They must have checked the records because they know she owned a Beretta."

"How'd you hear that?"

"One of the detectives called Terri this morning. They wouldn't keep asking her about it unless it was the same kind of gun that killed Weaver."

"It would help if she could produce it," I said. Unless, of course, it was the murder weapon.

Steven may have had the same thought. His voice, when he continued, was thoughtful. "She never liked owning a gun. But Arlo insisted she needed it for protection. He made sure we all learned to shoot. While other kids spent Sundays in the park, we'd have family picnics at the rifle range."

"Still, they can't pin this murder on her just because she once owned a gun similar to the one used as a murder weapon."

"You'd think not." Left unspoken was what we were both thinking. *There must be more to it.*

"You want me to ask around?" I said. "See what I can find out?"

"That would be great." Relief flooded his voice. "I'd do it myself but I've burned a few bridges over at the Hall of Justice."

I'd heard rumors to that effect. Steven Cross, transformed from grieving husband and father into total jackass. I could well understand the need to blame someone, however. And since the driver of the other car had never been identified, it wasn't hard to see how allegations of ineffectual police work followed.

"I hate to ask a favor," he said.

"Steven, please. It's the least I can do." Listening to my own words, which rang with a theatrical tenor I wasn't expecting, I felt a giggle spring forth out of nowhere. "Sounds like a line out of a soap opera, doesn't it?"

He laughed too. It felt good. We'd almost succeeded in browbeating the awkwardness into submission.

"I suppose it's not too far from the truth," Steven said. "The soap opera, I mean. You'd be hard pressed to come up with a tawdrier script."

I was suddenly silent. As if silence could banish the memories.

Steven seemed not to notice. "How about coffee sometime?"

"Coffee?" My mind was still immersed in the drama of our tawdry history, where the unexpected peal of Steven's cell phone five years earlier had wrenched open the gate of self-blame and guilt. A shiver inched across my shoulders, powered by the memory of Steven's hand tracing the contours of my face before he reached to answer on the fourth ring.

"You know," Steven said, "coffee. The beverage you drink hot from a cup. Or maybe you'd prefer wine. As I recall, that's more up your alley."

My throat felt tight. "Why are you doing this?"

"Hair of the dog, maybe." He laughed. I wasn't sure what but, he might be verging on hysteria. "Oops, got to go. Time for my eleven o'clock class."

Steven was gone but the mental reel continued to spin as unwelcome images flickered across my brain. I tried counting backward from one hundred, but got only to seventy-nine before I declared the exercise a failure. Second round of defense: focus my attention on Terri.

I called the San Francisco Police Department and got the runaround. They weren't about to reveal details of an ongoing investigation. Neither Dennison or Holbrook was available. I left a message though I suspected I'd get no more from them. My mind ran through the list of people I'd known in the District Attorney's Office. All had since moved on.

I buzzed Jared. "Who do you know in the San Francisco DA's office?"

"Couple of people. Why?"

I explained.

"Whoa. Guess we're not in adoption-land anymore, Toto." He gave a soft whistle. "We going to handle her defense?"

"Jared, back up. The police have questioned her. Period."

"But you're worried they think she did it."

I sighed. "That's what I'm trying to determine."

"Gotcha. So what is it you want to know?"

"What they've got on Weaver's death and why they're looking so hard at Terri Harper. Will you see what you can find for me?"

"Sure, boss. Consider it done."

It was past noon and I was suddenly ravenous. The six-ounce container of lemon-flavored yogurt I'd brought from home seemed paltry fare. I got into the car and drove to the burrito shop on College Avenue, where I wolfed down a veggie burrito and diet cola while sitting at one of the small tables clustered near the front sidewalk. Then, instead of heading back to the office, I drove across the bridge to San Francisco and the address where Bram Weaver had lived, and died.

Weaver's house was located on a narrow street, down a flight of steep stairs that led to a landing. The walkway and main entrance were at the side of the house. Thick foliage and the natural rise of the hillside provided privacy from both the street and neighbors. They also offered easy hiding for a gunman.

The papers had been full of news about Weaver's death, but had offered little by way of substance. From what I'd pieced together, Weaver's body had been found just inside the doorway. Speculation was that the shots had been fired by someone standing outside. Had Weaver opened the door from the inside? Or had he been going into the house himself when he'd turned at a sound behind him?

The crime scene tape was no longer up but I saw a piece that had torn off lying in the garden. What had the police found in their search of the scene? No fingerprints, I would guess, or they'd have taken Terri's for comparison. But nothing that would seem to rule her out, either.

I tried to determine the most likely spot for the gunman to have stood. Probably the flat area where the stairs met the landing. It was far enough from the door to be out of arms' reach, yet close enough for accurate aim. All he'd have had to do to blend into obscurity was take a few steps downhill behind the heavily vined concrete wall.

Positioning myself there, I gazed down at rooftops below. An unlikely angle for anyone looking back up the hill to where I was standing. The house to the left was screened by Weaver's own place and to the right the nearest window didn't come into view until I was halfway back up the stairs toward the street. Weaver had no doubt treasured the seclusion, but it might have cost him his life.

From Weaver's, I drove to the Harpers', timing myself from point to point. With midday traffic the trip took twenty-five minutes. At night it would be considerably less. Could Terri have driven to Weaver's, killed him, then driven home without her mother ever knowing? Clearly she could have.

Did I think she had? No, I didn't.

I fervently hoped those two convictions never had to meet head-on.

When I arrived back at the office, Jared was busily scribbling a note for me.

"I was just on my way out," he said, setting the pen aside. "I got the information you wanted. A guy who was a year ahead of me in law school."

I stuck my purse in the desk drawer. "What did you find out?"

"Probably not what you were hoping to hear. You were right about their interest in the gun. Weaver was killed with a .25 caliber Beretta, same as is registered to Terri. And a neighbor heard Terri go out a little before midnight. She doesn't know what time Terri came in because she was asleep by then. The cops have some fibers and stuff too. Just to warn you."

I tried to ignore the knot forming in my stomach. "Any idea what?"

"Nope. My friend didn't know either."

Didn't know or wasn't saying.

CHAPTER 11

Whatever it was the police had on Terri, they clearly hoped to find corroborating evidence by searching her house. She called me Tuesday morning, her voice pitched in panic.

"The police are here with a search warrant. What should I do?"

"If they've got a warrant, you have to let them in."

"But they're tearing the place apart."

Cops executing a search are sometimes far from careful. Since the vast majority are male, I suspect it has as much to do with their gender as their profession.

"Maybe you should take Hannah and sit on the deck," I suggested.

"And let them turn this place into a sty?" She sounded as though she were hyperventilating.

"Terri, you need to stay calm. There's not a lot you can do about it."

"There must be something."

"Have you got a camera?"

"Of course."

"When they leave, take pictures. If they've been out of line, we can sue for damages."

She humphed. "For all *that's* worth."

"Do you want me to come over there? I'd be happy to."

"It won't change anything, will it?"

"Probably not."

She sighed. "I'll be okay. But thanks for offering."

"Don't say anything to them. Don't answer their questions; don't volunteer information."

"Right."

I hesitated. "Terri, what about the gun? Is it there?"

"I told you, I haven't seen it in ages."

At least her story was holding up under pressure. "Did you ask Ted about it?"

"Last night when he called. He doesn't know either." She dropped her voice. "Why are they so interested in *me?* Certainly I'm not the only person in the country with a gun."

This wasn't the time or place to talk to her about physical evidence or the neighbor who'd heard Terri drive off the night of the murder. Especially when I didn't know, myself, what the cops really had.

"Note what they take," I told her. "And call me when they leave. Most importantly, stay calm."

"Just how do I do that?"

She had me there.

I left messages for both Dennison and Holbrook immediately after talking to Terri. By the end of the day neither man had called me back.

Aggravating, but not surprising.

Terri didn't call again either. Maybe she'd taken my *staying calm* suggestion to heart and was off doing something pleasurable. Or she'd gone to the other extreme and had a nervous breakdown.

Or been arrested. But then I'd have heard, wouldn't I?

I tried calling her and got the answering machine.

When I finished my four-thirty conference on another matter, a client who'd been injured when the deck of her rental home collapsed, I called it a day. I'd managed to garner a nice settlement for her. Better to end on a high note, I decided. It wasn't an opportunity that offered itself often.

Overhead, the late afternoon sky was clear blue and the sun was still bright, but a cool wind was blowing off the coastal fog bank—a fixture of Bay Area summers. I traded my skirt and blouse for jeans and a sweatshirt, then took Loretta for a walk. We didn't head into the parklands this time, but instead wound through the maze-like streets of my hillside neighborhood in Berkeley and down to the small block of shops at the base of the hill. Securing Loretta's leash to a parking meter, I dashed into Peet's and bought myself a decaf latte, then perched on the wide lip of the brick retaining wall in the courtyard. Sheltered from the wind, I could enjoy soaking up the last of the sun's rays.

It was, ironically, the same spot I'd come with Steven Cross in the early stages of our . . . I stopped myself. *Our what?* Our indiscretion? Our infatuation? Our cosmic bonding?

Except that when we'd stopped for coffee that crisp fall morning, it had been simple friendship.

When had it changed? Sometime during the Dickerson case, I'd have said then. Somewhere in those long hours together reviewing psychiatric evaluations and preparing witnesses; somewhere in the nooks and crannies of camaraderie over late-night pizza eaten in the office.

But with the clarity of hindsight, I'd since decided that the chemistry between us had been there all along, buoyed by our mutual love of the outdoors and bad movies, by the offbeat sense of humor we shared, and the bond of having lost a parent during our childhoods. It had been there, smoldering under the surface, but neither of us recognized it until it slapped us in the face.

When the Dickerson case settled, Steven and I drove to Tahoe for a day of skiing, with his wife's blessing. Caroline didn't ski, hated the cold, and was glad that her husband had someone with whom to share the drive.

Midwinter bright and crisp following a dusting of fresh snow, the day was ski-perfect. Though Steven was a stronger skier than I was, our abilities were evenly enough matched that we took the hills together, often with an edge of good-natured competition. At the end of the day I was pleasantly tired and greatly satisfied.

Sitting in the passenger seat on the way home, I dozed off-and-on during the last leg of the drive. There was a part of me that never wanted it to end.

Steven helped me carry my ski stuff into the house, where I told him to dump it in the front hallway. I would deal with it later.

"You want some coffee?" I'd asked. Steven still had to continue on into the city and I thought the coffee might help him stay awake. I remember thinking that, because what I really wanted was wine. And a roaring fire. And Steven's thigh pressed against my own.

He faced me, started to say something, then leaned one arm against the wall behind me and kissed me softly.

For a moment, I was too stunned to speak. I said the first thing that came to mind. "Whoa, that was a surprise."

He smiled. "Surprised me, too."

"A nice surprise," I added.

"Very nice." Steven leaned closer and kissed me again.

That was the pivotal moment. If I could go back and change what happened, that is where I would start. We could have laughed it off, said *gee, if only things were different.* We could at least have put up a fight. But we didn't.

Not that night. Not the nights that followed. Somewhere the thought drifted across my mind that what we were doing was wrong. The warning was faint, though, like skywriting turned to haze. In the weeks and months that followed the accident, I would be reviled by my moral failings. Not by Steven's, interestingly, but very definitely by my own.

But in those days and nights before everything changed, I lived only for the moment. Even in the quiet aftermath of our lovemaking, with Steven nestled at my side, I would pull the blinds on any thoughts but the here and now.

It was March. A rainy night. A good night to be indoors with someone you cared about. According to my bedroom clock, it was nine thirty-eight when Steven's cell phone rang, wrenching the sweetness of two-and-a-half months from our grasp.

I wanted to go with him to the hospital, but I knew it was wrong. I didn't even offer. Steven stumbled into his clothes and out the door almost in one movement. There were no good-byes, not even any muttered words of regret. Just loose ends and unfinished business.

Caroline was dead by the time Steven arrived at the hospital. Rebecca was taken off life support three days later. A wrenching decision I learned about only via the grapevine. By mutual, unspoken accord we hadn't seen each other again. Until last week.

What in the world had he been thinking anyway, asking me now if I wanted to have coffee? Was he out of his mind?

It wasn't necessarily a date, I reminded myself. Mature adults had friendships. But a voice in my head protested. Mature adults didn't find themselves in situations like the one we were in.

Maybe the invitation had simply been a slip of the tongue. Gratitude for my willingness to help Terri. Maybe he'd never mention it again and we could pretend the question had never been raised. I fervently hoped so. The memories, and the unrelenting guilt, were simply too painful to revisit.

A woman with a golden lab walked by and Loretta jumped up, her tail wagging. She had about ten seconds to sniff and make friends before the woman yanked on the lab's leash and continued on. Begrudgingly, Loretta settled herself on the pavement again.

In front of the bakery next door, a man with a baby stroller leaned against the building and smoked a cigarette, drawing glares and disdainfully wrinkled noses from customers exiting the store. First, a man with a commuter cup and then a woman carrying two cups of coffee and a bakery bag. I did a double-take.

Because I'd been used to seeing her pregnant, it took a moment for me to recognize the young woman. Melissa was dressed in shorts and a loose-fitting cotton tee. She was still plump, but I had no way of knowing how much of the weight was left over from the pregnancy. While I debated calling out a greeting, she headed across the street to the blue Explorer I remembered from the day we'd met over lunch in San Francisco.

Ted Harper's Explorer.

One of the fringe benefits the Harpers could offer and the first adoptive couple couldn't. It made me slightly uncomfortable to see that the Harpers had allowed her to keep driving it after the baby's birth, but I couldn't say why.

Melissa climbed into the driver's side, handed her passenger the coffee cups, and buckled herself in. As she pulled away from the curb, I tried for a glimpse of the passenger but saw only light-colored hair pulled into a ponytail at the nape of the neck.

When I hadn't heard from Terri by midmorning the next day, I called the Harpers, and reached Ted.

"When did you get back?" I asked.

"Last evening. Just in time, too. Terri was beside herself."

"About the search?"

"They left the place a real mess."

"How's Terri now?"

"Sleeping."

I checked my watch. Ten-thirty. "Is she okay?"

Instead of answering, Ted began peppering me with questions of his own. His tone was angry. "What in the hell is going on anyway? The airwaves have been full of the story, and the search was front-page news in this morning's *Chronicle*."

I'd seen the story too. Not as big as the one on Weaver's death in Sunday's paper, but police interest in Terri Harper had not gone unnoticed.

"How can they even *think* Terri killed Weaver?"

"She's got a motive," I told him. "At least from their perspective. And she owns a gun similar to the one used in the murder."

Ted grunted dismissively. "Terri hates guns. She doesn't even know where the thing is anymore. Neither of us do."

"That may have added to their suspicions."

"What do you mean?"

"If you could produce it, tests would be able to determine whether or not it was the murder weapon. I imagine the cops find it suspiciously convenient that the gun is missing."

"I told you we haven't seen it since . . . I don't know when. It's not like the gun disappeared right when Weaver was killed."

Ted did not sound like a man interested in rational discussion so I didn't point out that no cop would find "I haven't seen the gun in ages" as proof that it was so.

"And where do they get off searching our house anyway?" Ted's voice was growing louder. "Just because Terri *once* owned a gun? Gun ownership is legal last I looked."

"Ted, I am not the enemy. Stop yelling at me."

He continued to rant. "I can see why the NRA gets so upset. The cops have already turned gun owners into outlaws!"

I tried to redirect his focus. "Did Terri say what they took?"

"Some stuff from our bedroom closet, and from the car. Didn't sound like they found anything significant. They made a mess of things though. We spent last night straightening up." He took a breath and grew calmer. "I feel unclean. Like our home, *our life*, has been defiled."

"That's a fairly common reaction, if it helps any."

"It doesn't."

"It must be much worse for Terri," I added. I was tiring of Ted's wrath. "She was there during the search and she's the focus of this . . . this witch hunt."

"Yeah, I know." He took a breath. "Sorry I got kinda hot under the collar. I realize it's not your fault." He paused, took another breath. "The baby's crying. I've got to go. You'll let us know if you hear anything?"

"Absolutely."

"See you Sunday then, for the christening."

On Wednesday afternoon I finally reached Inspector Dennison, although I might as well have saved myself the call. Tight-lipped didn't begin to describe his response.

Either he was sitting on something big or he had nothing. I was hoping it was the latter. Hoping that whatever the police were expecting to find at the Harpers', they hadn't.

The news coverage had quieted some too. No longer a front-page story. A couple of inches of text rather than two columns. *A number of possible suspects* was the official line. Terri wasn't even mentioned by name.

At the office Friday morning, I set aside an hour to clean off my desk, which was beginning to resemble a free-form paper sculpture. I'd just poured myself a cup of coffee, smeared half a bagel with light cream cheese, and pushed back in my chair, when I got a call from the District Attorney's Office. A man by the name of Don Pelle.

"You representing Terri Harper?" he asked.

"That's correct."

"A warrant has been issued for her arrest. As a courtesy, we're going through you rather than having the police pick her up directly. She has until five o'clock today to surrender."

I set my coffee down hard, spilling it in the process. "On what evidence?"

"You'll get a report."

Eventually. "You chose Friday on purpose, didn't you?"

The bail hearing wouldn't be until Monday, maybe Tuesday. Terri would wind up spending the weekend in jail. Friday arrests were an old ploy meant to wear down suspects, make them more inclined to cooperate.

"What are we supposed to do," Pelle asked with sarcasm, "never arrest anyone on a Friday?"

"You won't make it past the preliminary hearing. Your office will wind up with egg on its face." This was bravado, but it might make him take another look at the evidence.

"There won't be a prelim," he said smugly. "We've got a grand jury indictment."

A beloved tool of the prosecution. Evidence was heard in private, away from the questioning eyes and ears of defense lawyers, and suspects themselves.

Given the high-profile nature of the case, I shouldn't have been surprised, but I was. And worried. They clearly had evidence tying Terri to the murder.

"When can I get a copy of the report?" I asked.

"When we've reached that stage. Right now all you need to worry about is making sure your client turns herself in by the end of the day."

CHAPTER 12

Terri huddled in the passenger seat of my car, staring silently out the side window. We'd driven the first four blocks from her house without exchanging a word.

"How are you doing?" I asked finally.

"I'm scared to death."

Stupid question. What did I expect? I glanced at the tiny overnight bag at her feet, filled no doubt with PJs, makeup, and a couple of paperback novels. Like someone trying to make the best of a stay in the hospital. Scared as she was now, I knew it was only going to get worse.

"Ted says there ought to be a way to get me out right away. So that I don't have to spend the night."

He'd made that point to me, as well. Several times. And he'd refused to listen when I'd told him it wasn't fair to raise Terri's hopes. He'd refused to listen to much of anything, in fact, including his wife's suggestion that he call Lenore to come help with Hannah. I suspected that he was merely trying to quell his own discomfort, but I'd found his snappishness irritating all the same.

"I think it highly unlikely you'll get a bail hearing today," I told Terri. I'd made a few calls already, to no avail.

"How long will I have to stay there?"

"Over the weekend at least."

"Till *Monday?*"

"Or maybe Tuesday."

Terri made a sound, something between a whimper and a groan. Her fantasy of an Eddie Bauer arrest had just taken its first hit.

"And they're probably not going to let you keep your things," I added.

"What do you mean?"

I gestured with my head. "The bag from home."

"But I . . ." She let the words trail off and sucked in a ragged breath instead. "This can't really be happening."

"Terri, we need to go over your story."

"My *story?*"

"What happened the night Weaver was killed. There are some points that need to be clarified."

"I told you, I was home in bed."

"But the police—"

"Later, okay. I can barely breathe right now, much less talk. Or think."

She was right. Now was not the time to plot strategy. "Just remember, don't talk to anyone. Not the police, not guards, not even cellmates."

"Cellmates." She shuddered at the very idea. "You're sure I can't get out before Monday? We've got the money. Posting bail won't be a problem."

"There needs to be a hearing before a judge. I'll see what I can do, but it's not likely to happen over the weekend."

Terri slumped lower in her seat and turned quiet again.

A photographer from the local paper had somehow learned of Terri's arrest and was there to record her misery as we entered the building.

"Keep your chin up and your eyes straight ahead," I told her. "Pretend you're walking into a room full of admirers."

"Don't worry," she muttered between clenched teeth. "I won't give those bastards the satisfaction of thinking they've gotten to me."

Terri was booked and fingerprinted, then escorted off to be stripped, searched, and doused with disinfectant—an indignity that was clearly unnecessary. The deputies were civil and efficient, but their sheer indifference to her was almost more demeaning than overt insults would have been.

"I'll be here first thing Monday morning," I told her. "If not before. And I will do everything in my power to get you out as soon as possible."

"Tell them Hannah needs me," she said, as if that were reason enough. As if the criminal system even took notice of human faces, or human hearts.

I saw Terri briefly on Saturday afternoon to convey the news. No judge would hear her request for bail until Monday. She wasn't surprised, she said. She'd learned a lot in twenty-four hours. None of it encouraging.

But she seemed to be holding up well. No tears, no panic, no crawling into a hole of depression. I was beginning to appreciate the steel fiber beneath the Junior League appearance.

Monday morning I sat at the cluttered, gray metal desk of Don Pelle, assistant DA assigned to the case. He was young, which surprised me; arrogant and brash, which didn't.

"I can give you five minutes," he said brusquely. "I'm up to my eyeballs in deadlines."

In other words, cut to the chase. I wondered if he'd have been as quick to bypass the social banter had I been a male.

"Theresa Harper," I said, matching his tone. "She was arrested on Friday. Arraignment is set for two this afternoon."

"What about her?"

"I was hoping we could work out something on bail before we got into court."

This was standard practice since neither side benefitted from a protracted and contentious argument before the judge. It worked smoothly in the majority of cases, but I could tell from the look on Pelle's face that this was not going to be one of them.

"Bail?" he roared. "She's charged with murder."

"Still, the court has discretion. She's hardly a risk to public safety—"

"How can you be sure?"

"For heaven's sake, she's got a five-week-old baby."

"The very baby who's the motive for murder. Besides, she's a flight risk." He held up a hand. "And don't bring up the baby again. Your client could take the baby with her. Like she did before."

It took a minute to figure out what he was talking about. "You mean her trip to Mendocino? That's ridiculous. She didn't know you wanted to talk to her until she got home."

"Right. Like, I've got a bridge to sell you."

"You know who she is, don't you? Terri Harper has got family here, connections to the community."

"If she killed Weaver, family's not going to make her stick around."

The kid had a knack for kindling my irritation. "There is absolutely no reason to keep her behind bars. She's got a clean record, ties to the area, no history of impulsive behavior. She can easily post bond."

"Right. And she could just as easily buy a one-way ticket to obscurity." Pelle checked his watch. "Sorry, I'm going to have to cut you off, I've got a meeting. It's going to be my recommendation that she be held without bail." Rising, he ushered me to the door with an unctuous smile. "See you in court, counselor."

The way he said it, I was willing to bet he practiced in front of the mirror.

At the arraignment that afternoon, Judge Simon followed the State's recommendation—despite my best efforts to the contrary—and denied bail. Terri let out a gasp.

I covered her hand with mine and gave an empathetic squeeze. "We'll try again," I whispered. "Don't lose hope." But first I was going to make my plea to the DA himself. I suspected the young prosecutor hadn't yet learned when it was appropriate to flex judicial muscle and when it wasn't.

"Nice try, boss." Jared fell into step beside me outside the courtroom. "Your arguments would have persuaded me. I don't think that judge even listened to you."

"This isn't nursery school, Jared. You don't have to boost my self-esteem." But I secretly appreciated his show of support.

"What now?" he asked, slowing his stride to mine.

"We need to file a motion for discovery. Find out what evidence they've got. Then maybe we'll have a better idea how strong their case is."

"They must have something pretty persuasive to charge her with murder."

"It's all in how you look at it. You know those black-and-white pictures that look like one thing until someone tells you it can also be something else?"

"Yeah. I remember one that looks like the profile of a beautiful young woman. But it's also the face of a witchy old hag." He laughed. "Funny that we always see the beautiful woman first."

"It's the other way around in criminal cases. Prosecutors are poised to see the hag. They string together evidence that paints a picture of guilt. But when you start looking closer, seeing other scenarios, you can sometimes make a pretty convincing argument for innocence."

We stopped at the elevator bank and I waited until the emerging cluster moved on before I continued. "We're going to have to anticipate what we think their best case will be, based on the evidence, and then reconstruct it to form a different picture."

"There's nothing we can do until trial?"

"In theory, we can quash the indictment if it isn't supported by evidence, but that's not very realistic. And I'll try again to get Terri free on bail. Other than that, we'd best put our efforts into preparing a dazzling defense."

He grinned. "You mean something along the lines of flying DNA and a police vendetta?"

"With luck, we won't find ourselves in such desperate straits. But first things first. Why don't you draft a motion for discovery. I'll take a look at it when I get back to the office."

"Sure. Where are you going?"

"To meet with our client."

There'd been no opportunity to talk at the hearing, and Terri and I had ground to cover.

Across the glass partition from me, Terri perched on the edge of a plastic chair. Her shoulders were hunched and her arms were folded in front of her—as if in retreat from the grim surroundings of the interview room. After a moment, she picked up the phone, holding it gingerly with her thumb and forefinger.

I sympathized. I was on the side where the good guys sat, and not any happier with the ambience than she was. Inmates didn't have a monopoly on oiliness and stale sweat. There was nothing fresh or alive about either cubicle.

"How's Hannah?" she asked right off. "Have you seen her?"

I shook my head. "I've talked to Ted though. He and Hannah seem to be doing fine."

"Without me."

"What I meant is, they're holding it together."

"Ted should have gone ahead with the christening, even if he did want to cancel the buffet afterwards."

"I'm sure he wanted you to be part of it."

"My mother will probably come stay with them now that I'm . . . now that the judge ruled against bail." She swallowed back tears. "I just want to get out of here!"

"I know. I'm trying."

"I didn't do it," Terri wailed. "I didn't kill Weaver. How can they think I did?"

"I'm sorry you have to go through this, Terri. I can imagine how awful it must be."

She bit her bottom lip.

"But they must have evidence. I'll know more after I see the police report. In the meantime, I've got some questions of my own."

She nodded, pulled her shoulders in even tighter.

"What time did you leave for Mendocino that morning?"

"Around ten o'clock, I think. I was up early with Hannah so it felt later, but I don't think it was."

"What made you decide to go?"

Terri shrugged. "I guess I was feeling at loose ends. My mother wasn't well. I thought she should go home. With Ted gone, the house felt empty. Besides, I wanted to show off Hannah."

"A spur-of-the-moment decision?"

"Right. I didn't even call Robin until we got there."

"Why didn't you tell Ted where you were?" I had a feeling that had only added to the cops' suspicions and probably underscored their concerns about her being a flight risk.

Terri dropped her gaze to the table top.

"He thought you were calling from home," I added.

"I know."

"That makes it look like you were intentionally concealing where you were."

She hesitated. "I was."

It wasn't the answer I'd expected. "Why?"

"Ted doesn't like me driving long distances by myself." She paused. "Also, he doesn't like that I visit Robin."

"Why, is she a bad influence?"

"He. Robin's a he."

"Ahh."

"But he's gay so it's not like Ted has any reason to be jealous."

Not logically maybe. But I'd found that men felt threatened by gay males in a different way. Nonetheless, her reasons for not telling Ted were apparently unrelated to Weaver's murder. If she was telling me the truth, that is.

"Robin and I used to teach together," Terri explained. "He had fifth grade; I taught third. The whole faculty was wonderful. Then the school board decided to reassign all the teachers. I lasted another year. Robin just quit last month. He bought a bed and breakfast place near the coast. It's going to be fantastic when it's all done."

"So you spent time reminiscing?"

"I spent the weekend scrubbing floors and helping him re-paint two of the bedrooms. And playing with Hannah, of course. Robin absolutely fell in love with her."

"He put you to work?" Not the kind of friend most of us go out of our way to visit.

"It was fun. Got my mind off my troubles."

"Troubles?" I was back to thinking about Weaver's death.

Terri looked up. "About Hannah, I mean. Whether we were going to lose her, whether we were even right to try to keep her."

I was mulling over her story, thinking about how it would play to the prosecution—and the jury. I could see where there might be some room for skepticism. The thought must have been evident in my expression because Terri leaned forward.

"You believe me, don't you?"

I had avoided asking myself this very question. What a defense attorney thought about her client's innocence wasn't supposed to be an issue. You tried to do the best you could by your client in light of the evidence. Sometimes this meant fighting tooth and nail at trial. Sometimes it came down to an acceptable plea bargain. But the role of attorney was that of advocate, nothing more.

Even so, you couldn't help but form impressions.

I looked into Terri's eyes and nodded. "I'm on your side, Terri. No matter what. And I don't think you killed Weaver."

But neither did I think she'd been entirely truthful.

CHAPTER 13

Three days later Jared and I were in his office sifting through the initial fruits of our motion for discovery. There were stacks of papers lining the floor along one entire wall. And this was only the beginning. Whatever else trials were, they weren't kind to trees.

Jared had taken the first cut at organizing the material—an important step because without a plan for tracking information, it was next to useless.

"Did you catch the press conference on the news last night?" Jared asked.

I nodded. The mayor and District Attorney Ray Shalla assuring their public that the case against Terri Harper would be pursued vigorously. Both were masters of the soundbite, but had come up short on detail and substance.

I slid my chair closer to the desk. "Guess now I understand why Shalla hasn't had time to meet with me."

"It's weird not seeing them nipping at each other's heels," Jared said, echoing my own thoughts. "Ever since the brouhaha over that article in the *Chron*, they've circled the wagons and made like they're on the same team."

In the spring the *San Francisco Chronicle* had run a special report comparing the treatment of rich and poor defendants in the city's legal system. Both the DA and the mayor had taken it on the chin and had been grappling to redeem themselves ever since. Terri, unfortunately, was a poster case for their cause.

But it had to be more than that. "The District Attorney's Office may have been a bit overzealous," I said, "but they wouldn't build a case out of thin air."

Jared looked at me. "They didn't." He reached into his desk for a bag of M&Ms, and poured a handful before tossing the bag my way.

"It's only ten in the morning," I told him, pushing the bag away.

"So?"

"What've we got so far?"

"You want to start with the gory stuff?" Jared asked.

I didn't. On the other hand, Weaver's body was a logical place to begin. "Okay. But just the highlights. I'll read the autopsy report later."

"Weaver was shot twice." Jared was reading from the report. "Once in the lower abdomen and once in the face. Entry wounds to the front in both instances." He slid the crime scene photos across the table to me.

I was glad to be drinking coffee and not grape soda.

Weaver was lying on his back amid a Rorschach spread of red. Blood had pooled on the tile floor of the entry hall and in the hollow above his neck where his face should have been.

"Geez," I said. "Looks like he was hit with a cannon."

"The blast to his face was at close range," Jared explained. He continued reading from the report. "A .25 caliber slug. Forensics says it's from a Beretta. Same manufacturer as the gun registered to Terri."

"That's prosecutor's logic," I told him. "Our job is to remind the jury that lots of people aside from Terri own .25 caliber Berettas."

"They don't list anything more on the gun."

"I don't think they're able to determine model. Did they find any casings?"

"Two."

"An automatic then." Which kept Terri in the running. "What else do they have?"

"Let's see. A Doublemint gum wrapper in the bushes by the walkway."

"Not necessarily dropped by the killer," I pointed out. "But if the prosecution learns that Doublemint is Terri's gum of choice, you can be sure they'll use it against her."

It was the kind of evidence that could only damage the defense, not help. We'd gain nothing if we could prove that Terri never chewed gum, because there was nothing to tie the wrapper to the crime. But if there was testimony that Terri chewed Doublemint, the jury would make the connection whether there was a basis or not.

Jared grinned. "Let's hope she's a Juicy Fruit kind of gal." He took another fistful of M&Ms. "You like the blue ones?"

"They all taste the same."

Jared shook his head. "Blue tastes different. I don't eat blue." He dropped two blue candies onto the table near my hand, then turned back to the report. "They found a pair of dark glasses near the body."

"Dark glasses and not reading glasses?"

"That's what it says."

It didn't make sense. Weaver wouldn't have worn dark glasses at night. That left the killer, who wouldn't have been wearing them either unless he was trying to disguise himself. Surely there were better ways.

"No sign of forced entry," Jared continued. "And no sign of a struggle."

"They think Weaver opened the front door to his assailant?" I put one of the blue M&Ms in my mouth, closed my eyes, and let it melt. Tasted like generic M&M to me.

"Who knows what they think? They aren't bothering to share their theories with us."

And because it was a Grand Jury indictment, we wouldn't even get a peek at those theories during a preliminary hearing. "Maybe someone was in the house with him," I said, thinking aloud. "They had a disagreement, and the killer shot him on his way out."

"Except there's no evidence of anyone else being there."

"A clever killer, maybe."

Jared shrugged. If he wasn't buying the theory, it was unlikely a jury would. Besides, it didn't help Terri.

"Prints?" I asked.

"Apparently none were Terri's. That's good news."

"Of course, if they're going to argue she shot him from outside, it doesn't matter."

"Unfortunately," Jared said, "that's where things get dicey. There was a handprint on the porch railing. Pretty small to be a man's."

"On the railing? How can they tell?"

"The railing's flat, about eight inches across. Apparently the board was dusty and then with the moisture in the air at night . . . Anyway, they've got a print but not enough detail to make an ID."

"Could have been someone selling magazine subscriptions," I pointed out.

Jared nodded. "But it's not going to look good if it's about the same size as Terri's hand, is it?"

"No, it's not." I'd been studiously ignoring the bag of M&Ms, but it was getting so that I was having trouble looking anywhere else. Finally I gave in and reached for a handful. "What about trace evidence?"

"Not much. Some black nylon fibers caught in a rose bush by the front steps. Again, not necessarily from the killer." Jared caught my eye and smiled like a student aiming to please. "Some short white animal hairs on Weaver's pant legs. No mention that Weaver had a cat or dog."

I tried to recall if I'd seen an animal at the Harpers'. I didn't think so. And black nylon was about as common as a winter cold.

"Coroner says time of death is between nine in the evening and about three the next morning," Jared continued. "But Weaver didn't get off the air until ten. And the couple who live down the hill from him remember hearing what might have been shots a few minutes after midnight."

"What *might have been* shots?"

"You know what it's like living in the city. There's always noise. Pretty soon you stop hearing it. And if you have your TV or radio on, you're not really listening to what's outside."

Jared reached down to the floor for another file. "This is the bad news," he said. "There's a witness, another neighbor of Weaver's, who says she saw a woman fitting Terri's description leaving the area about midnight. She was driving a dark-colored SUV."

"No shortage of SUVs or slender blondes in the city." Nonetheless, I felt a knot form in my stomach.

"Gets worse," Jared said. "The witness got a partial reading of the license plate. Letters were NMO. Same as the Harpers' dark blue Explorer."

The knot got tighter.

California license plates have seven places; a number, three letters, and then three more numbers. I'd forgotten how to do mathematical permutations, but I assured myself there had to be a lot of plates with those three letters. Given the popularity of sport utility vehicles, we might get lucky and find a dozen or so that fit the witness description.

While part of me was mentally countering the damaging evidence, another part was struggling to contain the uneasiness rising in my chest.

Was Terri actually guilty?

I tucked that thought away for later. Not that it should matter, I chided myself. My job was advocate, not judge.

"Still," Jared said, oblivious to the debate playing out in my mind, "we ought to be able to raise reasonable doubt. It wasn't like the neighbor got the whole license number. Or even the exact color or make of car."

"You're right. Besides, eyewitness testimony isn't the slam dunk most people think it is. In fact, most experienced cops say it's next to worthless. Memory plays tricks on people. They see what they want to see or what they think they should have seen."

But I could already see the state's case taking shape. Terri leaving the house the night of Weaver's murder, her mother drugged into heavy sleep with pills offered by Terri. She drives to Weaver's place, rings the bell, and when he opens the door, she shoots him in cold blood. Clean and quick, she's come and gone in the blink of an eye.

Next morning Terri sends her mother home and flees to Mendocino, conveniently removing the possibility of a forensic test for powder residue from her hands. As a further safeguard, she spends the day scrubbing floors with ammonia.

It was a lot of supposition, but that's what murder trials were made of. All you needed was a jury looking for an excuse to convict.

CHAPTER 14

Parking in Pacific Heights isn't easy, but after circling the block only once, I was lucky enough to find a spot a couple of houses from the Harpers'. As I was getting out of the car, a young woman in khakis and a navy cardigan trudged down the walkway pushing a baby carriage. At first I thought it might be a neighbor who'd been visiting Ted, then I recognized Melissa.

Why was she with Hannah?

Melissa turned and headed down the street in the other direction without noticing me.

I punched the doorbell sharply.

"Hey, Kali. What a surprise." Ted was dressed in sweats with a towel draped around his muscular neck. There wasn't a drop of perspiration visible.

"What's Melissa doing here?" I demanded, a little too sharply.

"Helping with the baby." He tossed the towel over a chair as he led me to a sitting room at the back of the house. Through the windows, I could see the towers of the Golden Gate Bridge, still shrouded in summer fog. The TV was on and he flipped it off.

"Are you out of your mind?"

Ted looked genuinely perplexed. "What do you mean?"

"That's asking for trouble."

"Melissa's no trouble. She was a real sweetheart to offer, in fact."

Could the man be so dense? "She's needy. And lonely." I wouldn't be surprised if she had a crush on Ted as well, but I wasn't going to flatter him by sharing that thought. "She wants to be part of your life instead of making one for herself."

"So? She's a nice kid." Ted plopped down on the sofa.

"She's also Hannah's biological mother. You don't think that's a problem?" Maybe he had a crush on her as well. Or an insatiable need for attention.

"What am I supposed to do now that Terri's in jail?" He sounded accusatory, as though she'd left him for a week in the Bahamas. "I can't care for a baby by myself."

"What about Terri's mother?"

Ted rolled his eyes. "God spare me."

"She can't be that bad."

"Lenore thinks she knows what's best for everyone. Bossy, opinionated—"

I cut him off. "Hire help then. Or learn to handle it yourself." The way women did. "What you're doing here isn't good for you, Melissa, or the baby."

"I don't see why not. Melissa was living here before." He was sounding defensive now, and a little piqued at my disapproval.

"Right, *before.* This is after. Melissa and Hannah should not be spending time together. Melissa should not be living here." I was surprised by my own vehemence. I knew next to nothing about babies, yet I was certain the current arrangement was fraught with problems.

"It was Melissa's idea," Ted explained.

"That doesn't change the fact that it's a bad idea."

Ted raked a hand through his thick, dark hair, turned to gaze out the window at the blue-gray water of the bay. Then he turned back to me.

"Are you going to stand there glaring?" he said. "Take a seat, why don't you." His tone might not have met the Miss Manners test, but it was friendlier than before.

I sat. The club chair was much too deep for my comfort.

Ted leaned forward. "There's this other couple who were interested in the baby . . ."

I nodded. "I know about them. The Coles."

"Right. Well, they contacted Melissa after they read about Terri's arrest."

"What?" I tried to keep the alarm from my voice. "They had no right to do that."

"They think she should reconsider."

"Too bad. Melissa made her decision, signed all the papers. She can't change her mind now." Though what Terri's arrest would do to the final decree was anyone's guess.

"It can't hurt to keep her happy," Ted said plaintively. "Besides, it's kind of nice having her around."

It struck me, not for the first time, that Ted's emotional maturity fell short of his years. And it made me uncomfortable. In part, I realized with dismay, because my mind was already testing the package of Ted and Melissa as conspirators in murder, intentionally letting Terri take the fall.

"I still think it's a bad idea," I told him.

"I'll take that under advisement."

I couldn't tell if he was brushing me off or not.

Ted leaned back, hands behind his head. "But that's not why you came."

"You said at one time that you'd done some digging on Weaver."

"Right. Back when I thought the judge might care what kind of father he'd be. Why?"

"Weaver is going to be the key to Terri's defense. We can argue the evidence against her, but if we can also come up with a plausible theory for his murder that doesn't include Terri, our case will be much stronger."

"I've got a file on him. Shall I get it?"

"Please. It will save me time if I don't have to duplicate what you've already done."

"Hold on. I'll be right back."

Ted was gone only a couple of minutes. He returned with a manila folder and two cans of soda. "Take your pick. I like 'em both."

Mountain Dew and Dr. Pepper. I opted for the Dr. Pepper.

"Anything new from the police?" he asked and handed me the soda.

I thought of the witness who'd gotten a partial plate off a dark-colored SUV, but I also remembered my earlier qualms about Ted and Melissa. I shook my head. "Nothing new."

Ted popped the tab on his soda. He took a gulp and set it on a *Sports Illustrated* at the end of the table.

I opened my soda as well, but used one of the cork coasters. The can was ice cold. "You don't have a pet, do you?" I asked.

"A pet?"

"Dog, cat, rabbit?"

"No." Ted shuffled through the papers in the folder. "I wouldn't mind a dog but Terri's allergic to them. Why?"

I didn't answer, and Ted didn't push. "Tell me about Weaver. I'll look through your notes later, but first I'd like to hear your thoughts."

Ted furrowed his brows. "He never finished college, something it seems he took pains to avoid mentioning publicly. He was raised in Missouri by his mother who, incidentally, he hasn't spoken to in years. Was in the Army for a while, worked a stint in a rehab program, then drifted into radio, first in Missouri and then in Bakersfield. Married, divorced, in pretty short order. He moved to the Bay Area about eight years ago. It's only been in the last couple of years that he developed a name for himself."

"I imagine the book helped. People who didn't listen to his program still knew who he was."

"Maybe. But I'd say as many people hated him as loved him. Heck, I turned up a whole web site devoted to dissing the guy."

"Mr. Popularity."

Ted nodded, took another slug of Mountain Dew. "He took potshots at just about everyone—feminists, liberals, gays, minorities. He tossed psychologists, educators, and the mainstream press in there too."

Plenty of people he'd ticked off. But you had to be a fervent believer to kill someone over theoretical differences. "How about closer to home? You mentioned an ex-wife."

"Yeah. And a kid. That's the part that really rankles. Far as I could tell, he never gave the kid the time of day, then he screams and kicks to get Hannah." Ted's wide mouth set in a line of outrage. "I still can't believe the judge didn't toss the jerk out on his ear."

"Do you happen to know when Weaver was divorced?"

"When the kid was just a baby. Must have been twelve, thirteen years ago."

"Wife live around here?"

"Sacramento. She's remarried."

"Where'd you get all this stuff, anyway?"

He tapped his fingers on the table like it was a keyboard. "Mostly online. With someone like Weaver, who's a celebrity, it's not hard."

"Did Weaver ever marry again?"

"No mention of it. But he's apparently had a couple of steady girlfriends over the years. He mentions what I assume is the latest in the front of his book. Her name is Ranelle." He paused for a gulp of soda. "You think maybe his ex-wife had it in for him?"

What I was thinking was that I had my work cut out for me.

The phone was ringing when I returned to the office. Jared was nowhere to be seen so I raced to grab it myself.

"At last," Steven said, "we finally make contact. You're a hard person to reach."

I felt my throat tighten. "Sorry. Things have been kind of hectic here." I'd picked up his messages, both at home and at the office, but I'd never found the strength to return the calls.

Steven hesitated. "I was beginning to suspect that you weren't any too eager to talk to me."

"It's awkward."

"Best way to handle that, Kali, is to confront it, not run the other way."

"It's also not a good idea."

"Good or not, you're representing my sister on a murder charge. I don't see how we can *not* talk."

He was right. If I'd wanted to keep Steven out of my life, I should never have taken Terri on as a client. I did want him out, didn't I? Or maybe it was just that I thought I *should* want him out.

"There are no new developments," I said, struggling to find the right tone. It felt both odd and comfortably familiar to be having a conversation with Steven. "The first discovery material was delivered the other day. We've just started going through it."

"What about another bail hearing?"

"I'm working on it. Shalla seems to be avoiding me."

"Terri's got to get out of there. She's got a baby, for Chrissake."

"I'm aware of that." Lenore, too, had been calling, urging me to work harder at freeing Terri. As if it were that easy.

"Sorry, I know you are." Steven paused. "I didn't call to complain anyway. I'd like to help with Terri's defense. Be part of the team."

"I've already got a team." Jared, myself, and Nick Logan, a private investigator I'd known since law school. And working with Steven again wasn't a good idea.

"You can use another pair of eyes and legs, can't you? We've done this before, Kali. We work well together."

Too well. It was what had led to our downfall.

His mind must have been following along the same track. "Caroline and Rebecca are dead," Steven said softly. "Our avoiding one another is not going to bring them back."

"No, but it doesn't seem right either."

"There's not a day goes by that I don't say to myself, if only I'd been home that night, they'd be alive. They wouldn't have driven out for pizza. Wouldn't have been in the middle of the intersection when that idiot driver plowed through a red light. Whatever guilt you feel, I feel a hundred-fold."

An unbearable weight, I thought. "I know there are—"

"But I didn't throw myself on the funeral pyre, Kali. And I'm not going to live my life as though I should have."

My head felt as though it were made of straw. Was I making an issue where none was warranted? Steven would clearly be an asset to the defense team. He was good at reading people—witnesses and jurors—and he knew his way around the system. Although Jared was eager and hardworking, he was inexperienced.

So it made sense. For Terri's sake, if nothing else. But on a personal level it left me feeling . . . feeling what? I tried to sort it out. Seeing Steven again made me feel scared, vulnerable, nervous. What really gave me pause, I realized, was that I still found Steven attractive.

"This is Terri's life we're talking about," he said. "I can't just sit idly by."

"But working as part of the defense team—"

"Is the only way I can really be involved. She's my sister, Kali."

The pain in his voice is what finally convinced me. "Okay," I told him. "If Terri doesn't have a problem with it, then it's fine by me."

"Thank you." He seemed ready to say something else, then changed his mind. "I'll come by tomorrow afternoon if you're free. You can fill me in on what we've got so far."

What we had so far wasn't much. I pulled out the file Ted had given me on Bram Weaver and began leafing through it. Not the ideology but the hard, biographical information. When I came across a newspaper article that alluded to Weaver's ex-wife, Judy

Monroe, and the gift boutique she owned, I picked up the phone and called, first Sacramento information and then the shop.

Judy wouldn't be in until later that afternoon, the woman answering the phone informed me. Perfect timing for me to make the drive and speak to Judy Monroe in person. I checked my calendar, left a note for Jared, then got into my car and headed east. The midday traffic was light enough that I could hit the speed limit most of the way there. The trip home would be a different story.

With the help of a map, I found Judy Monroe's store without difficulty. It was a trendy home-accessory and gift shop in one of Sacramento's older neighborhoods near the edge of town. While much of what she carried was too *cute* and countryish for my taste, she had some lovely ceramic and pewter pieces as well. If I'd been in a shopping mood, I might have been tempted. Instead, I browsed until a harried mother with four-year-old twins in tow had paid for the duck-motif towels she'd chosen, then approached the woman at the cash register.

"I'm looking for Judy Monroe," I told her.

"That's me."

She was a petite woman with a cap of stylishly short jet-black hair, a bit too much makeup, and a smoker's husky voice. On first impression, she appeared a bit older than Bram, but I couldn't tell if she actually was.

I introduced myself and explained why I wanted to speak with her.

"So long as you're not with the press." She took my business card, examined it briefly, then slipped it into her pocket without further comment. "Don't know what I can do for you, though. I've hardly seen Bram since the divorce."

"How long ago was that?"

"Thirteen years this October."

"Were you married long?"

"Less than a year." She laughed without humor. "Just long enough to get knocked up."

"A son, correct?"

She nodded. "Danny. He's fourteen going on thirty." Her face softened for a moment. "It's hard being a kid these days."

"Harder still being a parent, I hear."

"Yeah, there's that too." The phone rang and she called to someone in the back room. "Helen, can you get that?" Then she turned her attention back to me. "Listen, I was about to step out back for a cigarette. You okay with that?"

"Sure." Better she smoked it outside than in, at least. I followed her out an unmarked door to the parking lot at the rear of the store. It was like stepping into an oven. Sacramento is inland, and doesn't get the coastal fog and breeze that the Bay Area does. I'd grown up with summer heat, but after living in Berkeley, it was always a bit of a surprise.

"You smoke?" Judy asked, holding her pack of Marlboros in my direction.

"It's about the only bad habit I've managed to avoid."

"I've got the other ones too. Least smoking keeps the extra weight off. I'd be as wide as I am tall if I quit, and I figure being fat's not good for you either, right?" She lit her cigarette and dropped the match into a galvanized bucket filled with sand and cigarette butts that rested on the pavement. "So, your client is the one they're saying finally got to Bram."

"Finally?"

"She can't have been the first who wanted to off him. I thought of it myself, in fact. Did she do it?" Judy paused only a second. "That's okay, I know you can't say. She had reason enough to, if you ask me. What gall to think he could just walk in and take their baby."

"He claimed to be the father."

Judy made a noise of disgust. "He was Danny's father too. Never seemed to take much heed of that."

I leaned back against the stucco exterior of the shop. "Tell me about Bram."

"That's a hard one. He was a chameleon. He could morph himself into whatever was needed at the moment. Smooth as silk when he wanted to be, but underneath, self-centered and smug. And definitely not interested in having a kid, at least not fifteen years ago. He took off before Danny was even born. He'd send money every once in a while, but not regularly. And he moved around so much, it was hard to pin him down for child support."

An all-too-familiar story. Woman and kid barely making it while the father sloughs off responsibility like a snake shedding his skin. "How did you manage?"

"A little of this, a little of that. I sold real estate for a while, then kitchen cabinets. That's how I met my husband. Doug's a contractor. His company is putting in a new planned community west of town. Maybe you saw the signs on the way in?"

If I had, I hadn't noticed. There were so many new developments of late, I'd stopped paying attention. The beautiful oak-studded rolling hills of my youth had given way to a relentless stream of cookie-cutter houses on dinky lots.

Judy doused her cigarette in the sand. "We've been married three years now and financially things are a whole lot easier. I only wish Doug and Danny got along better."

"It must be hard on Danny after having you to himself his whole life."

"I'm sure that's part of it. The relationship's smoother now that he's at a year-around boarding school. Down in your neck of the woods, in fact. Pacific Academy in San Francisco."

"The same city as his father," I said, speaking aloud without realizing it.

"Not that it made much difference. I think they got together a couple of times, only cuz Danny called *him.* I gather they weren't quality-time encounters."

"Would you mind if I talked to Danny?"

Judy considered my request. She took a drag on her cigarette, careful to blow the smoke away from me. Then she shrugged. "I guess not. I have to warn you though, Danny's . . . well, he's got an attitude, if you know what I mean. He might not want to talk to you. It's got to be his call."

"I can't force him to."

"I'll contact the school and tell them to expect you." Judy checked her watch. "Got to get back to minding the store. Sorry I couldn't be of more help."

"You've got my card. Let me know if anything comes to mind."

She nodded, pushed herself away from the wall. "There were two guys Bram grew up with. The three of them remained close during the time I was married to Bram. I just remembered that Danny mentioned meeting one of them so I guess they're still in touch. You might want to talk with them. They'd probably know more about Bram than I do."

"What are their names?"

"Clyde Billings and Len Roemer. I don't know where either man is living now, but Len's the one Danny mentioned."

"Thanks, I'll try to reach them."

Judy walked me through the store to the door in front. "Losing a father has got to affect a kid, no matter how distant the relationship. You'd never know it to listen to Danny, but I'm sure on some level he's hurting. You'll be careful talking to him, won't you?"

I promised her I would. I knew from personal experience what it was like to have a father who turned his back on you.

CHAPTER 15

I hesitated at the freeway entrance. West, toward San Francisco—that was the direction I needed to go. But a part of me was tempted to head east toward Silver Creek, my hometown and the place I'd returned to three years ago when my fast-track life in San Francisco derailed. The town where Tom lived, now, once again, with his wife.

And his children, I reminded myself. It was because of them that he'd agreed to give his marriage another chance. I couldn't fault him for that.

I could be there in a little over an hour, maybe catch Tom still at the newspaper, where he worked. Before the return of his wife, I'd dropped in so many times it felt like I worked there myself. But all of that had changed when Lynn decided she wanted to give their marriage another try.

As I dithered, the light turned red, granting me a momentary reprieve from indecisiveness. Not unlike the upcoming trial, I thought, which had postponed my facing a more major decision. Silver Creek or the Bay Area. I was going to have to make a choice fairly soon.

Certainty and direction had come so naturally when I was younger. I marveled now at the ease with which I'd been able to tell black from white, what I wanted from what I didn't.

Back then there was no ambiguity. I hated my sister, avoided my brother, and scorned my father. My mother, who was dead, fared better since she wasn't there in the flesh to disappoint me. I'd marched off to college, sure that I was putting Silver Creek and the banality of my formative years behind me forever. That single-minded vision carried me through law school and seven years of practice. At thirty-one I'd learned the hard truth. That the past is never behind you, and life plans don't come with guarantees.

The car behind me tooted when the traffic signal turned green. I sent a wistful glance in the eastwardly direction of the Sierra foothills, then swung onto the Interstate back toward San Francisco. Predictably, traffic was heavy. But it moved along until we crossed the Carquinez Bridge, where it came to a complete stop. There had to have been an accident.

I pulled out the cell phone, called home, and told Bea that I wouldn't make it in time for dinner. She'd asked me to join them for homemade cannelloni, and I was sorry to be missing it.

"We'll save you some," she said. "Assuming it's any good."

"It will be fantastic."

"I don't know. There's a lot of places for the recipe to go wrong."

Since we still weren't moving, I punched the number for Nick Logan, a law school classmate who'd decided that investigative endeavors held more appeal than the practice of law. I'd asked him to work on Terri's defense and he'd agreed readily. He was a good man to have on our side.

"Hey, Kali. I was just thinking about you."

"Good news or bad?"

"Neither. I've just been looking over the reports you sent on Terri Harper's arrest. We're going to be busy in the months ahead."

"I know. See if you can track down addresses for two of Weaver's buddies. Clyde Billings and Len Roemer. They're probably local though not necessarily in the city."

"I'll get right on it. Any luck with the DA?"

"I haven't even been able to speak to him yet."

Nick made a noise of sympathy. "A power play and Shalla holds all the cards."

"Right. But I've got an appointment in the morning. With luck, we'll be able to work out something on bail. That's Terri's biggest concern right now."

"Must be rough on her being in jail with a little baby at home."

"The judge wasn't much concerned with Terri's emotional comfort, or the baby's."

"You at the office?" he said.

"In the car. Interstate 80 near the Carquinez Bridge."

"If you want to continue on into the city, I'll spring for sushi. Gail had to work tonight and I don't feel like cooking."

"I'd love to another time. Right now I'm about trafficked out." And I had another stop I wanted to make before calling it a day.

The apartment where Melissa had lived pre-Hannah was in Oakland near the Berkeley border. A three-story building with only six units, it sat in a mixed neighborhood of single-family homes and larger apartment houses. Melissa had told me she'd met Bram through a downstairs neighbor named Hank. Only last names were listed on the directory, so I started with unit one. A woman answered.

"I'm looking for Hank," I said.

"You've got the wrong apartment. He's next door in unit two." She slammed the door in my face before I had a chance to apologize.

I rang the bell for Hank's unit.

"Who is it?" he yelled over the sound of a television car commercial.

"You don't know me but I need to talk with you. I'm a friend of Melissa Burke's."

"Whatdy'a want?"

"Can you open the door? I'd like to speak to you in person."

I heard some muttering, then, "Okay, okay." The television volume dropped and the door opened.

As it turned out, Hank did know me. He was Bram's friend, the photographer.

We both did a double-take.

"Uh-oh," Hank said with a smirk. "Here comes trouble."

"Sorry to bother you. Melissa told me she used to hang out here. It was how she met Bram. I didn't realize you were the man who'd come to my office."

Hank's T-shirt was about two inches too short for his girth. A roll of white flab darkened with belly hair protruded above his belt. He eyed me skeptically. "A minute ago you said you were a friend of Melissa's."

"I am." More friend than adversary at any rate.

He leaned against the open door. "What is it you want?"

"To talk about Bram."

"Why should I talk to *you*? Bram was a friend of mine."

"Then you want to see his killer punished, right?"

"Punished and tortured." He gave an incongruous smile.

I ignored the smile. "I'm looking for information about Weaver and people who might have had disagreements with him."

"Your client had a major disagreement with him."

"People besides my client."

Hank laughed. "Hell, half the people who knew him had conflicts with him. The half that didn't thought he walked on water. Bram didn't pull any punches."

I nodded. "I'm interested in specifics, though."

Hank's eyes dropped to my chest, then returned to my face with a twitch of his mouth. He stood back. "You might as well come in."

I hesitated, but only for a moment. I wanted to hear what he had to say.

The apartment was bachelor basic. A living-dining area and open kitchen. Hank's ex-wife had obviously gotten most of the furniture, assuming they'd had any. There was a futon sofa, a pair of mismatched chairs, a chipped laminated dining table, and a newish-looking, black lacquer entertainment center. The walls were hung with matted and framed photos of nude women— some artistically rendered, most befitting *Hustler* magazine.

"You want a beer?" Hank asked. "I was just about to get myself another when you rang."

"I'll pass. You go ahead, though."

He disappeared into the kitchen and returned a moment later with a can of Budweiser. I pulled my gaze back from the wall of photographs. It made me uncomfortable to be in the same room with them.

"You've been admiring my work?" Hank asked.

"Just killing time."

"I'm always looking for new models. You interested? The pay can be pretty good." Another smirk. "Depending on the type of photograph."

"Not good enough," I said, waiting until he sat on the sofa, then choosing the chair farthest from his. He set his beer on a table marred with water rings. I couldn't imagine why Melissa and her roommates had wanted to party here.

On second thought, I could. They were nineteen.

"What was your connection to Bram?" I asked.

"We belonged to the same church."

"Church?"

"Metaphorically speaking." He rubbed his chubby cheek, raking several days growth of stubble. The unshaven look might have been cool in Hollywood, but on him, it was most unappealing.

"What does that mean, metaphorically speaking?"

"We had a lot in common," Hank explained. He took a slurp of beer. "Including a mutual friend, which, to answer your question, is how I knew Bram."

"How long had you known him?"

"A couple of years." He gave me an amused look. "Men don't keep track of stuff the way women do. How long they've known someone, when and where they met, what each of them was wearing, probably even what color the bathroom wallpaper was. They can tell you every fucking detail. And they usually do."

I didn't rise to the bait. "Were the two of you close?"

"*Close.* See, that's a woman's term." Hank rested his arms on his stomach. "We'd play poker, take in a basketball game now and then, shoot some pool. Sometimes we had conversations along the way but mostly we simply shared a good time."

"Do you share Weaver's political and social views, as well?"

Hank shrugged. "Some, not all. I don't think Bram himself agreed with everything he said. He liked controversy. The more people he offended, the happier he was."

Great, countless motives for murder.

"The callers who criticized him, the letters to the editor berating him—Bram ate it up. And when the book came out, heck, he loved it when the women's groups picketed his signings. Got him lots of press. Some great photos too. It was a riot to watch."

Perspiration had beaded on Hank's forehead and the band of exposed flesh around his middle had grown wider. The thought of standing before his camera, clothed or not, made my skin crawl.

"Did you see much of the girls upstairs?" I asked.

Hank sat up straighter. "What's that supposed to mean?"

"Melissa said she and her roommates came here to party. That's how she met Bram."

"It's a new group there now. Summer, you know, they all scatter."

"Nineteen is a little young for you guys, isn't it?"

He again reached for the beer. "What is it with women and age? Nineteen is legal."

"Was Bram dating anyone else?" Not that I'd have called his fling with Melissa *dating*.

"He was seeing a woman, a real looker, but they broke up, I think."

"Recently?"

"Coupla months."

"You know her name?"

"Ranelle."

The same name Ted had come up with. "Last name?"

"If I knew, I've forgotten. She lived out in the Sunset. But it wasn't anything serious. Bram had been burned once. He wasn't stupid enough to make the same mistake again."

"Then why did he want the responsibility of a child?"

Hank's expression turned serious. He leaned forward and tugged at his shirt. "Hard to tell. He brought his son around a couple of times, but never paid him an ounce of attention. Plopped him down like he was a suitcase or something. 'Course the kid didn't exactly make it easy."

"What do you mean?"

"He's a geek. Isn't that what they call them now? A loser. Skinny kid with Coke-bottle glasses. You'd think the least his mother could do was get him contacts."

"Or his dad," I said pointedly.

"You mean Bram? I doubt the thought ever crossed his mind."

Yet had he lived, Bram would have ended up with Hannah. So much for legal justice. "When did you last talk to Bram?"

"That afternoon, before he was killed. I called to tell him I couldn't make it."

"Make it where?"

"A bunch of us were going out to shoot some pool and then grab a bite before Bram's show. I had to bow out on account of my sinuses. I felt like shit."

"Did he say anything about expecting a visitor later that evening?"

"Nope."

"Or about anyone being angry with him."

"Just your client."

"He mentioned Terri specifically?" This was the kind of testimony that could hurt us at trial, despite its being of questionable probative value.

"Not by name. But it was clear what he meant."

"What did Bram say exactly?"

Hank shrugged. "That she'd threatened him, that she gave him the ice queen glare when he came for his visit."

Hank had finished his beer, his third from the number of the cans on the table, and was leering at me in a way that made my skin prickle. "I bet you photograph well," he said.

"Terribly."

"I don't believe it."

"I've seen the evidence."

Hank's lips parted in a smile. "You've just never experienced the hands of a master."

Right. No doubt he envisioned his hands-of-a-master persona extending beyond photography. I stood up, thanked him for his time, and headed for the door.

"Don't think for a minute that your client didn't do it," he called after me. "I've seen her kind before."

And I'd seen his.

CHAPTER 16

District Attorney Ray Shalla was as much politician as lawyer, and like most San Francisco politicians, he reveled in mixing with the rich and famous. But he was also ambitious. In light of recent allegations about double standards in prosecutorial diligence, he was now intent on playing an evenhanded game of hardball.

It was unfortunate that Terri's case happened to be crossing his desk when it did.

"I've got a conference call in fifteen minutes," Shalla said when I sat across from him Friday morning. His office was large and lined on two sides with books. A framed photo of himself with Bill Clinton hung on the wall behind him, a collection of diplomas and awards over the credenza.

"I'll talk fast." I smiled.

He didn't.

"Terri Harper," I said, getting directly to the point. "I'd like to see if we can't reach an agreement about bail."

Shalla leaned back in his chair. He was square-shouldered with a full head of black hair and olive skin. Despite the puffiness around his eyes, he was an attractive man in an old Hollywood kind of way.

"As I recall," he said, "the matter has already been addressed by the court."

"But the court could reconsider."

"Why should it? This is a murder charge." Shalla tugged at the sleeve of his suit jacket, an elegant and expensive, perhaps even custom-tailored, navy pinstripe.

"The court has discretion," I reminded him. "Terri Harper has a six-week-old baby at home. Think of the child if not the mother."

"Funny, I don't recall running for the office of social worker."

"She's not a flight risk," I added. "And she's hardly a threat to the community."

"That's a matter on which reasonable people may disagree."

I chose not to, and continued my argument. "Nor is the presumption of guilt so great as to prohibit bail."

"Again, our perceptions differ." This time he allowed himself a thin, smug smile.

I couldn't tell if he was posturing or speaking from inside knowledge. Nothing I'd seen so far pointed to a heavy presumption of guilt.

"Let's be up-front about this," I said. "You're using the case for your own agenda. You want to show the public that you cut no favors for people with wealth or influence. Throw Terri Harper in the face of your critics to get them off your back."

"That's hardly fair."

"You're the one who's not being fair."

"I'm simply doing my job. You asked for bail. My office recommended against it. The judge ruled. You can go back and ask again, but we're not going to change our position." He leaned forward slightly, his manner cordial. "Now, where we might be able to reach some agreement is in terms of a plea bargain."

"No way."

He frowned. "You haven't seen all the evidence yet."

"Not for lack of trying."

A nod of acquiescence. "You'll get copies of our files as soon as we put everything together."

"That's good, since it's the law." I kept the sarcasm light. "When do you suppose that might be?"

"It's a cumbersome process, there's no getting around it. And, of course, new facts emerge as we go along."

"Such as?"

He folded his hands on the desk. His nails were smooth and manicured. "The white animal fur they found on Weaver's body, for example."

I felt my skin prickle. "What about it?"

"It matches the sheepskin seat covers in Terri Harper's Explorer."

And Terri's Explorer fit the description of a vehicle a witness had placed a block from the crime scene on the night of the murder. I felt a dull ache beginning at the base of my skull.

"She's not the only person riding around on a sheepskin seat cover," I pointed out.

"No," he agreed, "she's not. And taken by itself, it might not mean much. But you take enough tiny scraps, tape them together, and pretty soon you've got a complete picture."

But if you taped them in a different way, you'd wind up with something altogether different. That was my job. To show the jury a different, and better, way to combine all the evidentiary pieces.

At the moment, however, I had a different objective. "You won't reconsider your position on bail?"

"I wouldn't be doing my job if I did. You, on the other hand, wouldn't be doing your job if you didn't at least consider a plea bargain."

Before I could respond, Shalla looked at his Rolex and stood. He moved from behind his desk and ushered me toward the door. He walked with a slight limp as the result of an old injury, but his stride was still commanding enough to carry me along.

"It's been a pleasure meeting you, Ms. O'Brien." He closed the office door as soon as I was through.

"The decision's final?" Terri sat on the other side of the dirty glass partition, clutching the phone so hard her knuckles were white. She looked as though she hadn't slept in days.

"We can go back to court and ask the judge to reconsider, but I don't hold out much hope."

She stared bleakly at the pocked counter on her side of the visiting booth. "So what now?"

"We prepare for trial."

"Trial. Oh, God." Her voice was choked, as though it hadn't previously dawned on her where this was headed.

I felt my own throat grow tight. It was always hard to represent clients I liked, and I genuinely liked Terri. Would have liked her even if Hannah hadn't been in the picture. But she was, and that gave a personal dimension to the case I felt in my gut, even if I couldn't fully understand it.

"You could enter a plea," I told her.

"What does that mean?"

"Admit guilt to a lesser charge. Maybe voluntary manslaughter."

Terri's eyes widened in protest. "But I didn't do anything!"

"They might cut you some slack on sentencing."

She hesitated. "I'd still have to spend time in jail?" Her voice plaintive, barely audible.

"Yes, you would."

She shook her head slowly. "No. I can't do that. I need to be with Hannah."

"The risk of going to trial is that we could lose. You could spend the rest of your life in prison."

Terri swallowed. "But I didn't kill him."

"It's not an easy decision, Terri. And you don't have to make it right now."

"It *is* easy. I'm not going to plead guilty to something I didn't do." There was a fiery determination in Terri's voice that hadn't been there earlier. That was good; it helped to be a fighter.

"Whatever the sentence," she added after a moment, "I wouldn't be part of Hannah's life. I can't let that happen."

"There are no guarantees, Terri."

She nodded. "How long before we get to trial?"

"The law says you can demand a trial within sixty days, but—"

"That's almost two months from now!"

Two short months from an attorney's point of view. "Terri, almost no one exercises their right to a speedy trial. It's not a wise thing to do. The longer we wait, the more time we have to prepare. Also, it's harder for prosecution witnesses to be sure what they remember."

"But I don't want to wait."

"Terri, listen to me. This is your freedom we're talking about. Maybe for the rest of your life. You don't want to rush things."

"Don't tell me what I want," Terri snapped. "I'm opting for an early trial. I have that right."

"Yes, you do, but—"

"If my math is right, we've got fifty-two days left."

Steven was due in my office at three o'clock. At two-thirty I combed my hair and freshened my makeup, then berated myself for being such an ass. What did it matter how I looked? To prove to myself I didn't *really* care, I studiously avoided looking at my reflection again during the intervening half hour. By the time Steven arrived, however, my stomach was tied in enough knots that I knew I wasn't fooling myself.

"Better office than you had at Goldman and Latham," he said. "Less pretentious, not as sterile."

"Most everything you see is Nina's." My law school friend whose illness had brought me back to the Bay Area from Silver Creek. I'd taken over her practice on what we all hoped was a temporary basis. As the weeks had dragged out, I'd added a few touches of my own—a clock radio, a bud base given to me by a friend, an electric fan—but I found Nina's office both functional and comfortable as it was.

Steven dropped into the chair closest to the desk. "I was sorry to hear about the cancer. How's she doing?"

"As well as can be expected."

"Her coach certainly turned into a pumpkin, didn't it?"

I nodded. Steven had met Nina through me. I wasn't anxious to start reminiscing about mutual friends and connections.

"I'll give you a rundown on what we've got," I said, all business. "Then you can go through the files yourself."

"Okay." If Steven felt any awkwardness at the situation, he hid it well.

I cleared a space at the corner of my desk for him to write. As he scooted the chair closer, I caught a faint whiff of something clean, like soap or shampoo. It wasn't a scent I remembered, and I was grateful.

"I appreciate this," Steven said. "Letting me help with Terri's defense. Makes me feel like I'm doing *something* at least."

"Terri was grateful to have your input."

"I hope it will prove useful. Anything more on bail?"

I told him about my visit with Shalla that morning. "He's not going to budge. And I doubt we can get a judge to reconsider without support from the DA's office."

Steven flinched. "All Terri ever wanted was to be a mother. Now that she finally has a baby, she's behind bars. It's worse than punishment."

He looked as though he felt some of her pain himself. Or maybe, underneath, he was as nervous as I was.

"She wants to exercise her right for a trial within sixty days," I told him.

"That's understandable."

"But foolish. We need time to prepare."

He gave a slight nod. "I take it you tried to explain the reasons."

"She wouldn't listen. I'm hoping you can talk some sense into her."

"I'll try," he said with an edgy laugh, "but I think we're facing a sixty-day marathon."

"Fifty-two days at this point."

Steven rubbed his chin. "It's interesting that Shalla raised the idea of a plea so early in the process. You'd think he'd be eager for the publicity of a trial."

I knew what Steven was thinking. That the DA's case wasn't as strong as they thought going in. But I'd dismissed the notion as wishful thinking on my part.

"Most likely," I said, "they're looking to boost their conviction rate. And maybe to save the taxpayers some money."

"That would be a new one. Does Ted know that Terri's pushing for a quick trial?"

"Not from me." I hesitated. "Last time I saw him, Melissa was there."

Steven raised an eyebrow. "Can't say it surprises me."

"Why?"

"Ted needs an audience."

"Do I detect a note of antipathy in there?"

Steven shrugged. "He's not a bad guy. Just a little stuck on himself. And Terri seems happy."

"I suggested Lenore if he needed help."

"I'm sure she's already offered, more than once."

"She likes playing grandmother?"

"That's putting it mildly. It used to drive Caroline crazy." Steven looked away, locked in a moment's private thought. I could see the pulse at his temple throbbing.

My own pulse had quickened too. I both did and didn't want to talk about that night.

But when Steven turned back, he was focused on the moment. "Tell me what you've got."

"Here are the basics of the state's case." I swiveled my chair to face the desk squarely. "They've got a witness who saw a car like Terri's a block from Weaver's house the night he was killed."

"What time?"

"Around twelve-fifteen."

"Do we know when he was shot?"

"One of Weaver's neighbors heard what he *thought* might have been shots sometime a little after midnight."

"Coroner got an estimated time of death?"

"They're kind of fuzzy there." Without corroborating evidence such as someone who'd seen or talked to the deceased, time of death was usually hard to pinpoint precisely. "In any case, the timing is close enough that it hurts Terri. Plus, the witness got a partial plate. NMO, same letter sequence as on Terri's car."

Steven's brow furrowed. A shadow of worry crossed his face. "What else?"

"Wool, on Weaver's clothing. I'd assumed it was cat or dog hair, and that we could use that to bolster Terri's case since she doesn't have a pet. I just found out this morning that it's from a sheepskin seat cover, like the ones in her Explorer. That's the prosecution's theory at any rate."

"Those covers are popular with Ted's crowd. Popular with lots of people, in fact."

"I know, but taken with everything else, it looks bad." I thought Shalla's analogy about piecing together a torn photograph wasn't a bad one. "There's also the gun," I reminded him. "Terri says hers was probably stolen. But she never filed a report."

"It *was* stolen," Steven said. "Or missing, at least. I remember last summer when Arlo wanted to take us all target shooting and she couldn't find it."

"Or didn't want to. You said yourself that she never liked shooting."

He shook his head. "She'd never have made Arlo angry if she could avoid it."

"I wonder if the jury will buy that."

Steven ran his palm along the arm of the chair. "That's the big spin, isn't it?"

The biggest and most critical variable in the whole process. An unknown in which we had little say. "Terri will be a sympathetic defendant," I said.

"I sure hope you're right."

I reached for the file and handed it to him. "Take your time. You can use the conference room." I hesitated just a moment before continuing. "I'm going to talk to Weaver's son tomorrow if you want to come along."

"Sure."

When Steven moved into the other room with the case files, I went back to work on the *Hawkins* pleading with a sense of relief. It had been awkward, but we'd pushed through it. Maybe Steven was right. It was time to let go of the past and to move on.

CHAPTER 17

Danny Weaver was clearly not happy about talking to us.
"I got a paper to write," he said, glowering sullenly. "This
better be quick."

"We'll make sure it is," I said.

Steven and I had met him in the lobby of his dorm, then immediately moved outside to the privacy of the campus garden. His
mother had called the headmaster, as she'd said she would, and
cleared the visit. She'd also talked to Danny so he was expecting
us.

The three of us started down the path away from the dorm.

"Pretty campus," I said.

"The school sucks."

"Why's that?" Steven asked.

"Everyone who goes here is a loser."

"That include you, Danny?"

"It's Dan," he snapped. "Not Danny."

"Sorry."

Dan Weaver had his father's slight build, narrow face, and cleft
chin, but he had his mother's liquid brown eyes, magnified by the
thick glasses he wore. His hair was stringy and bleached, almost a
flaxen yellow. He wore it pulled back in a ponytail, exposing a
small tattoo on his neck. He kept his left hand in the pocket of his
baggy cargo pants.

"Why do you stay at the school if you don't like it?" Steven
asked. "Are your parents making you?"

The boy shrugged. "It's better than living at home."

He shuffled over to a picnic table on the grass and plopped

down on the bench. His left hand fiddled with something in his pocket. "I don't know what you think I'm going to be able to tell you, anyway. I hardly knew Bram."

Whether Dan knew Bram well or not, the boy had lost his father. "I'm sorry about his death," I said.

"Really?" Dan laced the comment with sarcasm. "I'm not."

Steven eased himself down on the bench next to Dan; I sat across the table from them. The wooden surface was sticky and sprinkled with bits of food.

"You didn't like him?" Steven asked.

"What was to like?"

I brushed an ant from my arm. "You visited him, though, didn't you?"

"A couple of times. Except it wasn't really a visit. He'd say 'let's get together' and then we'd wind up spending the evening with friends of his. Most of the time, he acted like a total jackass."

"What do you mean?"

"Like he was Mr. High-and-Mighty. I think his friends were getting tired of it too. I heard them shouting at each other last time I was there."

"Could you hear what they were saying?" I asked.

"Just some stuff about outgrowing old friends, having his head up his ass, that sort of thing. Like one of them said, it wasn't like he was indispensable."

I could feel my inner ears pick up. "Who are these friends? Do you know their names?"

"Guy by the name of Len. He's the one who seemed really pissed. And another guy, Hank, who's actually pretty cool."

I'd met Hank. The photographer with the hairy belly and the leer that seemed to undress you. And Judy had told me about Bram's childhood friends, Clyde Billings and Len Roemer.

"Do you remember anyone by the name of Clyde?" I asked.

A shrug. "Maybe. I wasn't really interested in who they were." Dan shifted his body under the table, his left hand still hidden.

"Did your dad ever mention Melissa Burke or the Harpers?"

"Dad? My stepdad doesn't talk to me, and I didn't consider Bram my dad."

"But when he suggested the two of you get together," Steven noted, "you went."

"I called him first. And it was only a couple of times." The tone was defensive, as though we'd accused him of something illicit. "My whole life I barely saw the guy, but when I came here to school, my mother thought just cuz we were living in the same city we'd suddenly share a bond or something. Doesn't work that way."

"You're right," Steven said, "it doesn't. Bram was never there for you when you needed him."

Dan was quiet a moment, his sullen features drawn tight. He glared hard at the weathered and worn wood surface of the picnic table. "Doesn't matter," he said finally. "Who needs a father anyway?"

"Most of us would rather have one than not."

Dan ignored Steven and turned to face me directly. "About your question, Bram never said anything to me about the baby or about the Harpers."

"But he talked about Melissa?" I wondered if Dan had intentionally omitted the name after I'd included it.

"I met her," Dan said. "She lived upstairs from Hank." He shifted his legs again and extracted his hand from his pocket. He was holding a tiny black and white mouse. "This is Herman," Dan said. "You're not afraid of mice, are you?"

I shook my head.

"Herman was prince of the Third Kingdom before the evil master cast a spell on him."

"He seems to be taking it rather well," Steven said without a hint of sarcasm.

Dan held the mouse at eye level. "Not really. He's plotting revenge. Aren't you, Herman?"

I glanced at Steven, whose expression hadn't changed.

"How's he going to do that?" Steven asked. "Is he planning an attack?"

"Nah, he's too small. That would never work. But he knows how to cast magical spells."

"That's good," Steven said. "He knows you don't have to be big and strong to be powerful."

Dan grunted in disgust. "Spare the pep talk; I'm not a kid."

I shot Steven a questioning look. I wanted to ask more about Bram but all this talk about revenge and magic spells was making me nervous. I didn't want the boy to turn ballistic on us.

Steven was no help. He acknowledged Dan's response with

the glimmer of a smile and ignored me all together. I was on my own.

"So Dan," I said, "did you know that your da . . . that Bram was seeing Melissa?"

"Sleeping with her, you mean. I don't think he ever *saw* her."

Spoken like someone who'd never been seen himself.

Another boy was approaching from the west across the grass. He, too, was dressed in baggy cargo pants and a black T-shirt. The school uniform of the new millennium.

"Listen," Dan said, slipping Herman back into his pocket. "I gotta get going. But I'll tell you this, that lady, your client, she did the world a favor. 'Specially that little baby."

"He's one angry kid," Steven said as we walked back to the car.

"That kind of goes with being fifteen, doesn't it?"

"Only to a point. Dan's beyond that."

"Probably with good reason." I started the engine but didn't back out of the parking place right away. "It was interesting what he said about Weaver's friends."

"About them arguing, you mean?"

"Yeah. Wouldn't hurt to talk to them. Do you have time to devote to a wild-goose chase?"

"If I didn't, I'd make time."

"It'll probably end up going nowhere." Already I was back-pedaling, thinking that maybe we'd spent enough time together as it was.

The glint of a smile worked the corners of Steven's mouth. "Probably. But it's the only chance we have of finding that damned goose."

I used the cell phone to call Nick and got his answering machine. "Damn."

"Who are you trying to reach?"

"Nick Logan, remember him?"

"The guy who could do just about anything with a computer but get it to wash the dishes. Wasn't he dating a friend of yours?"

Memory lane again. It wasn't a place I wanted to be. "They broke up ages ago," I told him. I slipped the phone back into my purse. "Nick's not in. I guess we won't be chasing anything today."

We hadn't gotten to the corner, however, when Nick called me back. "I was taking out the trash," he explained. "It always happens that way. I stick around the house all day and the phone never rings, but the minute I'm in the can or outside for something, I get a call."

"That's the beauty of answering machines. Did you happen to get addresses for those friends of Weaver's I told you about?"

"Yep. I was going to give you a call this evening. Clyde Billings works in Silicon Valley. Not one of the guys who's made a fortune, from the looks of things. Lives in Mountain View. He's got a wife and two kids. A dog, too, if I had to guess, but that didn't come up."

I didn't even ask him where it would have *come up*. Nick had sources I deemed it prudent to know nothing about.

"Len Roemer is closer to home," he continued. "Lives in San Francisco, south of China Basin. This one's single. Works as a personal trainer at Fitness First downtown."

A computer nerd, a fitness buff, and a photographer who specialized in naked women. Weaver's friends were an odd assortment.

"He's also a male stripper," Nick added.

"You mean for money?"

Nick laughed. "Pretty good money, I'd bet. Mostly it's private parties although he occasionally fills in at one of the local clubs."

"Anything else I should know?"

"Roemer was arrested for indecent exposure about five years ago. He got a fine and probation. Billings is clean as far as I can tell. Here, I'll give you the addresses."

I motioned for Steven to grab a pen and paper from my briefcase. "Okay."

Nick read off the address and I repeated it for Steven. "Thanks. Talk to you later." I disconnected and turned to Steven. "Shall we start with Roemer since he's closest?"

"Sounds like a plan."

San Francisco's China Basin is a testimonial to the potential of urban renewal. This southern section of the city fronting the bay had been, until recently, a wasteland of abandoned shipyards, empty warehouses, and industrial plants gasping their last breaths. Now it was a bustling enclave of modern condos, freshly minted parks, an ever-expanding choice of restaurants, and smashing views. As well as home to the new PacBell stadium.

Len Roemer's piece of the district was not quite so gentrified. He lived on the fringe of the revitalized area, in a three-story building of live-work lofts. Instead of green grass and palm trees outside his windows, he had a PG&E substation.

I didn't really expect to find him home on a Saturday afternoon in the middle of summer, but he answered the door right away. I could tell from the look on his face that he'd been expecting someone else.

"I'm not buying and I'm not giving," Roemer said. "I'm not converting, either."

He was probably in his early forties with dark, closely cropped hair, a square chin, and a body that was a little soft around the middle but otherwise lean and muscular. We couldn't miss seeing the body, either. He was dressed in short shorts made of a soft, clingy fabric and a sleeveless, mesh shirt that covered very little.

Steven and I introduced ourselves. "We understand you were a friend of Bram Weaver," I said.

"Damn straight."

"We'd appreciate a few minutes of your time." I explained our connection to Weaver.

"I'm not talking to anybody working for that bitch who murdered him."

The venom in his voice stung. I tried to ignore it.

"You think Terri Harper killed Weaver?" Steven asked.

"I know she did."

I could sense the tension in Steven's posture. "How's that?" he asked.

"She threatened him. She hated him. She wanted to steal his kid."

I spoke up. "Terri considers Hannah *her* child."

"But she wasn't, was she? She was Bram's little girl."

"She wanted the baby," Steven said. "That doesn't mean she killed Weaver."

"The cops think she did." Roemer glanced in the direction of the stairway. "If that tight-assed bitch Melissa had told him about the baby in the beginning, none of this would have happened."

Steven scrunched up his forehead. "Why do you think she didn't?"

"Because she didn't think about Bram, that's why. It's like that with a lot of women, so cocky and full of themselves. About time somebody put them in their place."

It sounded like a line from one of Bram's radio shows. It also echoed Hank.

"There's some chance Terri Harper isn't Weaver's killer, you know." Steven was trying his best to sound nonchalant. "If we could just ask a few questions."

"Nuh-uh. Like I told you. I know it was her." Roemer stepped back and slammed the door in our faces.

"Well, that was useful," I said. We headed down the stairs.

"It does tell us something about Weaver's choice of friends. Was the guy you spoke to yesterday of the same ilk?"

"Not as rude, but about as unappealing."

"It'll be interesting to see how Clyde Billings compares."

Clyde Billings wasn't home, his wife informed us in a voice so soft-spoken I had to lean forward to make out what she was saying.

She was Asian, probably Vietnamese, although I couldn't be certain. A good foot shorter than me, with straight black hair that hung below her shoulders. A boy about seven and a girl about three clung mutely to their mother's legs.

"We're investigating the murder of one of your husband's friends," Steven said. "A man by the name of Bram Weaver."

The investigating part was technically accurate but misleading. I didn't bother to clarify.

"Did you know Mr. Weaver?" I asked.

She shook her head. "I know he was a friend of my husband's. From many years ago when they were children. I didn't know him myself, however."

"Do you know when your husband last spoke to Weaver?"

The little girl gave a shy smile and hid her face in her mother's leg. Out of the corner of my eye, I saw Steven smiling back.

"I think it was the day of his death," Mrs. Billings replied. She spoke slowly, looking between us. "Is there a problem?"

I hastened to reassure her. "No problem. We're trying to fill in Weaver's activities in the days before his death."

"He and my husband had dinner that night."

"In the city?"

She nodded.

"It's a long drive coming home," I said.

"Oh, he stayed the night. Clyde has an apartment there because he's up a lot on business."

Monkey business, I suspected, having met Bram's other buddies. But maybe I was misjudging the man.

"Will he be home this afternoon?" Steven asked.

She shook her head. "He'll be in Seattle all weekend."

On business, no doubt. The question was, what kind?

CHAPTER 18

Wednesday afternoon, while summer beckoned from outside, Jared, Steven, Nick, and I sat around the office conference table discussing strategy. I'd left the window open so we could enjoy an occasional caress of fresh air. A small pleasure denied to Terri in her jail cell.

Yesterday we had received another installment in the continuing flow of discovery material. Several stacks' worth. We'd also begun to amass our own collection of reports and files. It sometimes felt as though preparing for trial was nothing more than an exercise in organizational dexterity.

"We've got a tentative trial date of September 15," I said. "That gives us under seven weeks to pull together a defense."

Nick groaned and rubbed a palm along his jaw. "You couldn't convince Terri to go for a later date?"

I shook my head.

"I tried too," Steven added. "She won't listen."

I wasn't sure how strong a case Steven had actually made. He seemed torn between professional judgment and brotherly compassion. Though he knew waiting would give us more time to prepare, he was more than sympathetic to Terri's desire to be out.

"That leaves us with a lot of ground to cover," I said, "and not much time to do it."

Nick was sitting in the chair we'd pulled in from the front reception desk, the one with rollers. He'd been using his long legs to propel the chair forward and back in a kind of rocking pattern. Now he scooted the chair over to the window and gazed longingly toward the small city park across the road. Nick was a run-

ner, with a runner's lean build, and I suspected it was near tor-
ture for him to be inside on such a lovely day.

He pulled his gaze back into the room and turned to me. "You
got a game plan?"

"No specifics. My feeling, though, is that we should take the
two-pronged approach."

"Assuming we can pull it off," Steven said. He seemed edgy,
and I didn't know if it was because of his personal involvement in
the case or something else.

Jared unbuttoned his shirt cuffs and rolled up his sleeves.
Even with the open window, the room was warm. "Which two
prongs we talking about, boss?"

"We'll chip away at the prosecution's case—with luck, even
undermine it—but we should also try to come up with our own
theory about what happened."

"Give 'em a substitute killer?"

"Right." That was the hard part. But jurors, whose legal sensi-
bilities were often influenced by film and television, expected answers. If you wanted them to acquit, you'd better hand them
another suspect and a plausible explanation.

"What if we can't come up with one?"

"We can still raise reasonable doubt," Steven explained. "In
theory, that's what it's all about."

Nick snorted. "Jurors believe what they want to believe.
Witness the OJ trial. The real trick is to win the jurors' hearts."

It was a trick all right. The key to winning at trial was weaving
a magic spell that would captivate the jury. And it usually had
very little to do with evidence or logic.

Jared hefted a plastic tub of files onto the table. "So, where do
we start—with the case against Terri or the search for a different
killer?"

"Let's start with what the prosecution's given us," I said.

What they'd given us was, at this point, largely what the police
had given them. In due time we would get transcripts of the
grand jury testimony from the witnesses they intended to call at
trial, as well as their own witness lists, but the prosecution wasn't
inclined to hand over anything more, or sooner, than they had to.

Jared grabbed a clipped sheaf of papers and a manila envelope. "Coroner's report and crime scene photos." He spread the

photos on the table. "You guys seen these?" He was addressing Nick and Steven.

"Yeah," Nick said.

"Me too," Steven added, although he picked up one of the photos and studied it anew.

It was one of the least bloody ones—black and white rather than color, offering a wide-angle view of the foyer. Weaver's body occupied only a small part of the print. Still, the photo was disturbing. Especially when you knew what the dark splotches and spatters were.

Steven's face was a mask of detachment, but his gray eyes studied the image intensely.

"Nothing jumps out from the autopsy report," Jared continued. "Seems Weaver was shot twice. Once in the abdomen and once in the head. The shot to the head was at close range."

Nick grimaced. "Ouch."

"Weaver had a blood alcohol level of point zero eight." Jared ran his finger down the page as he read. "He was buzzed but not flat-out drunk, for what that's worth. Last meal, some six hours earlier, consisted of a burger and fries."

"He went out for dinner with his friend Clyde Billings," I noted.

Steven tossed the photo back onto the table and picked up another. "He's on the air what—seven to ten? So they must have eaten first."

I shot Steven an amused look. "Don't tell me you're one of Weaver's fans?"

"Hardly a fan, but I tuned in now and then. Especially after he made a stink about the adoption."

Steven was examining an eight-by-ten color shot of Weaver's front room. I looked over his shoulder for a moment in the hopes that something would jump out. It didn't. Couch, chairs, glass tables. Ultra modern. Ultra neat.

I turned to Nick, who'd positioned himself in line with a ray of sunshine that angled through the window. "Weaver's son says he overheard an argument between his father and his friend Len Roemer. It might be worth checking into."

"Will do."

"You might talk to a couple of other friends, Hank Lomax and Clyde Billings as well."

"It's one thing to argue with a friend," Jared observed. "Another to blow his face away."

Steven picked up a different photo. A close-up of Weaver's body. "Guess it depends on how impassioned the argument was," he said. "From the looks of this, I'd say the killer had some strong personal feelings about Weaver. Friend might fit that profile better than stranger."

"What about someone from the Women's Alliance?" Nick offered. "They've battled with him before, and they're certainly full of fire."

I rocked forward in my chair and looked at Nick. "They're what?"

He grinned. "You aren't one of them, are you?"

"No." And he was right that they were a vocal and militant bunch, but I felt stirrings of gender solidarity. "It seems to me more like a crime a male would commit than a female."

Steven raised an eyebrow. "What makes you say that?"

"The shot to the face at close range."

"You think women aren't capable of close violence?" It was a rhetorical question and he didn't wait for a response. "Let's just hope the jury shares your bias."

"Besides," Jared pointed out, "the police arrested Terri, and she's a woman."

"It's something we should definitely follow up." Nick tapped his fingers on his knee. "You want me to see what I can find out?"

"Good idea." I turned back to the task at hand. "What about blood at the scene? Any that wasn't Weaver's?"

"Doesn't mention any, boss."

Steven tucked the photo back into the stack. "Doesn't look like the killer gave Weaver much chance to inflict damage."

"Did the police find any blood in Terri's car?" I asked.

Jared scanned the file. "Appears not."

"Can you shoot someone at close range and not get blood on yourself?" Steven addressed the question to all of us.

I deferred to Nick, who scratched his cheek. "Good question. Maybe, if you were careful. I'll ask around."

Jared flipped the page of the report. "We've got a fuller description of the glasses here. Purple frames. Women's styling, whatever that is. An eight-inch blond hair caught in the hinge."

"But they are definitely *dark glasses?*" I asked.

"That's what it says."

"Weaver was killed at night. Why dark glasses?"

He shrugged. "Someone who's watched too many old movies."

"Or they weren't dropped by the killer," Steven said.

"Except they were on the floor, right inside the door near where Weaver's body was found." I made a note to ask Terri what kind of dark glasses she wore.

Nick stood up, stretched. "Let's just hope the hair doesn't have enough root to run a DNA match."

"Or that it does," I said, "and points to someone besides Terri." I turned to Steven. "By the way, does Terri chew gum?"

He looked surprised. "I imagine so. Doesn't everyone, at least once in a while?"

"What flavor does she prefer?"

He laughed. "I haven't the foggiest idea. She liked that fruit stuff as a kid. Why?"

I explained about the Doublemint gum wrapper found near the walkway to the house. "Of course, it could have been dropped by the paper boy, or Weaver himself."

Steven nodded thoughtfully.

In cases like this where the police had no hard proof, they had to rely on cumulative bits of evidence pointing in the same direction. If we could show that some of their pieces pointed to others as well as Terri, that was good. If we could show that they didn't point to Terri at all, that was even better.

"I don't recall her chewing Doublemint," he said after a moment. "I'll check with Ted if you like."

"Okay." I turned back to Jared. "Anything more on the white sheep wool?"

"Nothing."

With luck, that was because they didn't have anything. But it might be that they were holding disclosure for a time closer to trial. Particularly if they had something damaging like a dye lot match.

For all I knew, they might even be able to do a DNA test based on perspiration. The recent advances in forensic testing were phenomenal.

And frightening. Move a decimal point one way or the other and you were talking the difference between iron bars and curtains on your windows.

"I'm working on getting some statistics for us," Nick said. He leaned against the wall. "We're not going to get hard-and-fast numbers because there are several manufacturers of those seat covers and hordes of distributors, including mail order catalogs. But we'll definitely have ammunition to throw to the jury showing they are far from rare."

"What else?" I asked Jared.

"There's the neighbor who heard Terri leave in her car sometime before midnight. What does Terri say about that?"

"That she didn't go out."

"So maybe the neighbor is mistaken," Steven said. "That ought to be an easy one to undercut."

"I hope so." I could feel my chest growing tighter as the evidence against Terri mounted. "We've also got the witness who saw a woman fitting Terri's description and an Explorer with a plate that's a partial match to Terri's."

"Do we have a transcript of her testimony?" Steven asked.

"Not yet, for either witness. We've got their names but I don't want to muddy the waters by questioning them until I know what they've already testified to. Jared, you're working on the order for discovery, right?"

"The draft is on your desk."

I gave him a thumbs-up. "Nick, any luck with your own canvass of Weaver's neighbors?"

"It's a monkey jungle. Nobody saw anything or heard anything, and if they did, they don't want to talk about it." He pressed his fingertips to his eyes, ears, and mouth. "Except for one kid, about ten. Says he saw a man leaning against a lamp post a couple of houses down, smoking."

I rocked forward. "What time?"

"Right around midnight."

"Did the kid get a good look at the guy?" Steven, too, had grown more intent.

"Yeah, he knows him. Seems the man delivers pizza to the woman down the street on a regular basis."

"She ordered a pizza at midnight?"

Nick shrugged. "I'm just passing on what the kid told me. But he's a pretty sharp kid. And he's apparently talked to the pizza man some in the past. Says the woman's real old. He didn't think she'd be the type to eat so much pizza. Has it for lunch every Sunday."

"And Friday midnight, on at least one occasion." I felt the ember of hope. "We may have found our other suspect."

"Afraid not," Nick said. "The kid heard the same two shots as the couple down the hill from Weaver. He says the pizza man was there, smoking, at the time of the gunfire."

"He's a potential witness, then." Not as good as being able to point a finger at him as a possible killer, but useful all the same. Assuming he hadn't seen Terri leaving the crime scene. "Which house is the old lady's?"

"Down the block. I got the address."

"Did you talk to her?"

"I tried. She's deaf. Unfortunately, sign language isn't one of my strengths."

"Which pizza company?" Steven's voice was tight. Maybe he was thinking the same thing I was, that a witness was useful only if he didn't identify our client.

"Pizza Pizazz," Nick said. "The drivers stick those little plastic cones on the roof of their cars when they're making a delivery."

"Will you follow up on it?" I asked.

"I already have. None of it rings a bell with either of the Pizza Pizazz franchises closest to Weaver's neighborhood. I thought I'd hang around there this next Sunday. See if I can talk to the guy myself."

"Good idea."

"Do we know who inherits?" Steven asked.

"A couple of right wing causes get some," I told him. "So does the son, in trust. Most of it goes to the American Cancer Society, however." The faces around the table registered surprise. "Weaver's father died of the disease," I explained.

"Guess we're not going to find motive there," Steven said. "What about his girlfriend?"

"Ex-girlfriend," Nick corrected. "Ranelle Mosher. She moved to Boston two months ago."

"Have you got a phone number? I'll call her anyway. She might be able to give us some useful background on Weaver."

"Who's that leave us with then?" Steven looked around the table. "Weaver's buddies, on the basis of an alleged argument. His public persona, on the basis of the guy was a prick."

"His ex-wife and son weren't crying tears over his demise," I pointed out.

"How about Melissa Burke?" Jared asked. "She didn't want Weaver to have Hannah. And she was driving Ted's Explorer for a while. Maybe she had access to it that night."

I remembered what Steven had told me about Ted and seat covers. "Does that car have sheepskin covers?" I asked him.

"I think so."

I wondered what flavor of gum Melissa chewed, and whether she'd recently lost a pair of dark glasses.

CHAPTER 19

"No, absolutely not," Terri protested, repeating what she'd said at least half a dozen times already.

We were again seated in one of the glass-partitioned interview rooms. Terri's hair had lost its luster and her skin was sallow. She clutched the phone in her left hand, revealing nails bitten to the quick.

"I'm not saying we hog-tie Melissa and deliver her to the police," I explained. "Only that we hint at a scenario where she might have killed Weaver."

Following yesterday's strategy session, I'd confirmed that Melissa Burke did have use of Ted's Explorer on the night Weaver was killed, and that the car, like Terri's, had sheepskin seat covers. True, it was black rather than dark blue, but at night it might be difficult to tell. She didn't much like Doublemint, though she chewed it on occasion, and had a new pair of dark glasses, she said, because she'd broken the earpiece from her old pair. The night Weaver was killed Melissa had been home watching television. Alone.

But Terri was having nothing to do with using Melissa as a decoy.

"If she's as likely a suspect as you," I explained, "then the jury will—"

Terri shook her head. "No."

"Why not?"

"She's Hannah's mother, that's why."

"*You* are Hannah's mother," I said.

Terri was resolute. "You know what I mean."

"Do you think Hannah comes out ahead by having you go to prison for something you didn't do?"

Terri was quiet a moment. "That's not going to happen, is it?" Her voice had lost some of its starch. "Can't you get me off without implicating Melissa?"

"I'm working on it. But if we can find another suspect and explanation to hand to the jury, and if the evidence supports—"

"But not Melissa." Terri fixed me with a penetrating look.

I shifted position on the hard wooden chair and leaned forward. "What if she did it, Terri? What if she's the one who killed Weaver?"

"Then she did it for Hannah's sake. You think I could throw her to the wolves for that?"

I could see that it was an argument I wasn't going to win. "Okay, we've got time. Let's see what develops."

"There must be plenty of people with reason to kill the man."

"I'm looking into that, too." I slumped back into my chair, gathering strength for the next question. "Do you wear dark glasses, Terri?"

"Of course."

"Where are they?"

She gave a startled laugh. "Not here, for darn sure. I guess they took them when they booked me. Along with my purse, my clothing, my medicines."

"Medicines?"

"For migraines. They let me take the medication, I'm not saying that. Just that I have to ask and get permission each time."

I tried to call up a picture of Terri during our drive to the jail. Though my memory was fuzzy, I seemed to recollect a pair of dark glasses. "Do you have just that one pair?" I asked her.

She nodded. "They're from the optometrist. Good-quality lenses. It really makes a difference. Why?"

I told her about the dark glasses found at the crime scene.

"They can't be mine," she said. "Check with the police. They must have my glasses with my other stuff."

One more chip in the prosecution's case. That was good.

Terri switched the phone to her other ear. "Were you able to work it out so that I can attend the adoption hearing?"

"Not yet." I'd tried both the legal route and a personal appeal to the deputy, but the answer was the same. Terri's presence was not legally mandated.

"Do you think you'll be able to?"

I hesitated. "Probably not."

Terri crumpled. She held her free arm across her middle as if she were in pain. "It's not fair. I didn't do anything wrong. How can they take Hannah from me?"

"I'm not convinced they can," I told her. "Not at this point." The sticky part was that Hannah's adoption hadn't yet been offi- cially ratified. If it had, Terri's arrest would have no impact. But we were stuck in a muddy and untried no-man's-land.

"What if they do?" Terri persisted. "Shouldn't I be able to tell them how much I want her?"

"It will be a procedural issue. Your being in court or not won't tip the scale."

Her expression was sober. "That other couple, the Coles, they'll be in court, won't they? Ted says they're out to cause problems."

I'd spoken to their attorney briefly on the phone. According to her, the Coles weren't so much causing trouble as stepping in to remedy a terrible misfortune.

"We'd be having the hearing," I told her, "even without the Coles." Private or not, all adoptions were regulated by the state. But she was right, the Coles muddied the waters.

"At least Melissa still favors us over them," Terri said.

A fact that probably went a long way toward explaining why Terri was reluctant to entertain the notion of Melissa as a killer.

Terri curled her little finger through the phone cord. "I miss Hannah so much it actually hurts."

"But you've seen her, haven't you?"

Terri nodded, smiled even, although it was a sad smile. "Ted brings her sometimes. So does my mother. But it's not the same as being with her. Most of the time, I can't even touch her because of the glass barrier."

And now, on top of everything, the Coles were trying to make Terri out to be an unfit mother.

"Is that them?" Ted asked me, directing my attention to the man and woman who'd just entered the courtroom.

"We'll find out soon enough."

The couple, both in their late thirties, hesitated for a moment, then moved to join their attorney near the front of the room. A prune-faced woman dressed all in black. She'd introduced herself to me earlier.

"Margaret Thatcher," she'd said, without a hint of amusement. "Attorney-at-law." She'd actually used that phrase, presenting herself, I thought, more as a business card than a person.

I whispered to Ted, "It's them."

The Coles looked enough alike to be siblings. Both were large-boned and angular with pale coloring and hardened scowls. They glanced about the small courtroom, lighting immediately on Lenore Cross, who held her granddaughter Hannah, swaddled in a blanket. As the couple took their seats, the husband lifted his wife's hand into his own and whispered something into her ear.

A moment later, Judge Nye entered and took a seat at the bench. He wore the same stern expression he had at the last hearing. After a few preliminaries, Nye addressed those assembled.

"We are here," he said gravely, "on a matter that has not only become more complicated since our last meeting, but has taken on new dimensions. It is, to my knowledge, a situation which the courts have not been called upon to address before today." He paused, then directed his attention to the social worker. "Legalities aside, the child is doing fine, am I right?"

"Yes. She's being well cared for by Mr. Harper and his mother-in-law, Mrs. Cross. The baby's birth mother also spends time with her."

As if on cue, Hannah whimpered from the back of the room. Lenore rocked her gently and she quieted.

Judge Nye cleared his throat and donned a pair of half-frame glasses. His steely gray hair was close-cropped at his temples. "What we have here is a most unusual situation. Had it not been for Mr. Weaver's claim to paternity, the adoption would have proceeded on schedule, and would be final by now. With his death, the outcome would be the same—except for the fact that the adoptive mother is in jail awaiting trial for his murder. And now"—he turned to the Coles and their attorney—"we have a new wrinkle."

Ms. Thatcher saw this as an invitation to step forward. "Your Honor, my clients had initially been selected as the adoptive parents of the child in question, and they are still desirous of adopting her. They can provide a two-parent home and a stable family environment. They have one adopted child already who is five."

"The birth mother chose the Harpers," I said. "That is her right in an independent adoption. Social Services has made the requisite home visits and found the Harpers to be acceptable parents. Nothing has happened that should change that."

"Except that the adoptive mother is in jail," Ms. Thatcher prompted.

I donned an air of reasonableness. "If Terri Harper were in the hospital with pneumonia or had been called for jury duty in a case that required her to be sequestered, the court wouldn't intervene."

"But she's not. She is in jail for murder."

"She's in jail awaiting trial," I said. "Surely you, of all people, understand the difference. Or did you miss the lecture on presumption of innocence?"

Judge Nye turned his gaze in my direction. "Ms. O'Brien, I will not have schoolyard behavior in my courtroom."

"Sorry, Your Honor."

"I concede that you do have a point, but I'm hard pressed to equate being in jail with being in a hospital."

"But that's the fundamental tenet of our judicial system." It felt funny delivering this lecture to a judge, but I wanted to make sure he followed my argument. "People are presumed innocent until proven guilty in a court of law. Nothing has been proven against Terri Harper. Because she was arrested on a grand jury indictment, we haven't even seen the evidence against her, much less been able to question it."

The Coles' attorney scrunched her face tight. "Your Honor, we have to consider the welfare and happiness of the child. An innocent baby. Doesn't she deserve a mother's love and attention?"

"The child is not being abused or neglected," I pointed out. "In fact, she is being well cared for by people who love her. If she were the Harpers' natural-born child, the court would have no grounds to intervene."

"But she isn't!" Margaret Thatcher's tone was growing heated. "The adoption isn't yet final. The child is still, in a sense, a ward of the court."

Our exchange reminded me of childhood scuffles with my sister. Judge Nye must have had daughters himself, because he rapped his gavel and gave us both a cold stare.

"Enough. Both of you." He removed his glasses, rubbed the bridge of his nose, then slipped them back on. "I have given this situation a good deal of thought. I've reviewed the record and read the briefs submitted by both sides. I am mindful that a child's welfare and happiness are at stake here."

Ted's hand formed a fist under the table. "No," he whispered under his breath. "Please, no."

"If I were charged with reaching a decision simply on what is in her best interest," Nye continued, "I might well reach a different decision. But this is a matter of law, and I must, however reluctantly, put the law before my own personal feelings."

He paused. The silence in the courtroom was deafening.

"I'm going to hold this case over until after Mrs. Harper's trial. The adoption will remain open and the case worker will continue to monitor the child's care, but unless circumstances change, the child will stay with Mr. Harper during this interim period."

Ted's fist uncurled and he slumped back in his chair. Behind us, I could hear Lenore Cross let out a breath of relief.

The Coles looked as though they'd been struck. Margaret Thatcher frowned darkly and bent across the table to mutter something for their benefit. A moment later, Mrs. Cole turned to look at me. Her eyes were filled with hatred.

Ted leaned over and offered a heartfelt thanks. "Terri will be so happy. I can't wait to tell her."

Lenore, also, was ecstatic. "I don't know what I'd have done if the judge ruled against us." She tucked in the yellow flannel blanket around Hannah's feet where she'd kicked it loose.

Hannah liberated her feet again in short order. She focused her gaze on me with eyes wide open and alert—and the brightest robin's egg blue I'd ever seen. I felt a tickle of something in my chest, and wondered how Terri had managed the loss of her daughter as well as she had.

Lenore handed Hannah to her dad.

Ted kissed her tiny forehead. "Ready to face the press, Hannah?"

"You're going to make a statement?" I asked. Although reporters had been barred from the courtroom, they were present in force outside. We'd already waded through the cameras and microphones once on our way in.

"A short one. You think it's a bad idea?"

"No." It was probably a good idea in fact. Nothing warmer and fuzzier than father and infant daughter. Defense strategy wasn't supposed to concern itself with PR, but sometimes what happened outside the courtroom was almost as important as what went on inside. "Just keep it positive."

Ted propped Hannah against his broad shoulder with the ease of someone accustomed to caring for an infant.

Lenore touched my arm. "Things are moving along on Terri's trial, aren't they?"

"September 15."

"That's a long time still." She seemed lost in thought.

"Come on," Ted said. "Let's get out of here."

Lenore lingered a moment, as though there was something more she wanted to say. Then she followed Ted.

I found a quiet corner, pulled out my cell phone, and called Steven, as I'd promised I would.

"You know," he said after I'd told him the good news, "the Coles had a motive for seeing Weaver dead, too."

"To get the baby, you mean?"

"Right. If you think about it, it's a pretty good plan. Eliminate the birth father, and at the same time, make it look like the adoptive mother is the killer. You get rid of both obstacles in one move. Very efficient."

"Sounds risky, if you ask me. They might not end up with the baby in any event, and more importantly, they might get caught."

"Don't rule it out too quickly, okay?"

I remembered the hostile look on Mrs. Cole's face after the judge's ruling. Maybe Steven's suggestion wasn't so improbable after all. "I'm game for anything that will help Terri."

Steven was silent for a moment. "Are you by any chance free for dinner tonight?" He was trying hard to pull off a casual, spur-of-the-moment invitation. But I heard the tremor in his voice.

"I thought we weren't going to go there."

"*Dinner*, Kali. I didn't say anything about a roll in the hay."

I felt my cheeks grow pink. Had I read too much into a friendly overture?

"If you prefer," Steven added, "you can meet me at the restaurant."

"I—"

"We'll get a table for six and sit at opposite ends."

I bit back a laugh.

"And I'll eat with one hand tied behind my back."

"I, uh . . ." It was a good night to be out. Dottie and Bea were cooking dinner for Murray Parsons and one of his pals. They'd invited me to join them, cajoled me in fact, but I didn't really feel like being a fifth wheel, especially at a table where the conversation was more likely to revolve around hearing aids and hemorrhoids than things close to my heart.

"So, how about it?"

"Sure," I said, with the same casual offhandedness. And the same tremor.

CHAPTER 20

I gave serious thought to canceling. To calling Steven and pleading illness or a last-minute client deadline. Or even telling him the truth—that I'd been out of my mind to agree to have dinner with him.

That he'd been out of his mind to ask.

Instead, I snapped at Jared, slammed file drawers and cabinet doors, then left work early for the gym. There, at least, I could put my irritation to good use.

With an hour's workout behind me, I was calmer if no less confused.

What was I doing jumping into the firepit a second time? Not a problem, I told myself, Steven was no longer a married man. The heavens echoed with laughter. *Not married because his wife was killed while you were sleeping with him.* It's still not the same, I argued. Maybe not the same, a little voice argued back, but ill-advised nonetheless.

Why wasn't I willing to leave well enough alone?

That one was easy. Because I was attracted to Steven. Something about him tapped a reservoir of feelings I usually tried to ignore. The only other person who'd had the same effect on me was Tom. Also married.

Steven had suggested a relatively new restaurant near the Rockridge BART station in Berkeley. Neutral territory since neither of us had eaten there before. It had recently been written up in the *Chronicle* so I was surprised he'd been able to get a reservation on short notice.

I arrived at the restaurant ten minutes late, on purpose. Steven was already seated, sipping a glass of red wine, but he rose when I approached, clearly torn between a hug and a handshake. In the end, he offered a nervous smile and sat down again.

The tables were filled and the room was noisy, but we had a relatively secluded table in the corner by a window.

"I didn't order a bottle," Steven said, "because I wasn't sure what you wanted. Still drink red with dinner?"

I nodded.

He signaled the waitress and she took my order.

Steven looked good. Maybe it was the soft lighting of the restaurant or the gaiety of the people around us, or maybe it was that I'd finally allowed myself to really see him. To be present with the man he was today.

There was a touch of silver at his temples, and his face had filled out a little in the years since we'd last had dinner. He was wearing a teal silk shirt that brought out the blue in his eyes.

"To Hannah Harper," he said when my glass of zinfandel arrived. "Lenore says you did a terrific job."

"The law was on our side. It's likely to be a different matter if Terri is convicted."

"I don't even want to think about that possibility."

"It's a real one, though."

Steven's face was a solid wall, suddenly unreadable.

I swirled the deep red liquid in my glass. It shimmered with reflected candlelight. "There are a couple of things that worry me," I said after a moment.

"Such as?"

"Terri's trip to Mendocino, for example." It was one of those things that made sense and yet didn't. An ink drawing that was a rabbit one minute, the profile of a woman's face the next.

"You don't believe her?"

"It's not that." In fact, I'd spoken to her friend, Robin, and he'd confirmed Terri's visit pretty much as she'd described it. In answer to my questions, he'd conceded that she probably *had* appeared somewhat distracted, but not particularly upset.

"The lonely bluffs along the way," I explained. "Lots of them. Perfect for tossing a murder weapon into the ocean where it would never be found."

He dismissed the notion. "She could have done that from half a dozen places closer to home."

"The plan was for Lenore to stay the weekend. She was looking forward to spending time with her new granddaughter. Why would Terri suddenly head off on an unplanned trip instead?"

Steven smiled. "It wouldn't seem strange if you knew Terri better. My mother on the other hand"—he paused for a reflective sip of wine—"I have to admit I'm surprised she gave up so easily, even if she *was* feeling a bit under the weather."

"I'm sure the prosecution will make something of it. And if it seems suspicious to me, it's going to strike the jurors the same way."

"Not necessarily. You've been trained to be suspicious." The corners of his eyes crinkled, but his tone was grave. "Just remember, you've also been trained to present arguments so as to alleviate suspicion."

It was interesting the way the world seemed so logical when you talked only in the abstract. "It's not that easy."

"You're good with a jury," Steven said. "I've seen you."

"There's also the witness who remembers a Ford Explorer," I reminded him. "And a woman fitting Terri's description. We can discredit her testimony with statistics and cross-examination, but you have to admit it's an odd coincidence."

Steven looked up, studying me. "Sounds like you're beginning to doubt your own client."

"Not really. I mean, there are things that bother me, but I don't think Terri killed him." In theory, it shouldn't matter anyway. But I was more comfortable representing clients I believed in.

Steven tapped the table top with his fingers. "I know Terri," he said, looking me in the eye. "And I know she isn't capable of murder."

"There are those who would tell you everyone is capable, under the right circumstances."

He retreated into some private place for a moment. Wrestling with his own doubt, perhaps. Or puzzling how best to handle mine. Then he laughed. A hollow sound without humor. "Maybe that's true for some of us. But not for Terri."

Our food arrived—grilled salmon for me, lamb for Steven, along with a second glass of wine for each of us—and we turned our conversation to other topics. Safe topics like recent movies, current events, the weather.

By the time the waiter had cleared our plates, I was in a relaxed and lighthearted mood.

"Are you back in the Bay Area for good?" Steven asked.

"That's up in the air at the moment."

"You might actually return to Silver Creek, then? Small-town practice must have its attractions."

It did. But the real appeal for me had been that Tom was in Silver Creek. He was also a major deterrent to my return. I wasn't enthralled at the prospect of crossing paths with an ex-lover who'd since reconciled with his wife.

"It's more complicated than deciding where to work," I explained. "There's someone there I was dating."

"What happened?"

"He was separated from his wife when we started seeing each other. They later decided to try to make the marriage work. For their children's sake."

Steven grunted in sympathy. "I can see how that might be tough. Especially in a small town." His voice was soft, sincere. It was one of the things I'd always found so appealing about him.

"But I'm tough, too. I shouldn't let it get to me."

"You're not as tough as you think, Kali." He rested his forearms on the table.

"Do you think maybe I do this to myself on purpose? Subconsciously, I mean." I'd spoken without thinking, but it wasn't such a bad question. And Steven was a psychologist. Maybe he'd get to the heart of my troubled history and set me straight.

"Do what?"

"Fall for married men."

A hint of a smile tweaked his mouth. His eyes met mine. "I'm probably not the best one to answer that."

Right. Something like the chicken seeking counsel from the fox, I supposed. Only Steven was hardly wily, and I was far from innocent.

The waitress brought our coffee and we sipped in silence for a moment. "Someone puts flowers on their graves," Steven said suddenly. "Each anniversary of the accident. Pink carnations on Rebecca's. White daisies for Caroline."

Caroline and Rebecca. The names we'd avoided speaking all evening.

"At first I thought it might be you," he added.

I shook my head. "It's not me." I'd been too consumed with my own feelings of remorse to face even their ghosts.

"I know that now. This last year I kept a vigil at the graves hoping to see who it was."

"And did you?"

Steven nodded. "A man. When I tried to speak to him, he ran away."

"Do you think it was the driver of the other car?"

"Could be. Or it could be someone who . . ." Steven ran a finger around the rim of his saucer, then looked up. "Maybe I wasn't the only one fooling around."

I wondered if that made it easier for him to accept, or harder. "You shouldn't jump to conclusions," I said. "There are lots of possibilities."

He started to say something, then stopped himself. "He'll probably never show up again."

"What happened with the police investigation? Were there no leads at all?" I knew only what I'd read in the paper when it happened or gleaned secondhand from others who'd known Steven. And since reconnecting with him recently, I'd been studiously avoiding the subject.

"None that went anywhere," he said. "You have to remember that hit-and-run isn't a high priority for an ongoing investigation. Usually something breaks right away if it's going to happen."

"And nothing did?"

"The one witness was a young high school student. She'd only had her license a couple of months and was too busy watching the road to notice much about the other car. White, she said, or light gray. Solo occupant, male. She couldn't remember anything more."

"Young? Old?"

Steven shook his head. "Nothing."

"What about make of car?"

"She thought *maybe* BMW, but she couldn't be sure. She agreed to be hypnotized even. No luck. The cop in charge, Joe Moran, he seemed like a good guy."

"But he never made any progress?"

"He died of a heart attack about two weeks into the case. The guy who took it on never really took it on, if you know what I mean. New things came in and the accident kind of fell through the cracks."

"I'm sorry. That must have been very hard to watch."

He nodded, almost imperceptibly, and looked at his hands. "I'd go down there and rattle their cages, but nothing ever happened. I often wonder about the driver of the other car. What he's feeling. What he thinks about. Whether he remembers them at all. Some days I look at every stranger on the street—from the bike messengers downtown to the bigwigs in their Armani suits and imported leather loafers—and wonder which one of them is him."

I fought the urge to touch his arm, to cover his hand with my own. How could I offer comfort when I was part of the problem?

"I failed them," he said. His eyes had grown dark and flat. "Especially Rebecca. A father is supposed to protect his child, no matter what. To put her above all else."

Steven had told me he'd put what happened behind him. If he honestly believed that, he was deluding himself.

"Why did you suggest dinner tonight?" I asked. "Doesn't it make things worse for you?"

A small smile pulled at the corners of his mouth. "Actually, it's just the opposite."

"What do you mean?"

"I feel connected."

I wasn't sure I understood, but the waiter came with the bill and we moved on to less personal topics.

Outside the restaurant there was another awkward moment during which neither a handshake nor a hug seemed quite right.

"Thanks for coming," Steven said at last. "I enjoyed it."

"So did I."

"Shall I walk you to your car?"

"I'm just down the street."

"Okay, then. See you." He made a sweeping gesture with his hand—half wave, half shrug—and headed off to his own car.

With a twist of nostalgia, I watched him amble away.

At home, I found Bea, Dotty, and their two guests embroiled in a lively game of penny poker. From the sounds of things, it had turned out to be a very successful evening.

I cut myself a piece of leftover cheesecake and went downstairs feeling unaccountably lonely.

I changed into a pair of sweatpants and a T-shirt, and then sprawled out on the bed to read. After nine pages, I gave up and set the book down. Critical acclaim aside, I was finding the story tedious and boring.

Instead, I pulled out the case file on Hannah's adoption, something I hadn't looked at since shoving it into my briefcase this afternoon in court. I wanted to make sure everything was in order so that when I looked at it again, which would most likely be months from now after Terri's trial, I wouldn't be scrambling to find lost papers or missing information.

Would Terri be in prison at that point, or back home with Hannah? I felt a knot of tension form in my chest at the weight of what I'd taken on. Two lives, three if you included Ted. Their fate in my hands.

Enough, I scolded myself. Too much of that sort of thinking can be counterproductive. I drew a curtain across my mind and flipped through the sheaf of papers the court clerk had handed me. At the back was the lab report for Weaver's paternity claim, a matter no longer at issue. Judging from the attached correspondence, it had gone to Weaver's attorney first, and then to court, where it had been filed awaiting review.

There were several pages of numbers and grids. I was too tired to try to make sense of them, but my eyes were drawn to the summary at the bottom of the second page. A short paragraph set off by a Roman numeral.

I read the paragraph once, then moved closer to the light to read it again. I felt as though the air had been sucked from my lungs.

Bram Weaver was not Hannah's father.

CHAPTER 21

"It must be a mistake." Melissa's voice sounded hollow. I couldn't tell if this was because of the phone connection or the news I'd just dropped in her lap.

"No mistake," I told her. "I have the report right here in front of me. Bram was not the baby's father."

"The report is wrong."

"I don't think so, Melissa."

"It has to be." There was a desperate edge to her words.

"It's a sophisticated test."

"But labs make mistakes. Or maybe the person typing the results messed up. You know that stuff happens."

"Not very often."

She grew quiet. I could hear her breathing into the phone. "Anyway," she said after a moment, "it doesn't matter now."

"Maybe not in terms of Bram's challenge to the adoption. But I'm sure Ted and Terri would like to know who Hannah's father is. And to feel comfortable he won't be coming out of the woodwork at the last minute to cause new problems."

I waited for a response. None came.

"It might also prove useful in structuring Terri's defense," I added.

"How?"

That was something I hadn't worked out for myself. But it seemed as though the information could be a crucial piece of the puzzle. "I'm not sure yet. But knowing who the father is might lead us in a new direction. Maybe even give us an alternate killer."

"I already told you," she snapped. "It was Bram."

"Melissa, this isn't about reputation or morals or whatever you're worried about. There are legal ramifications. If the father was never notified of the pregnancy—"

"You asked me about Hannah's father and I gave you my answer. It's your problem if you don't like it." She hung up abruptly.

Monday morning I was at my desk reviewing a commercial lease when Weaver's attorney called. I'd left a message on Wednesday and was wondering if he'd decided to simply ignore it.

"Sorry I couldn't get back to you sooner," Trimble said. "Big trial. You know how that is. In fact, looks like your client's got you into a humdinger. You got a court date yet?"

"Mid-September. Mr. Trimble, I—"

"Bill. I don't stand on formality."

Allegiance among lawyers was apparently more important to him than the fact that my client was accused of murdering his. I was grateful not to be dealing with misplaced hostility.

"Bill, what can you tell me about Weaver's exchanges with the Women's Alliance?"

"You're thinking maybe one of them had reason to kill him?"

Lawyers' logic following lawyers' allegiance. "Possibly."

He chuckled. "I don't know, they loved screaming and yelling about him, but truth of the matter is, the publicity helped their cause more than it hurt."

"Was there anyone in particular, maybe, who took it more personally?"

"They take everything personally as far as I can tell. That's part of their problem."

"What about death threats, that sort of thing?"

"No, nothing like that." He paused. "About a year ago, though, there was a woman who was harassing Bram. Real in-your-face sort of stuff. She'd grab his arm at public appearances, try to speak to him one-on-one, show up on his doorstep. Always angry. We took steps to get a restraining order, but she backed off."

"You remember her name?"

"Suzze Madden. I had an address at one time, but I couldn't tell you what it was now. She worked at a rape crisis center in the city, though. A man hater. Tough as nails."

"Was she connected with the Women's Alliance?"

"Must have been, but I got the impression she was acting on her own."

I thanked him for the information, and had barely hung up when Nick Logan called with a report on the pizza man.

"His name is Peter Longfellow," Nick said. "He's worked for Pizza Pizazz about six months now."

I reached for a clean sheet of paper and began jotting notes.

"The boss says he's a conscientious worker, though he's apparently been playing fast and loose with his deliveries to the old lady, Mrs. Rudd. Pizza Pizazz doesn't show any orders for her, and the boss says Weaver's neighborhood isn't in their delivery zone anyway. Besides which, this guy Longfellow doesn't even work Sunday afternoons."

"Did he show up at Mrs. Rudd's again yesterday?"

"Right on schedule."

"Did you talk to him?"

"I tried. He wasn't in the mood for being social. Swears he wasn't even in the neighborhood the night of the murder."

I tapped my pen against my wrist. "You think the kid who saw him was mistaken?"

"No, I think Longfellow is lying," Nick said. "The guy was nervous as hell."

"Maybe he was the one who killed Weaver." That idea didn't hold water, though. The boy had said that Longfellow was standing on the street when the shots were fired. "Not the one who actually pulled the trigger," I amended. "But he could have been a lookout or something."

"Hard to tell until we know more. You want me to stay on this, right?"

"Absolutely." It could be just the break we needed. "I'll try reaching Mrs. Rudd. It will be interesting to see what she says about him."

Nick paused. "She's deaf, remember?"

"I have a friend who knows sign language. I think she'd be willing to help out." More than willing. If for no other reason than to lord it over her sister.

"Can't hurt."

I looked at my afternoon calendar. Nothing pressing. "I'll see if we can get over there today. And see what you can find out about a Suzze Madden. She works, or did work, at a rape crisis center in the city. She was causing trouble for Weaver last year."

When I phoned her, Bea leapt at the chance. "My signing may be a little rusty," she warned. "But I think I'll be able to communicate."

"Do you have time this afternoon?"

"Honey, I have nothing but time. You know that."

It wasn't so. Both Bea and Dotty led lives that would have had my head spinning. Classes, bridge groups, part-time jobs—in fact, I'd been surprised to find Bea home when I called.

"I'll pick you up in half an hour."

"I'll be ready." With a chuckle, she asked, "Shall I bring my trenchcoat and magnifying glass?"

"We're just going to visit an elderly woman." As soon as I said this, I realized Mrs. Rudd was probably not much older than Bea.

"One who might have information about a crime," Bea added, oblivious to my verbal stumbling. "It's all very exciting, if you ask me."

Bea was waiting by the front door when I arrived to pick her up. No trenchcoat, but I noticed she'd put on her new yellow dress and matching cardigan.

Dotty, who was also wearing one of her special occasion dresses, wanted to come along.

"I think not," Bea said curtly. "Too many people will scare the old gal off."

"Look who's talking."

"Kali *asked* me. She wants my help, don't you?" This last was addressed to me.

I took a stab at making peace. "I think Bea's right. It's better if just two of us go. And Bea knows sign language."

"She *knew* it," Dotty said with sisterly disdain. "A long time ago."

Bea was chatty on the drive across the bridge, but she grew quieter as we approached Weaver's neighborhood. I drove down the street, past Weaver's house, to the address Nick had given me. Mrs. Rudd lived on the ground floor of a four-unit wood-frame building set back from the street.

"She may not know sign language," Bea said, betraying signs of nervousness. She smoothed the skirt of her dress, pulling it taut across her lap.

"Nick saw her hands moving when he tried to talk to her."

"She could have been finger spelling."

"That's different?"

Bea nodded and again ran her hands over her skirt. "Or she might have been using SEE."

"See?"

"Signing Exact English. It's a different form of sign language from ASL, or American Sign Language, which is what I know."

I wondered if Bea had intentionally neglected to point this out before now for fear I'd change my mind about involving her.

"There are some others too," she added slowly.

"Great."

"But they're much rarer."

I sighed. "I guess we'll find out soon enough."

I rang the bell, then realized Mrs. Rudd wouldn't hear it.

"She probably has a signal light," Bea explained. "Most deaf people do."

The door opened not long after I'd pushed the bell. Mrs. Rudd was not as old as I'd been expecting. In truth, she was probably younger than Bea. But her skin was heavily wrinkled and her features were pinched in a scowl. She moved with the aid of a walker.

She stared at us a moment with deep-set gray eyes, then pointed to her ear and shook her head.

Bea's fingers started to move. Mrs. Rudd nodded and her expression softened. She steadied herself with one hand on her walker and responded with surprisingly quick finger movements of her own. They went back and forth a couple of times before I interrupted.

"What's she saying?" I asked Bea.

"I told her we were investigating the murder of a man in her neighborhood."

We were, sort of. But I was willing to bet Bea had embroidered our role considerably. Too late, I was beginning to doubt the wisdom of involving her.

"Mrs. Rudd says she didn't know Weaver but she knew he

was a celebrity of some sort." Bea looked at the dancing fingers and nodded. "She says we already arrested somebody. A woman."

We. I was right. "Bea, you can't impersonate a police officer."

"I'm not impersonating anyone."

"Where'd she get this *we*, then?"

"So maybe I'm a little sloppy with my signing."

"Bea, just ask her what she knows about the pizza delivery man."

More finger activity. Then suddenly the woman's face snapped back into a frown. Bea gestured more emphatically, but Mrs. Rudd ignored her. Bea stepped forward, as though to move inside. The door shut in our faces.

"What was that about?" I asked.

"I'd like to know myself."

"What did you say to her?" I didn't intend to sound accusatory, but I did.

Bea gave me a sidelong glance and ignored the question. "We were getting on so well, too," she humphed.

Exasperated, I turned and laid a hand on her arm. "Would you please tell me what's going on."

"Mrs. Rudd says it's nobody's business but hers how much pizza she eats."

"You asked her *that?*"

"Of course not. At least, I don't think I did."

I sighed. It was my own fault, I reminded myself. I was the one who'd asked for Bea's help.

We started back down the front walkway. "What about the delivery man?" I asked. "What did she say about him?"

"That's when she shut the door on us." Bea chewed on her cheek, perplexed. "I wonder if I said something obscene by mistake. Some of the hand signs are only a wiggle away from words you don't want to use. Sort of like 'luck' and that word that rhymes with it."

Mrs. Rudd's reaction was so swift and so sudden, it must have been truly offensive.

"I'm sorry, Kali. I guess maybe I've been away from it for too long." Bea's round shoulders slumped.

I was annoyed with myself more than Bea. "You did a better job than I could have done," I told her.

She gave me a disdainful look. "That's not saying much now, is it?"

"Tell me again what you asked about the delivery man."

"As I recall, I said something about his maybe witnessing the murder. I know I asked about him by name."

"I bet that's what upset her. It wasn't how much pizza she ate, it was the questions about the man who delivered it."

"Why would that upset her?" Bea asked.

"Beats me." If Mrs. Rudd had been younger, or less wrinkled, I might have surmised that she and the pizza man were enmeshed in a clandestine love affair. Perhaps they were anyway. Maybe he wasn't as superficial as I was. Whatever the reason, it was clear she didn't want to talk about him.

We'd reached the curb when a young, harried-looking woman pulled up in a station wagon full of kids and double-parked in front of the house. Holding a large, towel-draped basket, she stepped from the car, then leaned in to say something to the children, two of whom were scuffling in the backseat.

"Looks like you've got your hands full," Bea said to her.

"This is only the tip of the iceberg." The tussle escalated and one of the boys knocked against the baby, who began to howl.

"Elliot!"

"It's Jeremy's fault. He hit me first."

"Did not."

The baby's wails intensified.

"Stop it! Both of you." The young mother looked close to tears. She turned to us. "You weren't by chance visiting Sophia Rudd, were you?"

"Yes," Bea crowed, "we were just there."

I refrained from correcting her. I thought *visit* might have stretched the nature of our encounter.

"Would you mind terribly taking this to her?" the woman asked, holding up the basket. "It's my day to bring dinner, but there's no place to park and I've got to pick my daughter up from school in ten minutes . . ."

Bea grabbed the basket. "We'd be happy to. Who do we say it's from?"

"From the church. She'll understand. Three days a week we bring her food. She can't drive since her stroke. I feel bad about running out on her today. I usually stay and visit for a bit. Tell her I'm really sorry."

"You know sign language?" I asked.

The woman nodded and began signing. "My daughter is deaf," she said at the same time.

I was impressed that a young woman with so many demands took time to help another in need. "Mrs. Rudd must appreciate the company," I told her.

"I know she really appreciates that I usually stay a bit. Most of the members just drop off their meals and leave."

"She's lucky to have such a good support system," Bea said.

"She has a son who visits her, too," the woman explained. "He comes every Sunday. Other times as well, I imagine. But every Sunday, like clockwork. Alexander's visits are the highlight of her week."

Every Sunday. Like Peter Longfellow, the pizza man. An idea tickled my brain. "Does her son by any chance deliver pizza?"

"As a matter of fact, he does work at a pizza place. I think it's just temporary, though. To be honest, I don't really pay that much attention to what she says. I try, but there are so many things on my mind already."

"We'll take care of your meal," Bea soothed. "You go get your daughter."

"Thank you. You've no idea what a godsend you two are."

I thought the poor woman could probably use a little more help from God than just us.

Bea and I turned and headed back up the front walkway, basket in hand. I saw Mrs. Rudd peeking from behind a lace curtain, which is probably how she knew we hadn't returned to harass her further. She opened the door, took the basket, then shut the door firmly, without so much as a nod.

"So," Bea said, when we got into the car. "He's her son."

"It looks that way."

"Why couldn't she just tell us that? You think she's ashamed of what he does?"

"I think she doesn't want people to know he's her son, or that he's visiting her. I bet that's why he comes in his work clothes, so it looks like she's simply getting a pizza delivery."

"But why?" Bea asked.

That was the question pounding in my head as well.

*   *   *

I dropped Bea at the house and went back to the office.

"Mr. Billings has called twice," Jared said, looking up from his computer screen. "Isn't he the guy who's a friend of Weaver's?"

"Right. The two of them had dinner together the night Weaver was killed. A third friend as well, I think."

"He sounded angry. And he insisted on speaking to you directly."

I took the message slip Jared handed me and returned Billings' call. It was a direct line.

"The police have talked to me, and cleared me," he said. His words burned with outrage. "You've no right to bother my family. No right to harass me."

"Whoa. Mr. Billings, I'm not trying to harass you, I simply wanted to ask you a few questions."

"You stay away from me. Stay away from my family. Just butt out, you got that?"

Loud and clear.

CHAPTER 22

"Peter Longfellow is her son," I told Nick. I'd called Monday evening and left a message but he didn't return my call until late Tuesday afternoon. "At least, that's my guess. And his name is actually Alexander."

"Interesting, because he's also dead."

"Dead! What happened? You just saw him on Sunday." And we'd just talked to Mrs. Rudd on Monday. Had she known then about her son's death?

"Not that kind of dead," Nick amended. "Peter Longfellow died thirty-one years ago at the age of six. The man who might have seen something the night Weaver was killed is not Peter Longfellow. At least not the Peter Longfellow he claims to be."

"Who is he then?"

"You just told me, the old lady's son." Nick snickered at his own lame attempt at humor.

"You mean he's using an assumed identity?"

"Looks that way."

"Why?"

"I haven't the foggiest idea. Trouble with the law, an ex-wife he's trying to lose, could be just about anything. I can dig around, but the answer probably has no relevance to Weaver's death."

"Probably not."

"Though it does explain why he was reluctant to talk to me."

I grunted agreement. "And why Mrs. Rudd slammed the door in our faces when Bea asked about him."

"How'd that church friend of hers find out, then?"

"I guess Mrs. Rudd must have slipped up. The woman knows

sign language and comes to visit on a regular basis. Mrs. Rudd probably finds it difficult *not* to talk about her son."

"You want me to pursue this?"

"There's a chance he saw the killer, Nick. We'd be foolish not to." Although getting Longfellow to testify might prove to be a serious challenge. A man in hiding is hardly going to step forward in a court of law.

"Got it," Nick said.

"What about Weaver's friends, anything new there?"

"I've got feelers out, but no real progress yet."

I told him about the call from Billings. "That kind of overreaction sets off alarms for me. Len Roemer was pretty hostile, too, for what that's worth."

"Yeah. I had the dubious pleasure of talking to him myself. Good thing he has a strong body because he hasn't got much of a brain."

"When did you talk to him?"

"Yesterday. I dropped by the gym when he was at work."

"And?"

"Nothing. He did confirm that he was at dinner with Billings and Weaver the night Weaver was killed."

"Did they have an argument?"

Nick laughed. "No argument, no falling out. Says he doesn't know what Bram's kid was talking about. Roemer claims the three of them—Weaver, Billings, and him—have been best of friends since seventh grade. One for all, all for one, that sort of thing."

About what I expected. "How about the Coles?"

"Well, they're an interesting couple. Mrs. Cole's first husband died. Shot, in fact."

I'd been doodling in the margin of the paper. I stopped and leaned forward. "When? How? Who shot him?"

"About eight years ago. Someone followed him to his car in a dark parking lot."

"And?" When Steven had first proposed we consider the Coles as substitute killers, I'd been skeptical. Now, I was thinking we might be on to something.

"That's all I've got for now," Nick said. "But I'll keep you posted."

"This could be big. God knows they have a motive—Hannah.

With a little bit more, it might be enough to raise reasonable doubt about Terri."

"I'm working on it, Kali. This kind of information isn't just there for the asking, you know."

Could have fooled me. Nick seemed able to get anything on anyone.

"And you didn't let me finish about Roemer," he continued. "I talked to a couple of his coworkers at the gym. It's a very upscale place, by the way. Lots of gorgeous, well-toned women running around in skimpy clothing. Not a bad place to work."

"Or conduct interviews, from the sounds of it."

Nick laughed. "I've been in worse environments."

"What did his coworkers have to say?"

"For the most part, not much. But one of them, a young woman by the name of Darina, said Weaver came to see Roemer at the gym about a week before he was killed. Something about a business venture. She could tell from their body language that they were angry. They went outside to talk so she doesn't know any of the details. But she says that Roemer acted pissed the rest of the evening."

"Interesting. Tough to pin a murder on that, though."

"This is a work in progress, Kali. You gotta take the long view."

Hard to do with a trial date approaching. "Thanks, Nick. You're a wonder."

It was getting close to five o'clock. I pulled out the adoption file, something I'd avoided doing all day, and called the lab. I was transferred and put on hold several times before reaching someone who could help me. The man had a rich, mellow voice that reminded me of dark brandy.

"I've got the report in front of me," he said. "It's pretty clear. Weaver was not the baby's father."

"But the tests are based on probability, aren't they, not absolute certainty?"

"You're right, in part. With the older forms of testing, the probability standard was lower. That left wiggle room for those who were looking to use it. The RFLP method that we use is the most accurate form of paternity testing available. If you want to prove paternity, we can say with 99.9% or greater certainty that a given man is the biological father of the child. Theoretically, I suppose, that still leaves wiggle room though the courts don't see it that way.

"When it comes to excluding someone, however," he continued, "the results are conclusive. No question about it, Weaver was not the father."

"I don't suppose you can discern anything from the test about who the actual father might be?"

"You mean a profile based on genes—like dark hair, brown eyes, tall, with a strong jaw and a family pattern of baldness?"

"Something like that."

He laughed. "Someday maybe, but not yet."

"Didn't think so."

"Hey, it's always good to ask. New techniques are being developed all the time."

"Thanks for your help." I disconnected and started to dial Ted, then decided it was a subject better broached face to face. I closed up the office and headed for the city.

Ted was watching the evening news when I arrived. I could hear the television in the background when he opened the door.

"Something about Terri?" he asked with alarm.

"No. Nothing new there. Can I come in? I'd like to talk with you."

"Sure." Ted's good manners overtook his confusion. He stepped back and opened the door wider. "I'm in the den, with Hannah."

He ushered me to the back of the house. A different room than last time I'd visited. It was sleeker, more tailored. The paintings on the walls were bold abstracts.

I took a seat on the couch where I could steal glances at Hannah, who was propped in an infant seat on the coffee table. Round cheeks, rosebud mouth, and a tiny button nose. She'd filled out and her hair had grown thicker. She was no longer a newborn.

I reached out a finger and gently caressed a cotton-swaddled leg. When had my recent fascination with babies begun?

"You want a glass of wine?" Ted asked. "I've just poured one for myself."

"Thanks. A small one."

He filled a cut-crystal glass with rich, red liquid and handed it to me. "Shalla is really taking it in the teeth for keeping Terri locked up. Serves him right."

"The Women's Alliance protest?"

"Not only that. There was a letter to the editor in yesterday's paper. Shalla got hit with a question about it outside court today. They had it on the news just before you arrived. Not that the support is helping Terri. She's still in jail."

Hannah made a cooing sound. Ted touched her cheek and cooed back. "Hey, Hannah banana. You want your mom home, too, don't you?"

Hannah stared into Ted's eyes and kicked her little feet like a propeller. I felt it again, that stirring somewhere deep in my chest.

Ted flipped off the television with a stab of the remote. "Shalla is ambitious," he said, turning his attention my way once again. "District attorney today, who knows what tomorrow, maybe mayor. Or senator. A groundswell of support for Terri would make him sit up and take note."

Only we were a long way from that. For every voice critical of Shalla, I'd heard another in support of him. *No special treatment for the rich and privileged.* It was practically a mantra for a large part of the city's population.

"I can try for bail again, though I don't think it will do any good."

Ted sighed. He leaned back against the black and tan chenille seat cushion. "I wasn't faulting you. It's just so damned . . . so damned difficult. And there's so little I can do."

He paused, looked at the ceiling, then pressed his palm to his temple. "You can't imagine what it's like having someone you love in jail. Every time I pour myself a cup of coffee, or wine . . ." He lifted the hand holding the glass. "Every time I look out the window, or cuddle Hannah, or wake to the sunlight coming through the bedroom window, I feel a knot of dread in the pit of my stomach. Terri gets a hard bunk and prison food. I worry about her, about how she's being treated, and how unhappy she must be."

"I know it's hard. But we each have our roles, and you're handling yours admirably."

Ted made a sound, something between a grunt and a laugh. "You sound like Lenore."

"She said the same thing?"

"More or less, only I think she was referring to herself as much as me. So what brings you here?"

I stole another quick look at Hannah, then took a breath. "The results from the paternity test."

"He's dead, what does it matter?"

"Weaver isn't Hannah's father."

Ted set his wineglass down so hard I thought it would break. His eyes turned a shade darker. "Who is, then?"

"I don't know. Melissa insists the test is wrong. I talked to the lab, and they stand behind the results."

Ted rocked back, shaking his head. "Jesus. First it's some kid from the deli, then it's Weaver, now it's someone else altogether. How can she not know who she was sleeping with?"

"Maybe you'll have better luck talking to her than I did."

"Hah! I doubt it. I took your advice and told her she should stop coming around so much. I'm not her favorite person at the moment." He leaned forward, elbows on his knees, and pressed his forehead to his palms. "Why couldn't we have had a normal adoption? Is that so much to ask for?"

I shook my head, although he wasn't looking for an answer.

Footsteps echoed in the hallway. "Hannah's laundry is all folded," Lenore said. "And I remade . . ." She stopped partway into the room. "Kali. What are you doing here?" Her voice held the same alarm Ted's had earlier. "Has something happened?"

"It's not about Terri," Ted explained. "It's Weaver. The paternity test showed he wasn't Hannah's father."

"What?" The color drained from Lenore's face. "How can that be?"

Ted shot her a contemptuous look. "Guess Melissa Burke was screwing someone besides Weaver. That's how."

Lenore's expression was pained. "There's no need to be crude, Ted."

"It's my house. I'll use whatever language I feel like using."

"I only meant . . ." Her voice faltered. She sank into an over-stuffed chair by the fireplace. "Not her father? You're sure?"

"I spoke to someone at the lab myself. The test results are clear."

"What does this mean for Hannah's adoption?" Lenore seemed to have trouble getting the words out.

"I'd guess the chance of the birth father coming forward at this point is slim." They didn't need me to point out that a more worrisome, and perhaps more likely obstacle to the adoption, was Terri's potential conviction at trial.

"You're telling me that Bram Weaver had no claim to Hannah? He couldn't have stood in the way of her adoption?"

"Right. Without proof of paternity, he wasn't relevant to the proceeding."

"It can't be . . . it's not fair," Lenore moaned. "None of this is fair. All Terri wanted was a baby. That's all any of us wanted for her."

"For us," Ted corrected. But his tone had lost its earlier hostility.

I stole another peek at Hannah, who was beginning to whimper. Her skin was creamy white with a blush of pink at her cheeks. As I watched the dimpled chin and cupid-bow mouth quiver with helpless indignation, I could only imagine the pain Terri must feel at having been wrenched from her daughter.

Lenore had regained some of her color. She rocked the infant seat, and when that didn't quiet Hannah's fussing, she scooped the child into her arms.

My own arms hung at my side, like awkward appendages that needed to be tucked away. I rose from the couch. "I need to be getting back."

"Come on," said Ted. "I'll walk you to the door."

When we were out of earshot, I turned to him. "How is it with your mother-in-law staying here?"

He groaned. "Everything's got to be done her way. I understand that she knows more about babies than I do, but I'm not a complete incompetent. And Hannah is *my* daughter."

"How long is she staying?"

"She wanted to move in for the duration, until Terri is home again, but I put my foot down. She's going back to Carmel on Monday. She can come up and visit for a day or two each week if she wants, but that's the limit. I don't imagine Arlo likes having his wife gone all the time anyway."

"Can you manage Hannah by yourself?"

Ted nodded. "I've hired a nanny to help me out. Besides, I don't have a lot of work commitments at the moment. Seems having a wife on trial for murder makes me less appealing as a spokesperson. TelAm is even talking about pulling the commercials." This last was said with some bitterness.

He opened the door. "What do you think Terri's chances are of beating this?"

"It's early still. There's so much—"

"But what do you think they are?"

I hesitated. "Good," I said after a moment.

"I sure hope you're right."

So did I.

I didn't hear from Steven again until the end of the week. After half waiting for a call on the Sunday following our dinner, I'd relegated our date—if that's what it was—to the back of my mind. Not without effort at times, but I'd managed to do it.

So when he called Friday, catching me as I was flying out the door to meet a friend for lunch, I didn't run through my customary mental list of admonishments. I simply treated it like I would any other renewed friendship.

"I had a good time Saturday night," he said.

"So did I."

"Maybe we can do it again someday."

"Yeah. Might be nice."

Steven laughed. "Be careful, you almost sounded as though you meant it."

I took a breath. "I did."

"You're on, then. I'm having a barbecue a week from Saturday. Very informal. A mix of friends and neighbors. If you're free, it would be good to have you join us."

So nonchalant. *Good to have you join us.* Not a big deal one way or the other. If Steven could handle this, I ought to be able to as well.

"Thanks," I told him. "I'll try to make it."

"I went to see Terri yesterday," Steven said, turning suddenly serious. His voice thickened and dropped a level.

"How's she doing?"

"She's lost weight and says she isn't sleeping well. Doesn't surprise me."

Me either. I had trouble enough sleeping in a comfortable bed with a room to myself.

"She told me about Weaver's paternity. Or nonpaternity, I should say."

Ted and I had agreed it was better she hear the news from him than me. But I hadn't followed up to know that he'd told her. "How did she seem?"

Steven thought for a moment. "Worried."

I hadn't realized until then what I'd been grappling with subconsciously all week. If Weaver wasn't Hannah's father, and if Terri had actually killed him, then she'd done so in vain. Worried must be only a fraction of what she was feeling.

On some level, I think, I'd avoided telling her about the paternity results myself because I didn't want to see her reaction. I believed in my client's innocence, and that was the way I wanted to keep it.

"How did it all get so muddled?" Steven sighed, a ragged sound that brought home his personal involvement in the case. Terri was my client, but she was *his* sister.

"We need to keep focused on the trial," I said.

"I've been going over what we know about the crime. Trying to look at it in a fresh light. According to the reports, the first shot, in the abdomen, was enough to kill Weaver. The second shot, at close range and to the face, was personal. Borne of anger or hatred, I'd say."

"Which supports the State's case that Terri killed him because of Hannah."

"Except it doesn't fit who Terri is. She doesn't get angry and she doesn't carry grudges."

"You weren't there when she lashed out at Weaver after the hearing."

"Well, okay, maybe she gets a little hot under the collar now and then. But it's a big jump from that to killing the guy. Besides, she hates guns and she hates blood. She flunked biology in high school because she wouldn't go to labs. I can't imagine her standing in close proximity to a dying man and shooting him in the face."

"But if she thought she was protecting Hannah—"

"Not even then. What's more, the killer was a good shot. Terri, frankly, isn't. Half the time she'd close her eyes when she pulled the trigger."

"That's going to be hard stuff to play before a jury."

"I know, but here's something else. Remember the smudged

handprint the police found on the railing?" There was an excited quality to Steven's voice.

"Not clear enough to make an identification."

"No, but they could tell it was a left hand."

"And Terri is left-handed."

"Which would mean that she'd be holding the gun in her left hand. It would have been the killer's free hand that made the print."

Not exactly a slam-dunk for the defense, but it was something.

CHAPTER 23

Jared nudged me with his elbow as we left the courtroom Thursday the following week. "Hey, boss."

"What?" We'd struck out repeatedly that morning in pretrial motions to exclude evidence. I was not in a good mood.

"Isn't that the big man himself?" Jared gestured in the direction of the figure striding toward us with his distinctive, uneven gait. District Attorney Ray Shalla, in the flesh.

"No doubt coming by to gloat."

"Too soon for that," Jared pointed out. "Unless he has a direct line to the courtroom."

"Right. I forget it takes at least an hour for news to travel these hallowed halls."

Shalla's gaze drifted our way. He gave a nod of recognition, then with a casual oh-by-the-way change of course, he veered to meet us face on. Although it was a convincing performance, I would bet the meeting was anything but accidental. Maybe he had a direct line, after all.

Shalla smoothed his tie. It was an elegant silk in shades of ruby and teal. "How's it going, counselor? Gearing up for the big day?"

"I'm looking forward to it. So is my client. She's tired of being in jail for something she didn't do."

The tie got another pressing. "You know, it's not too late to talk about some sort of accommodation."

"Plea bargain, you mean."

He seemed to consider the term. *Accommodation* certainly had a better ring to it. Finally, with a half-shrug, he acquiesced. "Call it what you will."

"I don't think we're interested, but I'll run it by her."

Much as I would have liked to think Shalla's scrambling reflected a weak case, I suspected it was more a matter of bad press. He'd taken on Terri Harper in the hopes of boosting his ratings with the liberal electorate. No breaks for the rich and famous; District Attorney Ray Shalla played it straight. But he'd ended up shooting himself in the foot, at least with a large segment of women voters.

As the tide of public sentiment became clear, the mayor had begun to distance himself from the case. And now Shalla was alone in the hot seat. There'd be no chance for redemption if the prosecution lost at trial. If he could get Terri to admit guilt, however, his reputation would remain intact.

"Be sure you do that," Shalla said with a fatherly crinkle of his eyes. "The state's case is solid. She should think long and hard before rejecting the offer."

"I'll tell her that." Not that he'd actually made an offer.

He looked at Jared, male-to-male. "Tough lady you work for. And a good attorney. You can learn a lot from her."

Shalla's groveling surprised me. He was more eager for a plea than I'd thought. And not nearly as bright if he imagined he could manipulate me with flattery.

Jared looked amused. "She's also a good person."

"Well said, young man." A good-natured grin pasted itself onto his fleshy features. Shalla in public figure mode. "If you get tired of working for the defense, be sure to give me a call. There just might be room for you here."

Jared matched the smile. And probably the degree of sincerity. "Thanks. I'll remember that."

Shalla scratched his cheek, broadened his focus to address both of us. "You know, that witness list of yours is all over the map. If you're playing fast and loose—"

"The names are legit."

Both the prosecution and the defense were required to submit a list of potential witnesses. They weren't, however, required to give any hints as to the expected testimony. The upshot was a sort of witness scavenger hunt, where each side tried to garner information about the other side's witnesses.

"Clyde Billings and Len Roemer, for example." Shalla

frowned as if in concentration. "They were old friends of Weaver's, right?"

I nodded. That was hardly giving away the store. Besides, the police had talked to both of them.

"But Alexander Rudd, that's a name that hasn't come up in any of the reports that I've seen."

We'd listed Rudd although we'd had no luck so far in tracing him. Nick had learned that Sophia Rudd's only son, thirty-four-year-old Alexander, had supposedly died five years ago when his car plunged off a cliff and into the ocean near Big Sur. Yet we were fairly certain that's who the pizza man was. Bea, who'd been back to see Mrs. Rudd on several occasions, had tried to ferret out the truth, to no avail. Surprisingly, Mrs. Rudd had welcomed Bea's visits, but she refused to talk about her son or the man who had delivered pizza to her house each Sunday until recently.

"How's he connected to the case?" Shalla asked.

I gave an enigmatic smile. "Just one piece of a very complex puzzle."

"You aren't playing games, are you?"

Gamesmanship was the essence of trial work—but there were strict rules of play.

"Scout's honor, no games." I held up two fingers.

The muscle in Shalla's cheek twitched. His expression was hard to read but I could tell he wasn't pleased.

"For what it's worth," I added, "I have questions of my own about some of the names on the prosecution's list."

He seemed on the verge of saying something, then backtracked. "More pieces of the puzzle. Well, good talking to you." He turned and headed off, his limp slightly more visible from the rear.

Jared waited until he'd gone only a few paces before asking, "Whew, what was that all about?"

"I'm not sure. But I'd bet he didn't run into us by chance."

"He seemed pretty anxious to work out a plea," Jared said. "Must mean we have him scared."

I only wished I knew why. And why the district attorney himself, rather than the prosecutor of record, was the one asking.

When I got back to the office, I found a message on the machine from Ranelle Mosher, Weaver's ex-girlfriend. Just when I'd given up hope of ever hearing from her, she'd finally returned my call.

I dialed the number and she picked up on the second ring.

"Sorry to be so late getting back to you," she said. "I've been out of town all week. My answering machine really got a work-out." A laugh fluttered across the wire. I pictured a blonde, with pronounced curves and big hair. "You said it was about Bram."

I hesitated, not certain she was aware of his death. It had been all over the news locally, but Ranelle Mosher was living in Boston.

"Is it something about his will?" she asked.

So she did know. I forged ahead, equally uncertain about her reaction to what came next. "I represent the woman who is charged with his murder."

"The one who wanted to adopt Bram's baby. I heard about that." Her tone gave away nothing of her feelings about it.

I didn't bother to explain that Hannah wasn't Bram's child.

"I have no clue who killed him," Ranelle Mosher continued, as though I'd asked. "Not the foggiest. I only spoke to him once after I moved away, and that was . . . gosh, months ago."

"How long were you and Bram together?"

Her laugh was a bitter stab. "I don't think we were ever really together. That was the problem. Bram was interested in Bram. And in his own pleasures, which included proving everyone else wrong. But we dated for almost two years. I'm a slow learner."

She and I could form a club. "When did you break up?"

"Officially, the end of December. But things weren't going well before that. Looking back, it kills me the crap I took from him. And I'm only talking the stuff I knew about. Now I discover he was banging some eighteen-year-old at the same time. Jesus, she's only a few years older than his son."

I picked up a pen and began doodling. A stick figure, to which I added a skirt and curly hair. And then a very pregnant belly. Where had that come from?

"Have you met Dan?" I asked, tossing the paper into the trash.

"Just brief hellos. Weird kid. He started coming around occa-sionally after he switched to a boarding school in the city. Bram pretty much ignored him, except to belittle him."

"How'd Dan react? I imagine he'd be pretty hurt and angry."

"Hard to tell. Like I said, the kid's weird. Tell the truth, I don't know why he wanted anything to do with Bram." Ranelle Mosher paused, then made a sound of disgust. "Guess for the same reasons I did. Pathetic the way some of us are so hungry for attention."

Maybe not such big hair after all, I thought. And mentally toned down the curves as well. "Did you know any of Bram's friends?"

"I'd see them at parties and stuff. But mostly when Bram and I got together, it was just the two of us."

"How about the names *Len Roemer, Clyde Billings, Hank Lomax?* You know any of them?"

"I've met them. Roemer and Billings were friends of Bram's from way back. Boys' club kind of thing. Hank was initially a friend of Roemer's, I think. But they were all four pretty close by the time I met Bram. They'd get together about once a week. Mostly for poker or Monday night football, but sometimes they'd go out on the town, too."

"Womanizing?" The word sounded old-fashioned but it seemed to fit.

"I don't think so. I certainly didn't think so then. I wasn't so stupid I'd have put up with *that.* Billings is married. Kind of straightlaced and nerdy. Doesn't seem the type. Hank was married too, although his wife left him just before Bram and I broke up so I guess he might have been messing around on the side. Mostly, though, I got the impression it was just guys being guys. And some computer software company or something that they were trying to get off the ground."

"Computers?" Everybody and his brother, it seemed. At least in the Bay Area. High-tech startup was the goldrush of the new millennium.

"I don't know whether they ever followed through."

Nick had reported a heated discussion between Weaver and Roemer over a business venture. "Could this idea for a company have become a point of contention?" I asked.

"What do you mean?"

"Friendship and business. They don't always mix well."

"It wasn't something Bram and I talked about. From what I could tell, though, the four of them were pretty tight."

"Do you recall anyone Bram *did* have disagreements with?"

She thought for a moment. "Half the female population?"

"You talking about the Women's Alliance?"

"Actually, I was joking. The interesting thing is that Bram could be quite charming. I realize now how manipulative he was, but he had the tender, soulful stuff down pat. Sorry I can't be of more help."

"I appreciate the call. Thanks." Billings, Roemer, and Lomax again. And this time in connection with a software company.

Saturday afternoon I slipped into a rayon print sun dress and sandals—the sort of outfit that sits in my closet all year waiting for one of the rare opportunities I have to wear such things—and headed for Steven's. A barbecue in the East Bay wasn't exactly a Renoir garden party, but I took along my wide-brimmed straw hat with the satin band as well. Like I said, it was a rare opportunity.

When I'd known him five years earlier, Steven had lived in a tall Victorian on Broderick in San Francisco. He and Caroline had been in the final stages of a home remodel, but even with the missing baseboards and curtainless windows, their home had been stunning—although a little too lavish and decorator-perfect for my tastes.

Now Steven lived across the bay in a small bungalow in Berkeley's Elmwood district, not far from my own place in the hills. The houses along the tree-lined street were small, but they had yards, which his place in San Francisco hadn't. I pushed open the squat, white picket gate, and climbed the few stairs to the entrance. The door was open. Two men were standing just inside, discussing some fine point of rock climbing. I made my way past them to the kitchen, where the buzz of activity was louder, taking in what I could see of the house along the way.

It had potential, but Steven hadn't taken that route. Fresh paint, metal blinds, furniture that could have come off any budget showroom in the country. The place was well kept but not in any way remarkable.

"Hey, Kali. Glad you could make it." Steven was checking something in the oven, but he turned to give me an all-purpose hug and peck on the cheek.

I'd told myself the smart thing would be to play it safe and skip the party. Working together on Terri's defense didn't mean we had to socialize as well. But every time I'd thought about calling to say I couldn't make it, I'd wavered. What harm could come of an afternoon barbecue?

Now with the warm strength of that quick hug and Steven's familiar scent, I wasn't so sure.

Steven tossed a pot holder onto the counter and introduced me to a nearby couple. After a moment's small talk, he was called away outside. The couple moved on.

Beer was in an ice chest by the door, wine on a nearby table, along with bowls of tortilla chips and salsa. A dozen or so people were mingling in the kitchen and on the adjoining backyard patio. I poured myself a glass of Chardonnay and began to make the rounds.

The gathering was largely university people, I learned as the afternoon progressed, with a sprinkling of neighbors. I was a lawyer Steven had done some work for, I explained, though the conversation came inevitably to Terri. It seemed that everyone there was aware of the case, and Steven's involvement.

As I moved off to refill my wineglass, a short, curly-haired man with a pronounced New York accent seized the opportunity to catch me alone for a minute.

"You going to get Terri Harper off?" he asked.

I offered an enigmatic smile. "I sure hope so."

"Me too. Her arrest has hit Steven hard. The two of them are very close."

"I know." Since my own brother and I spoke maybe once or twice a year, the tenor of their bond made an impression on me.

"Crazy business, this legal system of ours," he said, reaching for a handful of chips.

"How so?"

"Don't get me wrong. I think it's far better than most. It's just that truth sometimes gets lost in the fray. You're a defense attorney. Your job is to argue as vehemently as possible for your client's innocence. But don't you ever wonder what truth is?"

All the time. But my response was standard law school rhetoric. "It's not a question defense lawyers are supposed to concern themselves with. That's for the judge and jury."

"Yeah, I know. I understand the theory. But my professional orientation is in getting to the bottom of things. Peeling away the facades and lies in order to learn what's really going on. I'd have a hard time operating only on the surface."

I smiled, happy for an entree to a different topic. "Psychology, I bet."

"Yep. Steven and I go way back. We were in grad school together. Then I went east when he came west. I've only lived in the Bay Area about five years." He shifted his wineglass and extended a hand. "I'm Martin Bloomberg."

"Kali O'Brien."

"I know." Martin's round face pulled to a wide grin. "Steven's told me all about you."

I swallowed uneasily, but offered light banter in return. "Only the good stuff, I hope."

"What else could there be?" There was a hint of unspoken knowledge in his voice that gave me pause. How much of our past had Steven told him?

"You knew him from before Caroline and Rebecca were killed," Martin continued.

"Right." I was on edge, waiting for the verbal blows I suspected he might deliver. Martin was, as far as I'd been able to determine, the only one at the gathering who'd known Steven before the accident. And he'd hinted that he was aware of our relationship. I wouldn't blame him for a little pent-up anger.

Martin seemed lost in thought for a moment. "You know the cops dropped the ball, don't you?"

It was so far from what I was expecting, I wasn't sure I'd followed. "The cops?"

"Investigating the hit-and-run. The first guy that had the case, Joe Moran, he seemed to be making an effort. In fact, he told Steven he'd made progress. But after he died, no one gave a damn. The case got reassigned and there was no follow-through."

"They may have done more than it appeared."

He looked at me with cynicism.

"It's hard picking up someone else's case," I explained. "And the chances of solving a crime, particularly one like hit-and-run, decline substantially after the first couple of days."

"I'm aware of that." The skepticism remained. "That doesn't change the fact that they didn't pursue it like they should have. I was still in the East so I got most of this secondhand, but I know how frustrated and discouraged Steven was." He paused. "Is, still."

I'd worked with enough victims' families to know that an unsolved crime was like an open wound. But I also knew that the closure families expected a conviction to bring was often elusive.

"It changed him," Martin said.

"Changed how?"

"It's not something I can put my finger on. He's still one of my best friends, but there's something missing. It's like there's a black hole deep inside him that tugs at his soul. You don't notice it?"

I shook my head. It made me realize how little I really knew Steven.

Martin picked up another chip and dipped it in salsa. He studied me for a minute while he swallowed his mouthful. "Do you think you could get a look at the police file on the case?" he asked.

"It's been five years," I reminded him.

Martin nodded. "Five years of Steven beating himself up. Five years of gradually losing his spirit."

"Even if he could find the driver at this point, you think it would make a difference to Steven?"

Martin swished the wine in the bottom of his glass. "Maybe not. But I'm worried about him. Especially with Terri's troubles. That black hole I was talking about wasn't more than a pinprick until she found herself in trouble. Now it's like . . ." He smiled. "I don't want to get too far out with this metaphor, but it's like the bad stuff is gaining fast."

A woman with her hair pulled into a single braid joined us. Martin introduced me to his wife, Peg. She was short and round, with apple cheeks and a generous smile.

"Steven's looking for you," she told her husband. "He needs some help with the salmon."

Martin made a gesture of salute. He turned to me as he headed off. "It can't hurt to try."

"Let me guess," Peg said. "Something to do with helping Steven."

"Your husband is worried about him."

"I know. So am I. But I think there's only so much any of us can do for him." She brushed her hands against her skirt. "I hate to run off, but Steven put me in charge of the salads, and I need to get working on them."

"Can you use some help?"

She smiled. "I'd love it."

We moved to the other side of the kitchen, where Peg set me to peeling and slicing an avocado.

"Personally, I think Steven will be fine once Terri is out of jail." Peg was wiping the nicked Formica counter top. She paused and raised her eyes to mine. "Assuming that happens."

I nodded. The idea of Terri spending the rest of her life in prison made me weak in the knees.

Peg took a Jell-O mold from the refrigerator. "How's Terri holding up?"

"Pretty well under the circumstances."

"She's a fighter."

I dumped the avocado pit into the garbage. "You know her?"

"Only through Steven. We see her maybe a couple of times a year. Usually at one of the big family events." Peg nodded to a framed photograph on the buffet. "Like that one this last spring. It was me behind the camera."

I wiped my hands and went to examine the photo. A headshot of Lenore and Terri grinning into the camera from the deck of the Harpers' Napa Valley home. With their sunglasses and wide-brimmed hats, they looked like they'd stepped from the pages of *Town and Country*.

"That was the day Terri and Ted learned Melissa had chosen them to adopt her baby. We were all giddy with excitement. Lenore and Terri spent the afternoon making up lists of things the baby would need. I think they had six pages by the time we were all finished giving them input. And now . . ." Peg's voice trailed off. "It's hard to believe all that's happened since then."

And harder still to contemplate what was ahead.

CHAPTER 24

I dreamed of Steven that night, though we'd barely exchanged two private words the entire evening. It was one of those sexy, arousing dreams, painted in bold sweeps of color and emotion. Incredibly vivid and intense; totally illogical. The minute I awoke, I was embarrassed at the memory, but eager to recapture the feeling. It had been a long time since I'd felt that way in real life.

But did I actually want to head in that direction with Steven? If he'd called me Sunday morning when I was still under the sway of my dream, I would undoubtedly have done something rash. But by mid-week, I again had both feet planted firmly on solid ground. I was lucky, I told myself, that he hadn't called. And I gratefully buried myself in work.

"Nothing," Nick said, peering at me over steepled fingers. He rested one leg on the corner of my desk. "No record of any business involving Roemer, Billings, Weaver, and Lomax. Not the four of them, not any pair of them. I checked official records as well as tapping into the gossip network. If these guys were into some sort of software or high-tech business, they've done a good job of keeping it quiet."

Nick had dropped by my office instead of calling because he was in the East Bay on other business. He'd brought bagels with lox and cream cheese—not the reduced-fat variety. And double lattes for both of us, whole milk instead of skim. For Nick, the calories didn't matter. He was a big guy, over six feet and athletic. With me, it was a different story. But I'd skipped breakfast and been ravenous all morning so I dug in anyway.

"I guess it never materialized," I said, using my finger to wipe up a smear of cream cheese.

"Or is still in the early planning stage. There's plenty of opportunity for disagreement even at that stage. Maybe especially at that stage. It's just harder for outsiders to find out what's going on before the thing is up and running."

Assuming there was anything going on at all. Friends argued; it didn't mean there was enough animosity to lead to murder.

Nick slid a thin stack of manila folders across the table. "These are reports on the key prosecution witnesses. No skeletons in anyone's closet, unfortunately. On the other hand, no one can positively place Terri at the scene of the crime."

"Any word on our friend Alexander Rudd?"

Nick shook his head. "Vanished into thin air, as far as I can tell. Hasn't shown up for his job at Pizza Pizazz and hasn't been to his apartment."

"What about the accident where he supposedly died?"

"Single car, rainy night. There was nothing ambiguous about the reports. Nothing untoward in his background either. No record, no impending bankruptcy, no nasty divorce. The guy was manager of an autobody shop. Lived alone, was active in his church, volunteered as part of the Big Brother program."

"So why fake his own death?"

"No idea. I've only researched records so far. If you want, I can try to locate people who knew him at the time."

To what end? Rudd had piqued my interest, but in terms of our case, the only important thing was whether he'd seen anyone on the street at the time of the murder. Anyone besides Terri, that is. No point chasing after a needle in the haystack when you weren't sure it was even there. In any event, we had more pressing matters to address.

"No," I told him. "Better to put your energies elsewhere."

"Speaking of which . . ." He reached into his briefcase. "Here's a preliminary report on the Coles. The gun that killed her first husband was a .44 caliber. Mrs. Cole was questioned, but never arrested."

"What about Mr. Cole?"

Nick shook his head. "Name didn't come up in connection with the crime. No police record. No complaints against the plumbing business. No Explorer either. One of their cars is a Toyota Camry, the other, a dark-colored van. Might be that someone could confuse a van for an Explorer though."

"Is there a gun registered to either of them?"

"No, but that doesn't mean much." Nick slid another sheet of paper in my direction. "Here's what I've got on Suzze Madden. Thirty-eight, single, no car. Active in the gay and lesbian community. Arrested once for protesting, but that's it. Here's the interesting thing though—she's a gun fanatic. Active member of the NRA. Teaches a marksmanship class for women and has three guns registered to her. One is a .25 caliber Beretta. "

I felt a jolt of excitement. "What about her connection with Bram Weaver?"

Nick shook his head. "Nothing I found, but based on what Trimble told you, she was at least a thorn in his side."

"Maybe I should go see her myself."

"Better you than me, for sure." He grinned. "I didn't fare so well with the other matter you mentioned."

"Which other matter?" We'd talked about several.

"The hit-and-run with Steven Cross's wife and daughter. The original investigating officer was a guy by the name of Moran. He may well have been making progress on the case, but he kept lousy notes. Anyone coming in after him would have had to start over, which is probably why the case fell through the cracks after his death."

I hadn't expected he'd find anything new, but the Bloombergs' concern about Steven had triggered my own. And since I'd been part of the initial problem, bringing some sort of resolution seemed the least I could do.

"You're saying it was bad luck rather than police incompetence, then."

Nick swung a leg over the chair's arm. "It happens. Some of us are sprinkled with fairy dust; some aren't. Life's not fair."

"You should have been a philosopher."

"I actually thought about it. Until I took a philosophy course." He grinned. "That cured me for good."

"There was nothing in the file that even hinted at what Moran learned?"

"Just the witness statement you already know about. Young woman saw a light-color car. Gray or white. Maybe a BMW. No license number, no distinguishing marks aside from a KEEP TAHOE BLUE bumper sticker, and you know how common those are. Plus the crime scene and autopsy reports. No surprises there either."

Steven had talked to the witness himself. Even under hypnosis she hadn't been able to remember anything more about the car or the driver. "Pretty thin investigative report, considering we're talking about two lives."

"Moran only had it about ten days, and like I said, he wasn't much for keeping records." Nick waded up his napkin and tossed it in the wastebasket. "His widow says she has a box of her husband's effects. She's happy to let us take a look. It's in storage, though, so we need to make an appointment."

"What kind of effects?"

"From his desk, locker, that sort of thing. She says Steven Cross looked through them already so I doubt there's anything there."

Nick checked his watch, then rocked forward abruptly. "Gotta scoot. I'll keep digging on Weaver's buddies, see what turns up."

"Good. But we're going to have to cut our losses fairly soon and prepare for trial with what we've got. September 15 is less than a month away."

That was how I intended to spend the remainder of the morning—preparing our defense. But after an hour, it became clear that I couldn't focus on trial preparation when other loose ends tickled my mind.

I called Moran's widow and set a time for Nick and me to look through the box of her husband's belongings. Then I climbed into my car and headed south to pay Clyde Billings a face-to-face visit.

Star Systems' headquarters were housed in a concrete low-rise with minimal landscaping and ample parking, a configuration that rendered it indistinguishable from hundreds of others in Silicon Valley.

Inside was a reception counter, empty. I waited, coughed, peered around the head-high partition to the vast warren of cubicles beyond. I heard the hum of conversation and the clicking of computer keys, but the people themselves were tucked out of sight behind sleek gray panels.

I tried making more noise. Nothing. Then a young man in

jeans and a white cotton crew-neck T-shirt emerged from what was presumably the coffee room. Carrying a steaming cup, he started to walk past me.

"Excuse me, I'm looking for Clyde Billings."

He slowed. "Talk to Gloria at the reception desk."

"She's not there."

A large sigh. "Is Clyde expecting you?"

"Yes." He must have been. Maybe not today, but he couldn't really expect that I'd let his threatening phone call be the end of it.

The young man shifted his coffee to his other hand and pointed. "Go down that way. When you get to a wall, turn right. Clyde's cube is on the left, just past the green exit sign."

"Thanks."

As I followed the directed route, I peered now and then into the interior work areas. I've never understood how anyone is able to work in a cubicle. To my mind, it's a shortsighted approach to cutting costs—though I've been told it's a management philosophy as much as an economic factor. But how often do you see a company president holding forth from a cubicle?

I found Clyde Billings' work space. His name was on the partition wall but he was nowhere in sight. I stepped inside anyway.

His space was neat as a pin, unlike many of the individual work areas I'd passed on my way there. Except for a small framed photograph of his wife and kids, there was nothing on the desktop. No Post-It notes stuck to the computer, no silly cartoons or personal mementos tacked to the corkboard walls. I peered into the trash can, which contained only an empty yogurt carton. Strawberry.

"You looking for something?"

The woman standing behind me in the entrance appeared to be in her mid-twenties, with spiky blue hair and a pierced nose.

"Clyde Billings." A some*one* rather than a some*thing*, but she might not notice.

"He's at a meeting," she said, giving me a wary look. "How'd you get back here anyway?"

"My feet." The words were out before I'd taken time to think.

The young woman made a face. It was clear she didn't appreciate glib humor.

"The receptionist wasn't in," I explained, endeavoring to counter my earlier flipness. "A man, one of your coworkers I presume, gave me directions."

"Figures. Gloria is never at the desk. I don't know how she's managed to hold on to her job as long as she has." The woman stepped into the cubicle. "My name's Jana. If you're here to see Clyde about the budget allocation, maybe I can help. I did all the work."

"No, it's . . . personal."

Jana giggled, which struck me somehow as an odd response coming from someone with spiky blue hair. "I didn't know Clyde had a personal life."

"What makes you say that?"

She shrugged. "He's here a lot."

"How is he to work with?"

"Okay." Another half-shrug.

"Except that he wants to take credit for your work," I said.

Jana narrowed her eyes at me. "The guy's a control freak. He doesn't make cooperative effort easy."

I gave her a girl-to-girl nod of understanding. "I know the type. Has he ever mentioned Bram Weaver?"

"That jerky radio guy who was murdered? Why would Clyde mention *him?*"

"Just wondering. How about a business venture he was involved in with friends. Any mention of that?"

She frowned. "Are you with the police or something?"

I debated stretching the truth a bit, then shook my head. "I'm an attorney."

It's an admission that often has an effect on people, sometimes positive, sometimes not. Jana wasn't reassured.

"You shouldn't be back here," she said, turning cool again. "It's company policy. I don't know which moron let you in but he shouldn't have."

"Let me leave a note for Clyde and I'll be on my way." First name only, like we had a standing and cordial relationship.

A voice from the corridor called to Jana. "I've been looking for you. You've got a phone call."

Jana hesitated. I grabbed a piece of paper from my purse and started scribbling. Finally, she left to take her phone call and I stuffed the paper back into my purse. I took another quick look around the cubicle. It was neater than any office of mine ever looked, even after I'd spent the afternoon cleaning up.

With a glance over my shoulder, I hit one of the keyboard keys. The screen saver vanished and a list of programs appeared. If I'd had time . . . But I didn't, I reminded myself. A flashing mailbox at the bottom of the screen caught my eye. With another look over my shoulder, I clicked on it.

Clyde Billings had three new messages. Two originated in-house and had been sent to multiple recipients. The third was from Hank Lomax. It was short and to the point.

"I still think we should reconsider. Especially now, with all that's happened."

He'd copied Billings' original message as well. *"Forget what Bram said,"* Billings had written. *"He's not part of this anymore."*

I heard steps in the hallway and clicked out of mail. But the screen saver hadn't come on, and it wasn't likely to do so in time.

In a desperate attempt to cover myself, I stepped back against the keyboard as if I'd knocked it accidentally.

The man who appeared in the entry to the cubicle was about my height, on the thin side, and prematurely balding.

"Who are you? And what are you doing in my office?"

I held out my hand. "Kali O'Brien. Pleased to meet you, Mr. Billings."

His anger apparently interfered with his eyesight because he said nothing about the computer screen. "I thought I told you to stay away."

He who must be obeyed. From his tone, it sounded as though that was the usual course of things.

"You may have," I told him. "But I wanted to talk to you about Bram Weaver."

"You're part of the conspiracy that got him killed. I've got nothing to say to you."

"Conspiracy?"

"Women who think men don't matter."

"Mr. Billings, I'm an—"

"I know who you are. And what you do. I'm warning you. Keep away from me." His voice was pitched low and tight. It radiated hostility.

If we'd been anywhere but in a sea of workstations, I might have been scared. As it was, I felt irritated rather than fearful. "I have a question about the business you're in with Len Roemer and Hank Lomax. The one Weaver was part of."

"Get out," he said. "Or I'm calling Security." He reached for the phone.

"If you won't talk now, I guess I'll have to subpoena you at trial." An empty threat since I'd be hard pressed to find a reason to do so.

"Get out."

I left my card on his desk. "In case you change your mind."

Nick had given me the address of the rape crisis center where Suzze Madden worked. I didn't know if I'd find her there on a weekday afternoon, but it was worth a try.

I drove north on 101 and got off near Market Street.

Once again, no receptionist. But I could see two women with coffee cups talking in a back room.

The woman facing the door had looked up when I entered. "Can I help you?"

"I'm looking for Suzze Madden."

"That's me," said the other woman, turning. She rose and came to greet me.

I'd been expecting stocky, maybe even burly. Features pinched into a permanent scowl. Trimble had said she was tough as nails. Nick had told me she was a gun enthusiast. I know it's not fair to think in stereotypes, but that doesn't stop my mind from forming images.

In this case, I was about as far off base as I could be. Suzze Madden was drop-dead gorgeous. Tall and slender, with emerald eyes and straight blond hair that fell just short of her shoulders.

"What can I do for you?" she asked.

"My name is Kali O'Brien. I'm an attorney representing the woman accused of killing Bram Weaver."

She raised a brow slightly, but said nothing.

"I'd like to talk with you, if I may."

"Me? Why?" Her voice wasn't as silky as her appearance. It was hard, almost reproachful.

"I was hoping you could tell me about Weaver. About your interactions with him."

She laughed harshly. "Sure I can tell you about Weaver. He was a prick. Among other absurdities, he claimed no woman could be raped against her will. As far as I'm concerned, he was a threat to public safety."

"Is that why you were harassing him last year?"

"He's the one who was harassing women." She eyed me with disdain. "Don't tell me you're one of those mousy things who went along with him."

"Far from it."

She crossed her arms and smiled. "Good."

"It must be kind of a relief for you now that he's dead."

"There's plenty more like him."

"But none quite so vocal."

She shrugged. "Vocal or not, men are always trying to impose themselves on women."

"So what was it about Weaver that got you so riled?"

"He's dead, what does it matter?"

"I'm trying to get a better handle on who he was."

"Slime," she said. "That about sums it up in my opinion."

I feigned a cough. "Do you by any chance have a stick of gum or something. I have this tickle in my throat."

Suzze Madden gave me an odd look, but went into the back room and returned with her purse. "No gum, but I've got a breath mint. Maybe that will help."

Tall, blonde, good with a gun. A stick of Doublemint would have been a nice addition, but it wasn't a necessity.

"Thanks." I took the mint and handed her my card. "And thanks for your help. My client didn't kill Weaver. That means someone else did. Give me a call if you have any ideas who it might have been."

In the next few days, I made an initial stab at outlining our defense case. The strategy was fairly straightforward. No tricks, no rabbits pulled out of a hat. We'd simply take the prosecution's case point by point and show at each step how the evidence was subject to a different interpretation. We would undercut the credibility of prosecution witnesses. And we'd raise the specter of a different killer by playing up disputes in Weaver's personal and professional life.

I took a break from the case Thursday afternoon when Nick and I met with Mrs. Moran at the storage facility.

It was a small concrete block with a corrugated metal door, but inside she'd made one corner into something of a memorial to her husband. His photo rested atop an oak bureau and his uniform, cleaned and pressed, hung inside a clear garment bag.

"I had to move into a studio apartment not long after Joseph died," she said, pulling her cotton cardigan around her ample frame. "Space was limited, but I couldn't bear to throw away things that were his."

She went to the bureau, pulled out a leather box, and opened it. "This is his badge. Being a policeman was his life, the only thing he ever wanted to do. Some of the newer recruits, they're drawn to police work because the pay is decent and there are good benefits. But Joseph wanted to make the world a better place. The day he died, in fact, he told me at breakfast how important it was to do what was right, even when it wasn't pleasant or easy."

"He had a heart attack?" I asked.

She nodded. For a moment her expression clouded, as though she were reliving the day. "It was completely unexpected. Joseph kept his weight down, exercised regularly. His last medical exam showed nothing. He was only fifty-six. His parents lived into their eighties."

"How'd it happen?" Nick asked gently.

"It was a Sunday. I'd gone shopping. Joseph was out in the garage, tinkering with his wood projects. When I came back, I found him crumpled on the floor. I called 9-1-1 immediately, but it was already too late." She paused to look again at his badge. "If only I hadn't gone shopping and left him alone. I wasn't even looking for anything in particular."

"It might not have made a difference," I offered. "Your being there."

"That's what the doctor said. It was a massive heart attack and there was nothing I could have done. But I'm sure I would have noticed that Joseph was out of sorts. Maybe I could have persuaded him to lie down or call the doctor."

"Out of sorts?" I asked.

"He must have been feeling a bit rocky. The side door to the garage was open. Joseph always kept it shut because the dirt blew in from the yard. He must have thought the fresh air would do him good. That's how he was. Hell could freeze over before he'd admit he felt ill. He'd just say he needed air or he'd eaten too much."

Another pause during which her mind seemed to drift. Finally she pulled a box from the stack of cartons to the left of the bureau. "Here's the stuff from his office desk. Not the official papers and reports, of course. Those were all retained at headquarters. But the department gave me what was left after they'd taken what they wanted."

"Did your husband keep a notebook that wasn't part of the official record?" It was not an uncommon practice, particularly among the older generation of cops.

"Sometimes he'd jot things down as he thought of them. On scraps of paper, though, not in any central place. Mostly he kept stuff in his head. Joseph had an incredible memory. I know that made things hard for the officers taking over his cases. I got an earful a time or two, like I'd been the one responsible."

Nick peered into the box. "Did your husband talk to you about his work?"

"I know you're interested in that hit-and-run. Joseph mentioned it to me in general terms, but not the particulars. Someone from the DA's office grilled me about it at the time, and Mr. Cross himself came to see me. He was understandably frustrated by the department's lack of progress."

"This was soon after your husband's death?"

She nodded. "Joseph worked hard on that case. It really bothered him because we have a granddaughter who was the same age. He never said anything about the case being stalled. In fact, he seemed pretty satisfied with the headway he was making."

As important as the case was to him, Joseph Moran had done a lousy job of documenting his progress. I could understand Steven's disappointment.

"Take your time," Mrs. Moran said, brushing dust from the top of the box. "I'm going to see if I can put some order to this box of old photographs."

While she sorted through photos, Nick and I went through the odds and ends from Joseph Moran's desk. There was a magazine of do-it-yourself home projects, a word-a-day calendar, an assortment of pens and rulers, an appointment card for an upcoming dentist visit, a business card from Henzel's Auto Works, receipts for postage, an ATM withdrawal slip, and an ad for leather jackets from Macy's.

I leafed through the calendar but it was blank. Something he'd probably used for building his vocabulary rather than keeping track of meetings.

Nick caught my eye and made an empty-handed gesture. I nodded.

I thanked Mrs. Moran for letting us look through her husband's things. Then Nick and I headed for the car.

Despite the fact I hadn't expected to find anything useful, I felt the weight of disappointment. And the cool shadow of my own guilt over the deaths of Steven's wife and daughter.

CHAPTER 25

Iwas sitting at my desk the next morning, staring at the phone and wishing I were barefoot on the beach instead of stockinged and office-bound. I'd intended to call Hank Lomax ever since I'd stumbled onto his e-mail in Billings' office, but I kept putting it off because I couldn't figure out what I was going to say. Certainly not that I'd been prowling around Billings' cubicle without his knowledge. With a sigh, I picked up the receiver and punched in the number.

"Change your mind about sitting for a photo?" Hank asked when I'd given my name. He managed to make even the question sound slimy.

"Afraid not. But I was hoping you could tell me a little about this business venture you and Bram were involved in."

Dead air on the other end.

"The two of you along with Billings and Roemer."

I could hear caution in the continued silence. "What venture?" he asked finally.

"Your foray into the world of dot-coms." I tried to make it casual. "I'd like to round out my understanding of Weaver."

"Why?" The tone was contentious. "What do you care about Bram?"

It was a good question. One better skirted than answered. "Has the business gotten off the ground yet? I imagine Bram's death set things back a bit."

Hank laughed harshly. "I don't know where you get your information, lady. But I hope you aren't paying for it."

"You mean Clyde Billings wasn't being straight with me?"

Hank's mood changed abruptly. "When were you talking to Clyde?"

"Couple of days ago. He seemed kind of distracted. Said he'd just gotten an e-mail from you. That's how the subject happened to come up."

"Clyde told you about the website?"

Website. I was making progress. "Only in general terms."

"What did he say?"

"That . . . well, you know, that it was something the four of you had a stake in. But I got the impression that there were some sore spots where Bram was concerned."

"If you've got questions, ask Billings," Hank snapped. "Let him explain since he's feeling so talkative." He dropped the receiver back into the cradle with a resounding thunk.

The phone rang again almost as soon as I'd disconnected.

"Good news, boss."

"Jared? Where are you calling from?"

"You wanted me to canvass Terri's neighborhood, remember?"

The defense attorney's due diligence. No stone unturned.

"Well, guess what? The housekeeper for the family that lives across from the Harpers says she remembers seeing Terri at home the night Weaver was killed."

"She remembers the night?"

"Yep." Jared sounded pleased with himself. "It was her birthday."

"What time did she see Terri?"

"Around midnight."

"She's sure?"

"Seems to be."

Hallelujah. It was about time we got a break. "Where's she been for the past month?"

"Out of town. The family she works for spends the summer at Martha's Vineyard, so Mrs. Hassan goes to visit relatives."

I swiveled my chair sideways and leaned an elbow on my desk. "The neighbor who heard Terri's car in the driveway. Didn't she say that was about eleven-thirty?"

"That's my recollection."

"It would be hard for Terri to drive to Weaver's, shoot him, and be back home by midnight."

"Unless she drove like a maniac. Besides, the woman who saw the Explorer with a plate like Terri's said it was a little after midnight."

I felt the glow of excitement. "You get a gold star for the day, Jared."

"Thanks, but I always liked the smiley face better."

I spent the next hour searching the Web, but discovered I hadn't the faintest idea how to locate a website by the folks who ran it. Finally, I called and left a message for Nick. Then I read my e-mail and typed out a brief note to my sister, Sabrina. I avoided talking about the upcoming trial, and about Steven, which left me with very little to say. I managed a couple of paragraphs nonetheless and felt virtuous, if not particularly creative.

At six o'clock, I closed up the office, then spent longer than necessary in the tiny restroom down the hallway freshening my makeup and fluffing my hair. I was meeting Steven for a drink after work.

When he'd called to suggest it the day before, I'd hesitated for less than a second. Whether this letting down of my guard was for the best or not, remained to be seen.

We met at the Claremont in the Berkeley hills, a grand old hotel that had managed to hang on through lean years by parlaying its facilities into a conference center and its spacious grounds into a resort. The evening parking there was readily available and the after-work drink crowd more subdued than boisterous.

Steven had a beer; I had a glass of Chardonnay.

"I thought you were a red wine person," he said when the waiter brought our drinks.

"Depends on the occasion."

"There's a lot of that in life, I guess. Adapting to meet the moment, I mean." His tone was philosophical and I assumed he was talking about more than wine.

About us, maybe? I wondered, but his expression was grave, and there was nothing intimate about his manner.

We were seated by one of the broad windows overlooking the bay. The sun was still well above the horizon, but a blanket of fog hung off the coast. The night would be chilly.

"Good news for Terri," I said, and relayed what Jared told me earlier.

A spark of emotion flashed in his eyes. "Thank God."

I was struck by the intensity of concern. "Must be nice to have a sibling you're so connected to," I said. "My sister and I have gotten to the point where we can now carry on a cordial conversation, but we're far from close. And neither of us talk much to our brother."

"It's a mixed blessing." Steven's expression had gone flat. He took a sip of beer and gazed out the window.

"Especially, I imagine, when one of you is in trouble."

He looked at me and I could see the fine lines around his eyes. Worry lines. Was it the sharp light of the setting sun, or had I never really noticed before?

"We weren't always close," Steven said. He reached for a fistful of nuts from the basket the waiter brought. "I used to tease Terri mercilessly. I can't begin to count the number of times I reduced her to tears. Or worse."

"You?" I tried to imagine Steven as an obnoxious older brother, and failed miserably.

"Makes me cringe to remember some of the things I did. I think that's what got me interested in psychology to begin with— trying to understand myself."

"Were you successful?"

He laughed with a trace of bitterness. "Distressingly so."

"You're being hard on yourself tonight, aren't you?"

"Maybe I'm just burned out on humanity." He lifted his glass in my direction and gave me a rueful smile. "With certain notable exceptions. Thank you for checking the police files and going to see Moran's widow. Martin confessed he'd twisted your arm."

"I was happy to do it, but I didn't learn anything useful."

"I looked at the file myself back before the department started circling the wagons the minute they saw me coming. I appreciate what you did all the same." He held up a hand. "And if you say 'It's the least I could do,' I will jump across the table and give you a knock on the noggin."

I bit back the response that had been on the tip of my tongue. "You're welcome."

Steven had finished his beer and now signaled the waiter for another. "You want more wine?"

"I'd better not. Got to keep my head clear."

He grinned. "Not on account of me, I hope."

"Don't flatter yourself," I said with a smile. But once again he'd hit close to the mark.

Steven leaned back in the heavy upholstered chair, turning serious again. "What rankles is that the investigation was subject to such bad luck. Maybe Moran wouldn't have found the driver, but he was at least putting forth the effort. And I got the impression he was getting somewhere. Then, out of the blue, he has a heart attack and it turns out he's a shitty record keeper. You'd think the department would demand better notes."

"I imagine they do, in theory."

Steven looked grim. "Yeah, for all the good it does. What am I supposed to do, bring Moran back from the dead and file a complaint against him?" He sighed. "Sorry, I don't mean to sound so harsh. I feel bad the guy passed away. And I'm grateful he gave the investigation as much as he did."

"His widow said it was important to him personally because they had a granddaughter the same age as . . ." I faltered, unwilling to speak Rebecca's name aloud.

"You can say it," Steven said, looking me in the eye. "You're not going to remind me of anything I don't already remember."

"The same age as Rebecca." A granddaughter who was now twelve, whereas Rebecca would be forever seven.

"My biggest gripe," Steven continued, "is with the guy who took over for Moran. He wasn't interested at all. There was a gang killing that came down about the same time. The District Attorney's Office was actively involved in that. Shalla had just won the election, in fact. All the energy was focused on gang crime. Very newsworthy, very flashy. That's where his energies went."

Life, as the saying went, was a crap shoot. Even in arenas where it shouldn't be. The judicial system; the police system; systems in general. They could look like gold on paper but in the final analysis it came down to people and luck.

And Steven had lost out on both counts.

CHAPTER 26

The weeks before a trial are always tense and jammed with last-minute preparations. I made lists for myself, lists for Jared and Nick, then made lists of the lists. Some days I ate nothing; other days it seemed I ate continually, dropping crumbs of cookies and chips onto the keyboard while I worked. Loretta got her exercise thanks to Dotty, who started each day off with a healthy walk. For myself, healthy was a concept I put off until another time.

I'd scheduled a meeting with Carla Hassan for two o'clock in the afternoon at the house across from the Harpers', where she was employed as a live-in housekeeper. This was easier, she said, than coming to my office since she didn't drive.

She greeted me at the door then led me immediately down the hallway to the right and up the back stairs to her rooms on the third floor. "My employer knows you are coming," she said, "but I feel more comfortable talking here. I hope that is okay."

"Fine," I told her. "It's better, in fact, because I can see for myself how the windows of the two houses are aligned."

Carla Hassan looked to be in her late forties or early fifties. She'd worked for the same family for eight years and considered herself lucky to have found such a good position. Though not particularly animated, she was cordial and attentive. I thought she'd make a good impression on the jurors.

I took a seat at one end of a small settee on the wall opposite her bed. "Tell me about seeing Terri Harper in the window the night Bram Weaver was killed."

"It was just before I went to sleep. I looked out and saw a light on in that room there." She pointed to a corner room on the second floor of the Harpers'. "Mrs. Harper was walking the baby. She crossed several times in front of the window."

I peered out myself. In daylight, the Harpers' window revealed only a darkened reflection but I knew it would be different at night. "She had the light on?"

Ms. Hassan nodded. "Not bright, but enough to see Mrs. Harper in the room with the baby. She came to the window and looked out. The baby was in a blanket against her chest." Carla Hassan positioned her own hands as if burping a baby. "Like so."

We went over the timing again—she'd just finished the ironing, which she'd started after turning off the television at eleven o'clock. I established that Mrs. Hassan recognized Terri by sight and had in fact previously spoken with her and seen Hannah on the street. I explained what I would be asking of her at trial, and wrote down for her the directions to the Hall of Justice.

"It's probably easiest for you to take a cab," I said. "I can give you money now or reimburse you afterwards."

She lifted her chin slightly. "Afterwards is fine."

My interview with Carla Hassan had taken only about twenty minutes, half of the time I'd planned. I'd arranged to meet Lenore at the Harpers' in order to go over her testimony prior to trial. I was early, but I rang the bell anyway.

Lenore answered the door herself and brushed away my apology for arriving ahead of time.

"It doesn't matter," she said. "I'm here. I was just getting Hannah her bottle." There were dark circles under Lenore's eyes and her cheeks were sunken. Terri's arrest had been hard on her.

I followed her into the kitchen.

"You talked to the neighbor's housekeeper?"

"I was just there. She'll be a good witness, I think."

Relief showed on Lenore's face. "It's about time something went right."

"I'd like to see the nursery, though. To make sure I understand the layout."

"Of course. Just let me test the temperature of Hannah's bottle and we'll go right up." She took the bottle from the stove and sprinkled a bit of formula on her forearm in a time-honored fashion. Then she grabbed a couple of paper towels and we climbed the wide, carpeted stairway to the second floor.

Steven was there, sitting in the rocker, with Hannah in his lap. He was singing to her softly.

He looked up when we entered and stopped singing, but my mind had captured that first image and held it in a sort of freeze-frame. I felt a tiny ping in my chest like the release of a spring, and a renewed rush of sorrow for the loss Steven had endured.

I'd known him as a lover and as a friend. Astute, perceptive, funny, but he'd been in many ways defined by the adult environment in which we'd traveled. This was something new. A man with an infant. Tender and loving. I wondered how much Hannah reminded him of his own daughter, and how he could possibly bear the memories.

"Hi, Kali." He rose. "Come take a look at Hannah. She's got the most amazing blue eyes. Just like Rebecca's."

I moved closer and peered into the folds of the blanket. Hannah's eyes were big and wide. She watched me with such intensity, I felt she might be able to read my thoughts. I sent a silent promise. *We're going to get your mother home to you.*

"Why don't I feed her," Steven said, "while you two go over what you need to."

"You have the time?" Lenore asked.

"Of course I have the time." Steven sounded almost grumpy.

I stepped to the window and peered out toward Carla Hassan's room across the street. The glass was darkened by the glare from outside, but I recognized the tie-back curtains I'd seen when I met with Carla. At night, with interior lighting, it would be easy to see from one room to the other.

Lenore and I headed back downstairs to the den. We sat on opposite ends of the sofa and I pulled out my notes.

"I'd like to go over this once more. Aside from Carla Hassan, you're the only person who can attest to Terri's being home the night Weaver was killed."

Lenore was sitting stiffly on the edge of the sofa, hands folded. "She didn't go out at all."

"After the visit in my office, you came straight home?"

"We stopped briefly at the grocery, but that was it."

"Did you watch television that evening? Read?"

Lenore sucked on her cheek, thinking. "We had dinner, though neither of us ate much as I recall. We were both pretty upset about

Weaver. We bathed Hannah, played with her some. Terri took a bath and went to bed early. Before ten. I wasn't up late myself."

"But she could have gone out after you went to bed."

Lenore shook her head. "I'm a light sleeper. And I was downstairs in the guest room. Near the garage. I'd have heard Terri leave."

"She gave you sleeping pills, though."

Surprise registered on Lenore's face. "How'd you know that?"

"Terri told me."

"I didn't take them until much later. I prefer not to take them at all. It wasn't until about two in the morning that I finally gave in. And I still didn't sleep well."

"Terri said you were agitated."

Lenore hesitated, then nodded. "About Hannah."

"How did Terri seem to you that night?"

"Worried. Sad. Scared."

"Angry?"

A small smile flickered across Lenore's lips. "Not as angry as I was."

"What about the next morning? Were you surprised when Terri suggested you head home?"

She shook her head. "I wasn't feeling well. I think I might have even suggested it myself."

Lenore was hardly an impartial witness, but I thought her testimony would help Terri. Especially since it corroborated what Carla Hassan had seen.

But there was so much uncertainty in a trial. Blind luck even. So much that had little to do with evidence and logic. I looked around the Harpers' home, Terri's home, and wondered if she'd ever see it again.

CHAPTER 27

On the first Monday after Labor Day, I met with Terri in the small attorney-client booth at the jail. The weather was hot; the room stuffy and stale. I could barely breathe, but Terri seemed not to notice.

"Tomorrow's the big day," she said, sounding almost jubilant. Even through the smudged glass partition, and in spite of the ill-fitting orange jumpsuit, she exuded energy. "Finally. For the longest time it felt like we'd never get to trial."

"Jury selection will take the first couple of days," I reminded her.

"But at least we'll be *doing* something." Terri leaned forward, not quite touching the glass. "I mean, I know you've been working all summer, but I've been just sitting here chomping at the bit. The waiting makes me want to scream."

"A trial puts it all on the line, though. It's not without risk."

"We've been over that, Kali. I'm not going to plead to something I didn't do. Not even for a reduced sentence."

"You should give it serious thought before you commit—"

"I want to be Hannah's mother. I want to be there when she's growing up. I want my life back. A plea bargain isn't going to give me that."

I could understand. In her place, I'd have made the same decision. But going to trial was a gamble. She could walk away a free woman, a mother with an infant and a wide-open future. Or she could remain locked up for life. A woman with only a past.

"I just want to make sure you've weighed the alternatives," I told her.

"I have. Believe me." Terri rolled her shoulders, whether from aching muscles or the burdens she faced, I couldn't tell. "Have you seen Hannah lately?" she asked.

"I saw her last week." The baby's dimpled limbs had churned with delight as Ted gave her a bath. I'd been half afraid to hold her for fear I might never hand her back.

"Ted says she rolls over now, and can scoot herself backwards along the floor. She'll be crawling before long." Terri gazed at nothing in particular, her expression a mix of wonder and sorrow. "I've missed so much already."

"There will be years ahead to catch up."

"It's not the same." Terri shook herself free from Hannah's image. "Tell me the truth, what are my chances?"

It was a question always on an attorney's mind, but one we were never comfortable answering. "Decent," I hedged.

"How decent?"

"The state's case will be based on circumstantial evidence. If we can show that their interpretation of the facts is only one of several possibilities, and I think we can, the jury will be hard pressed to convict." Assuming the jurors didn't form an opinion before hearing the facts.

"Our biggest stumbling block," I added, "will be the witness who saw a dark-colored Explorer with the partial license matching yours."

"There've got to be other cars matching that description."

"You'd think so. The trouble is, we haven't found one yet."

A flicker of worry crossed her face. "That's not good." Terri twisted sideways in her chair, arms crossed over her chest. "You mentioned before about trying to hint at a different killer. Someone with a reason to want Bram out of the way."

I nodded. "I wish I could tell you we had a candidate for that role."

"You've dropped the idea of dumping on Melissa, then?"

"For the moment." It wasn't so much that I'd deliberately dropped it, as that it hadn't quite jelled. Neither had my thoughts about offering Mrs. Cole or Suzze Madden as substitute killers. But I hadn't ruled any of them out, either.

"Is there any evidence against her?" Terri asked.

"The white fleece found on Weaver's clothing."

"Those sheepskin seat covers are everywhere. I mean real evidence."

I shook my head. "No real evidence one way or the other." And Melissa herself had been less than cooperative.

"What about Weaver's son? He had plenty of reason to be angry at the guy."

"He was at school." I'd had Nick look into that possibility.

Terri brushed the air with impatience. "Didn't you ever sneak out a window at night?" Then she sighed. "I don't want to dump on him either. He's just a kid. A kid who had a hatemonger jerk for a dad."

I frowned. "I hope you haven't talked about Weaver like that to anyone else."

"I've kept my mouth shut, just like you said. It's been hard, though. If you're too standoffish, people don't like it. And everyone's got an opinion about the guy."

"They're entitled to one. So are you. Just remember to keep it to yourself."

Terri rested her elbows on the table and propped her head in her hands. She stared at me in silence for a moment. "Let me get this straight. You're going to tell the jury you have no idea who killed Weaver or why, but it wasn't me." She sounded incredulous.

"Basically." Unless we got a last-minute lucky break.

"That's lame. It's like I'm guilty and trying to get away with something." She pressed a palm against the side of her face. "I don't see how you can say things look decent for us."

"They do, Terri. Trust me on this. There are no guarantees, of course, but the prosecution has to prove its case beyond a reasonable doubt. It'll be tough convincing a fair-minded jury that you're guilty."

The key was making sure we had a fair-minded jury.

"And we have the neighbor's housekeeper who saw you at home through the upstairs window, don't forget. An alibi of sorts. You can't be two places at once."

Terri gave me an odd look. "How will the jury know whether to believe her or the prosecution's witnesses?"

"Credibility. And how the testimony fits with other evidence in the case."

This was why trials were more art than science. Facts in dispute. Or unclear. Or both. Evidence that was contradictory. Loose ends that couldn't be explained. What you had to do was spin a web that drew the jurors to your side, and there was so much more to it than straight logic.

Terri looked down at her hands. Her expression was silent and impenetrable.

"If you're having second thoughts," I reminded her, "it's not too late to talk a deal."

She shook her head, slowly and almost imperceptibly. Then she sighed and raised her eyes to mine. "No. I'm not going to deal."

"You've got the clothes we picked for tomorrow?"

"Yes, my mother brought them by earlier today." A fleeting smile. "It's going to feel so good to wear something other than this ugly monkey suit."

"Try to get a good night's rest, Terri."

"You too. And thanks. For everything." She pushed back in her chair. "Steven says you're the best, and Steven is usually right."

It's common wisdom among trial attorneys that a case is won or lost with the selection of the jury.

Some attorneys prepare for voir dire as thoroughly as they do the trial itself. They hire consultants, assemble focus groups, invest heavily in research hoping to pinpoint the ideal juror for their case. We'd rejected that approach. Not only is it expensive and cumbersome, particularly on a tight schedule, but it's also far from foolproof. Instead, we were relying on our collective experience and gut reactions.

An approach that was equally far from foolproof.

Stepping into the courtroom that morning, I could sense the anticipation in the air, at once both electrifying and stifling.

I'd slept fitfully the night before, awaking hourly with a tight throat and a knot in my stomach. I didn't imagine Terri had slept well either, but she looked more rested than she had in months. She was dressed in a sage-green linen suit set off with a simple gold pin. We'd chosen the outfit because it was flattering and fashionable without being pretentious. Her hair fluffed softly around her face, and her complexion was highlighted with a dash of pink across the cheeks.

Ted and Arlo sat in the gallery directly behind the defense table. Lenore, after much anguish about where she was needed most, had decided to remain at home with Hannah.

Steven and I sat at the defense table with Terri between us.

Terri eyed the pool of prospective jurors nervously. "They look bored already," she whispered.

"How many people do you know who are thrilled to be called to jury duty?"

"Shouldn't they care, though?"

"They will, Terri. Try to relax."

We'd drawn Judge Susan Tooley, who had a reputation for fairness and for keeping trials on course. I didn't know her personally, but I thought that the draw was a good one, especially in light of some of the other judges we might have found ourselves before.

Tooley had been a public defender first, then a prosecutor. That was good, too, since I was wary of overzealous judges. She appeared to be in her early fifties. Salt-and-pepper hair cut short and brushed back from her face.

Judge Tooley addressed the assembled jurors briefly, then asked the bailiff to pull the first name.

Steven and I had reviewed the jury questionnaires, and now I pulled my notes from my briefcase. I could feel my heart pounding with anticipation.

The first juror called was Manuel Ortiz, a slender man of twenty-six who spoke with the hint of a Spanish accent and worked as the manager at the local Burger Boy. He was married, with two young sons. He had a brother with the Highway Patrol.

Judge Tooley questioned him first, followed by Don Pelle, who seemed inclined to accept Mr. Ortiz as a member of the jury. That didn't surprise me. Jurors with family ties to law enforcement were generally considered pro-prosecution. And if stereotypes held, a Latino male might find himself more naturally aligned with Weaver than a defendant who was white, rich, and female.

But I'd been impressed with Ortiz. His answers were careful and direct. What we wanted were jurors who would keep an open mind and not assume that arrest and guilt went hand in hand.

"Mr. Ortiz." I took two steps in his direction. "Have you followed this case in the media?"

"I heard about it from some people at work, but I don't get a chance to read the paper regular. The minute I come home, my little boys are all over me."

"Did you ever listen to Weaver's show or read his book?"

A charming half-smile. "Afraid not. Like I said, my boys are a handful."

"Do you know anything about Bram Weaver?"

"Just what people say about him."

"And what's that?"

Mr. Ortiz looked uncomfortable. "Men should be men, that kind of thing. He thought women were getting too much power."

"And do you agree with those statements?"

"Men should be strong, yes. Dependable. We need to take care of our families."

"And women?"

There was a twinkle in his eye. "What can I say, I'm married. My wife is a wonderful woman."

Not heavily macho, which was good. "Mr. Ortiz, from your answers to the questionnaire, it sounds like you are a devoted father."

"I try. Boys need a father."

"And being a father is more than just biology, is it not?"

He was nodding vigorously. "Much more."

I leaned down to confer with Steven. "I say we keep him."

"The family tie with law enforcement doesn't bother you?"

"A little. But we're not going to get everything we want in every juror."

Steven nodded. "I like him too."

I looked at Terri for her reaction. By previous agreement we'd arranged for her to have a say in the selection of jurors. But Terri appeared numb. It was a phase all defendants experienced—the punch to your gut when you recognized your future rests in the hands of twelve strangers.

"I can't do this," she whispered. "You two decide."

I turned to Judge Tooley. "The defense accepts Mr. Ortiz."

The next juror called, an active feminist, was dismissed by the prosecution for cause. We burned a peremptory challenge on the third juror, a man still licking his wounds from a bitter divorce in which he'd sought custody of his three children and lost.

Nancy Huntington was up next. Married without children, Ms. Huntington worked as a commercial loan officer at Bank of America. Her husband was a CPA with a large accounting firm.

On the jury questionnaire she'd indicated interests in golf, travel, and opera.

Pelle questioned her at some length. He pressed her about Weaver, but she'd hardly heard of him or his book, making it clear in the process that her time was spent on more important matters than radio talk shows. Nor had she heard of Ted Harper before his wife was arrested. Football was not one of her interests either. Nor, apparently, was television or she'd have run across his TelAm commercials.

On first impression, Nancy Huntington seemed a good choice for the defense. A woman about Terri's age, college educated and in the same general social strata. But she made me uneasy.

It's believed among those who study such things that female jurors are hard on other women. While I wasn't sure I bought the generalization, I had a feeling that Ms. Huntington might fit the pattern. There was a harshness about her, an aura of self-righteousness that suggested she made up her mind quickly, and rarely changed it. I was reluctant, however, to use another peremptory so early on.

I questioned her about her schooling—Wellesley; her family—a sister in Boston and parents in Arizona; her reading habits—she took my question about reading mysteries as an insult; and the extent of her political activism—she gave money to worthy causes and served on the boards of several local committees, including the Opera Board and the Council for a Better San Francisco.

"Sounds like a busy life," I said.

She allowed a smile. "I like it that way."

"Would you feel jury duty to be a burden?"

"On the contrary, I look forward to serving."

Sounded like someone in a job interview. Not the norm for jurors, especially those with demanding professional careers. It was a sure red flag. "Have you served on a jury before?"

"No. I was called to jury duty once, a simple insurance claim. A fender bender in a grocery parking lot. One of the attorneys asked to have me excused."

"A disappointment for someone who was looking forward to serving."

She managed to look disdainful. "It was only a civil case and not a very interesting one from the sounds of it."

"And you think this one might be interesting?"

"It's an important case."

"Important how?"

"It's been in the news a lot." Realizing she may have said more than she wanted to, she hastened to explain. "I mean, it's a big case. A serious matter."

With big names and star attraction. A case she could talk about over sips of champagne at the opera opening.

"Tell me about this council you serve on," I said.

"It's comprised of representatives from city government and local business. We're trying to work together instead of fighting each other."

I was under the impression that city government and businesses were already on the same team. One had only to look at the skyline to see how pro-growth interests had changed the character of the city.

"What specific areas of city government?" I asked.

"It's pretty broad. There's someone from the mayor's office, from Muni, that sort of thing."

"From the police department also?"

"Yes. Like I said, it's a broad-based coalition."

"How about the DA's office?"

"I don't believe so."

I looked at Steven, whose hands were folded, thumbs crossed. Our agreed-upon signal for a juror we didn't want. His assessment mirrored my own.

"Sidebar, Your Honor?" I found Ms. Huntington's responses troublesome enough to support a dismissal for cause, but I expected Pelle to disagree.

He did. "That's absurd," he argued to the judge when I'd finished explaining my reasons. "Counsel is trying to pick and choose jurors without having to waste a peremptory challenge."

Judge Tooley removed her glasses and wiped them on the sleeve of her robe. Then she put them back on and looked at me. "Ms. O'Brien, it's your contention that Ms. Huntington's willingness to serve on this jury is evidence that she ought *not* serve?"

"I think eagerness is a more apt term, and yes, I find that suspect. Moreover, she's got ties to the mayor and the police department, which indicates the potential for bias toward the prosecution."

"Ties?" Pelle rolled his eyes. "It's an advisory committee, for God's sake. One of those puff-and-fluff delegations that provides a photo op and not much else."

Judge Tooley pressed her lips together and nodded. "I agree, Ms. O'Brien. I don't find sufficient bias to excuse her for cause."

I returned to the defense table and leaned over to look at Steven's juror list. Based on the questionnaires the jurors had filled out, we'd drawn lines through a number of the names—jurors we didn't want. If we used a peremptory on Ms. Huntington, we might be stuck with one of these others down the road.

"On the positive side," Steven said, "loan officers don't, as a rule, jump to conclusions."

Terri had been sitting silently, eyes straight ahead. But apparently she'd been listening because she turned and said, "Let her stay. At least I recognize the type."

The smile on Ms. Huntington's face when she was seated as a member of the jury left me feeling less than confident, however.

By the end of the day we'd empaneled eight jurors—five women and three men. I felt really good about two of them, had minor misgivings about four, and serious reservations about Ms. Huntington and a young woman by the name of Judy Johnson, who reminded me of one of those wind-up dolls that spewed forth recorded phrases—in Judy's case, *I guess, I don't know,* and *I think so.* I could only hope that her brain marched to a different drummer than her mouth.

I'd hoped Steven and I might have a chance to talk after court adjourned, maybe even head out for a drink or an early dinner. The notion of unwinding with someone whose company I enjoyed seemed enormously appealing. I'd been too long alone and I was getting tired of it.

But Steven had dashed off with only a quick, "Good job, see you tomorrow." I was exhausted by the tensions of the day, and too keyed up to concentrate on the next stage. I pulled out my cell phone and tried three friends who worked in the city. I struck out three times.

Although it was five o'clock, the day was warm still. A rare event in San Francisco, where the fog rolled in most evenings, if not before. An evening for strolling. So that's what I did. I headed out toward Union Street for some serious window shopping.

I even meandered into a few stores, bought a pair of hammered copper earrings, checked the sales racks at the expensive clothing boutiques, and was admiring a hand-painted silk scarf when the woman standing next to me pulled the cell phone from her purse and looked at it blankly.

"Not mine," she said, turning her gaze in my direction. "Must be yours."

It was only then that I became aware of "Ode to Joy" playing softly in my purse. There aren't many people who have the number to my cell phone.

I pulled the phone from my purse and took a minute to remember which button I pushed to answer it. Once I got the thing working, however, I recognized Bea's voice at once. She sounded frantic.

"Kali, I've been trying to reach you. Then I remembered your cell phone."

"What is it?" I had visions of my house aflame. Loretta missing.

"It's Sophia Rudd," Bea said. "She was beaten up this afternoon. Badly."

CHAPTER 28

"Who would do such a thing?" Bea asked for maybe the fifth time since I'd arrived at the hospital twenty minutes ago. She'd been talking with a young police officer at the time, but we'd moved to the cafeteria when he left.

She headed for a table in the corner. "What kind of animal attacks a defenseless old woman? And for what possible purpose?"

Bea wasn't looking for answers, which was a good thing because I had none. "What did the police say?"

"Didn't say much of anything," Bea grumbled. She was agitated, and clearly exhausted by the afternoon's events. "Didn't even ask many questions. Not that I'd have been able to tell him much."

I'd managed to piece together enough of the story to know that Bea had discovered Sophia Rudd sprawled on the floor, bludgeoned and bloodied, when she'd dropped by there that afternoon. But I didn't know much more than that.

"How are you doing?" I asked, touching her arm. "You must be pretty shaken."

"I'm doing better than Sophia," Bea said, blinking back tears. She pulled the tea bag from her Styrofoam cup and set it on a napkin. "I can't imagine they thought the poor dear had anything worth stealing. It's a small apartment, very modestly furnished."

"Is that what the police think?" I asked. "That she was robbed?"

"The place was messy, like someone had been searching through it. Drawers emptied, books off the shelf, that sort of thing."

A midday burglary in an occupied apartment was unusual.

"Why don't you start at the beginning and tell me what happened."

Bea brought the cup to her lips, but set it down again without sipping. "I got there about two o'clock. I'd bought those currant scones from Nabloom Bakery that are so good, and some fresh strawberries. And a couple of tea bags, just in case, although I was sure Sophia would have plenty."

Bea had embraced the challenge of improving her signing skills, and Sophia had welcomed her company. The two women had apparently found plenty to converse about as long as they stayed clear of Alexander Rudd's identity and whereabouts.

"When she didn't answer after a couple of tries," Bea continued, "I figured maybe her signal light was broken. So I went around back to see if I could wave through the window and catch her attention. The door was partially open and I could see her lying on the floor, all twisted and hurt."

Bea's hands were shaking still, though her voice was steadier. "I used the phone to call 9-1-1, which I know wasn't smart. There might still have been someone in the house. But I wasn't thinking straight."

"Was she conscious?"

"It was hard to tell. She opened her eyes at one point and looked at me, but that's all. No recognition, no change in expression."

The cafeteria was filling up. Doctors and nurses, plates piled high, plying themselves for the long evening ahead. Their conversations were punctuated with gestures and occasional laughs. They were easily distinguishable from the bleary-eyed families and friends of patients. Visitors who made it to a hospital cafeteria were usually in for the long haul. They were absently sipping sodas or hot beverages, and if they'd bought food, it remained largely untouched.

With a sudden awareness, I realized how horribly familiar the surroundings would feel to Steven. In the days following the accident, when he'd found himself a newly widowed father with a young daughter on life support, the hospital would have been his world. A capsule of pain and grief.

I pushed the image away.

"Do you think Sophia keeps jewelry or valuables?" I asked.

"I wouldn't know, but she's a practical person. Why not give them what they were after? Nothing could be worth the beating she took." Bea's eyes teared up. "You should have seen her face, Kali. All bloody and swollen."

Unless they weren't looking for valuables.

I knew virtually nothing about either of the Rudds. They could both be running from the law or mixed up in shady dealings. It dawned on me that I might inadvertently have placed Bea in danger.

I covered her hand with my own. "How terrible for you. I should never have involved you in this."

She shook her head. "Don't even think such a thing. I want to help now, too. Now more than ever. If they weren't after valuables, what did they want?"

"Someone might have been looking for information about her son," I suggested, since it was a question prominent in my own mind.

Bea fingered the blue and tan scarf around her neck. "I suppose that might make sense. She'd want to protect him, I know that much. From the little she's said, he was . . . is, a lovely man. Very concerned for her. Always willing to help people in need."

Maybe. But there had to be a reason he'd faked his own death.

"Who do you think would be after him?" Bea asked.

"Could be whoever killed Weaver. He might be worried that Rudd will be able to identify him. Or possibly it's connected to whatever trouble Rudd was in before."

In theory, I supposed Don Pelle might be looking for Rudd as well. Rudd was a potential witness, after all. Supplied by the defense. And the DA himself had expressed interest. But I couldn't imagine Pelle bludgeoning anyone to locate a witness.

Bea looked at her watch. "I think we should go back upstairs and see if there's any news on Sophia. She should be out of surgery soon."

The small visitor lounge on the fifth floor had been empty when we left for the cafeteria. Now there was another couple there, holding hands, staring silently into space, their expressions strained.

Bea and I went to the nursing station across the hall. "Any word yet on Sophia Rudd?" I asked.

The nurse was a moon-faced woman with skin the color of rich espresso. She clicked at the computer keyboard, then looked up.

"The surgery went well. When she's ready to be moved from re-covery, they'll take her to intensive care, one floor down."

"She's deaf," Bea volunteered. "She uses sign language. I can interpret if you'd like."

The nurse looked at her with compassion. "I imagine it will be quite a while before Mrs. Rudd will be communicating with any-one."

"Oh." The word was a puff of air, as though Bea had been punched in the chest. She gripped the counter to steady herself.

"She's still unconscious?" I asked.

"Besides a broken arm and deep lacerations, she's suffered a major blow to the head. You'll need to talk to the doctor about the long-term prognosis."

"I gave the other nurse the name of her church," Bea said. "That's who her closest friends are. She has no family that I know of."

Unless you counted her son, I added silently.

"The information is right here," the nurse assured us. "We've already called and spoken to the pastor."

Over dinner, Bea recounted the afternoon's events for Dotty's benefit. Usually one to jockey for a place in the spotlight, that evening Bea was subdued. Her focus remained on Sophia Rudd.

I ate quickly, then moved downstairs to work. I also put in a call to Nick and explained what had happened. "You think you could keep an eye out?" I asked. "Alexander Rudd might show up at the hospital."

"I thought you'd given up the idea of finding him."

"I have. More or less."

"Aah." The voice of skepticism.

"At least in terms of the defense case."

Nick didn't press the issue. "Sure. I can hang around there this evening until they kick me out. But I'm booked solid tomorrow."

"I'll put Jared on the day shift."

Jared was less than thrilled at the prospect of spending the day in a hospital when he expected to be in court.

"Bo-oss." He made the word into two syllables, both delivered with a clear whine.

"Right. I *am* the boss, as you keep informing me, and I want you to do this."

Silence.

"Jared, do I need to remind you whose signature is going to be on the letter of recommendation you'll be asking for when you pass the bar?"

He laughed. "You're lucky I'm a nice guy. Otherwise I'd make you beg. But you owe me."

I arrived at the Hall of Justice early next morning in the hopes I might find an opportunity to talk with Don Pelle before court convened. But he appeared at the last minute, in the company of two assistants. Finally at mid-morning break, after three more jurors had been selected, I caught up with him near the elevator bank.

"Looks like we'll have a jury before the day is out," I said in an off-hand manner. This was lawyer small-talk, like backyard exchanges about the weather.

He nodded. "Tomorrow we begin battle. Maybe even this afternoon."

"You think she'd do that?" Most judges liked to start a trial fresh, with opening statements in the morning. But some, in an effort to ease perpetual backlog, forged ahead whenever there was an available time slot.

"Judge Tooley runs a tight ship. Doesn't believe in wasting taxpayer money. You'd better be ready, just in case."

I nodded and smiled. He sounded sincere. "I am ready," I offered. And paused. "The only hitch is that I haven't been able to locate one of my witnesses, a man by the name of Alexander Rudd."

I watched closely for a reaction. Pelle didn't blink. He didn't hesitate or show any signs of recognition. "You'll still have time. I figure my case will take several days at least."

He took the elevator down to the lobby. I went to the ladies' room. I hadn't really believed he'd been responsible for the attack on Sophia Rudd, but I felt an odd relief nonetheless that nothing in his reaction had made me reconsider.

The last juror was seated by eleven o'clock.

Steven leaned over. "Our fate is cast," he whispered with an edge of black humor.

"You sound like someone with little faith in your fellow man."

"Not far from the mark, my dear." While the words were meant to be light, there was an ominous vein to them.

All in all, it wasn't a bad jury. Five men and seven women, with a range in age from sixty at the far end to a woman in her twenties who looked about fifteen. All gave the impression of giving their task the serious and fair-minded attention it deserved. There were enough uncertainties in my mind, however, that I was far from confident.

Judge Tooley rubbed her temples. "Mr. Pelle, is the prosecution prepared to present its opening statement this afternoon?"

"We most certainly are, Your Honor." A little too kiss-ass, I thought, and wondered if the jurors' reaction was the same.

"Ms. O'Brien?"

"Ready, Your Honor."

"Fine. Let's take our lunch break and begin with opening arguments when we reconvene at one-thirty. I'd like to hear from both the prosecution and the defense today, if possible, so let's keep it moving on track, shall we?"

With that admonishment, she rapped her gavel, and court was in recess. I glanced at Terri and gave her a reassuring smile, which she didn't return.

"I'm scared, Kali." She looked it, too. Her features were drawn, her naturally rosy cheeks almost colorless. "Those men and women on the jury don't know me. They don't know anything about me. But they get to decide my future. They could so easily get the wrong impression."

I laid a hand on her arm. "It's my job to make sure they don't."

She took a deep breath and nodded obediently.

I didn't think I'd reassured either one of us.

The press was there in force when the afternoon session began. Camera crews in the hallway, reporters craning their necks from the seats on the far side of the bar. Word had gotten out that the trial was about to begin.

Ted, Lenore, and Arlo were in court as well. I assumed Steven had called them over the break. The remaining seats were crammed with spectators. Terri had told me she recognized a couple of friends.

Don Pelle strode to the jury box emanating confidence and

purpose. His shoes were polished, his white shirt crisp and starched, set off with a silk tie of red and black stripes. His suit that morning had been a light gray; the one he wore now was a fine worsted charcoal. He'd obviously had a fresh ensemble waiting in his office. A distinct advantage to working out of the same building that housed the courts.

Pelle began by thanking the jurors for their time and for their participation in such an important undertaking. He went on to talk about the jury process, its role in our society, and his part as a representative of "the people." It was not an original approach, but a wise one. It's human nature to want to feel appreciated, to be part of something important. By playing on these feelings, Pelle was hoping to win the jurors over to the side of justice. His side.

He then laid out the bare bones of his case. His presentation wasn't flowery or dramatic. In fact, it was a bit stiff. But it was effective.

Terri Harper and her husband wanted a baby, Pelle said. Arrangements had been made to adopt a baby girl born to Melissa Burke. Unfortunately for the Harpers, Ms. Burke had neglected to notify the baby's father, Bram Weaver, of the impending adoption—or even of the pregnancy. When he learned he had fathered a child, he immediately took steps to stop the adoption and assert his parental rights.

Terri Harper had lost one child already in a failed adoption, and she wasn't about to lose another. With Bram Weaver's death, Pelle explained, there would no longer be an impediment to the adoption.

"The State, ladies and gentlemen, will prove that the defendant murdered Bram Weaver because he stood in the way of the adoption. We will present witnesses who will testify that the defendant made threats against Mr. Weaver."

Threats. Plural. I stole a glance at Terri. As far as I knew, there'd been only one threat, such as it was—the afternoon at the courthouse when Weaver had asked for visitation rights.

But Terri's face remained a mask of stoic attentiveness. Either she hadn't picked up on the use of the plural, or she knew of threats I did not. I scrawled a note to myself.

"We will show that a weapon registered to the defendant is the very make and caliber gun used to kill Bram Weaver. A weapon that she is now unable to produce. A weapon, incidentally, that is not among those most commonly owned."

Pelle infused his words with just enough fervor to raise the specter of suspicion. He paused to let the points sink in, then continued.

"We will link evidence found at the crime scene to the defendant. Hair, fibers, a pair of dark glasses, for example. We will present witnesses who will testify to the defendant *not* being at home, where she claims she was that night. One of the defendants' own neighbors heard her leave the house a little before midnight. Another witness will place her near the murder scene about half an hour later. These times are well within the window of the crime."

The jurors were listening intently, some leaning forward in their seats, eyes riveted on Pelle. Their curiosity had been tweaked during voir dire and now, finally, they were being allowed to hear the elements of the case.

Pelle paced slowly across the breadth of the jury box, making eye contact with the jurors one by one. "We will show further that the defendant changed longstanding plans to spend the weekend at home with her mother. Instead, she left town unexpectedly less than twelve hours after the murder. She left without telling anyone she was leaving or where she was going. Not her mother, who she sent back to her own house in Carmel. Not her husband, who was out of town that weekend. By the time the defendant finally made herself available to speak with detectives, it was no longer possible to test her skin for powder residue, a test that might have been conclusive to guilt."

Or not. Pelle was treading dangerously close to argument, by innuendo if not directly. But my objecting would only reinforce the points he was making in the jurors' minds and lead to the appearance that Terri had something to hide.

"After you've heard all the evidence," Pelle said in conclusion, "I am confident that you will find Terri Harper guilty of murder." He again thanked the jurors, and sat down.

Judge Tooley seemed pleased with the brevity of the prosecution's remarks. She turned to me. "Ms. O'Brien, do you intend to make opening statement at this juncture? We have ample time in the afternoon schedule."

I'd given some thought to waiting until after the prosecution had presented its case. There are theoretical advantages to this approach, the biggest being you know by then the full extent of the state's evidence. But I didn't want the jurors sitting through the next several days of testimony with only the prosecution's interpretation of events ringing in their heads.

"The defense is ready to proceed, Your Honor."

"Good. We will take a fifteen-minute recess and then resume with the opening statement from the defense."

No sooner had the gavel struck, than the bailiff approached and handed me a note. *Ring me on my cell phone as soon as you're free. Jared.*

I gave Terri's hand a squeeze, then headed for a quiet corner of the hallway to return Jared's call.

"What's up?" I asked.

"Your man Rudd. He was dressed like an orderly. Stopped by to see his mother and now he's down at Pier 39 playing his harmonica."

"His harmonica?"

"For money. Only he's competing with a blues saxophonist on the next corner and a bronzed human statue across the street. I don't think he's going to pull in much."

"Have you talked to him?"

"Nope. I thought I should check with you first. I was afraid I might scare him off."

"Stay with him. I've got opening argument in a few minutes but I'll call you as soon as I'm finished."

"Gotcha. How's it going in court?"

"Pelle was good. No surprises, though."

"You're going to be better than good, boss. You'll be super."

The confidence of a neophyte is amazing.

Facing the assembled jury, I felt both a surge of hope and the terror of possible failure. As Terri herself had said, the jurors didn't know her. Didn't know what she'd done or hadn't done; didn't know what was on her mind or in her heart. I was the conduit by which they would come to know her, and decide her fate. It was up to me to convince them of her innocence, or at the very least, raise reasonable doubt about her guilt. And that was a frightening burden to shoulder.

I began by introducing myself and Terri. Not as attorney and defendant, but as human beings. It was an effort at establishing a bond, an attempt to erase the presumption of guilt which often lodges in a juror's brain after listening to the prosecutor's tale of murder.

I, too, thanked the jury. "I know you have other commitments, and places you'd rather be. I appreciate your putting those aside to help make our judicial system work the way it should. Terri Harper appreciates it, too."

I turned and gestured to include her in the delivery. The jurors' eyes shifted in her direction.

Terri was working hard at looking relaxed and confident, as we'd discussed. But not overly so. A trace of vulnerability was a good thing. She'd been practicing for days, without benefit of a mirror. And she was doing well.

"Terri Harper has, herself, sat on juries," I continued. Build a sense of identification between defendant and juror. It was a basic tenet of trial work. "She knows what a difficult job it can be, and how important. As you're aware, some countries have no jury system. If an innocent person is arrested, she goes straight to jail with no chance to question the charges or give her side of events. But in this country we know that police sometimes make mistakes, just like everyone else. Despite their hard work and best intentions, they sometimes arrest the wrong person. That is why our system requires the state to prove its case to you, the jury. To you as independent, impartial members of the community."

I paused, took several steps to the left. My delivery was, by intention, less formal than Pelle's. I wanted the jurors to see Terri as one of them.

It was difficult to judge how well I was succeeding. The jurors' faces were, by and large, masks of blandness. Mr. Ortiz yawned. A gesture that was picked up and repeated by several others behind the railing. Already the trial had lost some of its newness.

"This is one of the instances where the police have made a mistake." I paused and met the gaze of as many men and women of the jury as were looking in my direction.

"We will show you each step of the way, how they did that. This is a case based entirely on circumstantial evidence." I gave the term a slight inflection, as though there were something sinister in the concept.

"Each piece of evidence could, and does, have an explanation different from the one the prosecutor has given you. He's taken a collage of facts and arranged them a certain way, painting a picture of guilt. We will show you that there are other ways to arrange these facts, other interpretations that are consistent with Terri Harper's innocence.

"Mr. Pelle talked of motive. We will show that there were many people who had disagreements and run-ins with Bram Weaver. We will show you that the threat Mr. Pelle mentioned wasn't a threat at all, but an understandable, and entirely human, outburst of emotion. The kind of thing we all do on occasion, and feel ashamed about later."

I moved on to cover the other points raised by Pelle—the gun, the witnesses, the physical evidence raised at the scene—and walked them through the concept of reasonable doubt. Nancy Huntington observed all through narrowed eyes. I could only hope it was bad eyesight and not displeasure.

"Because there is no murder weapon," I said, "the prosecution has no way of knowing, or proving, what specific gun was used in the crime. That Terri Harper once owned a gun similar to the one used in the crime means nothing. A lot of other people own the same type of gun. The prosecutor has no eyewitness to the crime, no one who can positively place Terri anywhere near the crime scene the night of the murder. He has no fingerprints linking Terri to the murder, no traces of the victim's blood on any of Terri's clothing or belongings. The evidence he does have—fibers, hair, dark glasses—may have certain similarities to items that belong to my client. But you are all wise enough to know that similar is not identical. Without DNA, we can say only that a blond hair comes from a blonde, not which blonde. We cannot even say with certainty that a hair found at a murder scene belonged to the murderer."

I turned and walked to the other end of the jury box. "On the night of the murder, Terri Harper was at home with her new baby and her mother. Terri had asked her mother to spend the weekend because her husband would be out of town and because Terri knew how excited her mother was about the baby. Do you think she would invite her mother for the night she was planning a murder?"

I braced myself for an objection I felt sure Pelle would raise, but no voice rang out from behind me, so I continued. "We will present a witness who saw Terri Harper in her home close to the time of the murder. I don't have to tell you that she could not be at Weaver's, twenty minutes away, if she was at home."

Out of the corner of my eye, I saw Judge Tooley lift her arm to check her watch. I decided to wrap it up.

"Terri Harper is a wife and new mother. She is on the Library Committee and is an active member of several local charities. Previously, she taught kindergarten. Now she finds herself, unexpectedly and through no wrongdoing on her part, a defendant in a murder trial. Her world has been turned upside down. It is up to you, ladies and gentlemen, to make it right again.

"Allow me to tell you again how grateful I am that you are serving on this jury. That you are here to prevent a grave miscarriage of justice. I am confident that when you hear all the evidence and use your own sound judgment, you will find my client, Terri Harper, not guilty."

CHAPTER 29

Court adjourned at four-fifteen. Ten minutes later I was on the phone to Jared.

"Alexander Rudd still entertaining the folks at the wharf?" I asked.

"He's actually pretty good, boss. You should hear him."

"I'm on my way."

I headed out Van Ness, catching a string of green lights, and arrived at the appointed corner in under twenty minutes. The waterfront around Pier 39, just south of Fisherman's Wharf, is a warren of trinket shops and food vendors in a picturesque setting that combines both the best of old San Francisco and the worst of its new commercialism. The area was crowded with tourists, and the sun sparkled on the bay. September was truly one of the finest months in the city.

I could feel the warm sun on my back as I stopped to get my bearing. I spotted Alexander Rudd before I saw Jared. He was a man about my own age and height, solidly built, with high Slavic cheekbones like his mother and a head of thick, dark hair so curly it formed short, uneven dread locks.

Standing against the corner of a building, gaze welded to a point somewhere in the distance, he was playing a slow, aching tune that made me think of campfires and cattle drives. One of the men in the surrounding crowd dropped a folded bill into the hat at Rudd's feet. Rudd raised his eyes and nodded acknowledgment.

He played for almost half an hour more before he took a break, picking up his hat and emptying the cash into one pocket while slipping his harmonica into the other. As the crowd dispersed, I approached him.

"I enjoyed listening to you play."

"Thanks." It was said without enthusiasm.

"I wonder if we could talk for a minute."

He gave me an uncomprehending look. "Talk?"

"About your mother, among other things."

The look grew alarmed. "Who are you?"

"My name is Kali O'Brien."

"Are you with her church?"

I shook my head. "I'm an attorney."

"I'm not interested in suing anyone."

"That's not why I'm here. I represent the woman accused of killing Bram Weaver. I understand that you might have seen something that night."

He backed away. His eyes darted to the passing crowds. "Nuh-uh. Like I told that other fellow, I don't know nothing about that."

"You're not a suspect," I told him. "There's a witness who saw you on the street at the same time the shots were fired."

"Must have been somebody who looked like me." Rudd was walking away from me now, with a long, quick stride.

I followed.

Rudd picked up his pace, dodging people as he went. Out of the corner of my eye, I saw Jared, off to our right, jog ahead. Rudd must have seen him too, because he turned abruptly and darted between buildings.

I was half running, moving as fast as I could in low-heeled pumps and a narrow skirt, but I was losing him. "I think whoever beat up your mother was trying to find you," I called out. "You can't hide forever."

Rudd slowed, started up again, and then stopped abruptly. I caught up with him at the same time Jared met us coming from the other direction.

"I'm not trying to cause problems," I said, breathing hard. "But there's a lot at stake here. Your mother and my client are both in trouble."

His expression hardened. "You think they're connected, lady, you're way wrong."

"Think about it. I've been wanting to talk to you about the

night of Weaver's murder. Don't you think the killer might be looking for you as well?"

We were standing on a wooden walkway along the water's edge. I could hear the bark of sea lions beyond the railing. Jared had positioned himself so that it would be harder for Rudd to take off again, but Rudd seemed to have given up the idea on his own.

"Someone beat your mother to near death. I want to know why."

Rudd looked at me, then Jared. He didn't say anything.

"It doesn't appear that whoever did it took anything of value," I added.

"What would they take? She has nothing."

"Talking to me might help catch the person who attacked her."

He gave me a wary look. "Why do you care?"

"It was a friend of mine who found her. She's been visiting your mother." The explanation was suitably vague that he could make of it what he wanted. "It might also help my client," I added.

Silence.

"You may have seen something the night of the murder," I told him, "and not even recognize that it's important."

Rudd shoved his hands into his pockets and rolled his shoulders forward. He kicked at a spot on the asphalt. His face had closed in on itself, like he was thinking hard, or trying hard not to think.

"My client is a young woman with her life ahead of her. She's a new mother with a three-month-old baby. Terri's in jail now, standing trial for a murder she didn't commit. If you can identify the killer, or help—"

"I didn't see who killed him."

"But you might have seen something that could help our case."

More silence.

"There's a good chance the killer thinks you saw him, and that's why he's after you. You and your mother will both be in danger until he's caught."

Rudd turned and scanned the horizon over the water. I thought for a moment he might be contemplating a jump, but he shoved his hands deeper into his pockets and faced me.

"The paper said your client's brother is Steven Cross."

"That's right. Why?"

"Nothing. I just thought the name sounded familiar."

"His wife and daughter were killed about five years ago in a hit-and-run accident. Maybe you heard his name on the news." I was not above using whatever it took to win Rudd over, although it left a sour taste in my mouth.

Rudd rocked back on his heels, studied me a moment. His eyes were a soft, liquid brown. Like those of an old, family dog. Finally, he shook his head. "I wish I could help you, but I can't."

"Just tell me what you saw that night. Surely you must have seen or heard *something*. You were right there when it happened."

He sighed, pulled a hand from his pocket, and scratched the side of his head. "I heard shots, scuffling sounds from across the street. I went to check. When I got there, it was clear there was nothing to be done for the guy."

"Did you touch anything?"

"No. Didn't even have to touch the body to know that help was too late."

"You were standing across the street at the time of the shooting. You didn't see anyone?"

"I wasn't directly across, I was down the street a bit, not paying much attention to what was happening around me."

"Why didn't you call the police?"

He shrugged noncommittally.

"And you've avoided talking to me."

"I just don't want to get dragged into all this," he snapped.

"Because you're supposed to be dead?"

His cheek twitched. I could see an internal debate taking place.

"You've already admitted to being Sophia Rudd's son," I reminded him.

"I didn't admit anything."

"I asked about your mother and you didn't correct me."

"You did that on purpose. To trick me." Rudd was growing agitated.

"I'm not trying to cause trouble," I said. "What I care about is finding out who did this to Sophia. And who killed Weaver."

Rudd gnawed on his lower lip. "You asked," he said after a moment. "But you aren't going to like what I have to say."

"Try me."

"Only person I saw on the street that night was a woman."

My heart froze. "Did you get a good look at her?"

He shook his head. "She was dressed in a dark jacket, hat."

"But you're sure it was a woman?"

"I'm sure. She wore a large diamond solitaire on her ring finger."

Just like Terri.

My mind called up the old maxim, "Be careful what you wish for." I'd been looking for a witness in connection with Weaver's murder, and I'd found him. It was good that the prosecution hadn't.

"Maybe now you'll butt out of my life," he said.

"I don't know what you're hiding from, but I'm sorry about your mother." I handed him my card. "If there's anything I can do . . . I really would like to see whoever attacked her caught, and punished."

He licked his lips like he was getting ready to say something, then he slipped the card into his pocket, turned, and walked off.

"Jesus," Jared said as we walked to my car. "We'd better hope Pelle never finds this guy."

"Half the population is made up of women," I reminded him. "And a significant number of them wear diamonds. It doesn't mean he saw Terri."

"Yeah, but it does make a tidy package for the prosecution."

CHAPTER 30

When I arrived at the Hall of Justice the next morning, the street was jammed with television trucks and dark cars sporting PRESS placards on the dash. Camera crews were set up across the front steps, making a straight entry impossible.

I pushed my way through without comment, but began formulating a statement I'd make later in the day. Inside, the hallway was congested with more cameras and reporters, primed for action.

I spotted Lenore and Arlo by the water fountain. Lenore was blotting her mouth with a dainty hanky when she saw me. She gave a little wave, though the effort seemed to drain her.

"Ted should be here any minute," she said. "He came separately."

Arlo shuffled from one foot to the other, his hands making a similar journey in and out of his pockets. Though I imagined he was at ease in most social situations, his daughter's murder trial was clearly something different.

"How is Hannah?" I asked, more to settle the uneasiness in the air than anything.

"Wonderful," said Lenore. Her face, which was etched with worry, brightened at the thought of her granddaughter.

"The nanny is working out okay?" I asked. Ted had hired a young English woman through an agency that specialized in providing nannies to those who could afford the best.

"She's fine. But she's still just a nanny. I try to be with Hannah myself as much as possible." Another pause. Lenore's face pinched with emotion. "Since Terri can't be."

Ted caught up with us just as we were heading into the court-room. "It's a media circus out there."

"Did you talk to them?"

"Just a few words, nothing of substance." He was trying to appear calm, but I noticed a spot on his neck where he'd nicked himself shaving. Like his father-in-law, Ted was agitated and worried, and not on familiar ground in dealing with those feelings.

We entered the courtroom together.

Terri was brought in by a matron, followed by another guard. As soon as she was seated at the defense table, they melted into the background. It was a well-orchestrated ritual that took place out of the jury's presence in order to deflect any implication of guilt that might arise if she was seen with guards.

She had dressed each day with increasing simplicity. Today it was a gray jersey dress with a modest silver chain at her neck.

"How are you holding up?" I asked.

"Not well. I thought the trial would be easier than the waiting, but it's worse. Much worse." She didn't even try for a brave smile.

Terri had kept her makeup to a minimum and I could see the spread of freckles across her cheeks, and a flush of nervousness beneath the pale skin.

I checked the ring finger of her left hand, as though it might be the oracle of truth. It was bare, as I knew it would be. In order to avoid having it held in storage by prison authorities, she'd left the diamond at home when she surrendered. But I remembered it clearly. A large, emerald-cut stone that sparkled from across the room.

Had Terri killed Weaver? As much as I didn't want it to be so, I had to admit the scenario was not impossible. I fought to push the thought from my mind. This was not a moment for doubt.

Steven and Jared slipped into the room just as the bailiff asked us to rise.

Court was in session.

"Call Inspector Dennison to the stand," Pelle said. After establishing the inspector's credentials and taking him through the preliminaries of the investigation, Pelle came to the discovery of Weaver's body.

"Were you the first person on the scene?" he asked.

"No, a uniformed officer answered the call, then the paramedics. I arrived about twenty minutes later."

"What time was that?"

He looked at his notes. "A little after eight A.M. The deceased's gardener was the one who found the body and called 9-1-1. He'd gone to blow debris from the area around the door and discovered it open."

"Can you describe what you saw when you arrived?"

"There was a body, male Caucasian, sprawled on the hallway floor by the front door. A lot of blood. It appeared he'd been shot twice. Once in the mid-abdomen and once in the head."

"What else?"

"He was dressed in street clothes—khaki pants, polo shirt. The light was on in the living room as though he'd been in there before he answered the door."

"Objection," I said. "Lack of foundation. Nothing has been introduced into evidence about Mr. Weaver opening a door." I hated to raise an objection so early lest the jurors peg me as *one of those lawyers whose case was so weak she had to rely on technicalities.* But neither did I want the state's scenario planted in the mind of the jury without evidence.

Judge Tooley nodded. "The jury will disregard the last part of the witness's comment."

Pelle started to pose another question, then asked instead to have photographs of the crime scene admitted into evidence. Once they were identified by Dennison and properly tagged, he asked that they be projected onto a screen for viewing.

The lights were dimmed. The first photo flashed onto the screen.

There was an audible gasp from somewhere in the back of the courtroom, and several of the jurors turned away. The blood had spattered against the wall and pooled near the body on the floor. It was deep, dark red against the pearly gray tile of the entry hall.

Terri, looking a little green around the gills, gripped her hands tightly in her lap.

Judges have the discretion to keep upsetting or prejudicial photos from the jury. But gory as these were, particularly enlarged for the benefit of easy viewing, they fell clearly into the camp of acceptability.

"Inspector, can you tell us how far the body was from the door of the home?"

"Roughly three feet."

"Was there any sign of forced entry to the home?"

"None whatsoever."

"Any sign of a struggle?"

"None. No scratches or bruises on the body of the deceased. Nothing under the fingernails. His clothing was straight and unmussed."

I leaned back in my chair and surveyed the courtroom. It was filled to capacity. Weaver's son, Dan, was seated toward the back. I didn't see Melissa, but I did recognize Len Roemer and Hank Lomax sitting together off to my left.

"How about inside the house? Any signs of a scuffle?"

"Again, no. No overturned tables, fallen pottery, anything like that. You can see here." He pointed to the antique glass table in the center of the foyer. "There are some precariously balanced articles and they remained in place."

Pelle was ruling out self-defense, hoping to undercut any argument on our part about "heat of the moment," as well.

"Any indication that Mr. Weaver had company the evening of his death?"

"Nothing obvious."

"Moving now to the gunshot wounds themselves. Can you tell which shot of the two occurred first?"

"Yes, the shot to the abdomen came first." Dennison went on to describe the entry and exit wounds, the clotting and other factors he observed, concluding that the gun was fired at a distance of approximately twenty feet. "The head wound," he continued, pointing to the photograph on the screen, "came from a shot fired at close range, probably three to four feet. You can see the tattooing around the wound, but there wasn't the tearing that you'd find with a contact wound."

"I'm not sure I understand."

"When a person is shot at close range, the bullet entrance wound is surrounded by pinpoint hemorrhages caused by the gunpowder expelled from the barrel. We call this tattooing or stippling."

"So there were two shots fired. The first from a distance and the second at close proximity but not in contact?"

"Correct."

"In your experience, could either wound by itself have been fatal?"

I could have objected—Dennison had been qualified as an expert in firearms, not on cause of death. But maintaining a favorable image with the jury is sometimes more important than being a stickler for the rules of evidence. I kept quiet.

"The shot to the head would have been fatal by itself," Dennison said. "In all likelihood, the first shot would have killed him as well, but it's difficult to say with certainty."

Pelle wanted the jurors to understand that the killing was deliberate. Not a botched robbery or some misguided, unintentional act. The point was not lost on Ms. Huntington, who turned to regard Terri with a cold glare.

"In your search of the crime scene, did you find the murder weapon?"

"No, we did not."

"How much of the area did you search?"

"The whole area, inside and out."

"Do you know if Mr. Weaver owned a gun?"

"There were two guns registered to him. A Smith and Wesson .38 automatic and a Colt double action .45. Both guns were in the house at the time of his death. Neither had been fired recently."

"What did you conclude from this?"

"That the killer brought a gun to the house with intention of shooting Mr. Weaver, and took it away after the shooting."

This time I did object. "Calls for a conclusion."

"He's a homicide detective," Pelle responded. "This is his area of expertise. He has a right to draw conclusions."

"But he can't read minds, can he? He has no way of knowing anyone's intentions."

The judge sustained the objection and Pelle rephrased the question. But the message remained. Someone had come to Weaver's that night for the purpose of killing him.

"Can you identify the type of weapon used to kill Weaver?" Pelle asked.

"Yes, a .25 caliber Beretta, semiautomatic." Dennison launched into an explanation of rifling and twist, terms applied to the markings and grooves imprinted on a slug as it moved through the barrel of the gun.

"Do you know if the defendant owns such a gun?"

"A Beretta model 21 Bobcat, .25 caliber, was registered in her name in 1992."

Again, glances from the jury.

"Did you test the defendant's gun to see if, in fact, it matched the slugs found at the scene?"

"No, sir, we did not."

"Why is that?"

"She was unable to produce the gun for us. She claimed not to know where it was." Even delivered in a straightforward manner, the response carried an innuendo of suspicion.

"You find spent cartridges at the scene?" Pelle asked.

"Yes. Two of them."

Pelle picked up two small plastic bags from the evidence cart. "Inspector, are these those cartridges?"

"Yes, they are."

Pelle addressed the court. "I ask that these be marked as people's exhibit one and two."

"Any objection?" This was directed my way.

"None."

Pelle moved back into place for questioning. "What else did you find at the scene?"

"There was some white wool on Weaver's pant leg."

Pelle reached for another bag and went through a similar exercise to have the fiber admitted into evidence.

"Were you able to identify it?"

"Objection," I said. "The Inspector is not trained in identification of fibers."

"Your Honor, I'm simply trying to present my case logically."

Judge Tooley nodded, but her face was a scowl. "A commendable goal, Mr. Pelle, but we have rules about how evidence should be presented."

Pelle didn't push the issue. Instead, he went through the other items bagged at the scene—dark glasses, black fiber, and the gum wrapper—and had them admitted into evidence. Then he moved on other aspects of the investigation.

"Were you able to establish a window for the time of the shooting?"

"Based on the coroner's report and interviews with neighbors, it appears that Weaver was shot around midnight." Dennison checked his notebook. "One neighbor heard what she thought might have been shots at twelve-ten. Another remembers hearing two sharp bangs just as she was going to bed. She didn't look at the clock, but based on her television viewing, she estimates the time to be a little after midnight."

"The coroner's report is consistent with that?"

"Right. And we know that Weaver was on the air with his radio broadcast until nine o'clock. He didn't leave the studio until about twenty after."

Pelle walked back to his table, checked a note, and addressed Dennison from there. "Inspector, when did you first talk to Mrs. Harper?"

"My partner tried to reach her that morning, about eleven, but she wasn't home. No one knew where she was. I was finally able to talk to her Sunday afternoon."

"Where did she say she had been all that time?"

All that time, as if she'd gone underground for months. But raising an objection would only highlight the fact that Terri had taken an unexpected trip.

"She said she'd driven north to Mendocino."

"A long drive for such a short stay, wouldn't you say?"

I stood up. "Objection. Not only is the prosecutor editorializing, it's irrelevant."

"I'll withdraw the question." His expression bordered on smug. Withdrawn or not, the thought remained with the jury. "Did you do a trace metal or gunpowder residue test on the defendant?"

"No. By then too much time had elapsed for either test to prove useful."

One of the members of the jury, a school teacher I'd thought might be sympathetic to our side, nodded slightly. Pelle had apparently succeeded in making his point.

"Did you conduct a search of the defendant's home?" Pelle asked.

"Yes, we did."

"And what did you find?"

"A black nylon jacket."

Pelle again headed to the evidence cart and had the jacket admitted into evidence. "What was it about this jacket that caught your interest?"

"Well, we'd found black nylon fiber at the scene. It was caught in a rosebush by the front walkway. Looked as though it could have come from the defendant's jacket."

Pelle picked up another plastic bag. "Moving on, Inspector, can you identify this videotape?"

"Yes, it's from one of the security cameras in this building."

"Taken?"

"July 6."

"Ten days before Mr. Weaver's murder, is that correct?"

"Yes."

Pelle had the tape logged into evidence and then asked permission to play it for the jurors.

I was on my feet in a flash. "Could we have a sidebar, Your Honor?"

"What is it?" she asked when Pelle and I had gathered at the podium.

"The tape is prejudicial," I said, "and has been introduced without proper basis. He's going to select the soundbite that serves his purpose and—"

"Would you rather I showed the whole tape?"

"I'd rather you didn't show it at all."

"Your client threatened Weaver," Pelle said tartly. "The jury needs to know that."

Judge Tooley interrupted. "Your objection is overruled, Ms. O'Brien. We'll see the tape."

The judge instructed the bailiff to darken the room. A minute later the courtroom's attention was riveted on an enlarged closeup of Terri's face contorted with rage.

There's no way in hell you'll get my daughter, she said on film. *You'd better watch your back. I'd kill you before I let you have Hannah.*

Pelle let the film run long enough that we could see Ted pulling Terri away, restraining her while she thrashed to get free. Then he stopped the film and signaled for the lights.

In the silence that followed, three jurors glared accusingly at Terri. The others seemed to make it a point to avoid looking at her. Pelle took his time checking his notes, letting Terri's words echo in people's minds.

"That's all for Inspector Dennison at this time," he said, and sat down.

I suspect he had other minor points he'd intended to bring forth, but the tape had been more powerful than he'd expected. And if there was one thing Pelle knew, it was how to stage a prosecution for effect.

CHAPTER 31

"Cross?" Judge Tooley tossed the ball into my court.

I had been afraid she might call a recess, which would have allowed Terri's angry face and words to be imprinted in the minds of the jurors for longer.

I stood and approached the witness box. Best to confront the damning testimony face on, I decided. Especially since it was freshest in the jurors' minds.

"Inspector Dennison, were you present at the courthouse encounter between Terri Harper and Mr. Weaver?"

"No, I was not."

"Isn't it true that you have no way of knowing the details and circumstances of that encounter outside the portion that was taped?"

"I know they'd left a hearing—"

"But you don't know what happened just prior to the events shown on the tape?"

"Correct." It was a reluctant admission.

"Or just after."

"That's also correct."

"Or what else might have been going on at the same time that was *not* captured on film."

"Well, it seems pretty obvious—"

"Inspector, please. Just answer the question."

"No," Dennison said in clipped tones, "I do not."

I took a few steps to the side, adopted a more casual tone. "When did court personnel contact you about the existence of the tape?"

"I contacted them."

I frowned. I'd assumed it was the other way around. "How did you know to do that?"

"I got a call, alerting me to the fact that your client threatened Mr. Weaver after the hearing."

"A call from whom?"

"A friend of his. Len Roemer."

The name caught me by surprise. "When was this?"

"I don't . . . just a minute." Dennison checked his notebook again. "July 19."

After Terri's arrest. After I'd talked to Roemer myself. An interesting detail though I wasn't sure what I'd be able to do with it.

"How many other names did you come up with of people who might have reason to kill Weaver?"

"How many?" He wore a befuddled expression.

"Surely my client wasn't your only suspect?"

"Not at first, no." Dennison ran a finger under the collar of his shirt. It was a nervous gesture, although Dennison appeared confident and at ease as a witness.

"It did occur to you, did it not, that someone besides my client might have a motive to kill Weaver?"

"Sure."

"You talked about the possibility among yourselves?"

"We tossed around a number of ideas."

"How many names?"

"I couldn't say offhand." He pulled himself up straighter in his chair.

"Two? A dozen? Fifty?"

"Sorry, I can't remember."

"Did you question any of them?"

"The evidence pointed to the defendant."

"Is that a 'no,' Inspector Dennison?"

He frowned. The busy eyebrows met over the bridge of his nose. "I've lost the question, I'm afraid."

"Did you question any potential suspects besides Terri Harper?"

"We talked to people who knew Weaver—neighbors, friends, coworkers, and so forth—but the evidence persuaded us to focus on the defendant."

"The evidence." I shifted my gaze to the jury box, as though we were allied by our doubts. "You can't say for sure that it was Mrs. Harper's gun that was the murder weapon, can you?"

"Without having the gun in hand to run a comparison, it's impossible to say with certainty."

"Nor can you say for sure that the murder weapon was a Model 21 Bobcat. Isn't that so?"

"Correct, but there are—"

"That's fine, Inspector. You need only answer the question. Did you find evidence of additional shots fired, shots that missed the victim?"

"No, we did not."

"And you found only two casings?"

"Correct."

"So the person who killed Mr. Weaver was a pretty good shot?" I could use this later when I'd introduce testimony to show that Terri was not.

"Either that or lucky." Dennison looked toward the jury with a thin smile.

Not a one of them returned the smile, though there was a soft ripple of laughter from the spectator area.

I checked my notes. "Did you find anything unusual about the casings, Inspector?"

"Yes. They showed multiple tool marks."

"How do you account for that?"

"Most likely explanation is that the casings had been fired previously."

"Reloaded?"

"Right."

"Where does one purchase reloaded ammunition, Inspector?"

"Mostly, people reload it themselves. Hunters, gun hobbyists, that sort. But you can sometimes buy it at gun shows."

This, too, was something we could use later in Terri's favor. She was not a likely candidate for buying reloaded ammunition.

I glanced back to the defense table, knowing Jared would signal if I'd missed anything. Apparently we were on track. But at the other end of the table, Terri was clutching her stomach and looking glum.

"Inspector, you said there was no sign of robbery. How carefully did you look?"

The question appeared to amuse him. "We looked through the house and saw no sign that anything had been disturbed."

"But your focus was on the homicide, wasn't it?"

"Initially. However, it's standard practice in a situation like this to check for robbery."

"And nothing was missing?"

"Not that we could determine."

"Did you get a list of contents for comparison?"

Dennison gave a derisive laugh. "I don't imagine many people keep a contents list for home furnishings and personal belongings."

"Did you ask a close relative or friend of Mr. Weaver's to look through the house and tell you if anything was missing?"

"The television, his wallet, a pair of diamond cuff links—there were many things of value lying in plain view."

"But isn't it correct that you don't know what else might have been there, whether in plain view or not?"

Dennison sighed and delivered his response with heavy sarcasm. "You're right. There may have been a valuable Ming vase Weaver kept in his sock drawer, and we never knew about it."

"Or business records, letters, compromising photographs, a taped conversation. The list goes on, Inspector. It's possible, isn't it, that the killer was after something besides so-called *valuables?*"

Pelle rose behind me. "I have to object, Your Honor. Counsel is engaging in pure speculation."

"The prosecution's interpretation of evidence is also speculative, Your Honor. We know that Mr. Weaver was killed. We don't know the circumstances or reason for his death."

Judge Tooley pressed her manicured fingers together and tapped her chin. "Do you intend to pursue this line of questioning much longer, Ms. O'Brien?"

"With this question, I'm finished."

"Fine. The objection is overruled. The witness will answer and then we'll move on."

At Dennison's request, I repeated the question.

"Yes," he said curtly. "It's possible."

I could see several of the jurors nodding. I hadn't given them a different killer, but I'd opened the door to the possibility.

I began a new line of inquiry. "You say you first talked with Terri Harper on Sunday afternoon."

"That's right," Dennison replied. "We'd been trying to reach her all weekend."

"Did you question her at her home?"

"We were at the station."

"You brought her in for questioning?"

"She came down on her own." Dennison could see where I was going with this and worked to keep his answers as simple as possible.

"Came down voluntarily. On a Sunday afternoon, following a long drive home from Mendocino. Of her own accord, she got into the car when she learned you'd wanted to speak with her, and drove downtown to assist in the investigation. Isn't that so?"

"She came down on her own," Dennison said. His gaze narrowed. "And then called you, her attorney."

It always amazes me that calling an attorney is portrayed as a sign of guilt. I was on the verge of moving that Dennison's response be struck, when I decided the jury would only see it as defensive on my part. I nodded instead.

"She came to the station initially without an attorney, in a good faith effort to answer your questions. Wasn't it you who suggested she call an attorney?"

"I wouldn't say I suggested it."

I tapped my forehead. "Excuse me, you said she had a right to call an attorney, is that it?"

Dennison looked away. "I might have."

I headed back to the defense table, then turned as though a thought had just occurred to me. "One last question, Inspector Dennison. You are part of the prosecutorial team, are you not?"

"I'm a homicide inspector."

"But you've gone over your testimony with the prosecutor, and the two of you have had numerous discussions about evidence, witnesses' statements, and the like. Isn't that correct?"

"That's part of my job."

"Precisely. You and the prosecutor are working together to see that Terri Harper is convicted for this crime."

His mouth was tight. "That's the way it works."

"No further questions of this witness."

While Terri ate a boxed lunch alone in the small holding cell behind the courtroom, Steven, Jared, and I hunched over case files in the similarly Spartan quarters available to defense attorneys. But we had the benefit of thickly packed turkey sandwiches and Chinese coleslaw from a nearby deli.

As we were packing up to head back to court for the afternoon session, Steven turned to me with a look that blended hesitation and expectation with a touch of irony. His mouth pulled up ever so slightly at the corners.

"How about dinner?" he asked, shoving his hands into his pockets.

"We just had lunch."

He grinned. "I meant later, tonight."

"I don't know that we should go down that road." I'd been reminded of the perils, as well as the pleasures, unfortunately, when we'd met for drinks at the Claremont the previous week.

"Nothing fancy," Steven said. "I'll cook up some pasta and make a salad."

"It wasn't the food that worried me."

"This isn't a date, Kali. It's just dinner. And pleasant company. I don't particularly feel like being alone after court today."

In truth, neither did I. And though I was loath to admit it, I *did* feel a pleasant ripple of anticipation at the idea of being with Steven.

During the afternoon session we heard from the coroner, who described Weaver's wounds in technical terms that may have zipped over the heads of jurors in content but clearly delivered the message Pelle was after—the shot to Weaver's face was calculated, and probably unnecessary. What you'd expect from a killer with a personal vendetta, and not a simple burglary.

We also heard from the crime scene technicians, a gun expert, and the gardener who discovered Weaver's body. The testimony did little but reiterate what Dennison had said earlier.

Through all of it, Terri tried to appear relaxed and attentive, as I'd instructed, but she had trouble pulling it off. I could almost feel the agitation vibrating under her skin.

When the jury had filed from the room, she turned to me. "How long before I get a chance to tell my side?"

"We'll present our case when the prosecution has finished. Another couple of days, I'd say."

"Will my turn come at the beginning or the end of our case?"

I straightened the papers on the table before me. "I haven't decided yet whether to have you testify at all."

Putting a defendant on the stand was risky under the best of circumstances, and my faith in Terri fell somewhat short of that.

"I can do it," she said testily. "I won't say anything stupid. The jurors will wonder about me if I don't testify."

There was that, too. "Let's see how things play out first."

I stopped by home long enough to change out of my work-wear and take Loretta for a very quick walk. And to brush my teeth, completely redo my makeup, use the blow dryer on a few errant locks of hair, rub my skin with lavender-scented lotion, and try on and discard several outfits. I ended up, finally, settling on a pair of soft-drape black rayon slacks and an emerald green silk-blend tee.

I'd taken the shirt off the hanger and put it back again at least three times before slipping it on. It had been one of Tom's favorites—he liked the way the green accented my eyes and set off the red highlights in my hair—and it seemed somehow wrong to wear it to dinner with Steven.

But Tom was in Silver Creek, no doubt enjoying his own dinner with his wife, so what Tom thought about my eyes or hair didn't really matter, did it?

Steven greeted me with a quick kiss on the cheek. It was the sort of familiar but meaningless gesture Californians often used in lieu of a handshake. I wasn't even sure Steven realized what he'd done. He took the bottle of wine I'd brought and headed for the kitchen, leaving me a moment on my own to reflect on the softness of his lips against my cheek.

"You look terrific," he said when I joined him in the kitchen. "That green is a great color on you."

"Thanks." *Take that, Tom.*

"Are you any good at chopping mushrooms?" Steven asked.

"Depends if you're talking amateur status or something grander."

"The meal is most definitely amateur. I consider it an accomplishment that I can even boil pasta."

Steven pointed to the chopping block by the sink and passed

me a bag of mushrooms. "Knife is in the drawer to the left."
Handing me a glass of wine, he added, "It went pretty well in
court today, don't you agree?"

That was something I had a hard time gauging. We hadn't been
hammered over the head with irrefutable evidence, and we hadn't
been ambushed by new revelations or unexpected testimony, but
neither had I thrown any harpoons of my own.

"It certainly could have been worse."

"I have the feeling it will continue to go well," Steven said op-
timistically. He was washing leaves of butter lettuce and patting
them dry with a towel. "I watched the jury during your cross of
Dennison. That Mr. Ortiz we were concerned about kept nodding
at everything you said."

"Maybe he's got a tic."

"Have faith, Kali."

"Juries are unpredictable. You know that."

He frowned. "Guess I'm trying hard to forget it."

A large gray cat appeared at the kitchen doorway, yawned and
stretched, then idled over to Steven, weaving figure eights around
his legs.

I smiled. "Somehow I never figured you for a cat person."

"I'm not actually. But Felix came with the house."

"His owners left him here?"

"I don't think he had any owners. He just showed up the day
after I moved in and never left. I put up signs around the neighborhood, rang doorbells, but no one claimed him."

"So you took him in."

"Actually, I took him to the pound. Got inside the door before I
realized I couldn't do it."

"Sounds familiar. That's sort of how I ended up with Loretta."

"Rebecca always wanted a kitten," Steven added, somewhat
subdued. He opened the cupboard and stared blankly at the contents.

"Why didn't you get her one?"

"Caroline didn't want pets in the house."

There was nothing derisive about the words or their delivery,
yet I knew intuitively that the remark was the tip of a large iceberg. The first hint he'd given that things hadn't been storybook-
perfect between Steven and his late wife.

"I failed her," he said after a moment. "I was her father, and I failed her."

I had the feeling we were no longer talking kittens.

Steven reached for the olive oil and vinegar, and poured a little of each into the salad bowl. "I was supposed to pick her up that night. She'd gone home from school with a friend. I was going to stop by on my way home. Instead, I called Caroline and told her I had to work late. Then I went to your place."

I felt the punch of Rebecca's death anew. "I didn't realize that."

He busied himself with tearing lettuce leaves. "Do you know much about reincarnation?"

I shook my head.

"I don't either, but I've done some reading. An innocent child like that. Such a waste of a beautiful soul. That can't be the end of it."

"I guess not." Though I'd always wondered about the math. How could souls be recycled when there were so many more people alive now than in the past? Maybe God recruited from other planets.

"I'm sure it's not."

It wasn't what he said so much as the dark, pained timbre he gave the words. I wondered if I was seeing the edge of the black hole Martin Bloomberg had spoken of.

Before I could think how to respond, Steven shook himself free from whatever demon had hold of him. "The news is coming on. Shall we see if they've covered the trial?"

"Let me have more wine first. I think I'll need it."

He turned on the set but kept the volume low during coverage of an apartment fire, an attempted bank robbery, and ongoing conflicts between bicyclists and motorists throughout the city.

He peeled an avocado and began slicing it into the salad. "Are you going to build a defense that incorporates a different suspect?"

"Who would I point to? The vague, random-gunman theory isn't usually a winner." And my list of potential standins was just that—a list. Unless I wanted to hazard to pick a name, toss it to the jury, and see if it stuck, I didn't have much to offer.

"What about the three musketeers?" Steven asked.

"The who?"

"Weaver's friends—Roemer, Billings, and Lomax. They certainly *act* like they're up to something."

"There's nothing that ties them to the murder, though. All three claim to have alibis, and none of them drives a car with sheepskin seatcovers."

"Maybe we haven't pushed hard enough."

"Hit the volume," I said, jabbing a finger in the direction of the TV. "It's the trial."

The coverage began with footage from the courthouse steps. I caught a glimpse of myself striding past the camera as I headed to court that morning. I came across as more confident and sophisticated than I'd felt, but could see that I badly needed a haircut.

The anchorwoman outlined the basics of the case, then switched to a reporter in the field who held a mike for Ted while he delivered what amounted to a pep talk for the defense. He managed to look attractively weary while still flashing plenty of white teeth.

The reporter then summarized the day in court—the prosecution's methodical presentation of evidence and the defense's uneventful attempts to chip away at the state's case. There were, she concluded, no surprises from either side.

The screen shifted to an impromptu interview with Len Roemer in the hallway outside the courtroom. "I want to see justice done. I want my friend's killer held accountable." Roemer was close to a rant. The knife edge of hostility didn't make a lot of sense in light of the rather bland day in court. Then he got to the heart of the matter.

"A woman judge," he continued, "a woman defense attorney, and a jury that's over half women. Against those odds, justice doesn't stand a chance. Terri Harper is going to get away with murder because women stick together. Our whole country is a conspiracy of women, and if we don't stand up and fight—"

The camera swung back to the reporter in the field, who wrapped it up with a smile and a "Back to you, Susan."

"What's Roemer talking about?" I grumbled. "The judge hardly played favorites. As for the jury, women are harder on other women than men are."

"He's nuts." Steven flicked off the television set. "All three of them are. Like I said earlier, I also think they're up to something."

"Such as?"

"I don't know. But we *do* know that Roemer and Billings had a falling out with Weaver." Steven drained the pasta into a colander. "You want to toss the salad?"

"I finally spoke with Alexander Rudd," I told him. I hated to spoil our evening, but if Steven was going to dissect defense strategy, he needed to know the whole picture.

"How'd you find him?" Steven asked.

"I had Jared keeping an eye on his mother's room at the hospital. I figured he'd show up at some point."

Steven drizzled pesto sauce over the pasta and topped it with sautéed mushrooms. His earlier balloon of enthusiasm deflated. "I guess if he'd seen a different killer, you'd have said so by now."

I swallowed against a mouth that was suddenly quite dry. "He says he saw a woman leaving the vicinity of the crime."

Steven stood still, sauté pan held midair. Like a marble tribute to the joy of cooking.

"A woman?"

I nodded.

"Can he identify her?"

"No. He says he didn't see her face at all."

The pan landed back on the stove. The marble became flesh.

"But he said she was blond," I added. "And that she wore a large diamond on her left ring finger."

"That describes a hell of a lot of women," Steven grunted, giving the pepper shaker a heavy twist over the pasta.

"But taken with everything else—"

"Don't even go there." His tone was sharp. "Terri would never kill anyone. And she most certainly didn't kill Weaver."

"I'm not saying we should give up and roll over."

He looked at me with skepticism. "What are you saying then, exactly?"

Good question. That Terri might be guilty? It was the thought I was dancing around. But I didn't want to give voice to doubt. Not as a friend of Steven's, and certainly not as Terri's attorney.

I shrugged. "I'm not sure I'm saying anything, really. Just passing on what Rudd told me."

Steven nodded. "Fine. Just as long as you realize it doesn't mean much."

Steven had set the table before I arrived. Black and white check tablecloth, striated pillar candles, and a small arrangement of sweet peas and zinnias from the garden. Now he lit the candles, put a Mozart concerto on, and dimmed the lights. Simple and informal as the dinner might be, the ambiance was anything but.

"I know very little about your life these last five years," Steven said. "Except that you moved home to Silver Creek when Goldman & Latham broke apart, and now you're back."

"That's about it."

He laughed. "That's like saying Ulysses took a trip and returned again."

"My years away were nothing like his, believe me."

"I'm glad to hear it." Steven's eyes met mine and held my gaze, bringing a tingle to my skin.

I began to talk, simply in order to break the spell. I told him about my father's death, the event that had taken me home to Silver Creek in the first place, and the family secrets I'd discovered quite by accident. I talked about the cases I'd tried, the practice I was building, and even, briefly, about Tom.

Steven said very little about himself.

After dinner I helped him clear the table. "Leave the dishes," he said, "I'll get them later. You want some coffee?"

I shook my head. "Actually, I should be getting home."

"It's early still."

"I'm in the middle of a trial, remember?"

He put a hand on my waist and drew me close, brushing his lips against my hair. "Stay just a bit longer, why don't you."

My forehead rested on his shoulder. "I wish I could."

What was interesting, I noted with almost clinical detachment, was that my reluctance had almost nothing to do with Caroline and Rebecca but with the work awaiting me. I wondered whether that was progress or not.

"Maybe another time," I said, reluctantly pulling away.

He kissed me on the forehead. "I can wait."

CHAPTER 32

M rs. Lucille Campe, the witness who claimed to have seen a
dark color Explorer with a license number similar to Terri's,
took the stand amid a tinkle of bells and bangles. She was a large
woman dressed in a flowing batik caftan and a collection of
beads, baubles, and bracelets reminiscent of the sixties.

"Mrs. Campe," Pelle began, "can you tell the court what you
were doing the evening of July 10 at a little before midnight?"

"I was taking my Penny out for her late-night constitutional."

"Penny is—"

"A Welsh corgie."

A few of the jurors smiled. Perhaps amused, as I was, that
she'd overlooked the more generic response *dog.*

"Did you notice a car parked in front of your house that
evening?" Pelle asked.

"Yes, I did. It was a Ford Explorer, dark blue. Real clean and
shiny, too."

"And did you happen to notice the vehicle's license plate?"

"I didn't get the whole thing. But the middle letters were
NMO. I think there might have been a 7 in there too, but I could-
n't say for sure."

"Was anyone in the car at the time?"

"Not to my knowledge." Lucille Campe was basking in the
role of eyewitness.

"Did you see anyone enter the car?"

"No, I did not."

Pelle frowned. It clearly wasn't the answer he'd expected.
"You didn't see anyone approach the car as you returned from
your walk?"

It was a leading question, but raising an objection was the kind of hairsplitting that turned off jurors. And it wouldn't make any difference in the long run. I let it go.

Mrs. Campe's face lit with understanding. "Yes, I did. But I didn't see her actually get into the car. It looked like she unlocked the door, but by then Penny was doing her business and I had to clean up. I wasn't paying much attention to the car by then."

Pelle relaxed. "Did you get a look at the woman?"

"From a distance."

"Can you describe her for us, please."

Mrs. Campe looked at Terri and then away again. A subtle, probably unintentional gesture that no doubt made its mark on the jury. "She was maybe five-seven or thereabouts. And slender. Her hair was a light color and she was wearing dark clothing. Pants and some kind of jacket."

"Was she approaching from the north or the south?" he asked.

"From the south. To my left as I came down the walk."

From the direction Bram Weaver lived.

"No further questions," Pelle said.

Judge Tooley looked my way. "Cross?"

I stood and took a few steps toward the witness. "Do you walk Penny every evening, Mrs. Campe?"

"Most evenings. Sometimes my husband does it."

"And do you always notice what type of car is parked in front of your house?"

"I look to see if they've blocked the driveway. People figure they can hang over a foot or two and it doesn't matter, but it does."

I went for an end run. "Did you walk Penny last night?"

"Sure did. She doesn't take 'no' for an answer." Mrs. Campe smiled fondly.

"Was there a car parked in front of your house last night?"

"Of course. There's never an empty parking spot in this city."

"What kind of car was it?"

Her face constricted, as though she'd just been stung by a wasp. "A sedan, I think."

"Make? Color?"

Mrs. Campe folded her arms in her lap, setting off another round of jingling. "I'm not sure. A compact maybe. Or a sports car. Something small. Didn't hang over the driveway, even by an inch. And the color was gray, or maybe beige."

"Can you be more specific?"

She squared her shoulders. "Some cars stand out, like the VW bug, a BMW, or an Explorer. This was just a small sedan. I don't remember what make."

"Or what color?"

"Only that it was a neutral color."

"Do you recall the license number?"

She didn't meet my eyes. "No, not really."

"Yet you are absolutely sure the car you saw the night in question was a dark blue Ford Explorer with an NMO on the plate?"

"Absolutely." She fingered the many layers of beads at her neck.

"Mrs. Campe, in your original statement to the police, didn't you say that you recalled seeing a dark-colored SUV?"

She looked to Pelle. "I'm not sure what my exact words were."

I pulled her statement from the papers on my table and asked that it be admitted into evidence. Then I read it back to her.

"If that's what they wrote down," she acknowledged, "it must be what I said."

"So at the time, you weren't sure the car was blue?"

"I knew it was blue. Maybe I didn't say it, but I knew."

"Nor did you identify it at that time as an Explorer."

"I'm not a person who knows the names of cars right off the top of my head. But later I recognized another one on the road and looked to see what it was."

I pulled out an envelope of photos I'd taken earlier in the week, handed one set to Pelle, and another to the witness. "Mrs. Campe, there are six pictures here. Which one, if any, is the type of car you saw in front of your house the night in question?"

She studied the photographs intently, then selected one with confidence and handed it to me.

"You're sure this is the one?"

"Yes, I am." She nodded vigorously, amid more tinkling and jangling.

"Let the record show that the witness has selected a photograph of a Chevy Blazer."

Pelle jumped to his feet, waving his copy of the photos.

"Objection. This little demonstration is nothing more than cheap theatrics. Counsel is purposely trying to confuse the witness."

"How so?" the judge asked.

"There isn't a picture of a Ford Explorer in the lot of them."

I thought it likely Pelle had been as confused as the witness. "I didn't say there was," I reminded him. "I merely asked which, if any, was the car she'd seen."

"That's a cheap trick and you know it!"

Judge Tooley rapped her gavel and directed a hardened gaze on Pelle. "You're out of line, counselor. The objection is over-ruled."

"I'd like it noted for the record," he protested.

"So noted."

I turned my attention back to Mrs. Campe, who was glaring at me so intensely I thought her eyes must hurt.

"Did the police at any time show you a picture of the defendant?" I asked.

"They showed me a bunch of pictures."

"And were you able to identify the defendant in any of them?"

"No," she said icily. "I was not."

On redirect, Pelle attempted to repair some of the damage.

"Mrs. Campe," he asked, "do you make a habit of memorizing license plates?"

"No."

"Can you tell the court, then, why you remember the plate you saw the night in question?"

"It struck me that if the first two letters were reversed, the sequence would be alphabetical. M-N-O. That sounds silly, but it's how my mind works."

"So you are sure the plate you saw was NMO?"

"Yes, I'm absolutely sure." This time her response rang true.

Terri seemed visibly shaken. "It wasn't me," she whispered. "It wasn't."

Pelle returned to his seat. "No further questions."

Steven leaned forward and touched my shoulder. "Good job, Kali. You did a lot of damage."

It was, I was afraid, a drop in the bucket.

Next, Pelle called Terri's neighbor Margo Poller, a high-strung woman with a voice to match. She testified that she'd heard the

Harpers' garage door open about eleven-thirty the night of the murder and had heard their car backing out the driveway.

"She hates me," Terri muttered as Pelle was winding down. "She'd say anything to cause trouble."

"Why?"

"They left their teenaged son home alone last spring while they went to Europe. After putting up with loud music and drunken rowdiness for a couple of days, I called the cops."

"I should think she'd be grateful."

"Well, she wasn't."

Pelle turned to me. "Your witness."

"Did you see the car?" I asked Mrs. Poller. "Or just hear it?"

"I didn't look, if that's what you mean."

"So it might not have been Terri Harper's car you heard."

"There's only hers and Ted's in the garage, and Ted was out of town." She fell just short of sounding like the neighborhood busybody.

"Did you hear the car return?"

"No, I went to sleep pretty quickly."

"Isn't it possible then, that the car you heard about eleven-thirty was coming into the garage rather than leaving?" Never mind that Terri had said she hadn't gone out at all, I was trying to raise questions about the credibility of the witness.

Margo Poller, however, wasn't about to entertain other possibilities. "No," she said emphatically, "I'm sure the car was leaving."

"Did you think it odd, someone going out at that hour?"

"Not at the time, no."

"If it wasn't unusual, how did you come to notify the police about what you'd heard?"

She folded her hands on her lap. "They came around the next morning looking for Terri."

"In your statement to them, you reported you'd seen her leave that morning. With a suitcase and portacrib, if I'm not mistaken."

"Something to that effect, yes."

"I'm a little confused, then, as to why you also volunteered that you'd heard her go out at night since it hadn't struck you as odd at the time."

"I'd heard about Weaver's death on the news," she explained. "I figured that's why they wanted to talk to Terri."

"And you wanted to be helpful?" I added a thin veneer of sarcasm but it was lost on Mrs. Poller.

She nodded. "They said he had been shot during the night."

The meddling neighbor. From a purely logical perspective, that didn't invalidate her testimony, but jurors instinctively treat such witnesses as less credible.

"Are you and Terri Harper close friends?" I asked.

"We're neighbors, not friends."

"Congenial neighbors, would you say?"

"I suppose." Her jaw tensed, belying her words.

"Wasn't there an incident this last spring that caused some hard feelings?"

She shot Terri a smoldering look. "Your client called the cops on my son because he and a few friends got a little loud. They are teenagers, for God's sake. They like to have fun. If she's going to get upset about kids having fun, she should move to the country."

The venom in Margo Poller's words spoke for itself. I knew enough to quit while I was ahead. "No further questions, Your Honor."

I'd caught a glimpse of Melissa sitting in the back of the courtroom, and when we broke for noon recess, I looked for her again. Finally I gave up and headed for the stairs rather than fight the crowds at the elevator. The quiet of the stairwell was a pleasant change from the din of voices in the hallway. I was partway down the first flight when I heard the rapid beat of footsteps descending from behind me. I turned to look just as Len Roemer caught up with me, knocking me against the wall with his shoulder.

"Better watch your step," he said, breathing in my face.

"Why don't *you* watch where you're going?" The guy was a jerk.

"You wouldn't want to take a nasty spill, would you?"

"Is that a threat?"

His teeth bared in a grin. "I'm worried about your safety is all."

I tried to duck around him but he stepped to the left, blocking my passage.

"Of course, lawyers who defend killers probably don't think much about safety."

Anger gave way to fear. I could feel a band of perspiration at the back of my neck. I worked to sound calm. "Don't do anything you're going to regret, Mr. Roemer."

"Life's too short to waste time on regrets. Never look back— that's my motto." He stepped aside, but just barely, so that I had to brush against him as I passed. "Oh, and tell your flunkies to stay away from me. I have another motto, and that's *Don't put up with crap.*"

I was half a flight below him by then and I kept on going. By the time I had pushed open the door on the main floor, my legs were shaking so badly I could barely stand.

CHAPTER 33

L en Roemer didn't make it back to court for the afternoon session, but Billings and Lomax were there, glowering from the second row, along with a handful of faces I'd not seen previously. It looked like they'd brought along new recruits.

Weaver's son Dan was there again too. I scanned the rows of spectators in search of Melissa, but didn't see her.

The afternoon session opened with testimony from Chuck Russo, the chief criminalist for the city and county of San Francisco. A short, wiry man with a trim mustache, he sported a red bow tie and delivered his responses in a direct, almost folksy manner.

Pelle introduced into evidence the white wool found on Weaver's pant leg, along with the black nylon fibers and the dark glasses with attached blond hair. At Pelle's prompts, Russo expounded on the similarity between the wool found at the crime scene and that taken from the seat covers of Terri's Explorer, but much to my relief, he didn't spring any fancy corroborative tests on us. Under cross, he admitted there was no way of knowing with certainty whether or not the fibers had come from the same source.

The testimony with respect to the black nylon and the blond hair were similarly inconclusive. Although Terri owned a black jacket, tests had not established a clear match. Terri was a blonde of similar shade, but nothing more could be stated with certainty. And I was careful to point out in my cross the sizable number of people who were blondes, owned black nylon garments, and covered the seats of their cars with white sheepskin.

Still, the cumulative effect of the prosecution's evidence against Terri had to have had an impact on the jurors.

Next in line was Irene Kontos, Terri's manicurist. She'd been added at the last minute, so that Nick had only had a chance to speak with her briefly by phone.

"Miss Kontos," Pelle said, holding out the dark glasses admitted into evidence earlier in the trial. "I ask you to examine this pair of purple-framed sunglasses. Can you tell me if you recognize them?"

Irene Kontos, an attractive young woman of Mediterranean descent, raised her gaze from her lap, where she'd been staring since being sworn in, and looked at the glasses. "I can't say for sure."

"Did you ever see the defendant wearing a similar pair?"

Biting her lip, she again lowered her gaze and nodded.

"You'll have to speak up," Pelle said. "For the record."

"Yes," Irene Kontos whispered.

"That's a 'yes,' you saw the defendant wearing a pair of glasses like these?"

"They were purple," she said. "With reflective glass. I'm not sure they were identical."

"Do you notice anything distinctive about the glasses in front of you?"

"What do you mean?"

"On the frame, near the right earpiece. Is there a logo of some kind?"

She took her time examining the glasses. "It looks like a lightning bolt or something. In silver."

"And did you notice a similar logo on the glasses the defendant was wearing?"

Irene Kontos shifted uneasily in her seat. She was clearly a reluctant witness. "There was some kind of silver accent on Mrs. Harper's," she said, "but I didn't really look that closely."

"Thank you." Pelle returned to the counsel table and I rose for cross.

"Miss Kontos," I asked, "how many clients do you have each week?"

"Oh, it varies. Maybe thirty on average."

"And you remember the type of dark glasses each of them wears?"

She smiled, causing her cheeks to dimple. "No, of course not. But I admired Mrs. Harper's. They were new. This was right around Easter and they looked very springy. I went right out and bought myself a pair. Well, not exactly the same, I'm sure. I got mine at Target."

"Do you have them with you?"

"Yes, I do."

"Would you mind showing them to me?"

"Objection."

Judge Tooley arched an eyebrow and addressed Pelle. "On what ground?"

"It's highly irregular."

"I don't recall 'irregularity' as being in the Rules of Evidence," she said.

There was a titter from the courtroom.

"Irrelevant then."

"I'm going to allow it," Tooley said, without asking for an explanation from me. "The witness will show counsel her glasses."

Irene Kontos dug her glasses out of her purse and handed them to me. They were purple with square styling and reflective glass like the ones found at the scene. But side by side, the differences between the two pairs were obvious. Among other things, Miss Kontos's glasses lacked the arched bridge and thick frames of the pair in evidence. Hers were also a lighter-weight plastic and much brighter purple. But there was a silver dot by the earpiece.

I handed them back to her. "Can you say for sure that the glasses you saw Terri Harper wearing were *not* identical to your own pair?"

Irene Kontos smiled again. "I doubt Mrs. Harper buys anything at Target."

"But aside from that, can you be sure?"

"No. All I remember is that they were purple and I wanted purple glasses. Also, that they had reflective lenses."

"Did you have trouble finding a pair?"

"Not at all. I checked a couple of places, then found these."

"So purple glasses with reflective lenses aren't uncommon?"

Pelle voiced another objection. "The witness is hardly an expert on dark glasses," he protested.

"I'll withdraw the question, Your Honor."

* * *

The final prosecution witness, Ellen Talbot, was a woman from Terri's book group— a brassy and shrill wife of the CFO of a local bank. She struck me as the kind of person who would never voluntarily pick up a book except to throw it. I mumbled as much to Terri, who explained that Ellen came for the socializing and the food, and at every meeting offered a new explanation as to why she hadn't been able to read the current month's selection.

Pelle had taken her through the preliminaries and was now questioning her about a book club meeting that had taken place at the Harpers' home just prior to Weaver's death.

"She was holding the baby," Ellen Talbot said, making Terri's mothering sound like an outrageous act, "and when one of the women mentioned something about Mr. Weaver, she said 'that man should be shot.' "

"Those were her exact words?" Pelle asked.

"Word for word. This was right after that shooting at the McDonald's, so it struck me as pretty reckless."

Pelle turned to the judge. "Nothing further."

I glanced at the jury. None of the members were exactly nodding off, but several wore glazed expressions.

I approached the witness. "Did my client elaborate, Mrs. Talbot?"

"What do you mean?"

"Did she expound on the idea of shooting Bram Weaver?"

"No."

"Did she talk further about Mr. Weaver at all?"

"She called him callous, and a troublemaker. She went on and on about how it wasn't fair that this should be happening to her." Ellen Talbot tossed her head like an adolescent, something she clearly wasn't. "As if *she* should be immune from bad things."

"Did anyone in the group try to dissuade her from using violence?"

"We thought she was just talking."

"Just using an expression, in conversation, the way we all do from time to time. Is that what you mean?"

"That's what we *thought*. Now we know that wasn't the case."

"Your Honor, I ask that the witness's last remark be stricken."

The judge instructed the jury to disregard the comment. Judging from the glazed expressions and nodding heads, I thought it likely that many of them hadn't heard it to begin with.

When the witness stepped down, Pelle checked his notes, conferred briefly with an assistant, then addressed the court. "The prosecution rests."

He'd ended where he'd begun, with Terri's motive for murder. He'd delivered a tidy package, neatly wrapped. I'd managed to poke holes here and there, though I'd hardly dealt the case a fatal blow. All in all, I thought it was a draw.

But I couldn't read the faces of the jurors. What they thought was anyone's guess.

CHAPTER 34

Lenore grabbed my arm as we made our way out of the court-room. "What was all that about the glasses, Kali? Do you think Pelle swayed the jury?" Her voice was high-pitched, nervous.

It's always difficult to predict what a jury will make of evidence. "It was a direct, by-the-book presentation," I said, erring on the side of caution.

"They're going to find Terri guilty?" Lenore sounded almost frantic.

"I don't know what they will do. Juries are notoriously unpredictable. For what it's worth, though, none of the prosecution's evidence is air tight."

Lenore wasn't mollified. "But they might! They could decide she killed him."

"All we need is reasonable doubt in the mind of one juror."

"You think you can do that?"

Before I had time to answer, Arlo, Ted, and Steven caught up with us. We gathered in the hallway outside the courtroom.

I touched Lenore's shoulder. "I think there's a good chance I can. Try not to worry too much."

"Easier said than done." Lenore turned to her son. "Steven, darling, you're coming for dinner tonight, aren't you?"

"I don't know, I've got some—" He shot me a quick look out of the corner of his eye.

"I insist," Lenore said.

He gave her an indulgent smile. "Mom, you can't insist. I'm a grown man, remember?"

She returned the smile with a pat on his cheek. "Right, you are."

"But I'll try to make it."

When the Cross family moved on, I turned to Ted. "How are you holding up?"

"I wouldn't wish this last couple of months on my worst enemy. But I'm muddling through, one day at a time."

"Good."

"It's much harder on Terri. I worry about her."

I nodded. "Of course you do."

"And I miss her more than I thought possible. I didn't realize how she filled out my life."

I'd once thought Ted to be all show and no substance, but that opinion had changed over the months as I'd come to know him better. He was a genuinely nice guy, although the packaging sometimes tripped him up.

"Having Hannah helps," he added, with a glimmer of a smile.

I offered a noncommittal grunt. It was the *baby* thing again. Lately, I'd found it difficult to simply toss the subject off the way I had in the past.

Loretta was asleep in the front window when I pulled into the driveway. She raced to meet me at the door, tail waving frantically.

"Okay, girl. I'm glad to see you, too."

Dotty called from the kitchen. "Don't let her fool you. That dog gets plenty of attention during the day."

"I know she does. More than she gets from me lately, I'm afraid." Dotty and Bea had taken to Loretta the way a young boy takes to mud. They couldn't get enough of her.

Dotty was chopping tomatoes. She had the television on and turned to the news. I grabbed an apple from the fridge and joined her.

"You just missed coverage of the trial," she said. "They had their legal analyst on, too."

"What did he say?"

Her expression made it clear she didn't like to be the bearer of bad news. "The short of it was that the defense had its work cut out."

"Great." Not that I hadn't already known that.

"He said you'd done a good job so far," she hastened to add, "but that the real proof would come when the defense presented its case."

If only the defense *had* a case.

Loretta sat at my feet, her eyes focused on the apple.

"You don't like apples," I told her.

"Actually," Dotty said, "she does."

I bit off a small chunk and handed it to her. Sure enough, she ate it and came back for more.

"Well, it can't be good for her."

I picked up the mail and began sorting through it while we watched news of a pilot who'd safely landed his single-engine plane on a busy freeway in San Jose. A Mastercard statement, a bill from my dentist, an ad for aluminum siding designed to look like a check, and a Victoria's Secret catalog. I'd been dropped from their mailing list years ago because I hadn't bought anything, but it looked like now they were trying again.

"How do *you* feel the trial is going?" Dotty asked.

"I'm afraid that legal analyst was pretty much on the mark. It's going to be an uphill battle."

"You sound discouraged."

"It's a big responsibility." Made worse by the fact that I liked Terri and, for better or worse, her brother.

I tossed all the junk mail into a stack and flipped open the catalog. Then froze.

Someone had doodled in pen on several of the pages. The kind of thing I remember boys doing in high school. Only instead of horns and mustaches, the models were gagging, bleeding, holding in their spilling guts. A couple of them, with my photo pasted onto the picture, had their throats slit.

My hand was shaking as I turned the catalog over to look at the mailing label. Blank. I went back to the front. It wasn't even a current issue.

"When did you pick up the mail?" I asked Dotty.

She looked up from the screen. "About two."

"Did you see anyone hanging around?"

"No. Why?"

"Any unusual calls this afternoon?"

"A couple of hangups. But that's not so unusual anymore. Why, is something wrong?"

I didn't want to scare her. It was probably just a prank. Some kid who'd seen me on television. "No, it's nothing," I told her.

She laughed. "Those lingerie ads must be really something, given the expression on your face. No offense, but you're not exactly a prude."

"I think I'm just tired. I had a hard day."

Swallowing against the sour taste in my mouth, I took my mail and went downstairs.

What if it wasn't a simple prank?

I could feel my heart racing in my chest, but my mind refused to operate at all. I knew I should call the police and make a report, for the record. But I also knew there was nothing they'd be able to do, even if they were so inclined.

What I wanted most was to share the experience. To receive sympathy and comfort, and to be told there was nothing to worry about. Or that there was lots to worry about, but that someone else cared and was standing by, willing to help.

I thought of calling Steven, then remembered he'd be at dinner with his parents. I also passed over Tom—who would, at this very hour, be sitting down to dinner with his wife and children.

Instead, I changed into shorts and a T-shirt, brushed my teeth, splashed water on my face, and took Loretta for a walk. I kept a careful eye on my surroundings, however. There was nothing like the threat of a slashed throat to make one circumspect.

Because of Judge Tooley's schedule, there was no court the next day. I went to see Terri instead.

"Monday is our turn," I reminded her.

"I know."

We were in one of the small rooms reserved for attorneys and their clients. Windowless and dreary, it was nonetheless a private room, without a shield of plastic between us.

I'd taken out a pen and pad of paper, but now I pushed them aside. "What are you not telling me, Terri?"

She blinked. "What do you mean?"

"I'm not sure, except I have the feeling you're not leveling with me." It wasn't that I needed, or even wanted, *the truth*. If Terri had, in fact, killed Weaver, I was better off not knowing. But I liked the pieces of the puzzle to fit snugly, and at the moment, they didn't.

"You think I'm lying?" Terri asked. Her voice was soft but steady.

"No, but I sense that you're holding back. That you know something you're *not* telling me."

"Like what?"

It wasn't so much any one thing as the whole picture. A kind of instinctive reaction on my part.

Or maybe I was beginning to feel the evidence against my client carried weight. Beginning to see some validity in the State's scenario.

The room was stuffy. I took off my jacket and draped it over the chair, but that didn't help with the breathing.

"You never left the house at all that night?" I asked.

"Right."

"Then how do you account for the two witnesses who say you did?"

"You did a great job with that, Kali. The woman who supposedly saw the car couldn't even get the make right when you showed her those pictures. And Margo Poller would say anything to get back at me." She leaned forward. "Besides, we've got Mrs. Hassan. She saw me in Hannah's room, right?"

"But she's unsure of the time."

"Around midnight, isn't that what she said?"

I nodded. What she'd actually said was after she'd finished the ironing, which she'd started after the ten o'clock news.

I picked up my pen and rolled it between my fingers. "Why did you give your mother two of your sleeping pills that night?"

"She was wound up, agitated. You don't know how she gets. It's almost like a manic state."

"But two pills? That's twice the standard dose."

"I wanted her to get a good night's sleep. One pill wouldn't have made a dent given the state she was in."

"She slept well?"

"What's the problem?"

"If she was in a drugged sleep, Terri, she wouldn't know if you left the house."

"But I didn't!"

"That's what you say. Pelle has paraded out witnesses who say you did." And Lenore claimed not to have taken the pills, but the jury might not find that credible.

Terri's tone turned angry. "You think I'd leave my baby alone in a house with someone who was drugged?"

"I'm telling you how it might look to others. It's the little things, Terri. Like your spur-of-the-moment trip to Mendocino. The jurors are going to have a hard time understanding that."

"I *told* you. My mother wasn't well. If you want to know the truth, she was driving me crazy."

"What about the sunglasses? You told me you didn't own a pair like the ones found at the scene."

"I don't." Terri licked her lips, then gave a little shrug. "Maybe I did once, but I'd honestly forgotten about them. I lose glasses so often I ought to buy them by the case."

It wasn't that the answer didn't make sense, but the delivery was off. A trifle too glib. An edge of nervousness. Or maybe I'd let my own doubts color my thinking.

"Have you talked to Melissa?" I asked.

"Not recently. She used to come visit, but that's sort of tapered off."

I pressed my fingertips together. "Has she given you any clue as to who Hannah's father might be?"

Terri shook her head. "Last time we talked, she was still insisting the test was wrong, that Bram had to be the father. For what it's worth, I believe her. All it takes is a lab tech mislabeling a vial of blood, or someone on the other end punching in the wrong numbers. These things happen. I know they do. And Hannah does look a little like him. She's got his cleft chin and same coloring."

I could feel my blouse sticking to my skin in back and under the arms. I leaned forward and pulled at the collar to let the air circulate. It didn't help much.

"Terri, these next days in court will be our only remaining chance to win over the jury. Maybe we've raised a few red flags in their thinking about the prosecution's case, but I don't know if it's enough."

"What do you mean?"

"Juries are made up of people. People don't think and behave like machines. The jurors are going to want some substitute theory about what happened. They don't necessarily have to believe that *is* what happened, but subconsciously they'll find assurance in knowing it *could* have happened. And that will make it easier for them to come down on the side of acquittal."

Terri's body tensed ever so slightly. "What do you have in mind?"

"I'll certainly point to the fact that Weaver offended people, but I'd also like to raise Melissa as a possible suspect."

"But if Bram wasn't Hannah's father—"

"Right. But as you just told me, he might have been. Or maybe he wasn't, but Melissa honestly believes he was. She wouldn't be the first woman to have drunk too much, or been drugged, and wind up in the bed of someone she couldn't remember."

Terri pressed her palms to her cheeks. She stared at the table in silence for several moments. "We can't do that to her, Kali. She's a sweet, lonely kid. I think Ted and I may be the first people in her life who've treated her decently. It would be devastating if we turned on her."

"Even if she killed Bram?"

"She didn't."

"How can you be certain?"

There was, again, the shadow of a thought passing over Terri's face. "I just know, that's all."

Our eyes met briefly, then Terri turned away. "Besides," she said. "The evidence doesn't fit."

"Maybe not perfectly. But it's closer than nothing at all. Melissa was still driving Ted's Explorer at the time. With sheepskin seat covers. She's a blonde. She could easily have had a pair of purple sunglasses. Your manicurist found some easily enough."

"There are hundreds of people who fit that description."

"Melissa had access to your house. She could have taken your gun."

"She didn't," Terri said emphatically. "The gun was stolen several years ago."

"There's nothing to show that, though, but your word."

Terri folded her arms and rocked forward in her seat. Her face had taken on an ashen hue. "I didn't do it," she said. "I didn't kill him. That's what's important."

"What's important, Terri, is convincing the jury that you didn't."

CHAPTER 35

Jared was working away furiously at the computer when I got
back to the office. He had the window open and Santana playing not so softly in the background.

"Hey, boss. How'ya stepping?" He turned the volume down.

"I'm stepping just fine, Jared. One foot after the other. Any
phone calls?"

"Two. Nick wants you to call him when you get a chance. And
Alexander Rudd was looking for you."

"Rudd?" I dropped my briefcase onto a chair. "Did he say what
he wanted?"

"Only that you'd given him this number and he needed to
speak to you. He sounded kinda weird."

"Weird how?"

Jared thought for a moment. "Nervous maybe, or upset.
Emotional, I guess. That's probably a better description."

"I hope to God he hasn't suddenly recognized Terri as the
woman he saw outside of Weaver's place."

"If that was the case, wouldn't he contact Pelle's office rather
than you?"

"Under normal circumstances, yes. But Rudd's a dead man, remember? Twice dead, in fact. I don't imagine he wants to get too
close to the law."

Jared tipped backward in his chair. "In that case," he said with
a smirk, "he wouldn't be calling *you*, would he?"

"Smart ass."

"Damn straight." Jared turned his attention back to the computer screen.

"Did he say where I could reach him?"

Jared shook his head. "Said he'd call back later. I gave him your home number, I hope that was okay. But with this being Friday and all, I figured you'd want to talk to him sooner rather than later."

"Thanks."

I opened the window in my own office, letting the afternoon breeze filter through, kicked off my shoes, and returned Nick's call.

"Are you fixed for Monday?" he asked.

"I hope to be by the time Monday arrives."

"Does that mean there are a few holes that need plugging?"

I opened the office door and motioned for Jared to turn down the volume, which had crept back up as soon as I'd picked up the phone. "It's more that we have no explanation of our own to offer," I told Nick. "I don't suppose you've come up with anything on Roemer?"

"The guy acts like he's pissed at the world so his quarrels with Weaver might not mean much. And the waiter at the restaurant the night Weaver died said all three of them seemed to be in good spirits."

"Maybe. But Roemer is eager to see Terri convicted. He tried to intimidate me in the stairwell after court the other day."

"What happened?"

I draped a leg over the arm of the chair in a most unladylike fashion. But I was wearing slacks, and I was alone in my office. "He bumped into me, intentionally. Then blocked me in a corner for a few minutes. I wasn't hurt but I was shaken." Just talking about it caused a tremor of anxiety in my gut.

"Want me to break his kneecaps for you?"

I started to laugh, then stopped short. "You don't do that sort of thing. Do you?"

"So far, only in my fantasies. But I'd like nothing better than putting a guy like Roemer in his place."

"There's more." I told Nick about the Victoria's Secret catalog with bloodied models and my photo.

"And you think that was Roemer, too?"

"It sort of fits his level of maturity."

"If you're not going to let me go after the guy, Kali, at least be careful."

"Believe me, I intend to be. But you called for a reason."

"Yeah. Remember when we talked to that hit-and-run cop's widow?"

"Sure."

"There was a business card in the box of things she was keeping. For an auto repair shop. Do you happen to recall the name?"

"Something with an H, I think. Handel?"

"How about Henzel?"

"Yeah, that's it. Why?"

"Well, I'm sitting here typing up my notes on this case, and suddenly it hits me. That's where Rudd worked before his car went into the ocean."

"At Henzel's?" I swung my leg back to the floor and sat up straight. Rudd had worked in an autoshop, so that part fit. But it was an awfully big coincidence that Moran had been holding on to a card for that particular shop. "Do you suppose he was a customer?"

"I doubt it. Moran drove a Chevy. Same one his wife drives now. Henzel's specialized in foreign makes. Audi, BMW, Porsche, probably Volvo, as well. Here's something else. I did a little research in the newspaper archives. Seems the place burned down a few days before Rudd's car went over the cliff."

My pulse jumped. "Was there talk of arson? That might explain Rudd's faked death."

"There was speculation to that effect, though nothing was proven. Henzel was mostly retired by then, left the day-to-day operations to his staff, with Rudd in charge. Police apparently questioned everyone who worked there, as well as Henzel himself, but nothing came of it."

"If Rudd wasn't a suspect, why would he fake his own death?"

"Might not be connected at all."

It almost had to be, given the timing of the two events. But what was Moran's connection to the shop?

"Was the fire before or after Moran's death?" I asked.

"The fire was three days after. Rudd's accident four days after that."

"So Moran couldn't have been investigating the fire."

"Not unless he was psychic."

"Which leaves the possibility that he was investigating something else."

"Or someone else, namely Rudd."

"He called me this afternoon," I said.

"Rudd? What did he want?" Nick's interest was clearly piqued.

"I don't know. I wasn't in. I'm hoping he'll call back."

Hoping, too, that he wasn't about to throw a monkey wrench at our case. Rudd's involvement with Henzel's autoworks didn't worry me nearly as much as his role as witness to Weaver's murder.

Jared and I were back at work early Saturday morning. Whatever else we might be by the time Monday rolled around, we'd be organized. Thanks to Jared, all crucial case information was at our fingertips, detailed and cross-referenced on the laptop. He'd also made hard copies of key documents and filed them in color-tabbed folders.

Our expert witnesses were on board and ready to testify; we'd reinterviewed our character and evidentiary witnesses; we were prepared to present Terri's account of her movements throughout the night of Weaver's murder. What we didn't have was another suspect to offer the jury in place of Terri.

Steven joined us in the afternoon while we fine-tuned the sequence of witnesses and the questions I would ask. By four-thirty I was exhausted.

"I think we should call it a day."

"Fine by me." Jared reached for his car keys. "If you think of something else, save it for tomorrow, okay? I've got plans for this evening."

"Linda?"

"Linda was last month."

"So now you're on to Miss September?"

He grinned. "She could be, boss. She's something else."

Jared took the stairs like a man in a hurry. I could hear the clatter of his boots all the way into the bottom lobby.

Steven reached into his pocket for a quarter. "Heads or tails?"

"What are we deciding?"

"Whether we eat out or I cook." He flipped the coin into his palm and quickly slapped it against the other arm. "Actually, you can have your choice, but knowing you, you'll say either is fine."

"Whoa, back up. I haven't even agreed to have dinner with you."

"You will, though, won't you?" He proffered his bad-boy grin. It wasn't totally irresistible, but it *was* charming. "And don't give me this work stuff. Your brain functions better when you give it a break."

"I might have plans."

"You could cancel them." He raised an eyebrow and gave me a long, flirtatious gaze. Then he lowered his arm and stuck the quarter back into his pocket without bothering to look at it.

"Seriously," he said. "I'd really like your company this evening. We can go to a movie if you'd like, or a jazz club. We can even play miniature golf." An allusion to an evening we'd spent together five years earlier. "I'm just agitated and anxious about the trial."

Bea and Dotty had left that afternoon for another Tahoe excursion. I'd be alone for the night, and would probably end up working.

Or bouncing off the walls with worry about Monday.

"It's my turn," I told him. "I'll cook."

He grinned. "You drive a hard bargain. I'll bring wine and dessert."

You'd think people would have better things to do on a lovely Saturday afternoon in early fall than shop for groceries. But the store was packed. Not that it should have surprised me—eating is serious business in the Bay Area.

I bought salmon, string beans, salad mixings, and ingredients for wine-scalloped potatoes—one of the many recipes my sister Sabrina was forever sending my way in hopes of domesticating me. Hummus and a sourdough baguette for predinner munching, and fresh flowers for the table. I selected a bunch of white daisies, then remembered Steven's comment about the daisies that mysteriously appeared on Caroline's grave each year. I decided on a mixed bouquet instead.

At home, I spooned teriyaki marinade over the salmon, took Loretta on a quick spin up the road, then grabbed the mail from the box in front on my return. I sorted through it with a sense of trepidation, and was relieved to find nothing more ominous than a bill from the phone company.

Loretta lapped water from her bowl with the gusto of someone who'd been lost in the desert, then curled up in the corner under the table. I straightened the kitchen and moved the recycle bins out to the porch, then went downstairs to take a shower.

My bedroom was as I'd left it that morning—my gray sweater draped over the chair, a discarded pair of socks balled on top of the dresser, the current issue of *Newsweek* on the floor next to the bed. But the corner of the comforter was bunched against the bedside table in a way I was sure it hadn't been when I'd pulled it into place before leaving for work.

A small thing, yet it gave me pause. I pulled back the comforter, lifted the pillow. Nothing amiss. I went so far as to pull back the sheets. Then I remade the bed, gave the room another visual sweep, and decided my experience with the catalog was making me paranoid.

If Bea or Dotty had been downstairs when the phone rang, they might have come here to answer it rather than trudging back upstairs, and mussed the comforter in the process. Or maybe I'd just been distracted that morning and hadn't been as thorough as I usually was. I flashed on a mental picture of Goldilocks, and laughed. What was I imagining anyway, that someone had been sleeping in *my* bed?

After my shower and a careful redo of my makeup, I dressed in a short-sleeve black jersey top and raw silk black pants. Then I plumped the bed pillows, and removed the sweater and socks, as well as the panty hose hanging from the bathroom towel rack.

I recognized what I was doing and I didn't like it. Steven wasn't going to see this part of the house, I reminded myself. But like a good Girl Scout, I wanted to be prepared, just in case.

CHAPTER 36

I managed to avoid overcooking the salmon. The potatoes were baked to perfection, and the green beans tender but crisp. Our dinner conversation flowed as easily as the wine. All in all, the meal was a success.

But I was never able to forget that Monday I would be making a case for Terri's innocence. It was a weight that followed me around like a lead shadow.

Steven poured the last of the wine into our glasses and looked at me across the table. "You've gone quiet on me. What are you thinking?"

"That I'm glad you invited yourself for dinner."

"Ah, but I didn't, really."

"Close enough."

The corners of his mouth twitched in a faint grin.

"And that Terri's case would be a lot more convincing if we could hand the jury an alternate killer."

He was silent a moment, thoughtful. "Do you have any players auditioning for the part?"

"Melissa. But Terri won't hear of it."

"They got pretty close during the pregnancy. Almost like Melissa was a younger sister. And Terri is loyal. Fiercely loyal."

"So I've discovered." I took no delight in pointing the finger at Melissa myself. "For a while I thought we might be able to use the Coles, but they've got a pretty tight alibi for the night of the murder. And Nick managed to get his hands on a casing from Suzze Madden's Beretta. No match with the gun that killed Weaver."

"What about Weaver's band of friends?"

"Melissa is the only suspect who might conceivably fit the prosecution's evidence."

He gave me a long look. "Could be someone you haven't even considered, you know."

It almost had to be, if Terri was actually innocent. When push came to shove, I wasn't convinced that any of the killers we'd considered, Melissa included, were true contenders.

I wrapped the fingers of both hands around my wineglass. "Do you think Terri could be protecting someone?"

Steven looked surprised. "Who?"

"I don't know. At one point I thought it might be Ted."

"He was in San Diego."

"It's only an hour's flight away."

Steven ran a hand through his hair. "He doesn't fit the prosecution's evidence either."

"I know. Except for the sheepskin seat covers. And maybe access to the gun."

"My brother-in-law is all braggadocio and bluster. I can't see him putting himself on the line for anything, even Hannah."

"Braggadocio?" I smiled to cover my ignorance. "Is that Italian?"

"Means he's a braggart. It was in *The New York Times* crossword puzzle a couple of weeks ago. I kinda like the sound of it."

I mentally filed the word away, knowing I'd be looking for an opportunity to use it myself. Then I took a sip of wine. "Alexander Rudd called yesterday afternoon while I was out. I wish he'd left a number."

"About what?"

"He didn't say. Jared talked to him and said he sounded nervous. I worry he's recognized Terri's picture, that he'll tell me she's the woman he saw the night of the murder."

Steven leaned forward. His gaze was intent. "She didn't do it, Kali."

"You're her brother. It's hard to be objective."

"Anyone who knows Terri well would tell you the same thing. She simply isn't capable of cold-blooded murder."

"Well, Rudd hasn't called back in any event. But there is an interesting twist." I hesitated, reluctant to bring up painful reminders, then decided that Steven lived with the past every day.

"Back before he supposedly drove his car off the cliff, Rudd was head mechanic at a place called Henzel's Autoworks."

I paused, but Steven showed no sign of recognition at the name.

"Did Joseph Moran ever mention it?"

"Henzel's?"

"Right."

Steven frowned. "Not that I recall. Why would he?"

"Maybe it's totally unrelated. But Moran had a business card for Henzel's Autoworks among the personal effects his wife packed away. The shop burned down three days after Moran's heart attack and four days before Rudd's supposed death. I know life is strange and all, but still . . ."

Steven frowned. "This is more than strange. It's dammed spooky." He thought for a moment. "What does it mean?"

"I was hoping you might have some ideas."

"Not off the top of my head, for sure."

We spent the next ten minutes dissecting and rearranging the facts as we knew them, exploring possibilities and then ultimately discarding them. Finally, we put them aside.

Steven had brought a pear tart from Grace Baking. After we'd cleared the table, we moved out onto the deck for dessert and brandy. The evening air was cool and scented with wood smoke, a reminder that despite the warm days, fall was fast approaching.

I'd grabbed a sweater and draped it over my shoulders. Steven seemed comfortable in shirt sleeves.

"Being back in this house doesn't feel as strange as I thought it would," he said, breaking a short but comfortable silence. "Those evenings we spent here listening to music, dancing and talking, it's part of another lifetime, and yet it isn't."

The evenings he'd told Caroline he was working. And I had blithely gone along with the lies. Well, maybe not so blithely, but certainly with my eyes open.

"I'm not proud of what we did," I told him.

"Nor am I." He glanced my way. "But that doesn't stop me from remembering the good things that you and I had going."

When I didn't say anything, he continued. "My marriage was in trouble long before you came into the picture."

He'd never mentioned that. We'd made it a point not to talk about his family, as though we could simply erase them from our world. Though in retrospect it made sense that he wouldn't have been involved with someone else if he'd been happily married.

What had I thought at the time, I wondered. That I was irresistible?

"For Rebecca's sake," Steven added, "Caroline and I both wanted to pretend that everything was fine. But it wasn't, and hadn't been for years. In fact, we were on the verge of splitting when Caroline discovered she was pregnant with Rebecca."

Sometimes silence is the best response. It was the only response that came to mind at the moment.

"I realize now we should have dealt with it directly. But you know the saying about the shoemaker's children."

"They have no shoes?"

"Right. And those of us in the psych field are certainly not immune from delusional behavior."

"I'm sorry." Finally, I found the words. "Maybe if I'd been less willing to—"

"It's not your fault, Kali. You're not responsible for my problems with Caroline or for the accident. That's what I'm trying to say."

Maybe not entirely. Maybe if it hadn't been me, it would have been someone else. But that didn't exonerate me.

Steven was quiet for several minutes. "I've made my peace with Caroline. We've had those conversations in my head, the ones we should have had while we were married. But Rebecca . . ."

His voice choked and he paused for a breath. His expression was unnatural, tight and twisted. "Her spirit . . . it isn't settled. She's searching . . ." He paused and looked at me. "I sometimes hear her crying out to me, waiting for me to help."

I felt my skin prickle, whether from the breeze or Steven's mood, I couldn't tell. I recalled his friend, Martin Bloomberg, talking about the black hole that tugged at Steven's soul. I was beginning to understand.

"Maybe dinner wasn't such a good idea," I said.

He smiled at me through the growing darkness. Grounded again, the Steven I knew. "Sorry, don't let me spook you. Dinner was, and is, an excellent idea."

We were seated next to each other, our chairs facing west toward the vast expanse of glittering lights below. Steven reached for my hand.

"I haven't quite figured this out," he said, lightly rubbing his thumb against my palm. "Why being with you makes it better, but it does. Like somehow Rebecca is nearby." He turned to look at me. "I'm talking nonsense, aren't I?"

I shook my head. But it made me uncomfortable to think I was somehow guardian of Rebecca's soul.

Loretta wandered out onto the deck and settled between us. Steven let go of my hand to rub the top of her head. "When did you get a dog?"

"She was my father's dog. I inherited her when he died. I wasn't the least interested in having a dog. And I'd built up layers of resentment toward my father because he ignored us for all those years, but now Loretta is, well . . . she's family, I guess. And I feel closer to my father than I ever did while he was alive." I laughed self-consciously. "Talk about nonsense."

"People are funny like that. The shapes and connections in our mind are powerful influences, even if they defy logic."

"Or maybe, especially then."

Steven nodded, rubbed his hands over his arms.

"More brandy?" I asked.

"I don't think so."

"Another slice of tart?"

Steven gave me a sidelong glance. I could see the corners of his mouth turn up slightly. "How about the hot tub instead?"

I shook my head vigorously. "No way."

"Why not?"

"Because it's not a good idea." In fact, I was sure it was a very bad idea, but I could already feel the flicker of something pleasant just behind my breastbone.

"You still keep it heated?"

"Yes, but that's not the problem."

"We'll make it chaste, okay? We'll admire the view, listen to the sounds of night, commune with our inner selves."

I started to laugh, but he appeared to be serious. "I'm not sure I want to know my inner self," I said instead.

"Concentrate on the view, then." Steven had already moved toward the tub and was now folding back the collapsible cover, as he had so many evenings in the past. Then he started to unbutton his shirt.

"Steven, I really don't think—"

"I'm going in. You can sit there and watch me, or you can join me."

Or I could go inside and start washing the dishes. "I'll go get towels," I said.

By the time I'd returned, Steven was already submerged in the steamy water. I flipped off the inside lights, cloaking us with darkness. Then I quickly undressed and joined him.

He'd turned on the jets. I eased back against the powerful fingers of water and began to relax. For several minutes, neither of us spoke. The hum of the jets, the gurgle of the water, a lone airplane overhead—the sounds that filled the silence between us were soothing.

"Kali?"

"Hmm."

"Your inner self is beautiful and intelligent. And she's not your enemy. Maybe you *should* get to know her a little better."

"This isn't Marin. Hot tub therapy is against the Berkeley city charter."

He laughed. "Point taken. I'm hardly one to give advice anyway."

I couldn't read Steven's mood clearly, but I could tell there was something rattling around inside him. Had been all evening. I decided I should probably have sent him on his way as soon as we'd finished dinner.

Steven's foot brushed mine.

I angled my legs the other way. We gazed at the lights of the city in silence. Then his foot grazed the inside of my calf.

"I thought this was going to be chaste," I said.

"It's just your leg."

I closed my eyes and a moment later felt Steven's hand on my thigh. My eyes stayed shut. As did my lips. The words of protest that sprang to my mind were never spoken.

And then his lips grazed my neck, sliding just to the water's surface near the tops of my breasts. "I guess it's not going to be chaste, after all," he murmured.

It wasn't too late to change course.

He touched my cheek. "You think that's going to be a problem?"

Yes. A chorus of voices inside my head sang out in unison.

"No," I breathed softly. "No problem."

Steven reached for a towel. "Let's go someplace more comfortable."

The chill of the night air was refreshing against my steamy skin. But it didn't bring either of us to our senses.

We toweled off quickly, then went inside and downstairs.

Steven laughed, a kind of uneven breath that betrayed nervousness. "Different bedroom, I see."

"Dotty's using the other one now."

He sat on the bed and took my hand, pulling me down beside him. "I've thought of you so often over the years. I think the reason I gave Terri your name was because I was hoping it might somehow bring us together again."

He grazed my neck and shoulders with the palm of his hand, stroked my back, my legs.

I didn't return the caress, but I didn't protest either.

Moving slowly, whispering in my ears between kisses, Steven gently eased me back onto the bed.

His skin was soft and warm, his breath sweet. My hand traced the arc of his shoulders, the curve of his spine.

His kisses became more passionate. My body responded with growing hunger. But in my head there was a persistent ringing, like Steven's cell phone the night of the accident. I felt myself stiffen.

"What's the matter?" Steven asked. His hand stopped moving, suspended at the base of my spine.

"I can't . . ." I rolled onto my back. "This isn't going to work," I told him.

"I was rushing it?" He raised himself, leaning on an elbow.

I shook my head. "It's that I keep remembering . . . what happened."

"We can't change that."

"And I can't silence the voices in my head."

Steven ran a finger along my collarbone in a moment of silence, then he, too, rolled onto his back.

"Are you angry?" I asked.

"I'm only sorry about the way everything has turned out."

"Me, too."

"Maybe things will change with time." He picked up my hand and kissed the palm. "I guess each of us has to exorcize the demons in our own way."

"I'm working on it," I told him.

"So am I, Kali. So am I."

After Steven had gone, I tried to sleep, but couldn't. Tried to make sense of my behavior, and couldn't do that either. I'd been eager enough to jump into bed with Steven when he'd been married. Now, ironically, it was the absence of his wife that stopped me.

Or maybe it was simply that I was no longer as young and impetuous as I had once been.

I straightened the kitchen and made myself a cup of herb tea, thinking I'd get into bed to read for a bit. That's when I noticed the blinking message light on the answering machine. In my haste to prepare for Steven, I'd forgotten to check it.

I hit play.

This is Peter Longf . . . I mean, Alex Rudd. My mother died yesterday. His voice came in gasps, like each word drained him of energy. *I don't . . . I think . . .* Another pause. *I would like to speak with you. I will be on the Berkeley fishing pier Sunday at one o'clock. I hope you will come.*

I played the message a second time. It was going to take a lot more than tea to lull me to sleep.

CHAPTER 37

I called the hospital immediately, and got the runaround—which wasn't surprising considering it was two o'clock in the morning. When I called back at the more reasonable hour of nine-thirty, I finally managed to connect with someone who confirmed that Sophia Rudd had died Thursday morning.

Though I'd barely known her, I felt a wash of sorrow. Weighted with self-blame. Had I stirred up trouble by asking about her son? He'd obviously had his reasons for going underground.

Maybe tomorrow I'd learn what they were.

In my days as a law student at UC, I would occasionally take afternoon walks along the waterfront to clear my mind and escape the confines of academia. Although I wasn't a fisherman, I often found myself heading out on the pier, which had been a Berkeley institution long before the city fathers had turned the mudflats of the bay into a marina and park.

The pier is a straight stretch of plank and asphalt, like a deserted highway, positioned several feet above the water. It gives you the feeling of walking on water, as though San Francisco were only a short stroll's distance across the bay. The people who come to drop their lines into the water are not the fishermen of L. L. Bean and *Sports Illustrated*, but the city's less affluent, and often foreign speaking. They trudge to their spot along the railing with buckets of live bait and coolers of beer.

On weekdays they are mostly men, but weekends draw whole families. The radios are louder, the coolers packed with sandwiches and soft drinks as well as harder liquid refreshment. By the time I'd arrived, about quarter to one that afternoon, both sides of the pier were lined with family encampments. Snatches of dialogue—Spanish, Chinese, and several languages I didn't recognize—caught my ear as I passed by.

Every now and then an image from the previous night would float to the surface of my mind and I'd push it away. I did not want to think about Steven just yet. Or about my own feelings and motivations. Maybe with a little distance it would all be clearer.

I walked to the end without finding Rudd, then turned and started back again. The pier was maybe half a mile in length, and he hadn't said where he would be.

Ahead, I could see a commotion of some kind. A flurry of activity and a gathering crowd. By the time I reached the spot, the crowd had grown considerably. I craned my neck to see what they were looking at.

A dark-haired woman of Asian origin, Pakistani perhaps, was sitting on the asphalt looking dazed. Her head was bleeding slightly and she held her elbow with the opposite hand.

A uniformed officer approached not thirty seconds after I got there.

"Are you hurt, ma'am?" he asked.

She bent her elbow a little and winced. But she shook her head. "It's not serious."

"He just knocked her down," one of the bystanders said. "Didn't stop. Just kept right on running like he never even seen her."

"What did the man look like?" the officer asked.

"Not too tall. Skinny. Had a knit watch-cap pulled low over his forehead. Kinda unkempt, like he lived on the streets."

A man brought the woman some ice and some paper towels to clean up the scrapes.

The officer's gaze swept the circle of onlookers. "Anyone else see him?"

"Adidas running shoes," an older black man said. "New. Flashy. They didn't look nothing like the rest of him."

"He came out of nowhere," said another man. "He was kinda ambling along, looking in trash cans, you know, minding his own business. Then suddenly, wham, like a horse with a burr under his saddle. He went that way." The man pointed toward shore. "Plowed right into that poor woman."

As the police officer took down names for his report, I continued my trek back down the pier.

Could the man have been Rudd? He was about my height, and slender—so that part fit. But he'd been wearing heavy boots when I'd seen him at the wharf. More to the point, why would he suddenly bolt after suggesting we meet? Had something, or someone, frightened him?

I'd returned to the base of the pier. It was now one-twenty. Maybe we'd simply missed one another in the throng of people.

The sun was bright. I could feel it baking my skin, and cursed myself for not bringing a hat.

I started toward the far end of the pier again. By now the crowd had dispersed and the injured woman and her husband were packing up.

Still no sign of Rudd.

I completed my second tour, then found a spot near the entrance and leaned against the railing. If he passed by, going or coming, I'd see him.

Vibrantly colored kites danced overhead. Equally colorful windsurfing sails skitted across the water. There was lots of activity, but no Rudd.

By three o'clock, I decided he wasn't going to show. Or had shown, and then fled. Both scenarios left me with unanswered questions.

Monday morning I put aside any lingering thoughts of Alexander Rudd and focused on the trial.

The first witness for the defense was Jane Parsons, a friend of Terri's for more than ten years. Pelle had presented his case within the narrow confines of motive and direct evidence. Not surprisingly, the picture that emerged was one-dimensional and distorted—Terri as a vindictive killer. I wanted the jury to see Terri as a fleshed-out human being, a compassionate and well-liked woman. Someone with whom they could identify.

Jane Parsons spoke of meeting Terri when they were volunteers in a church-sponsored literacy volunteer program. Both women had gone on to become teachers, Jane at the high school level, Terri favoring kindergarten. They remained close friends to this day. Jane acknowledged that Terri had seemed upset by

Weaver's claim of paternity, but she insisted that Terri would never have killed him.

"She won't even step on a spider," Jane said. "Terri is one of the most nonviolent people I've ever known."

"Did she talk to you about the possibility of losing Hannah?" I asked.

"Yes, we discussed it. Obviously that wasn't what she wanted, but she knew it might come to that. I think she'd begun the process of bracing herself for the loss."

Pelle kept his cross-examination to a minimum. He underscored the fact that Jane Parsons was there as a character witness at the request of her friend.

"Did you speak to the defendant on the day of Weaver's murder?" he asked.

"No, I didn't."

"How about the day before?"

"Not then either." Jane Parsons had short, dark hair and the remnants of a Texas accent.

"Did you speak to her at any time during the preceding week?"

Jane shook her head. "No, I did not."

"And why is that?"

"I was in France at the time."

"Then you don't know what she might have been thinking or planning at the time of Weaver's murder, do you?"

"I know Terri, and I know she would never resort to killing."

"Never? Not even in self-defense?" Pelle asked, sounding astonished.

Jane hesitated. "Well, maybe then."

"Or in the defense of an innocent child?"

I raised my voice. "Objection."

Pelle smirked. "I'll withdraw the question. That's all for this witness, Your Honor."

I called two more witnesses—another friend and the principal of the school where she'd taught—to attest to Terri's good character and solid moral values. Both times, Pelle declined the opportunity to cross-examine them, giving the jury an amused, we-all-know-this-is-meaningless glance before declaring, "No questions of this witness."

I spent the remainder of the morning calling a parade of defense experts in order to put the State's evidence against Terri in proper context. Sheepskin seat covers were widely distributed; there were countless .25 caliber Berettas registered to owners in the greater Bay Area; three out of seven digits in a license plate didn't narrow the field much; a killer shooting at close range would be likely to end up with blood spatters on his or her clothing.

I called to the stand a criminalist who reiterated what I'd brought out earlier on cross, that there was no way to know with certainty whether the black fibers found at the crime scene had come from Terri's nylon jacket. Another expert attested to the popularity of nylon clothing.

There were no bombshells and no "aha" moments. In fact, it was fairly mundane stuff. I tried to keep it lively by keeping it short. Pelle's approach to cross-examination was methodical and thorough. I wasn't at all sure on which side I'd come down, had I been on the jury.

But the foundation was laid for reasonable doubt. Nothing in the State's case was conclusive, and for every element of testimony they had presented, there was an alternative, and in most cases equally logical, explanation presented by the defense. I was counting on the neighbor's housekeeper, Carla Hassan, who would be testifying that afternoon, to begin pulling the jury over to our side.

Steven had come into court after the morning session had begun. When I looked for him at noon recess, he was already gone. Happenstance or avoidance? The latter was certainly easy to understand in light of the awkwardness of Saturday evening. Though he'd said he wasn't angry, a dark mood had settled over him by the time he left.

I'd almost called him on Sunday, using Rudd's message as a cover, to apologize. But since I could never get a handle on what I was apologizing for, exactly, I'd let it go. And in truth, I was just as glad that I'd been spared the embarrassment of a face-to-face encounter today.

"Turkey on rye?" Jared asked as we packed up our portable office—the laptop and plastic case of files.

"Without mustard this time." I'd never understood the attraction of mustard on turkey. "And fruit salad if they have it."

I carted our stuff to the conference room while Jared went to pick up lunch. Rather than reviewing my questions for witnesses one last time, I picked up the crime scene photos and went through them anew. No matter how many times I saw Weaver's body crumpled on the entry floor amid the spatters of blood and brain, each viewing made me catch my breath. I forced myself to ignore the body and look at the rest of the room, to put myself there.

Beyond the foyer was the living room. Although the photos had been taken in daylight, the lights were on, as they had been at the time of the crime. No open book or magazine, however. And the television was off. A lone bottle was on the buffet. Courvasier, according to the crime scene report. But no glasses. Unless Weaver drank straight from the bottle, it was there from an earlier occasion.

But the autopsy report had shown a blood alcohol level of point zero eight. Could he have drunk enough at dinner six hours earlier to account for that? Not if he'd been sober when he was on the air that evening.

Maybe he'd stopped for a drink on the way home from his show and been followed. Someone he'd insulted or angered. Or inadvertently attracted with a thick wad of bills.

As I was jotting a note to myself, Jared returned looking grim. He set the deli bag on the table. "Bad news, boss."

"What is it?" The realm of "bad news" possibilities was almost infinite when Jared was the arbiter of "bad." Anything from a riot on the streets to mustard on my turkey sandwich.

"I checked our messages," he said. "Carla Hassan called this morning. She says she's not feeling up to testifying."

"What? We've subpoenaed her. This isn't an optional after-noon diversion." I shoved my chair away from the table. "I'd better call her."

"Done that," Jared said.

"And?"

"No one answered."

Keep calm, I cautioned myself silently. A flustered attorney is no good to anyone.

"Go on over there," I told him. "Maybe she's unsure about get-ting downtown." The woman didn't have a car, and relied on the bus to get around. I'd offered to reimburse her taxi fare, but I realized now that if she wasn't accustomed to taxis, which she probably wasn't, it would be a daunting undertaking.

Jared eyed the deli bag longingly.

"Take your lunch, for goodness' sake. You can eat and drive at the same time, can't you?"

"Not if I'm going to appear in court this afternoon in a clean shirt."

"Then I'm afraid lunch will have to wait."

I took one bite of my own sandwich. It landed like lead on my stomach. I wrapped it up and set it aside. Without Carla Hassan, there was nothing to refute the testimony of prosecution witnesses who claimed to have seen Terri on the night of the murder. I spent twenty minutes going over my notes, but it was a rote exercise. Hardly one word stuck.

Finally, I tossed my remaining lunch into the trash and headed downstairs to the room where trial evidence was stored. After signing myself in, I took the evidence box to the table and went through it, as I had before, baggie by baggie. When I came to the purple sunglasses, I was again struck by the sense that they were somehow familiar. Had I seen Terri wearing them at some point? I closed my eyes and tried to call up her initial visit to my office, then moved to the afternoon not long after that I'd spent at the Harpers' place in the Napa Valley. Nothing clicked. I had a vague association of the glasses and blinding sunlight. But that was obvious—sunlight was the whole reason for wearing dark glasses.

Maybe I'd spent too much time mentally playing with the evidence in this case. It was sometimes hard to draw the line between memory and imagination, and perhaps I was simply confused.

I was back in the courtroom in time to offer a few words of encouragement to Terri. I managed to sound upbeat, in spite of the knot in my stomach.

Jared and Carla entered the courtroom minutes before the judge. I heaved a silent sigh of relief.

"Good job," I whispered to Jared. "What did she say?"

"Not much. She wouldn't talk to me on the trip over. Mostly she clutched some sort of prayer book and muttered to herself."

I turned to give Carla a reassuring smile. She avoided my gaze.

Judge Tooley emerged from her chambers and opened the afternoon session.

"Your Honor," I said. "Could I have a few minutes to confer with my next witness?"

The judge looked at me as if I'd bungled the punch line of a joke. "You just had a ninety-minute recess."

"But the witness only arrived a moment before court reconvened."

"Ms. O'Brien, you had months to prepare for this trial. Surely, you've had time to talk with the witness before now. Let's proceed."

With some hesitance, I called Carla Hassan to the stand. She moved slowly, head bent. Maybe she *was* ill, I thought with a wave of guilt. She looked a little green around the gills.

"Mrs. Hassan," I asked when we'd dispensed with the preliminaries. "Can you please tell us where your bedroom window is relative to the Harpers' house?"

"I work for people who live across street. I have two small rooms on third floor." She spoke without inflection.

"From your window, can you see any rooms in the Harpers' house?"

"The corner. Upstairs. Is now the baby's nursery."

"Did you see anyone there the evening of July 10?"

She hesitated. "About midnight, I look out and see light on in baby's room. Someone pick up baby and walk with her."

"Did you recognize that person?"

Carla Hassan lowered her eyes. I could see the long, thick lashes against her cheek. "Then, I think it Mrs. Harper. Now, I'm not so certain."

I was taken aback. "Mrs. Hassan, didn't you tell me that you recognized Terri Harper?"

"Maybe I think it her because that what I expect." She paused. Her lips moved silently for a moment, then she added, "I cannot say for sure it Mrs. Harper that I see."

I was living a trial attorney's nightmare. A witness who changes her story on the stand. My hands were sweaty, my throat dry. "What *can* you say for sure?" I asked, trying to keep my agitation in check.

Silence.

"Did you see *someone* in the room around midnight?"

"Yes."

"A female?"

Mrs. Hassan looked at her hands. "I think so. But could be someone else. Mrs. Harper's mother maybe. She is staying there, I think. Or a friend."

I turned to the judge. "Your Honor, I ask that the witness's comments be stricken." Not that it would do any good. The jury had heard what she'd said, and Pelle would undoubtedly raise the possibility on cross.

The judge directed the court reporter and then advised the witness that she was to answer only the question put to her.

"Has something happened, Mrs. Hassan, that makes you less sure now than you were when we first spoke?"

Her eyes scanned the courtroom quickly, almost involuntarily, but she shook her head. "I realize now I was too hasty. I may have been mistaken."

The response sounded canned, which I suspected it was. The big question was who had fed it to her, and why had she agreed? But I was afraid to push at this juncture for fear I'd lose more ground. "No further questions," I said, stepping back to the defense table.

Pelle was in pig heaven. "Are you acquainted with the defendant's mother, Mrs. Hassan?"

"I have spoken to her. A few words here and there."

"Can you describe her for us?"

Mrs. Hassan looked quickly at Lenore and then away. "Blond hair, slender. Young for her age."

"The defendant is also blond and slender, is she not?"

"Yes."

"So you might have seen the defendant's mother, and not the defendant, in the Harpers' house on the night of the murder?"

Pelle was hammering home the point—our witness was no longer sure it was Terri Harper she'd seen in the nursery. Our alibi, such as it was, didn't hold water.

"Is possible. Like I tell the lady attorney, I am not so sure anymore."

Pelle smirked and sat down.

I had planned to put Lenore on next, but to do so now was out of the question. It would only add credence to the logic of Carla Hassan's confusion.

Instead, I called the marksmanship and gun safety instructor for the gun club where Arlo Cross was a member. A beefy ex–military man with clipped gray hair, he had given Terri shooting lessons at the time her father had given her the gun.

"She was a lousy shot," he said. "And she wasn't interested in improving. Acted like she was afraid of the gun. It was clear she was there against her will."

Under Pelle's cross, he conceded that the last of the lessons had been five years ago.

"Isn't it possible then," Pelle asked, "that she could have become an excellent marksman since that time?"

"I suppose so, but it would surprise me. Terri Harper wasn't comfortable around guns and didn't much like them."

"Are most of your clients comfortable around guns initially?"

The witness shifted in his seat. "It varies."

"It's not unheard of, is it, for someone who is nervous around guns to become more relaxed about them? For that person's skills improve with practice?"

"Not unheard of, no."

"Thank you." Pelle sat down.

When we were leaving the courtroom at the end of the day, Jared turned to me. "I think we need the cavalry, boss."

"For what?"

"Didn't you ever watch Westerns? At the last minute, they come charging forward in a flurry of hoofbeats and trumpets, and save the day."

"What we *need* is someone else to point the finger at."

"Got anyone in mind?"

I shook my head. "I think I'll start with Melissa." Despite Terri's reservations, she seemed the most likely substitute.

"Desperate times call for desperate measures, huh?"

"Right. Call Nick. Have him recheck both of the Coles' alibis for the night of the murder. Tell him to keep digging on Weaver's three buddies, too. I'd like you to talk to Weaver's producer, see if Weaver might have stopped for a drink somewhere after work. And check the bars in the area. Find out if anyone remembers seeing him that night."

"Guess we've got our work cut out."

We certainly did.

CHAPTER 38

With the start of school in late August, Melissa had moved from her apartment into one of the dorms. She was finally getting the college experience she'd wanted. I wasn't happy about the prospect of dragging her back to a more troubled period of her life.

When I called, I reached a roommate who told me that Melissa was at her job, a work-study position in the undergraduate library. I headed to campus and asked for her at the main desk.

"She's on her dinner break right now," a brunette with a winsome smile told me. "With that four-eyed weirdo who's got a crush on her."

"Do you know when she'll be back?"

The woman checked her watch. "Should be any minute now."

Instead of waiting in the library, I took a quick walk through campus. The law school, where I'd gotten my degree, was housed at the edge of the main campus, a five-minute uphill trek from the library. My head echoing with memories, I crossed Strawberry Creek and wound through Faculty Glade to the familiar doors of Boalt Hall.

I'd been so optimistic as a law student, so fired up with notions of truth and justice. Fired with romantic notions about love as well. How had I gotten so far off course?

My career wasn't floundering exactly, but neither was I a pillar of the legal community. Instead of a résumé marked by pivotal accomplishments, mine lurched first one direction, then another. But it was the personal realm that most troubled me. It wasn't that I'd set my hopes on marriage, two kids, and a picket fence—in fact, I'd been known to scoff at the notion—but I'd always assumed that I would find someone with whom I connected. Someone who would be there for me, and I for him. Lover, friend, playmate, advocate. A companion along the winding and sometimes lonely road through life.

I thought back over the men I'd known, and with those memories I was once again brought face-to-face with my feelings for Steven. Sooner or later we'd have to discuss what had happened Saturday night. Talk through our past and explore the direction, if any, of our future.

Steven hadn't returned to court for the afternoon session. While I was in some ways relieved, I was also hurt that he hadn't made some sort of overture. But then, I chided myself, neither had I.

I started back, heading down Bancroft Avenue, then turned by Sproul Hall, the main entrance to campus. The evening sky was beginning to darken. Students crisscrossed the open plaza, some heading home, others to libraries and classes.

I was approaching the undergraduate library when I spotted Dan Weaver sitting on the steps with another boy about the same age who was pulling on a cigarette. They both had skateboards.

I waved and meandered over. "Hey, Dan, you get around."

"As much as I can. You'd have to be nuts to stay at that shit-ass boarding school any more than you have to."

"Berkeley's clear across the bay, though." It was also a mecca for high school kids, so I shouldn't have been surprised.

He shrugged. "It's easy on BART."

"My folks used to live in Berkeley," the other boy said. "I coulda gone to Berkeley High if they hadn't moved." Berkeley High School clearly scored higher points as a happening place than Pacific Academy.

Dan laid his skateboard across his knees and reached into one of the deep pockets of his cargo pants.

I remembered the mouse. "Did Herman come with you?" I asked.

Dan raised his head, and looked at me through narrowed eyes. I was struck by how much he looked like Bram. "Herman's dead," he said in a flat voice.

"What happened?"

"He escaped from his cage and the dorm parents went totally krazola. They poisoned him."

"How awful." A loose mouse was probably a hazard when you were responsible for a houseful of kids, but surely they could have come up with something short of poison.

"They knew he was my friend," Dan added. "But it didn't matter." I could hear the pain in his voice.

"I'm sorry," I said, and meant it. Strange as the kid was, there was an appealing vulnerability about him.

Dan opened his hand. I noticed a thin black friendship bracelet around his wrist. "Sunflower seeds, you want some?"

I didn't. Especially ones that had been in a pocket that might not have been washed since Herman lived there. And in the boy's hand, which looked as though it hadn't been washed any more recently. But I hated to turn down an offer of friendship so I took two from the top.

Dan turned to his companion. "This here's the lady that's defending my dad's killer."

"Alleged killer," I corrected. "She didn't do it."

Another shrug. "Whatever."

"I didn't see you in court today."

"The teachers noticed I was gone." He made a face and turned sarcastic. "Bad, bad me. Geometry theorems and verb conjugations, can't miss those or the world might come to a standstill."

His buddy laughed.

Dan stood up. "Besides, it was kinda boring sitting there all day." He motioned to his companion. "Hey, good luck. We gotta fly, like a kite."

I went to the main desk and inquired about Melissa.

"She got back right after you left," the young woman at the desk told me. "She's on the second floor, in ancient civilizations."

"Huh?"

"We're reorganizing the stacks. Melissa is moving books."

I found Melissa pulling books from the shelves and piling them onto a book cart. "Sorry," she said, concentrating on the books and not looking up, "you'll have to go around." Then she saw it was me. "Oh, hi, Kali. What are you doing here?"

She was looking good. She'd cut her hair and lost the weight from the pregnancy. Probably a few additional pounds as well.

"How are classes?"

"Great. My psych professor is incredible, and in English we're reading *St. Joan,* a play by George Bernard Shaw. I'm loving it. Me and my roommate get along fantastic. She's from Los Angeles. I'm going to go home with her over Thanksgiving." Melissa was animated, her cheeks flushed.

"Sounds like you're enjoying yourself."

She brushed the hair from her face and gave me a quick smile. "Finally."

"That's great."

She nodded. "For the first time in my life, I'm where I want to be."

"Melissa, I hate to dredge up the past when things are going so well . . ."

"Then don't." Her tone was almost playful.

"I'm afraid I have to. I need some answers."

She went back to pulling books off the shelves, her mood subdued. "Bram's murder has nothing to do with me."

"Terri might be convicted. You don't want that, do you?"

A moment's silence, then finally, "No."

"Help me by telling me who Hannah's father is."

She turned and snapped at me. "It's Bram. I told you that."

"The tests say it wasn't," I reminded her.

"The tests are wrong." She pulled a dusty blue volume from the shelf and stacked it on the cart. Her hand was shaking.

"Is it Ted?"

"Ted?" Melissa's laugh was shrill. "Is that what you think?"

"I'm just asking."

She rolled her eyes. "Wouldn't that be something. Geez, me and Ted."

"It's not so far-fetched."

"You're crazy."

"Maybe a one-night stand then, with some guy whose name you don't even know?"

"Puh-leese."

"Melissa, I've done plenty of stupid things in my life. Nothing you say is going to shock me."

She drew in a breath and hesitated. Then abruptly, her manner shifted and she turned her back on me. "I've told you who Hannah's father is. If you don't like my answer, tough. Now if you'll excuse me, I've got work to do."

I leaned an arm on one of the bookshelves Melissa had emptied. I could see the line of dust that ended where the books had stood. "Maybe you're right about it being Bram," I conceded.

"I've been telling you that."

"You didn't want him to stand in the way of the adoption," I added. "And you didn't want him raising your daughter. That gives *you* a motive for killing him."

"Me?"

"Think about it. There's a witness who saw a blond-haired woman a block from Weaver's place. And a dark-colored Explorer. They found white wool fibers at the scene. What's to say it wasn't you?"

"Well, it wasn't."

"Can you prove it?"

She gave a nervous laugh. "You're serious about this, aren't you?"

Desperate, was more like it. I nodded.

"I was on the phone practically the whole night."

"With whom?"

She looked away. "Someone."

"Last time I asked you, Melissa, you said you were home alone. Now you conveniently remember a phone call."

She gave me a dirty look, as though I were the one who'd changed my story, not her. "Check with the phone company if you don't believe me."

"Why don't you just tell me who you were talking to?"

"Why don't *you* just leave me alone. You're acting totally krazola over this."

Krazola. I'd never heard the term before, and now twice in the space of fifteen minutes.

That's when I noticed the packet of sunflower seeds on the book cart.

So obvious, once you knew. Like that old saying—*plain as the nose on your face.*

I'd remarked to myself how much Dan looked like Bram. How they both had the same chin, like Hannah. Dan was here in Berkeley. Dan wore thick glasses. The woman at the desk had said Melissa was on her break with some "four-eyed weirdo who had a crush on her."

"It's Dan, isn't it?" I asked, certain that I was right. "He's Hannah's father."

She looked at me. Wide-eyed and open-mouthed. Like I'd tossed a bucket of water at her.

I expected her to deny it. To lash out at me in anger, or to challenge me with a dismissive laugh.

Instead, she slumped on the floor and buried her head in her hands. "I thought it was Bram. I really did. I never considered the possibility that . . . that . . ." Her voice grew faint.

"So it *is* Dan?"

Melissa looked up. "It must be. I mean, if the test is right that it isn't Bram." She rubbed her hands over her arms, as though she were cold.

"Does he know?"

"Dan? I don't think it's even crossed his mind." She was sobbing now, and shaking. "He's only a kid. They'll arrest me, won't they? There was a case in the newspaper not long ago. The woman went to jail."

"She was forty years old, Melissa." Although technically it didn't matter. Adult was adult, and Dan was a minor. "I think your case might be perceived in a different light. But I'd certainly put a stop to it now, if I were you."

"I have! I mean, we're not . . . you know, sleeping together or anything. But Dan's like calling me, coming to Berkeley to see me, wanting us to do things together. I'm afraid to make him mad because he might tell someone."

That was always the problem with stepping over the line. "How did you end up with Dan?"

She shook her head. "It just . . . happened. Bram used to bring him along to Hank's sometimes. That's how we met. Bram treated him terribly. And then one day Dan showed up without Bram, and we went to a movie, just for something to do. Next time he came over, we started goofing around, and . . . It was only that one time."

"That you slept with him?"

She nodded. "Both of us were real mad at Bram, though for different reasons. I guess we were trying to get back at him, or something. And Dan is nice. He's a geeky kid and all on the surface, but he's probably the first person who's ever *liked* me. I may have been the first person who liked him, too. And I do, but not like *that*." She made a face, as though she were looking at something grotesque.

"Was it Dan you were on the phone with the night Weaver was killed?"

She nodded. "It was right after his visit with Hannah, remember? Dan was so hurt that Bram was making this big deal about Hannah. He'd hardly ever sent Dan a birthday card, even. He called me during Bram's show to tell me to listen. Bram was going on and on about the importance of fathers, and how children need men in their lives." She took a breath and exhaled slowly. "We were on the phone for a long, long time. I felt sorry for Dan. And I was lonely myself. You can check the records if you want. I'm sure the phone company keeps tabs."

I would, though I knew in my heart that she was telling the truth. Too bad, because she and Dan would have made good surrogate suspects.

CHAPTER 39

Bea and Dotty returned home a little before eight o'clock. I'd fixed myself a spinach omelette for dinner and had just finished cleaning up the frying pan when I heard them coming in.

"I'm in the kitchen," I yelled. "How was your trip?"

"Wonderful!" they called out in unison. There was a flurry of dog barks and the rattle of luggage wheels on hardwood flooring. Then they appeared at the kitchen door.

"I hit the jackpot," Dotty said with a grin. "Sirens and lights and everyone was looking at me. I thought I'd broken the machine."

"She would have run off if I hadn't grabbed her arm," Bea added. "Should have let her go and claimed the money for myself."

"I bought you a fancy dinner afterwards, didn't I?"

Bea humphed with good-natured humor. "One measly dinner." She turned to me. "How's the trial going?"

"Could be better. I'm afraid I've got some bad news of a different sort, however." I told them about Sophia Rudd's death. As I expected, Bea was shaken. Tears sprang to her eyes.

"Do you know when the funeral is?" she asked.

I hadn't even thought to ask. "I don't. I had a call from her son asking me to meet him Sunday afternoon, but he never showed up." For the first time, I thought to wonder if he'd met with foul play as well.

"I'll call the church in the morning," Bea said.

Dotty shook her head sadly. "You just never know when life is going to up and punch you in the face, do you?"

They headed off to unpack and digest the news while I went downstairs to check my e-mail.

Invitations to join "I'm so hot," and "Barely eighteen," at their respective websites, a couple of get-rich-quick proposals, notes from friends, one from a reporter with the suggestion we collaborate on a book about the trial, and a message from my sister, Sabrina, telling me to check her website for the latest in family photos.

I deleted the spam, ignored the note from the reporter, and punched in responses to the personal messages from friends. Then I clicked onto Sabrina's web page.

My sister is a techno-phobe. Well, actually, it's less that she is afraid of technology than that she hates challenges. But her husband gave her an easy-to-use digital camera for Christmas, and since then I've been privy to a steady stream of family photos. I clicked through the snapshots, rather quickly for the most part, paying only enough attention so that I could tell her I'd seen them.

But one shot caught my eye. Sabrina and her sixteen-year-old son, mugging for the camera on the back deck of their home. She had her hair piled loosely on top of her head, and she shielded her eyes from the sun with her hand. My sister is better looking than I am, although there are people who find her appearance too polished. But what struck me about this photo was how strong the family resemblance was. I tried to imagine myself there on the deck with a teenage son. A husband ten feet away shooting pictures. For the first time that I could remember, I envied her life.

I started to disconnect, then went back to the photo. Sun, deck, vista beyond. Mother and child mugging for the camera. It reminded me of the photograph I'd seen on Steven's bookcase. Terri and Lenore, taken the day they'd learned Melissa had chosen the Harpers to be the parents of her baby. Different setting, of course, but a similar feel.

Suddenly, I remembered where I'd seen the purple sunglasses before. They weren't Terri's; they belonged to Lenore.

My heart did a two-step. Could it really be Steven's mother who'd killed Weaver? She had the same coloring and build as Terri, and I'd noticed the flashy diamond on her ring finger. She doted on Hannah. That gave her as much a motive as Terri. And she didn't share her daughter's abhorrence of guns.

The more I thought about it, the more the pieces fit. Reloaded ammo. Arlo would have access if he didn't actually reload it himself. And Lenore was staying with Terri the night Weaver was killed. She could easily have driven Terri's car.

A film of perspiration prickled my skin. My mind was a jumble of conflicting thoughts. One thing I knew, I had to tell Steven.

How would he react?

I couldn't do this to him, I thought.

Did I have a choice?

I was shaking as I picked up the phone. My embarrassment about Saturday night paled by comparison to what was yet to come.

CHAPTER 40

"Yes." Steven's greeting was curt, his voice sharp.

"Hi, it's Kali."

His tone softened, but only marginally. "I don't have time right now."

"Steven, I'm sorry about the other night."

"Can we deal with this later?"

There was such a flat quality to his words that I was sure he was angry with me. Or hurt.

"That's not really why I called, anyway. I have to talk to you."

"Not tonight, Kali."

"It's about the trial. I know who killed Weaver."

He didn't even ask. "Tomorrow. We can meet first thing, before court."

"Steven, are you all right?"

He laughed. A hollow sound that brought to mind the black hole of despair his friend Martin Bloomberg had talked about.

Then he was sober again, sounding like the Steven I knew. "I'm fine."

"I need to talk to you."

"I'm not upset with you, if that's what you're thinking. Sorry that we can't go back to what we had, though. So sorry." His words were thick.

"This can't wait until tomorrow, Steven. It's important. I could be over there in fifteen minutes."

"I'm on my way out. It's going to have to wait." He paused. "I'm sorry, Kali. But it can't be helped."

He hung up before I could get another word out.

I stared at the phone, half thinking he might ring back and explain his odd behavior. But the line remained silent.

Did he have someone with him? That would explain part of it. But not the black edge of depression I'd detected. Maybe Steven was really over the edge. His friend was worried about him. Even I'd seen glimpses of his dark moods.

I tried to work, but I felt uncomfortable. Like my skin had shrunk. My mind wouldn't focus.

Talking to Steven had scared me. I couldn't put my finger on why, exactly, but there was an almost crazed tenor to his mood.

Before I'd actually decided what to do, I grabbed my car keys and was heading down the hill toward Steven's.

What if he wouldn't talk to me? What if there was a woman there with him? I didn't know how I'd handle it. But there was something going on that didn't feel right.

I took Ashby down to College Avenue, cursing leisurely drivers and red lights, both of which I faced in abundance. I pulled onto Steven's street and parked in the first open space I found, near the end of the block. I headed for his house on foot. Partway there, I saw a dark figure scurry down his walkway.

"Steven?"

He didn't answer. Didn't even look my way. But the figure climbed into Steven's car, and in the brief flash of light when the door opened, I saw that it was, indeed, him.

The car pulled away from the curb in a hurry, with a screech of tires. I trotted back to my own car, and followed. Maybe I was going to look like a fool when all was said and done, but there was no way I could turn around and head home at this point.

Steven got onto the freeway, headed toward San Francisco. I stayed a couple of cars behind. When he got off at the Embarcadero, I did too, then slowed to leave more distance between us. He parked along the waterfront. A bustle of activity during the day, the place was deserted at night. I didn't see another person anywhere in the vicinity.

I parked a little distance away and followed him out toward the ferry slip, staying in the shadows of the construction equipment parked along the way. My first thought was suicide, and I wondered if I would be able to stop him. But as I approached, I saw Steven take a seat on a bench. He was huddled in a heavy coat, the collar up around his neck to keep out the damp wind.

I hadn't even thought to bring a jacket. I shivered and shook my arms in a futile attempt to stay warm.

Several minutes I stood there feeling the icy fingers of night slice across my skin. Either I had to return to my car, or confront Steven. He wasn't acting like a madman exactly, but neither was he acting in a manner I would call normal.

Nothing ventured, I said to myself, and called out his name.

He looked up, startled. "Kali? What are you doing here?"

"I was coming to your house, to see you. But you were leaving just as I got there."

"So you followed me here?" His voice contained something more than disbelief.

"I was worried about you."

"Worried." He made a funny sound, like a strangled laugh. "That's a good one."

"I was. Am."

This time he laughed for real, but there was nothing merry about the sound. "So am I, Kali. Real worried. But I'm worrying enough for both of us, so why don't you just go on home."

"I can't—"

"Do it, Kali."

Steven—"

"Now."

I hesitated. This wasn't the Steven I knew. I wanted to reach him. "Why don't we get a cup of coffee somewhere."

He shook his head, looked over my shoulder. "Go on. I'm not in a mood for company."

"Steven, I can't just leave you. Something's clearly—"

He pulled his hand from his coat pocket and I saw the shimmer of smooth metal.

"Turn around, Kali. Walk back to your car and go home."

I wasn't going to argue with a gun.

But this was Steven with a gun. What was happening?

Still facing him, I stepped back. I was shaking so hard now I could barely move. And it wasn't just the cold.

"That's good, Kali. Keep going."

When I was maybe twenty feet from him, I again slipped into the shadows and started to sprint for the street.

Then I saw another figure coming toward us. Tall and broad,

with a slight limp. Instinctively, I knew who it was even before I saw his face.

Why was Steven meeting with Ray Shalla?

Or was it something else?

I pulled back into the shadow of a construction crane, then inched out toward the plaza, taking cover in the darkness of the boat ramp. Shalla stopped short of where Steven was sitting.

"So Rudd," Shalla said. "We meet at last. Better you should have stayed dead."

Steven raised his head. "You shouldn't have fled the scene of the accident."

Shalla did a double-take. "Where's Rudd?"

"I'm here in his place."

"You've talked to him?"

"He called me Sunday."

When he was supposed to meet me at the Berkeley pier.

"He told me about the damage to your gray BMW and the cockamamie story you made up when you brought the car to the body shop. Complete with its KEEP TAHOE BLUE sticker. You were driving the car that killed my wife and daughter, Shalla, and you didn't even stop."

Steven's words hit me like a bolt of lightning. So that was Rudd's secret!

"You can't prove that," Shalla said. I couldn't see his face, but his voice was scratchy. Bravado mixed with alarm.

"Close enough. Rudd took the evidence to Joe Moran, a dedicated cop. When Moran tried to talk to you, you killed him and made it look like a heart attack."

"You can't prove that either."

"And I'm betting you set the fire at Henzel's autoshop as well."

"You've certainly got an active imagination."

"Oh, I've got more than that." Steven sounded like he was enjoying himself. "Rudd took copies of the photographs and work order home with him. They weren't destroyed in the fire, Shalla. He still has them."

"Not for long." Shalla pulled a gun and held it on Steven. "You didn't really think I'd go for that 'let's make a deal' proposition Rudd suggested, did you?"

It was only then that I realized I'd stopped shaking. My body was numb but fear was what had turned me to stone. What had Steven been thinking? That he could stand up to Shalla and convince the man to turn himself in?

I slid my hand into my purse and found what I hoped was the emergency dial button on my cell phone. It was hard to tell, since I was working literally in the dark. The electronic beep was so loud it made me wince.

"What was that?" Shalla asked.

"What was what?" Steven either hadn't heard, or was doing a good job of covering.

"That noise."

"The voice of God coming to get you." Steven laughed.

"I'll be gone by the time He gets here. So will you."

"I don't think so."

"Come on," Shalla said. "You're taking me to Rudd."

"Can't do that."

"Why not?"

"I don't know where he is."

My heart was pounding like a jackhammer. I started to move away and Shalla turned.

"What's that noise?"

"Jumpy, aren't you?" Steven said. "Must be the guilt."

Shalla looked over his shoulder again. "I can shoot you now and find Rudd on my own, if that's the way you want it."

"Won't be easy. When you showed up at the pier yesterday, Rudd got scared. He thought Kali had told you he would be there. What did you do, put a bug on her phone?"

It took me a second to realize he wasn't talking spiders.

"Shut up." Shalla was growing agitated.

"Anyway, that's why Rudd finally called me. He wasn't sure about Kali."

"What does he want?" Shalla asked.

"Justice."

Shalla snickered. "Justice? Is it just that one moment of bad timing should ruin everything I'd worked so hard for?"

"Is that what it was to you, bad timing? A man in your position should know better than to drive drunk."

"I wasn't drunk." Shalla was angry, defensive. "Maybe a little over the limit, but not drunk. If your wife had looked to her left before she pulled through the intersection, she'd have seen me coming."

"Hit-and-run, Shalla. And two people died."

"I didn't mean for it to happen."

"What about Moran? Did you not mean for him to die either?"

"Moran had evidence. He knew it was my car. I didn't have a choice."

"And Sophia Rudd? You shouldn't have touched Rudd's mother, Shalla. That's what made him finally come forward."

"The old lady was a mistake. All I wanted was to find her son."

Steven stretched one leg forward. "Her son, and the evidence, will be at the office of a reliable public official at eight in the morning, along with a television camera crew. Your future is about to take a tight turn for the worse."

"Better than yours, Cross. You'll be dead by then."

Fear stuck in my throat like a wad of wax.

Steven smiled. "You may be right about that, Shalla." The hand came out again. The gleam of metal. Only it wasn't a gun, but something small and square. "Shoot me and you blow yourself up as well."

"You wouldn't dare."

"Want to try?"

Shalla looked uncertain. "What would be the point of killing us both?"

"Justice."

Another snicker. "What's to stop me from simply walking away?"

"You won't get very far. I'll throw myself on you and the result will be the same."

Steven's voice was so calm it was almost otherworldly. He had to be insane. He and Shalla were locked in a battle that allowed no winners.

I needed to get away before I went down with them. Shalla would hear me if I tried to run. He'd shoot. I'd be a moving target, though. That gave me a chance.

But it meant abandoning Steven. Could I do that?

My fingers were numb from the night chill. My body achy from standing stone still in the shadow. I wasn't sure that I could still move, but I knew anything I tried would have to be quick.

The slightest sound or shuffle from my direction, and Shalla would swing the gun and fire.

As if I even had any idea what to try.

Even as that thought ran through my mind, another took form. I'd spotted a long pole hanging from the railing near where I was standing. The sort of pole used in an emergency rescue of someone who'd fallen into the water. How to reach it without attracting Shalla's attention.

I don't watch B movies for nothing. Bending over, I picked up a couple of pebbles from the ground at my feet and tossed them to the pavement out toward the water. When they hit, Shalla turned toward them and fired.

In that instant, I grabbed the pole and swung with all my might. Shalla fired again, but the pole hit him first and the shot went wide. The gun flew to the ground. Shalla started running.

I swung again and sent him to his feet.

Steven grabbed the gun. I whacked Shalla once more for good measure. He sprawled on the ground, holding his head. Blood trickled from his temple.

"What are you doing here?" Steven sounded more angry than grateful. "I thought I told you to leave a long time ago."

"I did leave. But then I saw Shalla . . . was it really him who killed Caroline and Rebecca?"

Steven drew in a breath. The dim light overhead illuminated only one side of his face, and that was strangely contorted by shadows.

"He killed them," Steven said. "As well as everyone who could tie him to it. That's why Rudd faked his own death—to avoid being killed himself. He moved away for a while, but then with his mother's stroke, he came back home."

And accidentally became a witness to Weaver's murder. When I'd put his name on the witness list, Shalla had known Rudd was alive. I remembered his questioning me about Rudd in the hallway of the courthouse.

I caught the flash of blue and red lights out on the street. My 9-1-1 call had apparently gotten through.

"Shit," Steven said. "Cops."

Relief flooded my body. "Better late than never."

Shalla lifted his head and groaned. "These guys know me. You're going to have a hard time making your story stick, Cross."

"Too bad they won't recognize you with your face blown away," Steven said.

I looked at him. "What are you talking about?"

"Get away from here, Kali." He raised the gun. His voice was cold.

"You aren't going to shoot him, are you?" Or me? The fear returned like a sudden storm.

"He'll find a way to get off. His kind always does."

"But he practically admitted to the killings. I heard it myself."

"It won't matter."

I heard the doors of the police cars slam. A strong-beamed flashlight cut a swath across the darkened plaza where we stood. They were still far enough away that I wasn't sure they could see us.

"Let the system handle it, Steven. Don't throw your life away."

"What life?"

"What do you mean?"

"I thought you knew."

"Knew what?"

"Who killed Weaver."

I hesitated. Steven's mood was unpredictable.

"You said you'd figured it out."

"It was your mother, Steven. It was Lenore."

"Wrong. It was me."

My heart stopped. "No."

"I couldn't let him have Hannah. Not after I failed to protect Rebecca. I had to do it."

"You let Terri stand trial for murder?"

"I felt awful about it. And I was going to come forward if she was convicted."

The flashlight made another arc. Stopped, like a theater spotlight, framing the three of us.

"Police," one of the men shouted. "Put down your gun."

"It's me," Shalla shouted, not moving. "District Attorney Ray Shalla. I'm hurt."

"Go on, Kali. Leave."

I held my hands over my head and headed toward the source of the light. "Don't shoot him," I yelled. "He's got explosives."

It took me less than a minute to reach the sidewalk. But it was a long minute. A minute of silence broken only by the soft tread of my shoes and the crackle of the police radio.

When I reached the string of police officers, the one on the end handcuffed me immediately and threw me against the side of his car.

"Shalla was going to kill us," I screamed. "It's his gun."

"Does that other guy really have explosives?"

"He says he does."

"Clear the area," said one of the cops. "And call for a negotiator." He turned to the cop next to him. "And take her downtown."

The cop who'd handcuffed me shoved me into the back of his cruiser. Then he climbed in the driver's seat and sped off, lights flashing.

It couldn't have been more than a second later that I heard the shots.

And then a loud, deafening blast.

CHAPTER 41

The days following Steven's death were like a dreamworld. There was a crazed logic to events that under scrutiny made no sense at all.

The early news accounts focused on the shootout at the waterfront. There was even video footage, grainy though it was. An enterprising reporter had apparently been listening on the police scanner and had arrived at the scene, camera in hand, just as I was being whisked off to police headquarters.

It was on every newscast for days running. I made it a point not to turn the television on at all.

I ended up watching the footage only because the police insisted. Internal affairs was involved, as they were in every police shooting, and they wanted me to walk them through my recollection of the events.

It was too dark to see Steven's face on film, but I could read his movements. And hear his voice clearly.

"I've got a bomb here," Steven said, still holding the gun on Shalla. "I need to get rid of it."

"First, drop the gun."

Steven started to lower it, then hesitated.

"Now," the officer shouted.

Steven looked to his left, out at the water. He seemed uncertain.

"The man's crazy," Shalla shouted. "He lured me down here and tried to kill me."

"Drop it," the officer yelled again.

Shalla moved slightly, gripping the side of his head. "The

guy's looking for a scapegoat for his wife's death. Came up with some harebrained story about how I'm to blame."

In one quick movement, Steven raised the gun and fired at Shalla. He got off two shots before a fusillade of police bullets hit, triggering a deafening explosion.

There was a flash of light. A ball of fire. I was grateful for the cover of night. I didn't even want to think about what the camera might have showed had it been daylight.

In later reports, other details began to emerge. Rudd came forward to attest to Shalla's role in the hit-and-run. An inquiry was opened into Joe Moran's death. A search of Shalla's papers revealed notes he'd made about Sophia Rudd. My phone had, indeed, been bugged.

The charges against Terri were dropped three days later, and the jury excused. Steven had left a taped confession on his kitchen table, along with the murder weapon. Since it provided a perfect ballistics match, there wasn't any real question about continuing with the trial. If there had been, Lenore's statement would have clinched it.

She'd gone to see Weaver the night of Weaver's visit with Hannah, thinking maybe she could persuade him, or bribe him, to relinquish his claim. She'd driven Terri's car, she said, because hers was parked on the street and she was afraid that if she moved it, she'd never find another parking space. Terri had gone to bed early and never knew Lenore had left the house.

Weaver had been cordial, Lenore said. He offered her a glass of brandy. They'd been in the living room when the doorbell rang and Weaver went to answer it. She'd barely had time to register the fact that he'd opened the door, when she heard a shot. And then a second one.

Frightened for her own safety, she looked for someplace to hide, and glanced out the window in time to see Steven slipping down the path at the side of the house and over a neighbor's fence.

Afraid to be placed at the scene, Lenore had taken the brandy glasses with her. An illogical, moment-of-panic decision that in retrospect had cast further suspicion on her daughter. If the police had seen signs that Weaver had company, they might have gone looking in a different direction.

* * *

I dropped by to visit Terri the day after she'd been released from jail. If anything, she looked worse than she had during her incarceration. Her eyes were puffy and her coloring was uneven. She wore her hair pinned back behind her ears, and no makeup.

Lenore was there too. Grief and worry had taken their toll on her as well, but she'd managed to pull off the Hollywood version, with rouge and eyeliner, and hair that was well styled.

We had tea in the sun room off the den. Ted stayed around long enough to be sociable, then kissed Terri and Hannah, who was sleeping in an infant seat near Terri, and took his leave.

"How are you doing?" I asked. I'd been hoping to find Terri alone.

"Not so good," she said. "Though I'm grateful to be home. To be with Hannah again." She held the blue ceramic mug in both hands, as if warming herself. "I still can't believe Steven is dead."

"Me either."

Lenore looked pale. Her lips moved but her words were inaudible.

"Or that he killed Weaver," Terri added. "That he did it for me."

Her eyes brimmed with tears and she wiped at them with the back of her hand. "It's so horrifying, like, I don't know . . . like I should be grateful, and then I feel bad that I'm horrified."

"He wasn't rational, Terri. And the last thing he'd want is for you to feel guilty."

"I'm so confused." She turned to her mother. "You really were there?"

Lenore took a sip of her tea. Her hand shook. "I went to see Mr. Weaver. To plead with him. I was so upset, I didn't know what else to do."

"That's why I gave you those sleeping pills, to help you relax."

"How could I relax when that man might have gotten Hannah? I didn't *want* to relax. I wanted to set things straight."

"It wasn't your place to set things straight." Terri's voice had an edge to it.

"I only wanted to help."

Terri stared into her mug. I could see a pulse jumping in the hollow of her neck. "You knew it was Steven all along?" she asked.

"Yes." The answer was slow in coming. There was no mistaking the pain in Lenore's voice.

"You let me spend all that time in jail when you knew I was innocent?" Terri's pale skin was flushed.

"I didn't have a choice."

"You were here with my baby while I was stuck in some cell thinking I'd never see her again."

"How could I tell them it was Steven?" Lenore asked. "How could I point to my own son?"

Terri dropped back against the couch cushions like a rag doll. "How could you *not* stand up for me?"

"I would have, Terri." Lenore moved to the sofa, held her daughter's hand in her own. "I would have said something if you'd been convicted. I saved the brandy glasses, as proof that I was there."

Terri stared at Lenore. Her mouth was slightly agape, as though she'd meant to speak and then found the words wouldn't come.

"I would have done anything to help you," Lenore said.

"Except tell them who the killer really was."

"It wasn't easy, Terri. There was you, and there was Steven. Then when that neighbor's housekeeper said she saw you . . ."

"But that wasn't until right before the trial!"

Carla Hassan had changed her testimony because Roemer had threatened her. More convincingly than he had me with his confrontation in the stairwell and the altered catalog. He was convinced that Terri was guilty, and would never be convicted because she was a woman.

"With all Steven's troubles," Lenore lamented, "I couldn't add to them."

"*He* committed murder." A shadow of distress crossed over Terri's face. She bit her bottom lip and swallowed. "*I* was the one in jail."

"But don't you see? I couldn't choose one of you over the other."

Terri's eyes welled with tears. She took a gulp of air, then turned to Lenore and pulled her hand free. In a voice devoid of emotion, she said, "No, of course not."

But Lenore *had* chosen. She'd protected Steven over Terri, at least in the short run. I could see from Terri's expression that she recognized that as well. There would forever be a rift in their relationship, a chasm between them so large I wondered if either would be able to see to the other side.

"I had a feeling you might have gone out that night," Terri said. "I could tell that my car was parked at a different angle. But I never said a word. I didn't want to cast suspicion on you."

"I'm grateful, but—"

"And when they showed the dark glasses they'd found at the crime scene, I thought to myself, '*Gee, those are kind of like Mom's.*' The ones I wore for a week last spring when you left them at our house. I could have said as much, cleared up the manicurist's confusion about my glasses. But I didn't."

"Honey, if I'd thought—"

"I was trying to protect you!" Terri rubbed her hands over her arms, hugged herself. Blinked back tears. "I was looking out for you. Which is more than you did for me."

"That's not so, Terri. I had no choice."

"You did, and you made it."

Hannah stirred, then woke with eyes wide open. Her little arms began thrashing like a dog pawing at the air.

"Look who's awake," Lenore said, reaching for Hannah.

Terri beat her to it, almost snatching the baby from Lenore's grasp. "Come to Mama, sweetie."

Lenore's arms fell back to her lap. "You want me to change her?"

Terri held her daughter to her chest. "I'd prefer to do it myself." Her tone was cold, distancing.

Lenore gave Terri a long look, then excused herself, and left the room.

Terri cuddled Hannah, patting her back and cooing until the baby stopped fussing. "Hannah will never know her uncle," Terri said sadly.

"I should think you'd be angry at him. He let you sit in jail for all that time."

"On one level I am. But I know he'd have never let them send me to prison. And he was a good man. That's the side of him Hannah will never know. She'll only know the stories. Her uncle, the murderer."

"He was unbalanced," I said. "Friends of his saw signs of it. In retrospect, I did too."

Terri nodded. "He went through a deep depression. Right

after the accident. He was totally irrational sometimes. His behavior was erratic. Then he got better. Or mostly better. There were times I'd wonder, though. He'd be talking along like the old Steven, and then, out of the blue, he'd say something totally off the wall. Usually about Rebecca."

"I think by "saving" Hannah, he felt he was atoning for his sins with Rebecca."

"There was an incredible bond between them. Much more so than with Rebecca and her mother. The only person Caroline really cared about was herself."

"I can't imagine the pain of losing a child."

"It wasn't just grief with Steven," Terri said. "It was guilt, too. He blamed himself for the accident. Thought he'd failed Rebecca. He'd berate himself for putting his own happiness before hers. It made no sense at all."

Maybe not to Terri and the rest of the family, but I understood the source of Steven's remorse. Shared it, in fact. Now layered with guilt about Steven's death. How much had I contributed to his suicide by turning away from him on Saturday night? I'd never know.

"Dan Weaver signed the adoption papers," I said, grateful to move on to a less painful subject. "There won't be any problems getting the final order."

"Wonderful. We're hoping he'll come meet her someday."

"I'm sure he will, in time. Alexander Rudd would like to meet her, too," I said. "And you. He feels he's partially responsible to Steven's death. He had no idea what Steven was planning."

"None of us did."

"He was the one who put flowers on Caroline's and Rebecca's graves each year. Did Steven tell you about that?"

She nodded, then gave me a questioning look. "You knew Steven pretty well, didn't you?"

I shook my head. "Not as well as I thought."

I didn't go back to the office. Wasn't sure I'd ever go back.

Instead, I headed to Tahoe, which was beautiful, and quiet, in the fall. I stayed at a cabin on the north shore, and spent my days hiking and my evenings reading. No computer, no e-mail, no television.

Jared had come through like a trooper. He was fielding calls, handling clients, following through on important pending matters as though he'd been at it for years.

He'd also managed to unravel the mystery of Weaver's high-tech business venture. Along with his good friends Billings, Roemer, and Lomax, Weaver had set up a pornography website. It was apparently a lucrative undertaking. But when the other three wanted to push the envelope into child porn and realtime video feed with unsuspecting women, Weaver had resisted. None of them were happy about our prying into what they were doing.

As for myself, I tried not to dwell on anything but the moment. The trill of birds greeting the sunrise, the blue lake water lapping against the shore, the scent of pine warmed by the sun and, in the evening, of woodsmoke in the air.

It didn't work, of course. I ended up spending a lot of time thinking about what had happened. About Steven. And about my own role in all of it.

Steven had said he'd made his peace with Caroline. That they'd had conversations after her death they should have had much earlier. I tried in my own way to reach Steven. Dialogue, both imagined and remembered, floated through my mind in an endless reel of remorse. But Steven remained elusive.

On my last night in the mountains, I stopped at the 7-Eleven for a soda and caught the top-of-the-hour news on the store radio. A gay rights rally in San Francisco, a Marin woman beaten and raped in a grocery store parking lot, a lost child reunited with her parents. Life moved on. The deaths of Steven Cross and Ray Shalla were no longer stories of the hour.

My cell phone rang as I was getting back into my car.

"Hi, boss. Sorry to bother you." Jared sounded tentative. I'd left strict instructions—don't bother me unless it's absolutely necessary.

"Not a problem. I'm just sitting in my car drinking a Dr. Pepper."

"I know you said you wanted to be alone, and I didn't know if I should call or not, but then I thought—"

"It's okay, Jared. Really." It was actually nice to hear his voice.

"Steven Cross's memorial service is day after tomorrow. I thought you might want to know."

"Thanks."

"You coming back soon? You've got a lot of messages."

"I'll probably head home tomorrow."

I ended up leaving that night instead. The quiet bubble of time away from time had been burst. I decided I might as well move forward.

Wherever that took me.